FALLING IN LOVE AGAIN

They slowly strolled down the street. His hand accidentally brushed against hers, and he quickly shoved it in his pocket.

He could smell her perfume, something soft that mingled sweetly with the jasmine. Ryder remembered it from the first time they'd met. And later, when they'd clung to each other outside the Ponderosa.

"I'm right here." She pressed her fob, and her red SUV beeped.

He opened the driver's-side door for her. But instead of moving away, he boxed her in. He knew even before he caught her mouth with his that he'd regret this moment. That it would upend any professional boundaries he'd tried to set. Yet he was powerless to stop himself.

He pulled her against him and kissed her. She moaned against his lips and laced her hands behind his neck. Ryder rocked into her as he took the kiss deeper, letting his hands caress her sides and resting them in the dip at her waist.

She was soft and curvy, and he itched to touch her skin instead of the fabric of her dress. He cupped the back of her head while he explored her mouth with his tongue. She pressed against his groin, silently pleading for more. He wanted to lift her onto the hood of her car, but they were in a public place. So, he settled for the taste of her kiss. It reminded him of springtime. Warm, like a May morning with all the comfort of coming home...

Books by Stacy Finz

The Nugget Series
GOING HOME
FINDING HOPE
SECOND CHANCES
STARTING OVER
GETTING LUCKY
BORROWING TROUBLE
HEATING UP
RIDING HIGH
FALLING HARD
HOPE FOR CHRISTMAS
TEMPTING FATE
CHOOSING YOU
HOLDING ON

The Garner Brothers
NEED YOU
WANT YOU
LOVE YOU

Dry Creek Ranch
COWBOY UP
COWBOY TOUGH
COWBOY STRONG

Published by Kensington Publishing Corp.

Holding On

Stacy Finz

LYRICAL SHINE
Kensington Publishing Corp.
www.kensingtonbooks.com

LYRICAL SHINE BOOKS are published by

Kensington Publishing Corp.
119 West 40th Street
New York, NY 10018

All Kensington titles, imprints, and distributed lines are available at special quantity discounts for bulk purchases for sales promotion, premiums, fund-raising, educational, or institutional use.

Special book excerpts or customized printings can also be created to fit specific needs. For details, write or phone the office of the Kensington Sales Manager: Kensington Publishing Corp., 119 West 40th Street, New York, NY 10018. Attn. Sales Department. Phone: 1-800-221-2647.

Lyrical Shine and Lyrical Shine logo Reg. U.S. Pat. & TM Off.

First Electronic Edition: May 2021
ISBN-13: 978-1-5161-0398-0 (ebook)
ISBN-10: 1-5161-0398-X (ebook)

First Print Edition: May 2021
ISBN-13: 978-1-5161-0399-7
ISBN-10: 1-5161-0399-8

Printed in the United States of America

Prologue

Joey Nix hopped out of her car and watched as the man she'd nicknamed Matthew McConaughey alighted from his 18-wheeler. His brown suede cowboy boots stepped off the running board, and a pair of long, denim-encased legs followed.

He tipped his hat and graced her with a grin that showed off those pearly whites. "Fancy meeting you here."

She moved in, took a fistful of his collar, flattened him against his tractor trailer, and caught his mouth with hers. He tasted good, like coffee and man. And he felt even better. Big and strong and something else Joey couldn't quite identify. Perhaps a little dangerous but at the same time safe. It didn't make sense, but she didn't dwell on it. Instead, she closed her eyes and let him take her away.

Unlike her ex-husband, who didn't want anything to do with her, McConaughey kissed her back, cradling the back of her head with his hands. He angled her face so he could take the kiss deeper, exploring her mouth with his tongue. The scent of his aftershave, or maybe it was just soap, drove her up.

She moved closer, feeling the evidence of his arousal pressing against her. Long and hard. The hot pull of his mouth made her whimper. She could've sworn she heard him laugh, but she was too enthralled with his kiss to care.

Even the chatter of the men gathered outside the Ponderosa had faded into the background, their voices nothing more than a dull whisper.

His hands moved down her sides and around to her back, where his fingers reached her backside. His mouth, hot and hungry, continued to devour her. It was then that she realized she didn't even know his name, even though they'd been flirting with each other for weeks.

She started to ask him, but his lips had moved to that sensitive spot behind her earlobe and she forgot her own name. He left a trail of kisses across her jaw and recaptured her mouth, his hands skimming the waistband of her jeans.

If they weren't careful, they'd be arrested for indecent exposure.

Somewhere in the distance a car backfired, the sound so jarring that they pulled apart. She immediately missed the warmth of his body and the intoxicating pull of his mouth.

"I thought you were married." He cocked one booted foot against his rig and grinned in that slightly sarcastic way of his, giving her naked ring finger a scan for good measure.

"I was." She pressed her key fob to unlock her car door. Five more seconds in his presence and she'd follow him to the hotel down the street or any other place he wanted to go. How could she feel that kind of longing for a stranger and only a mild sensation of nostalgia for the father of her child?

"Yeah?" He gave her a long appraisal. "What does that mean?"

"It means that I'm not anymore." With that, she got in her car and drove away.

She was halfway to Reno when she remembered she still didn't know his name.

Chapter 1

"So, this is it, huh?" Ryder tossed the keys in the air. Thirty days ago, with the scrawl of a signature, he'd signed his life away.

"It's all yours, Ryder. Congratulations, and welcome to Nugget," said Dana, his real estate agent.

Ryder switched his gaze from the small Craftsman cottage to the detached one-car garage. Dana had called it a carriage house, which sounded a whole lot fancier than it was. If he squeezed it in real tight, he might be able to fit a John Deere tractor mower. Definitely not his truck.

The house was also pint sized. But he'd purchased the place for the property, ten acres of mostly flat land. Enough for a couple of buildings to house his long-haul trucking business. The location was also primo. Smack-dab in the middle of his route and a quick drive to Reno. Only a mile from the Feather River—good fishing—and about five to the main highway, which in less than an hour could get him to Interstate 80, a major transcontinental corridor that connected California to New York. His trucking route rarely took him that far east, but depending on how he grew the business, it could. He had all kinds of plans.

His company had started small, just him and a Peterbilt truck and a livestock trailer. Back then, he'd driven solely for rodeo contractors, delivering bucking stock to arenas across the country. He'd bought the rig with his own National Finals Rodeo championship winnings. But over the last five years, his business had expanded to livestock hauling of all kinds and included sixteen tractor units, fifteen semitrailers, fourteen drivers, and a bookkeeper. He wasn't wealthy by any stretch, but he made a good living. Enough to afford a nice piece of California real estate.

"Thanks, Dana. And thanks for the gift." He held up the basket that had been elaborately wrapped in cellophane and tied with a big bow.

"It's my pleasure. I hope you're happy in your new place. When's your mom coming?"

"A week." He needed the time to give the house a good scrubbing. But first on his agenda was an in-home caregiver.

"If there is anything you need, just holler," Dana said, her hand idly resting on her protruding stomach. A month ago, when they'd started shopping for property, he hadn't even noticed she was pregnant.

Ryder raced ahead to open her car door. "Say hi to your husband for me."

"I will. We're all excited to have you as our new neighbor."

For the last year, he'd been making pit stops in Nugget to either pick up livestock from surrounding ranches to deliver to feedlots or to park his big rig overnight. Through his old rodeo buddy, Lucky Rodriguez, he'd gotten to know many of the locals while enjoying the hospitality of Nugget's only bar and sit-down restaurant and its only inn. It was a small town and a crew-change site for the Union Pacific Railroad. But a good many of its residents were cattle ranchers, or like Lucky, raised rodeo stock. They'd provided Ryder with plenty of business.

As he watched Dana's car jackknife down his long driveway, he thought about the possibilities here. Roots. Something he hadn't had in more than half a decade. He'd been renting space in a trailer park in Oakdale and living out of his fifth wheel. Most of the time, though, he bunked in his sleeper out on the road.

Staying in one place too long had been difficult after the accident. It had made him feel like he was drowning in quicksand.

Ryder didn't know if it would be any different this time around. But for the sake of his mother, he had to at least try. It was just a place—an inanimate object—to hang his Stetson when he wasn't on the road, he reminded himself.

He carried the basket up the porch steps, bouncing up and down on the treads to test their strength. Solid but ugly. Nothing that a little sanding and painting couldn't fix.

He opened the door with his new key and let himself in. It was as stuffy as hell. Putting the basket down on the kitchen counter, he went around the house, opening windows, mentally adding screens to his shopping list. At some point, he'd have to install central air-conditioning. It was May, and the temperature was still tolerable. But here in the high Sierra, June was hotter than a pancake griddle.

He looked around, taking stock of the house. It was a hundred years old, according to Dana, and had once been the foreman's residence when the property was part of the old Montgomery sheep ranch. The ranch had since been divvied up into smaller parcels, many of which had been sold years ago for grazing land. His had been listed to appeal to a residential buyer and had sat on the market for years. He didn't know why.

Although the house wasn't much—just twelve hundred square feet of nasty, mismatched carpet, kitschy wallpaper, and chipped tile countertops—it had a wide front porch and a sunny interior. And it still had the original moldings and baseboards from the 1900s, great wainscoting, coffered ceilings, and quarter-sawn white oak flooring underneath the ratty carpet.

The kitchen had been updated in the fifties, complete with one of those O'Keefe and Merritt stoves, which he kind of liked. The trashed linoleum flooring, not so much. But it wouldn't take a lot of effort—or cash—to bring it into the twenty-first century. A fresh coat of paint on the wooden cabinets, new countertops, and it would be like new.

He'd already lined up a local contractor to refinish the old wood floors. He could peel off the wallpaper himself and plaster and paint. That was just cosmetic. His top priority, though, was making the house safe for his mother.

Since her stroke, she had problems with coordination, balance, and dizziness. The doctor had suggested twenty-four-hour in-home care while she worked with a physical therapist to get her mobility back.

Before the stroke, Siobhan Knight had been a spry sixty-six-year-old. Now, all it would take would be one bad fall, and she'd be back to where she'd started. Ryder wasn't taking any chances.

He eyed the bottle of wine in Dana's gift basket, thinking it would be nice to celebrate his new acquisition. On further reflection, he didn't want to drink alone. He'd spent two years doing that and little else. Bad habit. He stuck the bottle in the pantry and unpacked the rest of the basket, hoping he wouldn't be sharing his treats with nesting critters. According to Dana, the house had been vacant for at least three years.

He had a good two hours before the first—and only—caregiver candidate arrived for an interview. He'd been warned it wouldn't be easy finding someone in the wilds of Nugget and hoped that Comfort Keepers, the agency he'd hired out of Reno, had come through. Originally, he'd used a home-care company from the neighboring town of Quincy, figuring a local firm would net better results. But he hadn't gotten so much as a bite.

It was getting down to the wire. He didn't want to leave his mother alone while he was on the road. And he had six hauls on the books between now and the end of June.

Deciding that he might as well get lunch before his interview showed, Ryder hopped in his truck. It was only a few minutes to the Bun Boy. The drive-through hamburger stand was in downtown Nugget on the square, a four-block commercial district anchored by a grassy park, the Lumber Baron Inn, and the Ponderosa saloon and restaurant. There was also a barbershop, a sporting goods store, and a smattering of other assorted businesses. The town's sole grocery store was a few blocks away, near Dana's real estate office, and the Gas and Go, the only fill-up station in town. It was hardly a metropolis. But as far as Ryder was concerned, it had everything anyone would ever need.

As usual, there was a line of cars waiting to pull up to the speaker box at the Bun Boy. "Screw it," Ryder said aloud, pulled out of line, and parked in the lot, deciding it would be quicker to order at the counter.

On his way in, he noted the redwood tables on the lawn were all taken. The Bun Boy didn't have indoor seating. And even though it wasn't all that warm for dining al fresco, the sun was shining. In Nugget that was enough for a picnic. Instead of waiting for a table to free up, Ryder would just take his to go.

The owner, Donna Thurston, greeted him with a big smile. "Today moving day?"

"Yep."

"Colin Burke said he's doing your floors."

Ryder chuckled. "Word gets around here quick."

"Small town, big mouths." Donna flipped the page on her order pad. "What'll you have?"

He listed what he wanted, including the joint's legendary fries.

"It's nice you're fixing up the place." In no hurry to get his order in to the kitchen, she put the pad down and leaned across the counter. "I always thought it had potential, maybe add on to the house when you start your family."

He nodded just to be agreeable. But the little Craftsman was more space than he would ever need.

"Anything I should know about the neighbors?" he asked. If Donna didn't care about the line forming behind him, he might as well learn what he could about his new neighborhood. She had a reputation as the town busybody and probably had enough intel to write a book.

"That would be the Lamberts," she said, warming to her subject. "Wyatt is a police officer for Nugget PD, and Darla cuts hair over at the barbershop. She's Owen's daughter. Thank God she takes after her mother. They're a sweet couple. Go over and introduce yourself. It's good to have a cop next door. On the other side of you is that weekender couple. Shoot." She snapped her finger in the air. "I can't remember their names. Nice folks. Hope to retire here someday. And down the road a piece are those daft Addisons. They own the Beary Quaint off Highway Seventy."

He'd seen the place. Chainsaw bears littered the front yard. A few times, he'd considered pulling in and getting a room for the night, instead of crawling into his sleeper. But the motor lodge gave him the creeps. It wasn't like he hadn't stayed in plenty of skeevy places over the years. Rodeo cowboys weren't too picky. Truckers even less so if there was a hot shower involved. But something about the motel reminded him of the movie *Psycho*. So, he'd opted for the Lumber Baron, a more expensive alternative but worth every freaking cent.

"Watch out for those two," Donna continued. "They're always looking to make trouble."

Donna finally put in his order, and he moved away from the counter so the next person in line, who'd been patiently waiting, could have his turn. That was the part about Nugget that was going to take some getting used to. It was a chatty town. After keeping his own company for the last five years, he wasn't used to a lot of conversation. But his ma would whup his behind if he wasn't respectful. And despite Donna's gossipy nature, he got a kick out of her. She was a good-hearted woman.

He took his food to his truck and ate in the cab. The agency texted while he scarfed down the last of his fries, confirming that its candidate was en route. He dashed off a reply that he'd be there and sent directions, even though the place was easy to find with a GPS.

Then he hit the road, pulling into his driveway a short time later. He sat in his pickup for a few minutes, surveying his new land. There was a copse of pine trees, nice for hanging a hammock in the summer. An old barn that looked ready to fall down. And post-and-rail fencing that needed repairing. But the land was beautiful. Green and lush from winter's rain.

It was hard to believe he'd actually pulled the trigger on buying the place. There was a time when a house and a small plot of land had been the dream. It was a time he didn't like thinking about.

Now home ownership was no longer a dream, just a good tax shelter.

He cut the engine, grabbed his toolbox from his truck bed, and went inside. He was installing his second grab bar in the shower when he heard a car pull up. From his window, he could see it was an SUV. He checked his watch. She'd passed the first test—punctuality. He was kind of a stickler for it.

She didn't get out of the car, and he wondered if it was a safety precaution. Perhaps he was supposed to meet her outside. He'd never really thought about it until now, but he supposed it was kind of risky for a woman to come into a stranger's house. Especially in the middle of nowhere. Then again, he and his mom had been fully vetted by the agency.

Unable to make out much from a distance, he waited a few seconds, then crossed the living room. He opened the front door to find her standing there. And…shit! He knew her. Well, not exactly.

Last spring, they'd shared an intense kiss outside the Ponderosa. But hell, he couldn't even remember her name. He'd run into her a few times at the bar. She'd always been by herself, and he'd gotten the impression she had hit on hard times. She'd had that sad, hangdog look about her. Though she was hot as hell. Blond, blue eyed, fantastic body, the whole package.

If he remembered correctly, he'd propositioned her with an offer to come back to his room at the Lumber Baron. Dick move. And totally out of character for him. There was just something about her.

And here she was, standing in his doorway. Judging by her wide eyes and the little *O* forming on her lips, she was as surprised as he was.

After a long pause, she finally managed, "You."

He quickly scanned her naked ring finger. She'd never been clear on whether she was married or not. Initially, she'd told him she was. Then a few weeks later, she was kissing him six ways from Sunday. Not that her marital status mattered anymore. Because nothing was going to happen between them. Not now. Not ever.

"I thought you were a nurse." At least that was what she'd told him.

"And I thought you didn't live here. 'Just passing through,' remember?" There was a glint of disgust in her eye.

"At the time, I was. Just closed escrow today." He didn't know why he was explaining himself to her. It wasn't as if she'd been honest with him. She'd told him her husband was a surgeon and she was a pediatric orthopedic nurse. "You lose your job in the children's ward?"

She blinked a few times and turned away. "I am…was…a nurse."

He hitched a brow. "Yeah? Isn't keeping a sixty-six-year-old stroke victim company below your pay grade, then?"

She didn't respond, just took a deep breath and looked him in the eye. "The truth? Yes. But I need the job."

That sort of knocked the fight out of him. Maybe because he was pretty sure it was the first honest thing she'd ever told him. He wanted to say that under the circumstances—the circumstances being that he was already wondering what a second kiss with her would be like—there was no way in hell he was hiring her to live under his roof.

He didn't want to piss off Comfort Keepers or have Janine, the case agent, think he was too high maintenance, so he planned to go through the motions of an interview, then make up an excuse why the candidate they'd sent him wouldn't work. Something other than the fact that not too long ago he'd had his tongue down her throat and a hard-on the size of Mount Whitney.

He moved over so she could enter and realized he had no chairs or anything for them to sit on. "Sorry, I don't have furniture yet. There's the kitchen counter or the porch."

They went back outside. She smoothed down her skirt and sat on the top step. He crossed to the other side of the porch and sat with his legs dangling off the edge.

"Tell me about your credentials." It seemed like a good interview starter.

"Okay." She swallowed and cleared her throat. "I have more than ten years of nursing experience. I started in the ER and eight years ago went on to get a master's degree to become a nurse practitioner. My specialty is orthopedics. And while I know your mother is a stroke survivor and will be working with a physical therapist, I, too, can help her regain mobility and balance. I'm responsible, hardworking, and have always been praised for my bedside manner. I also have excellent recommendations."

She was making it hard to say no. But it would never work, given their weird history. Okay, "history" was an overstatement. If you added up all their interactions, they might take up a space of thirty minutes, max. But every damn one of those contacts had been a prelude to sex, even if they hadn't actually wound up in the sack together. No, having her around 24/7 was a terrible idea.

"What else would you like to know?" she asked.

Plenty, like why was she applying for a job as a caregiver when she was supposedly a nurse? But what was the point in asking? He wasn't hiring her.

"Comfort Keepers talked to you about the compensation package, right?"

"Yep." She brushed her hair back from her eyes.

"And you're okay with running errands and light housework?"

She nodded. "All part of the job."

"I assume you're certified in CPR?" Ryder knew damn well that all the caregivers for Comfort Keepers were. It was one of the first things Janine

had told him during her sales pitch. Despite it being a Comfort Keepers'
requirement, he suspected CPR was Nursing 101.

"Of course." She stifled an eye roll.

"Why don't I show you the accommodations?" He turned his head and
pointedly stared at the front door, where cobwebs dripped from the overhang
like rope hammocks. "Maybe after you see them, you won't be interested."

She sure didn't strike him as the roughing-it type. Her leather boots
were high-end, her handbag had a designer logo on the front, and her Ford
looked like this year's model. Hopefully, the state of the house would
scare her away.

He led her through the empty front room to the hallway and showed
her the first of the two bedrooms. "This'll be my ma's room. And the one
next to it is where you'd stay." He showed her the ten-by-twelve room and
watched her quickly glance at the putrid green carpet and then up at the
ugly-ass floral wallpaper.

"This is great."

Liar. But he'd give her points for pulling it off with a straight face.

She cleared her throat again. "Where are you staying?"

"Out there." He nudged his head at the window. "In the fifth wheel."

"Oh," she said, slightly taken aback.

The fact was, the camper was a freakin' mansion compared to the
house. He'd bought it after winning his first saddle bronc world title, tired
of sleeping in fleabag hotels or in the cab of his pickup while chasing the
next rodeo.

"Let me show you the bathroom. There's only one, so you and my ma
will have to share."

The bathroom, though dingy, was probably the best room in the house.
It was comparatively large for a home this small and had a clawfoot tub
and a separate walk-in shower. The black and white tile could use some
caulking, but all in all it had held up well over the last hundred years. A
little paint and a lot of cleaning would go a long way. But he reckoned
whatshername went in for something a little sleeker.

"You know, I don't think we ever introduced ourselves." He grinned
at the awkwardness of the situation. Just a year ago, he'd had a tour of
her tonsils and his hands up her shirt. "I'm Ryder Knight. And you are?"

"Joey Daniels...I mean Nix."

He gave her a long, sideways glance. "Is it Daniels or Nix?"

"Nix. Daniels was my married name."

"You sure? Or are you running from the law?" He was only half kidding.

"Ha-ha." She flipped her blond hair.

"So, what happened to the surgeon?" It wasn't any of his damn business. This was a job interview, not speed dating. But for some odd reason, he felt the urgent need to goad her. Or at the very least, find out if anything she'd told him was the truth.

"We're divorced. He's one of my references if you'd like to call him."

"References for what?" He hitched a brow, and one side of his mouth slid up.

"A job reference. We used to work together," she said, refusing to take the bait. She opened the shower door and looked inside. "The grab bars are good, but you need a stool in here for your mother to sit on. I'll give you a website where you can order one. The tub is out of the question for her."

She walked out of the bathroom and headed to the kitchen. "Cute rooster wallpaper."

He leaned his hip against the counter as she explored the rest of the room, including the inside of the empty refrigerator, which Ryder planned to replace with something from this decade.

"I'm getting a new one," he said, annoyed at himself for feeling the need to tell her that. What he did with his refrigerator was his business.

"Hopefully some furniture, too." She continued to nose around, popping open cabinet doors and closing them with a thud. "You'll also need an alert button for your mom. Even though the house is small, you'll want to make sure your mother can call out for help any time of the day or night."

He hadn't thought of that. "Okay. Anything else?"

"Lots." She pursed her lips. "Do I have the job?"

He rubbed his hand down the back of his neck. "I'd like to take a couple of days to sleep on it." Which would give him time to find someone else. Someone he hadn't pinned against his big rig and kissed into tomorrow.

She nodded. "You should know that I have a few requirements."

"Yeah? Like what?"

"I share custody of my daughter with my ex. I'd like to know that she would be welcome here when the relief caregiver is working. My daughter will be eight in June, is well behaved, and won't be any trouble."

In general, he considered himself kid friendly. But since he wasn't planning to hire Joey Nix, her little girl wasn't an issue.

"I've got no problem with that," he said, leaving out that she was the problem, not her daughter.

He watched her drive away in her red SUV, cursing his luck. As soon as her taillights were out of view, he phoned Janine and asked her to send someone else.

Chapter 2

Joey pulled over to the side of the road, grabbed a wad of tissues from the dispenser on her visor, and blotted her face. It wasn't a particularly hot day, but she was sweating like she'd spent forty minutes on a treadmill, going full speed.

Ryder Knight. Damn.

Twelve months ago, he'd simply been Matthew freaking McConaughey, the silly name she'd given him because he looked a little like the movie star. A tall, lanky, broad-shouldered cowboy with pale blue eyes and a square jaw. Well, to be truthful, he was better-looking than the real Matthew McConaughey. And probably a better kisser, if she had to guess.

After initiating a brazen make-out session with him in the middle of downtown Nugget—one that had left her feeling more than a little exposed—she'd hoped to never see him again. For months, she'd stayed awake at night, fantasizing about that kiss. And wondering what the hell was wrong with her. The man had been a total stranger. Someone she'd flirted with in a bar while trying to get over her ex-husband.

And there he was today in all his virile glory, standing between her and the best job Nugget had to offer someone with her qualifications. Wasn't that just her shitty life these days?

If she didn't get the job, she'd have to find something in Reno, nearly an hour away. Too far from Veronica's school for overnights on the weekdays. After months of pressing, Ethan had finally agreed to let up on the court order that gave him full custody, allowing Joey to take Roni a few nights a week. Ethan's only caveat was that Joey got a place nearby, so Roni wouldn't be uprooted. Fair, and the best thing for their daughter. But she couldn't move here without employment. In Reno, she lived with her parents. Free.

Ethan gave her alimony, but after monthly student loan and car payments, there wasn't enough left over for her to be a woman of leisure. Then, there was the small matter that she needed to work to feel useful again. To build her self-esteem. It was key for a recovering drug addict.

She nosed back onto the highway, wondering where she could kill time until Roni got out of school. They had a mommy-daughter dinner date. Ordinarily, she would've headed over to the Circle D Ranch and hung out there. But Ethan's fiancée lived with him now. She and Brynn were still navigating the whole "he was mine first" road.

She settled on Farm Supply. The feed store was the closest thing Nugget had to a Macy's. Joey figured she could blow an hour or so, trying on clothes. In the parking lot, she called Comfort Keepers, even though it felt a little desperate.

"Hey, Janine, it's Joey Nix."

"Hi, Joey. How did the interview go?"

"Good." If you counted the fact that it could've been way weirder than it was. All things considered, Ryder had been mostly professional. "I was just wondering if perhaps Mr. Knight had called with a decision." He'd said he needed a few nights to think it over. But in her deluded dreams, he was so blown away by her credentials that he was afraid of losing her to another employer.

"I've been out, hon, and haven't checked my messages. But I'll call you as soon as I hear something. In the meantime, I have an opening in Sparks. An eighty-four-year-old man who is experiencing early stages of dementia. His daughter is meeting with candidates tomorrow. Should I book you a slot?"

Sparks was more than an hour away from Nugget. "I think I'll wait to see what happens with this job, Janine. I really want to stay in the area. But thanks for thinking of me."

"Of course. It's not every day we get employees with advanced nursing degrees."

Joey imagined not, since the pay was roughly a quarter of what she'd made at Renown Children's Hospital. But you couldn't be a nurse without a license. Hers had been suspended for injecting herself with the narcotic waste she was supposed to be dumping at the end of her shift. And then there was the small matter of her forging Ethan's name on scripts for opioid analgesics. Like the saying went, "Go big or go home." Or in Joey's case, a rehab facility in the desert.

She got out of the car and crossed the lot. Rocking chairs lined the front porch of the store. A display of barbecues stood off to one side, next to an elaborate chicken coop. On the other side was a small nursery, popping with bursts of color from the flats of flowers.

The place was crowded for a weekday afternoon. Two toddlers stood by a cage filled with chicks, sticking their fingers between the wire mesh, trying to touch the birds' downy feathers. The sight of it made her ovaries tingle. She headed straight for the clothing department. For a small-town feed store, it had a great selection. About ten different brands of jeans, racks of dresses, and a variety of Western shirts. They even had footwear—and not just cowboy boots.

Joey browsed through the sales rack. She really shouldn't be spending money, but she told herself there was nothing wrong with looking. A woman she vaguely recognized was pawing through the jeans. Joey tried to place her but couldn't remember where she knew her from.

"Oh, hi," the woman said when she caught Joey glancing at her. "You're Roni's mom."

"I am, and you're…"

The woman smiled. "Annie Jenkins. I own the farm stand up the road."

"That's right." Joey had been in the store several times with Roni, who loved running down the aisles, eating the free samples. "You have a daughter, too, as I recall."

"Emerson. She's with her dad today." Annie beamed. "Raylene's minding the store to give me a little break. I can finally fit into jeans without an elastic waistband and thought I'd check out the offerings, though I hate the idea of buying new. I'm a thrift store kind of woman."

Not Joey. She had a closet full of designer jeans left over from her days of being the wife of a renowned surgeon. Back then, even she made close to six figures and spent it like a drunken sailor.

"Where's the closest thrift store?" she asked.

"Quincy. The week before Easter, the Catholic church on Pine holds a rummage sale. But other than that, it's either Reno or Sacramento. Too far for one pair of jeans, so I thought I'd take a peek. Grace's daughter is the buyer and has great taste."

Joey had no idea who Grace was but nodded as she joined Annie in sorting through the jeans. "These are cute." She held up a pair with rhinestones on the back.

"Too blingy for me. But they are adorable. So, do you live in Nugget?"

Joey shook her head. "Reno. But I just interviewed for a job here. If I get it, I'll be relocating."

"What's the job, if you don't mind me asking?"

"Not at all. In-home care. That's probably all I should say about it because of privacy rules."

Annie wore a knowing smile. "For the mother of the guy who just bought the place next to Darla and Wyatt's house, right? I think the guy is a trucker. Anyway, he's friends with Lucky Rodriguez. I think they used to ride in the rodeo together."

Ryder rode in the rodeo? Why was she not surprised? The first time she'd met him, he was glued to the television at the Ponderosa, watching professional bull riding. As far as she was concerned, it was among the stupidest sports in the world. Eight death-defying seconds for a meager purse and only if a cowboy was lucky enough to win. Sure, the guys who made it to the big leagues made millions. But in comparison to other sports, the earnings were chump change.

And Joey would bet everything she had that Ryder Knight had never made it to the big leagues.

"According to the Nugget gossip mill, his mom had a stroke and is coming to live with him as soon as he gets the house ready," Annie continued.

Joey just smiled because she really wasn't at liberty to say more.

"Who's Lucky Rodriguez?" she asked, hoping to change the subject.

"He's a world champion bull rider and owns a dude ranch in Nugget that caters to corporate types. His wife, Tawny, makes gorgeous custom cowboy boots. Her clients include Mick Jagger and Beyoncé. You should check out her studio. She has racks of seconds she sells. They're not cheap, but they're amazing."

Joey wasn't in the market for boots, just a job and a place where she could live close to her daughter. But she was mildly curious. Who knew Nugget had a designer who catered to the rich and famous?

"Where is it?"

Annie gave her directions, and Joey made a mental note to check out the place the next time she was here and needed to kill time. She was dying to ask Annie more about Ryder, who apparently was a topic of conversation in town, but didn't want to seem too interested. She told herself it was for professional reasons, even though she knew better.

"How long have you had the farm stand?" she asked instead. The country store was charming and filled with local gourmet products, flowers, wreaths, and even kitchenware. When she first visited the stand with Roni, she didn't know how a place like that could make it in such a small town. But every time she'd gone since, the stand was crowded with customers.

"A little over two years now. It's done so well that I'm branching out with an online store. Brynn Barnes...uh, I guess you know Brynn."

Joey tried not to gnash her teeth. "Yep. What about Brynn?"

"She's helping me with the advertising side of it."

Of course she was. Perfect Saint Brynn. Okay, that was unfair. Brynn was a nice person, who'd had more loss and heartache than anyone should ever have to endure. She also happened to be the love of Ethan's life. And although Joey wasn't in love with her ex, she never really got over the husband-and-wife bond she'd had with Ethan. The finishing each other's sentences, the bad habits that she secretly found endearing, and the closeness they'd shared. The worst part was that Roni woke up in the same house as Brynn every day instead of with Joey.

That was Joey's fault, not Brynn's. But it still left a gaping hole in her heart and a modicum of unintentional resentment. And a truckload of guilt and regret.

"That's great," Joey told Annie. She was genuinely happy for her. "I'm rooting for your success. It's a wonderful store. If I move here, you can bet I'll be a regular."

"I hope you get the job. And in case you couldn't tell, I adore your little girl. She's such a sweetie pie."

Joey's chest expanded with pride. The one thing she'd done right in this world was Veronica. Though she owed Ethan much of the credit. He and his stepmother, Alma, had raised her during the years Joey had struggled with addiction. But now she was back in her daughter's life to stay.

On her way to Nugget Elementary, she took a detour to the market and bought Roni a cupcake. In general, she wasn't a dessert-before-dinner kind of mom. But occasionally it didn't hurt to indulge. At least that's what she told herself. Later, she would let herself wonder if she used treats and presents as a way to buy Roni's love. Deep down inside, she knew her daughter adored her, but it was difficult keeping up with Ethan and Brynn, who could offer Roni ten times more than Joey could.

A trail of cars had already lined up at the curb of Roni's school. Joey joined the queue and kept her eyes peeled for a towheaded seven-year-old. A few vehicles ahead of her sat Brynn's minivan. Brynn stood outside on the grassy lawn, chatting with a group of women. As usual, she was completely put together in a tailored skirt, white blouse, and knee-high designer boots. It was her New York City wardrobe, Joey assumed. Yet, in its elegant simplicity, it worked in a country town the size of a postage stamp. Her dark hair was tied back in a smooth ponytail that would've taken Joey hours to perfect but on Brynn appeared effortless.

Joey watched Brynn's easy way with the other women and felt a wave of envy wash over her. It wasn't enough that she was beautiful and accomplished, she was clearly also popular with the other moms. *Popular*. It was such a ridiculous thing for Joey to be jealous of. Her high school days were long past, yet here she was, bemoaning the fact that someone else was homecoming queen.

But before the pills, before the stealing and the lying, Joey had been well-liked by the other nurses at the hospital, the moms at Roni's preschool, and the neighbors in their planned community in Reno. She'd been invited to all the happy hours, parties, and potlucks and had often played hostess.

But after being strung out on opioids, she'd become a disheveled mess, living for her next fix, forsaking her friendships. Even now that she was clean, it was too awkward and humiliating to rekindle any of her old relationships. For the most part, she stuck to herself.

Her parents had been a great support. And although her brother, Jay, was a competitive blowhard, he'd been good to her throughout her ordeal, even offering to pay for an attorney to fight Ethan for shared custody of Roni. Thank goodness they'd avoided a court battle and had worked things out on their own.

Brynn caught a glimpse of Joey and waved. Joey waved back, hoping that it fulfilled any further obligation. But nooooo. Brynn came walking over to say hello.

It would've been rude to remain in the car, so Joey got out and self-consciously let Brynn hug her. "How's Henry?" she asked lamely. She'd seen Brynn's nine-year-old just a few days ago while picking up Roni. He was a sweet little boy and had been Ethan's patient after an accident had crushed both his femoral shafts.

"Great. You can say hi when you get Roni. How'd the job interview go? Ethan said it sounded promising."

It had been promising until she'd found out her interviewer was none other than kiss buddy Matthew McConaughey. Now who knew? Though she was banking on the prospect that Nugget had a dearth of qualified candidates. And that judging by Ryder's kissing skills, he got around and wasn't as freaked out about their brief encounter as she'd been. Besides, she'd be working for his mother, not him.

"We'll see." She tried to sound optimistic.

"And the living situation…that would work?"

The place had been a dump. Old, dirty, and tiny. But its proximity to Roni couldn't be beat. "Uh-huh. And it's only a few miles from the Circle D." *So, we'll all be one big, happy family.*

"That's terrific," Brynn said. "I'm keeping my fingers crossed."

"Thank you. But if it doesn't work out, I'm sure I'll find something else."

"Absolutely," Brynn said brightly. She was trying too hard.

Joey gave her credit, though. Not every woman pulled off magnanimous with such aplomb. Then again, Brynn—a wealthy woman in her own right—had landed Ethan, his ranch, and his spectacular home. She could afford to be magnanimous.

"Where are you and Roni going for dinner?"

There were only two choices if they wanted to stay in Nugget. "Probably the Ponderosa. Unless Roni wants a burger."

"She had one last night," Brynn blurted, then quickly fell silent.

"Oh. Well, then, the Ponderosa for sure." It took all of Joey's willpower not to add sarcastically, "Unless you took my daughter there for breakfast."

Over Brynn's shoulder, Joey spotted Roni running toward them. Henry was close behind. Both of them looked so happy that it made her momentarily forget her resentment.

"Mommy!" Roni wrapped her arms around Joey's waist.

"Hey, pretty girl, how was school?" She reached for Henry to bring him into the huddle, and like Roni, he gave her a great big hug. He was walking so well; she hadn't even noticed a limp. Her ex was a brilliant surgeon, so she wasn't surprised, despite Henry's massive injuries.

"I thought we could go hang out in the square for a little while before dinner," she told Roni. It was still too early for dinner, and they didn't have anywhere else to go. "What do you think?"

"Can Henry come?"

Brynn exchanged an apologetic glance with Joey. "Oh, that's so sweet of you, Roni. But Henry's got homework and chores."

"I could do them later," he said and looked from Brynn to Joey imploringly.

The kid went straight to her heart. She didn't want to countermand Brynn, but Henry was welcome to join them. Trying to be sly about it, she gave Brynn a nod to let her know it was okay if Henry came along.

But Brynn ruffled his hair and said, "Next time, buddy."

Joey wondered if Brynn didn't trust her with her kid or if she was simply trying to give her alone time with Roni. She tried not to dwell on it. This was all about spending time with her daughter, not Brynn Barnes.

Joey and Roni headed to the park in the middle of the square. There were a few benches and a gazebo, but no playground, not even a swing set. Other than running around on the grass, there wasn't a whole lot for a kid to do.

"I brought a snack." Joey parked the car and presented Roni with the cupcake she'd bought at the store. "How 'bout you eat half now and we'll save the rest for after dinner?"

"Is it vanilla?" Roni peeled back the paper.

"Of course it is. Your favorite. Let me split it in half, and we'll keep the other half right here." Joey patted the passenger seat. "You want to eat outside and walk around?"

"Okay." Roni released her seat belt and jumped out of the car.

"Be careful, Roni. We're in a parking lot." Joey got out and went around to Roni's side, and then handed her a slice of the cupcake and a couple of napkins she kept on hand in the glove box.

They strolled around the perimeter of the greenbelt, Roni eating and talking a million miles a minute.

"Mommy, can you get a house here with a swimming pool?"

Joey laughed. From what she'd seen at Ryder Knight's house, she'd be lucky to have running water. "Geema and Geepa and your grandma Alma have pools. We don't need another one."

"They're so far away, Mommy."

"It's only Reno, baby. Plus, there's a river and a lake here." And someone had told her there was a millpond in the neighboring town. This summer they'd have to go.

"We're going to have a pool in Hawaii and a giant ocean."

Joey jerked her head up. "Hawaii? Is Daddy taking you to Hawaii?"

"For his and Brynn's moon."

"You mean honeymoon." She wiped pink frosting from Roni's mouth with one of the napkins. "You guys are going to Hawaii?" It was the first she'd heard of it, but she wasn't exactly in the loop.

"Daddy and Brynn are going first. And then me, Henry, and Grandma are meeting them for a vacation in a big hotel with three swimming pools and a million restaurants. Daddy said me and Henry can order whatever we want, and we might see dolphins."

"How fun, Roni." And how nice of Ethan to let her know. "Maybe you and I should go on a vacation, too." The words were out of her mouth before she could stop them. Not only didn't she have disposable cash for dolphins and fancy hotels, but a new job didn't allow for time off.

"Disneyland!" Roni jumped up and down.

She and Ethan had taken her when she was three, barely old enough for her to remember. "Good idea." She tossed Roni's cupcake wrapper in the trash and rummaged through her purse for a wet wipe. "Maybe before you go back to school." At least that would buy her a little time and give her a chance to win the lottery.

They managed to burn another hour and then had a nice dinner at the Ponderosa, where Roni told her about her day at school, including a story about a girl who fell off the monkey bars and broke her knee.

"Do you think Daddy can fix it?" Roni asked as Joey drove her home.

"Are you sure it's broken and not just bruised?"

Roni shrugged. "A bunch of blood came out."

"Well, if it's truly broken, Daddy can fix it. But she probably has her own doctor."

It was still daylight as she took the turn to the Circle D Ranch. She edged up the paved driveway and admired the array of flowers blooming on both sides of the road. She couldn't tell if they were wild or had been planted, but all the lovely colors—blues, violets, pinks, whites, and oranges—were incredible. The whole ranch was.

Ethan, normally a barebones kind of guy, had spared no expense. The house with all its picture windows was something you'd see on one of those home shows. The horse barn was better than most people's houses. And the grounds were spectacular. Dense with trees and green rolling hills and a bird's-eye view of the Feather River, which wound its way through the property. It was nothing like the suburban tract home he and Joey had shared in Reno.

The cozy sight of Ethan and Brynn, drinking wine on the front porch, greeted her as she crested the hill. Henry was in the front yard, playing fetch with Simba, the dog she and Ethan had raised from a pup. The whole picture was like a still shot from a Hallmark movie.

"'Bye, Mommy." Roni jumped out of the car, even before Joey could kiss her good-bye, scampering off to join the fun. To join her new family.

With a lump in her throat, Joey unrolled her window, shouted good-bye, waved to Ethan and Brynn, and hung a U-turn, hauling ass out of there as fast as she could fly. The whole way back to Reno she cried.

Chapter 3

It had been four days, and Ryder hadn't heard a word from Comfort Keepers. He was moving his ma in Monday and then was heading out with the cattle wagon for three days on the road. He needed a caregiver, and he needed one quick.

At least the work on the house was going smoothly. The floors were done and looked brand new. The guy who'd refinished them…Colin Burke…knew his stuff. He'd also helped Ryder spruce up the tilework in the bathroom and had built a ramp to make it easier for Siobhan to get up on the front porch without having to climb the stairs.

The cleaning crew was coming later today. After the place got a good scouring, Ryder planned to move in his mother's furniture and give the house some semblance of hominess.

In the meantime, he was panicking. He dialed Comfort Keepers, even though he'd been exchanging texts with his case agent.

"Hey, Janine. It's Ryder Knight again. Hey, I'm getting a little worried." The other agency in Quincy hadn't come through at all, and Janine had only sent him one person. Albeit a perfect person, if not for the small matter that once upon a time he'd had his hands and his mouth all over her.

Janine let out an audible sigh. "I'm sorry, Mr. Knight. As I've explained, your remote location makes it difficult. If you were in Reno, you'd have your pick of caregivers."

"What if I offered some kind of incentive? Like a signing bonus. Would that help?"

"It might, but the real issue is there just aren't many qualified caregivers out your way. Unfortunately, seniors and patients in rural areas tend to rely on friends and neighbors. But that's not something I would recommend, especially given your mother's twenty-four-hour needs. I had hoped that you would find Ms. Nix a good match, but I'll keep searching."

Ryder had rejected the idea of putting an ad in the local paper. He didn't want just anyone caring for his mother. He wanted someone with serious bona fides, someone who could properly administer his mother's medication, someone who would recognize the signs of a stroke if, God forbid, his mother had another one. And here he was, turning away a freaking nurse with a master's degree.

"Is there any way I could hire Ms. Nix until we found someone else?"

"Umm, I could ask, though I think she's anxious to find permanent work. Someone with her credentials is in high demand," Janine said. Ryder didn't miss the sound of exasperation in her voice. If she only knew.

The funny thing was, he didn't get why someone with Joey's credentials wouldn't be working in her own field. A nurse for Siobhan was overkill, not that he didn't consider it an added plus. But he assumed the job of caregiver was below Joey's usual pay grade. The woman was a goddamn mystery. A mystery he didn't need. But desperation called for desperate measures.

"Can you let me know?" he asked Janine. "If she'd be willing to work on a trial basis, it would be great to get her in here by Monday."

"No promises, Mr. Knight. But I'll see what I can do."

He had an hour until the cleaning crew came and figured he might as well go to town and grab lunch. Fifteen minutes later, he slid onto a bar stool at the Ponderosa. The chief of police was jawing with the bartender and bobbed his head at Ryder in greeting. He'd seen him here a couple of times, but they hadn't formally met. Now that he was a resident, it was probably time he introduced himself.

"Ryder Knight." He stuck out his hand and shook the cop's. "I just moved into the old Montgomery place."

"Yep, that's what I heard. Rhys Shepard. Welcome to Nugget."

"Thank you, Chief."

"Lucky says you're a legend...a world champion saddle bronc rider."

"That was a lifetime ago." Ryder stared down at his boots, then looked up. "I own Knight Trucking now. We haul livestock across the west."

Rhys nodded. "I've seen your rig parked outside the Lumber Baron. My wife owns the place."

Ah, Maddy Shepard, the innkeeper. He should've put it together. "Beautiful inn. A hell of a lot nicer than what I'm used to."

"You should've seen it when Maddy and her brother first bought it. The place was ready to be condemned." He grinned, obviously proud.

Ryder whistled. "You'd never know it."

"One of my officers is your neighbor. Wyatt Lambert. Good guy."

Life in a small town was a lot like the *Cheers* theme song. Everyone knew everyone else's name. If he hadn't grown up in Oakdale, California— "Cowboy Capital of the World"—it might've felt intrusive.

"That's what I hear. My ma is moving in, and it would be great if you could keep my place on your radar when I'm out of town." Nugget seemed like a safe place, but it didn't hurt to have the law looking out for his mother.

"We sure will. When will she be here?"

"Next week. I'm just getting the place fixed up before I bring her home. A few months ago, she had a stroke. It landed her in the hospital and then a rehab facility. She's still not up to full speed, but we're working on it."

"Sorry to hear that. Glad she came through it okay."

"Thanks. There will be someone staying with her at the house, but I'd sure appreciate it if someone from the department drove by every now and again."

"You can count on it," Rhys said, looked at his watch, and grimaced. "I've gotta get going. Hope to see you around."

"Back attcha." He grabbed a menu and gave the bartender his order.

The restaurant, which reminded Ryder of a Western theme park, was quiet. Then again, it was late for lunch and too early for dinner. A baseball game played on the television behind the bar. The sound had been turned off and a Hayes Carll tune filled the dining room.

Over the last year, he'd spent a good amount of time here at the Ponderosa. It's where he'd first laid eyes on Joey Nix.

She'd come in with that shiny blond hair of hers swinging, along with a pair of denim-clad hips, and had sat alone in the corner. There'd been a lot of women since Leslie. Mostly ladies he'd met in truck stops, who, like him, were looking for a few hours of recreation and nothing more. But no one had stirred him the way Joey had.

Maybe it had been her looks—he'd always been a sucker for a pair of baby blues—or her confidence. Or maybe he'd recognized loneliness when he saw it. Whatever it was, he'd made it known he was interested in taking her to bed.

She'd been tempted. He could see it in her eyes, in her body language, in the way she flirted with him. But something had held her back. And then one night, out of nowhere, she'd waylaid him as he was getting out of his rig, grabbed him by the collar, pushed him against his truck, and kissed him into kingdom come. Then, just as calm as you please, she got back in her little red SUV and drove away.

He hadn't seen her since. Not until she'd shown up at his front door, sent by Comfort Keepers.

His tri-tip sandwich came, and he plowed through it, hungrier than he'd realized. Keeping one eye on the clock, he drained his beer.

"You want another?" The bartender cleared away Ryder's glass.

"I'm good. Just the bill, thanks."

He squared up and made it home in time to let the cleaners inside the house. While they did their thing, he unloaded furniture from the U-Haul he'd rented and stacked it up near the front door.

Around four, he took a break, grabbed a cola from the cooler in his truck, and sat on the edge of the porch, listening to the birds sing. Colin, the local who'd done his floors, made slick-looking rocking chairs. One of these days, Ryder planned to swing by Colin's workshop and buy a few to put on the porch so he could stare out over his land and up at the Sierra mountain range. It was beautiful here, that's for sure. And the air was so clean it was cleansing.

The ring of his phone broke the stillness. He thought about letting it go to voice mail, but it was Janine.

"Hey," he answered. "You got news for me?"

"I have another candidate. I know you wanted a woman for your mother, but Peter Crenshaw has excellent credentials. He's been with the agency for five years and until recently had been the caregiver for an elderly gentleman who passed two weeks ago. The family adored him, and I can get you letters of recommendation from them as well as other clients he's worked with. Ordinarily, he works with terminal patients, but the death of this last gentleman hit him hard and he's looking for someone who's…" she trailed off. But Ryder could fill in the blank. *Someone who wasn't circling the drain.* "I thought they'd be a good match until your mother moves to a senior community."

"And he's willing to come out this far?" Ryder asked, though he was hesitant. A man helping his ma in the bathroom, the shower, getting dressed; she wasn't going to be comfortable with that.

"He is. Frankly, I think he's anxious for change."

Ryder blew out a breath. "I don't know, Janine. I don't think my mother will go for it. I'd like to keep searching for a woman. Did you talk to Ms. Nix about a trial basis?"

"I did." She paused. "Because she's eager to be near family in Nugget, she's willing. But, Mr. Knight, if you decide to replace her with someone from outside of Comfort Keepers, we'll have to charge you for the remainder of our three-month contract. So please keep that in mind. Are you sure you and your mother wouldn't like to speak with Peter?"

Siobhan wouldn't even let him help her in and out of the bath. And he was her freaking son. No way in hell was she going to let a male stranger do it. The screwed-up thing about it was that he was pretty sure his mother would like Joey. Besides the fact that she was female—very female—Joey had a no-nonsense air of confidence about her that would put his mother at ease.

"Level with me, Janine. What are the chances you'll have another female caregiver for me in the next four days?" He pressed his soda bottle against his forehead.

"I'm trying the best I can, Mr. Knight. But not to sound like a broken record, given your rural location, it'll take time."

He banged his head against the porch railing a few times. Desperation was driving him against his better judgment. "For now, I'll go with Ms. Nix." He knew he'd regret it. But what choice did he have? It was her or nothing.

"Excellent. I'll let her know. When would you like her to start?"

"If she could be in before my mother gets here, that would be great." The transition would be difficult enough for his mom, who, before the stroke, had been a hardheaded independent woman. She hadn't been thrilled about leaving her home, her community, and her freedom. And she'd balked at having a full-time "babysitter." Best not to turn it into an ordeal with Joey moving her stuff in at the same time he brought Shiv home.

"Let me see about this weekend. And how would you feel about using Peter as relief for Ms. Nix? It would only be two eight-hour shifts a week."

Ryder squeezed the bridge of his nose. "Yeah, okay, we'll see how it goes." Because what choice did he have?

By the time he got off the phone, the cleaning folks were finished. In two hours, the six-person crew had knocked down all the cobwebs, removed the dust and grime, and left the place smelling like bleach and lemons. While not the most attractive bungalow, it was now habitable.

Tomorrow, the new refrigerator, dishwasher, washing machine, and dryer would come. He was keeping the stove, which, according to Colin, worked like a charm. And then there was the fact that Ryder just plain liked the vintage feel of the antique stove. It had seen some life, just like Ryder.

He spent the remainder of the evening moving in his mother's boxes and setting up the furniture. His ma's stuff was old and a little worse for wear, but when she'd bought it, the pieces had been quality. Siobhan Knight had worked her whole life scrimping and saving to make a good life for her and her son. Ryder's dad hadn't stuck around long enough to celebrate his kid's first birthday. Last Ryder heard, the old man owned a small ranch in Colorado with one of his sons from his second family. Well, they could have him. Tanner had never done Ryder nor his ma much good.

Shiv, though, had more than made up for the old man's absence. With not even so much as an associate degree, she'd managed to get a job with the Stanislaus County Superior Court, working for Judge Morgan Lester as his court clerk. She'd been in his courtroom for more than thirty years and had read the verdicts in some of the most high-profile civil and criminal cases that county had ever seen. When she retired, Judge Lester threw her a party at his private club, and everyone from the sheriff to the district attorney had been there.

On her single salary, she'd managed to buy them a small house with enough yard for him to have a swing set and later a basketball hoop. When he was old enough, he worked weekends and summers at a neighboring ranch to pitch in with the expenses. It was there that he'd found his love for all things horses and ultimately riding bucking broncs.

His ma had supported him through the California High School Rodeo Association, putting a lot of miles on their old car attending his events. And when he'd gotten a rodeo scholarship to Cal Poly, she'd made sure he had enough spending money to keep up with the other kids. When he'd won his first million, he upgraded her from their small house in Oakdale to a two-story, luxury town house in Modesto. She'd been so damned proud of that place. And now she couldn't live there anymore. Climbing the stairs was too much after the stroke.

So it was his turn to look after her the way she had him.

He hung pictures on the wall, including a few of him as a kid, hoping it would make her feel more at home. By the time he finished, it was past eleven. The place needed a few more lights. Tomorrow, after the appliances came, he'd go on the lookout for lamps. Maybe get that bench for the shower Joey had recommended.

He did a walk-through to admire his handiwork. The living room wasn't half bad furnished. There'd been enough room for his mother's sofa and love seat. He'd hung the flatscreen over the fireplace and positioned the recliner so his mother could comfortably watch her shows. Her bedroom could still use some personal touches, but at least the bed was made with fresh linens and he'd gotten most of her clothes hung in the closet.

Not bad for a day's work.

He shut out the lights and headed across the yard to his fifth wheel, more tired than he'd been in a long time. It wasn't the physical labor; it was all the decision making. For so long, he'd only been responsible for himself. And the biggest choices he'd had to make was where to eat and sleep. Or whether to drive the whole night through.

He preferred it that way. The last time he'd made a decision for someone he loved, it had cost her her life.

Chapter 4

Saturday was moving day. Jay, Joey's brother, had offered to help. Between her SUV and his pickup truck, they were able to move her bed, dresser, toiletries, and clothes in one trip. She didn't want to go crazy in case the job didn't work out. Besides, the bedroom she'd be using wasn't much larger than the bathroom she had all to herself at her parents' house.

But it was a job close to Roni, and that's all she cared about. She planned to make herself so indispensable that Ryder wouldn't have any reason to can her.

In the nicest of ways, Janine had conveyed to her that Ryder had reservations about Joey. She knew it had nothing to do with her qualifications. No, Ryder's issues had nothing to do with her professionally and everything to do with one very hot kiss.

She couldn't say she blamed him. The kiss made for an awkward employment situation and a potentially unprofessional one. But she wouldn't let it become a problem. She needed the job—and especially the living situation—too badly.

For the last eight months, Comfort Keepers had gotten her work all over Reno. But this was the first opening in Nugget, and she wasn't about to screw it up. The prospect of being only a couple of miles from Roni, from being able to attend her school events and regularly take her for dinners and sleepovers was beyond perfect.

Whatever attraction she and Ryder had once felt for each other would just have to be set aside.

The second they got to his home, she could feel Jay's disapproval emanating off him like a bad odor.

"This is it?" He stared at the house with distaste, then under his breath said, "That son of a bitch is getting away with murder over what he pays you in alimony."

Ethan was under no obligation to pay her anything. At the time of their divorce, the court had awarded her rehabilitative alimony, meaning that once she was able to work again, she'd be on her own. Ethan continued to pay her support out of the goodness of his heart. But he was starting a new family, and Joey had no intention of taking advantage. She'd been the one to ruin their marriage and had nearly cost Ethan his career. It was understood that as soon as she was financially solvent, she'd stop mooching off him.

"Shush, I don't want the owner—my new employer—to hear you. Let me go find him so we can start moving this stuff inside."

"I don't know what you're working for. If you'd played your cards right, pussy boy would've had to pay you the rest of your life."

Joey rolled her eyes. Her brother didn't have the first clue about Nevada divorce laws. But at the rate he was going with his own marriage, he should definitely get himself acquainted with them. In addition to Jay's naïveté, he could be a vindictive jerk. It was no secret that he and her ex-husband despised each other. Joey had always suspected that Jay was jealous of Ethan. The famous surgeon thing really rankled Jay.

Ryder came out of the house and onto the porch. He shielded his eyes with his hand against the sun as he surveyed the back of Jay's pickup. "Howdy."

"Hi," Joey said, her pulse unexpectedly quickening. "This is my brother, Jay. Jay, this is Ryder Knight, Ms. Knight's son."

Ryder and Jay sized each other up the way guys do. Then Ryder came down the steps and shook Jay's hand.

"You need some help?" Before she or Jay could answer, Ryder had started untying the straps her brother had used to secure her mattress and box spring.

Together, the two men carried in the bed while she grabbed a few boxes. It took less than thirty minutes to unload everything. Jay used the time to try to sell Ryder one of the new Ford F-450s on his dealership lot. Her family had grown used to Jay's cheesy sales pitch. But to give him credit, it's probably why Nix Ford did as well as it did.

With her boxes, chest of drawers, and bed, there was hardly room to move in her new bedroom. She planned to spend the next couple of hours putting things away before picking up Roni for the day. They would have so much more time together now that she didn't have to commute.

She walked Jay out to his truck. "Thank you for doing this."

He turned and gave the house another appraisal. "It isn't as bad on the inside, but are you sure you want to do this? You're practically a doctor for Christ's sake."

"Jay, I've been doing *this* for the last eight months." Though it was the first time she'd be a live-in caregiver. "You know why?" It was a rhetorical question because he knew as well as she did that she'd been stripped of her nursing license. "Because this is the only vocation I have." And she liked it. At the end of the day, she was still helping people. And that's why she'd gone into nursing in the first place.

"I say you make that bastard pay. Lord knows, he can afford it."

She clamped her jaw together. It was futile arguing with him, so why even bother? "Drive safely." She opened his truck door and managed a tight smile.

He got in and nudged his head at the front door of the house. "Watch out for that guy. I don't trust him."

"Yeah, okay," she said and walked away, wishing she'd handled the move on her own.

Inside, she found Ryder stretched out on the couch, drinking a beer, watching pro rodeo.

"Do you miss it?" she asked and just as quickly wished she hadn't. They weren't friends. He was her employer and she his employee. The end.

He turned to look at her, his expression surprised. "You've been doing your research, huh?"

"People talk." She shrugged.

"Nah, I don't miss it. It's a young man's sport."

She'd wondered about his age and was tempted to ask but stopped herself. If she had to guess, the crow's feet dancing around his eyes put him somewhere in the vicinity of forty. A good forty, though, with a full head of hair, a lean physique, and facial lines that told a story.

"You miss nursing?"

"This is similar enough," she said, desperately wanting to extricate herself from the conversation.

"I was wondering why you quit."

Shit. She'd promised herself she wouldn't lie if the question came up. Lying was grounds for immediate dismissal. Besides, a successful addiction recovery required honesty. "A few years ago, I had an accident. I slipped on a wet floor and threw out my back. The pain…well, it was beyond anything I'd ever experienced. I became addicted to painkillers, and my nursing license was suspended. I'm in the middle of appealing to be reinstated."

He didn't respond at first, just sat there assessing her, making her feel like she was under a microscope.

"I'm clean now," she stuttered. But even to her own ears, she sounded defensive.

"It would've been good if you'd told me that from the beginning."

"All you had to do was ask. But if it's a problem, I'll pack up and be on my way." Her chest tightened. She wanted this job with every fiber of her being.

There was a long silence, then, "You and I both know that would leave me in a bind. We'll see how it goes."

But Joey sensed her days were numbered. He'd already made it clear that he was uncomfortable with her in the first place. Add the new revelation that she'd been a druggie and...Ryder was going to find someone else. It was clear as the newly cleaned windows.

"I'm going to unpack my stuff now," she said and headed to her bedroom.

She shut the door and sat on the edge of her bed. At least her past was out in the open, she told herself. When he slapped her with a pink slip, she'd be prepared. Monday, she'd tell Janine to start looking for something else. Insurance companies required caregivers to work through a licensed agency, but it didn't mean she couldn't put the word out that she was available for in-home care in the general vicinity.

In the meantime, she kept busy by hanging up her clothes in the stingy closet. When she finished, she made up the bed and displayed a few pictures of Roni on the dresser and nightstand. It was a drab little room. But why cheer it up when she'd only be leaving soon? The worst part of getting canned would be Roni's disappointment. Her daughter had been over the moon that Joey was moving "next door" as Roni liked to say. And Ethan and Brynn...she was so tired of being the loser ex.

There was a tap on the door. Joey girded herself. Now that Ryder had had time to think, he'd probably come to deliver her walking papers. "Come in."

He opened the door but remained at the threshold as he glanced around the room. It was cramped but neat. "I'm going to the market to stock up on food for the week. Is there anything you'd like me to get? Meals are part of the compensation, right?"

"Yes. I'd like to focus on your mom first. I'll go over it with her when she gets here. But to tide us over, I can make a list or I can just do the shopping, which is technically part of my duties. It's up to you how you want to work it."

He reached up and hung his hands from the door casing, deliberating. "For now, why don't we just go together? Maybe I can set up some kind of account there for you."

Most of her clients just gave her a credit card. But whatever. "Sure." She glanced at her watch. Roni was expecting her. "I'm ready to go."

"I'll drive."

She grabbed her purse and followed him out to his truck. It was a Ram, which was probably why Jay didn't trust him.

"The house looks good," she said as he made his way down the driveway. It had been cleaned, and polished hardwood floors had replaced the old, disgusting carpet since the last time she'd been here. The furniture and pictures in the living room lent the cottage a cozy air. "It's important. Patients tend to recuperate better in a tidy and cheerful environment."

"My ma had a nice place in Modesto. Modern. She'll miss it. What about you?"

She turned in her seat. "What about me?"

"You leaving a good setup for this?"

"I've been living with my parents in Reno." It had been important for her to have a safe, nurturing place to land after six months in a rehab facility. "After my divorce, I needed time to restructure."

"I gather the ex lives here."

"The Circle D Ranch. You know it?" In her experience, everyone knew everyone else in Nugget.

"Ethan Daniels? That's your ex?"

"Uh-huh." She might as well get everything out in the open. It was a small town, and folks here loved to talk.

"I've only been there once. Nice place."

"Yep."

He slanted her a glance. "You two on good terms?"

"We are." It was true, not that it was any of Ryder's business. "If you have any doubts about me, feel free to give him a call."

"Why? He'll just say nice things about you whether they're true or not."

"No, he wouldn't. He's a respected surgeon, he wouldn't risk his credibility like that." Even though she'd had no compunction torpedoing his reputation to get a fix.

"Why'd you two get divorced? Was it the pills or the brunette?"

She assumed he meant Brynn. The fact that Ryder was comparing them hurt more than she was willing to admit. "He didn't meet Brynn until long after our divorce. As for why we broke up, that's kind of personal, don't you think?"

He hitched his shoulders. "So, you two have a kid together?"

"Veronica. We call her Roni."

He looked at her again, and she waited for the inevitable question. *Why isn't she with you?* But it never came. She suspected he already knew the answer and was saving her from the humiliation of it.

"What about you? Divorced? Kids?" A year ago, he'd told her he was single. But his status could've changed.

"Nope" was all he said.

She was about to ask him if he had a girlfriend but thought better of it. "How's the trucking business?" she asked instead.

"Busy." He was quite a conversationalist when the questions were aimed at him.

He slid into a parking space at the Nugget Market. The lot was the most crowded she'd ever seen it. A late spring weekend in the Sierra, she supposed. People came to look at the wildflowers and get their nature on. The market, which carried everything from bug spray to charcoal briquettes, catered to the tourists as well as locals.

She didn't wait for Ryder and grabbed a shopping cart, heading directly to the produce aisle. "Is there any fruit your mother doesn't like?"

"Not that I can think of." He squeezed an apricot and threw a few in a plastic bag.

"What about dietary issues? Is she allergic to anything?"

"She's not a vegetarian or a vegan, if that's what you mean. As far as allergies, I've never known her to have one. She doesn't like peas or fishy fish. Not a fan of venison, either."

"Okay, that's a good start."

She loaded the cart with a carton of strawberries, a honeydew melon, and any other fruit that looked fresh. Then, she perused the vegetable offerings. Next time, she'd visit Annie's farm stand.

She went from aisle to aisle, Ryder tagging along as she selected healthful ingredients. Whole grain bread, nuts, beans, and foods that would help control blood pressure and body weight. In the meat section, she stuck with poultry and ground turkey.

"For now, we're going to avoid most dairy and foods high in saturated fat," she told Ryder, who'd been throwing his own choices into the cart, including a couple of steaks. "If she really misses something, I'll work it into her diet sparingly and a little at a time. It's important that she doesn't feel deprived but at the same time maintains a healthy diet to reduce the risk of another stroke and to help her recovery."

"Okay. She's not much of a drinker, but I know she enjoys a glass of wine every now and again. Can she have that?" He stopped, as though suddenly remembering that Joey had a substance abuse problem. "Or will that be an issue for you?"

She couldn't tell if he was being thoughtful or acerbic but decided to answer with honesty. "As a recovering addict, I don't drink. But alcohol was never my problem, opioids were. In any event, you and your mother should pose the question of wine to her doctor. I don't know enough about her medical history to advise you on whether drinking, even in moderation, would exacerbate her condition."

He nodded. "We 'bout done here?"

Hey, shopping on a Saturday when Joey could be spending time with her daughter wasn't her idea of fun either. She was just about to tell him that when she thought better of it. Best to stay a hundred percent professional. "I just want to get a few cans of low sodium soup and we're out of here."

Ethel, the market's owner, rang them up. As Ryder paid, Joey couldn't help but notice the appreciative glances coming his way. Even Ethel, who had to be in her late sixties, was flirting with him.

She would've sworn she heard a sigh as the two of them passed a young woman on their way out of the store. Jeez, the man wasn't that good-looking.

"Here." Ryder handed her a credit card when they finished loading the groceries into the back of his truck. "This is for you to use on food and household items. I don't want my mother paying for anything."

The credit card made her feel like she'd passed a test with Ryder. Or maybe she was overanalyzing. He was hard to read.

On the way home, he turned on the radio to a country-and-western station and drummed his fingers to the beat of the tune. He drove with a lazy nonchalance, only one hand on the wheel, that for some crazy reason she found inordinately sexy.

Shut it down, girl.

"I'll be out of town for a few days next week, so you'll have to hold down the fort. My ma has an appointment with her new doc in Quincy. You'll need to drive her."

"Of course." That was all part of the job description. "I'll want to get a list of her appointments and the numbers for your cell and any other family members that I can contact in case of an emergency."

"Just me." His voice was almost a growl.

"Okay." Apparently Ryder didn't have any siblings. "Are you going on a business trip?"

He slid her a glance. "Cattle run. Wyoming. And hopefully a load on my way back to California."

"To Nugget?" She had no idea how livestock trucking worked.

"Nope. Coalinga. Feedlots."

"Do you ever speak in full sentences?" She simply couldn't help herself.

His mouth ticked up. "Nothing wrong with being spare."

"I bet you're a blast at parties."

"Don't go to 'em."

"Why's that?"

He shrugged. "No one ever invites me." Again, that wicked smile.

The man was a natural-born liar. Judging by the reactions he got at the Nugget Market, she'd say it was a pretty safe bet that he got all kinds of invitations.

"That's too bad." She started to say that maybe if he worked on his personality, he'd make more friends, but stopped herself. It was bordering on flirting, and there would be none of that.

By the time they got back to the house, she was ready to get out of his truck. The roomy cab had started to feel tight.

Together, they carried the groceries into the kitchen. He'd done work in here, too, she noted. Except for the old-timey stove, the appliances were new. The sleek stainless-steel refrigerator and dishwasher looked slightly out of place in the vintage kitchen. But they were so clean, they shined. And the place smelled like disinfectant, which reminded her of the hospital.

"It looks good in here." She turned in a circle. "You've been busy."

"I hired cleaners. And a local guy did the floors."

"Nice." She zeroed in on the wallpaper. "This is starting to grow on me. There's something about roosters...they're happy."

He eyed the wall, then her. "If you say so."

"We'll see what your mom thinks. Janine said Ms. Knight is hoping to move into a senior community in Reno once she fully recovers." A lot of seniors moved from California to Nevada because the cost of living was lower and there was no sales tax on food and medicine.

He nodded. "Cascade Village. You know it?"

She shook her head. "I'm sure it's very nice, though."

"Yup, lots of activities, along with a couple of restaurants, tennis courts, a pool, a spa, a gym, the works. And it's about half the price of similar places in California. She's pretending to be excited about it, but I know she's not too thrilled."

"Wasn't it her idea?" Joey asked, surprised that Ryder had suddenly opened up so much.

"Nah, she's been too sick. So, I checked it out and showed her pictures and a video tour. When she's a little bit more mobile, I'll take her to see it. It's a pretty swanky place."

"I'm sure when she visits in person, she'll be more enthused. Change is hard."

"Yeah, I guess. I just figured it was the best way to go. She'll be close to me and yet go back to having her independence. The place also has assisted living apartments and medical care on the premises if it winds up that she doesn't...well, anyway, I was trying to cover all the bases."

"It's a good plan," she reassured him because he seemed to be second-guessing himself. "And if she decides it's not what she wants, you'll come up with a new plan."

He let out a sigh. "I wanted to at least get her on the list. The place is full right now, and the director said it could take up to a year for something to become available."

"Absolutely." She was impressed with his compassion. He clearly loved his mother and wanted what was best for her, which was really sweet. It didn't match his rough exterior, but that was a cowboy for you. She'd known many cowboys in her time and had dated plenty. Hell, she'd married one. Ethan might be a surgeon, but he'd grown up in a multigenerational ranching family. "I'm sure you'll get it all settled. In the meantime, we'll take good care of her."

His response was to give her a look that said, *Don't get too comfortable here.* "You hanging around today?"

Was that a subtle hint that he wanted the house to himself? "I'm taking my daughter out."

"I'm planning to grill for dinner. If you're interested, let me know and I'll throw something on for you."

The man clearly had a split personality. He couldn't make up his mind whether he wanted to be friendly or aloof.

"I didn't see a barbecue," she said. Except for the overgrown grass, the yard was a wasteland.

"Nope. But by the end of the day, there'll be one."

"Thanks for the offer, but like I said, I've got plans."

"Suit yourself."

She stashed the nonperishables in the pantry. It was bigger than her clothes closet and might just be the best feature of the house. Joey assumed that when the home was first built, it had been a cold storage room for canned fruits and vegetables from the garden.

"If you don't need me for anything else, I'm going to take off," she said.

"Have a nice time with your daughter."

She took her cosmetics bag to the bathroom and applied some light makeup, then changed into a summery dress. It was overkill for a day out in Nugget with Roni. But Brynn brought out the competitive in her. The woman was stunning, even first thing in the morning. Joey had never considered herself a beauty by any stretch. But she'd always turned heads, especially male ones. Lately, though, she'd been less confident in herself.

She'd spent a lot of time in counseling, talking about it and exploring why Ethan had ever loved her in the first place. A truth not lost on her was that he could have had any woman he wanted. A doctor with a résumé equally as good as his. A supermodel. A movie star.

Yet he had chosen her and loved her like crazy. But that hadn't been enough for her. After Roni was born, she'd felt so low that she'd begun posting her picture on dating sites just to see if she could attract interest. Even before she'd become pregnant, going to bars with her nurse friends and counting the number of men who hit on her had become a game.

What kind of person did things like that? A very insecure one. It had taken her months of rehab to learn that about herself. She was working through it a little at a time, but she still had moments of doubt that were paralyzing.

And here she was, dressing up to impress her ex-husband's fiancée. It was beyond ridiculous. But as her therapist would say, if it made her feel good, it was harmless. So, she applied a little lipstick, grabbed her purse, and headed out.

Ryder was back on the sofa, watching rodeo again. For a man who didn't miss the sport, he certainly seemed obsessed. He looked up as she was leaving and took a long visual stroll over her dress. "See you."

"Bye."

The thought of spending the rest of the day with Roni cheered her. And by the time she got to the Circle D Ranch, she'd managed to shove her insecurities to the back of her mind and only focus on her daughter. Ethan came onto the porch when he heard her car pull up. She got out and waved to him.

"How'd the move go?"

"Good. It took longer than I thought it would, though."

"It always does."

Ethan looked good. He'd always been one of the best-looking men she'd ever known. But today, there was so much happiness coming off him that it was infectious. She should've been jealous but instead felt a surprising warmth for him.

"Come on in," he said.

She climbed the front porch. The house never failed to floor her.

"Where's Roni?" she asked, noting how quiet it was. Between Roni, Henry, and the dog, there was always a ruckus.

"We didn't know what time you'd get here, so Roni went with Brynn to get her wedding dress altered. She was excited about it."

"Oh. Why didn't you call me?" It was her day with her daughter, not Brynn's. She didn't want to make a federal case out of it, but it was presumptuous of them.

"I did. But you didn't answer your phone. I figured you were caught up in the chaos of the move. Look, if it's a problem, I can have Brynn bring her home or you can run by the seamstress shop in Clio. It's only a few miles past Nugget. You're the one always lecturing me about being too regimented with Roni's visitation schedule." It was his crafty way of saying that he'd been flexible with Joey, even though the court had granted him full custody. And that she in return should be flexible with him.

Because she hoped he would continue to be flexible, especially now that she could see Roni every day, she didn't argue. They'd spend all of Sunday together.

"I suppose it's good. I still have a ton of unpacking to do at the house," she lied.

"You want a cup of coffee or a soft drink?" He crossed the foyer and headed to the kitchen. Joey obligingly followed.

The rooms were so Ethan—the understated comfy rustic décor and muted colors—and yet so unlike Ethan. Her ex had always believed in living light on the land. And this house was anything but light. It fairly shouted, *"Look at me. I'm an architectural marvel."* Big open spaces, cathedral ceilings, exposed beams, ginormous windows that let in the views.

It was much fancier than the tract home Joey had had with Ethan in Reno. When they'd bought it, Ethan hadn't yet reached the pinnacle of his career. After the divorce, they'd sold it and split the proceeds, which hadn't amounted to a whole lot. Between what they owed to the bank and the slowing real estate market, they were lucky to have broken even.

He'd inherited the Circle D, which had been in his family for ages. The Danielses used to run their cattle here in the summer when there was no grass to be found in the arid Nevada countryside.

"Do me a favor," he said. "Write down the address of your new place." Ethan handed her a pen and a notebook.

She didn't know it by heart and rummaged through her purse for the slip of paper she'd written it on when she'd first interviewed with Ryder. She jotted it down and handed the notebook back to Ethan.

"That's the old Montgomery place," he said as he read her scrawl. The only person who had worse handwriting than her was him.

She shrugged. "It's the Knight place now."

"I'd heard that Ryder Knight bought it." He looked at her quizzically. "Last time I saw him, he was in perfect health."

"I'm working for his sixty-six-year-old mother. She recently suffered a stroke. He's bringing her home Monday."

Ethan gave her a long, assessing look. "There's nothing new on your nursing license?"

She tensed. It had been a year since she'd started the appeal. They both knew the California Board of Registered Nursing had no intention of reinstating it. "No. Who knows? It might turn out that I like this better." It was certainly less stressful than working at the hospital. The only drawback was not having her own place with a room for Roni. But one step at a time.

"Will the union get you an advocate?"

The question irritated her. The first thing she'd done in trying to reclaim her career was bring in a union rep. She didn't need her ex-husband mansplaining how she could fix her broken life. It wasn't broken, thank you very much. It was merely bruised and on the mend. "I've done that already." She changed gears because she didn't want to talk about her work anymore. "So you know Ryder Knight, huh?"

"Only in passing. He hauled my calves last summer, and I used to watch him compete in the PRCA. He's one of the greatest saddle bronc riders in recent history." He grabbed a mug from the cupboard. "You want coffee?"

"No thanks, but a glass of water would be great." She wanted to know more about Ryder. "One of the greatest, really?"

"Two-time world champ."

Whoa, she'd definitely called that one wrong. She'd assumed he was your run-of-the-mill rodeo bum, not a big timer. "Why'd he quit?"

Ethan hitched his shoulders. "You can only do it so long. The guy had more broken bones than all my patients put together. And I seem to recall there was some kind of family tragedy."

"Like what?"

"I don't remember, and I may be confusing him with someone else. It was at least five years ago. He's been out of pro rodeo for a while now."

He grabbed a glass, filled it with ice and water, and motioned for her to pull up a stool at the center island. "Brynn and I wanted to talk to you about the wedding."

"Roni already told me. You're all going to Hawaii. Do you think that from now on you could at least notify me of these things in advance? It would be nice to know when you're taking my daughter out of state without having to hear it from her first."

There was a long stretch of silence. She knew Ethan well enough to know that she'd overplayed her hand and that he was one inch away from letting her have it. He had sole custody of Roni, after all. And for good reason. At the height of her addiction, she'd put their daughter in imminent danger. Ethan had never fully forgiven her for it. And she hadn't forgiven herself. What she'd done was terrible. But slowly, she was earning back both their trust. And although he'd agreed to unsupervised visits with Roni, even allowing Joey to keep their daughter overnight, he was in charge.

"I should've told you," he said, surprising her. "It wasn't intentional. But with everything going on—work, the ranch, planning a wedding—it slipped my mind. It's not an excuse, and I'll do better in the future."

"Thank you." He'd caught her completely off guard.

"What we wanted to talk to you about, though, was the wedding itself. If it's not too weird for you, we'd like you to be there. We think it'll be good for Roni...show that it's amicable between you and Brynn...that it's okay for her to love both of you."

That last part was like a punch to the gut. He might as well have said that Brynn was as much Roni's mother as Joey was. Well, she wasn't. Not even close.

Joey's first inclination was to tell Ethan that he and Brynn could both go to hell. But one of the many skills she'd learned in rehab was impulse control.

She put down her glass of water and as calmly as she could, said, "I'll think about it." Then she picked up her purse and walked out.

Chapter 5

Ryder had just turned off the TV, ready to take off in search of a grill, when Joey came through the door and headed straight to her bedroom. It didn't take a genius to tell she was upset about something.

He deliberated for a few minutes, not wanting to get involved in whatever her problem was. But in the end, a sense of humanity he didn't know he had won out and he knocked on her door. "You okay?"

There was a long pause, and then in a faint voice, she said, "Yes."

He was about to walk away, satisfied that he'd done the right thing and was now absolved from giving a shit. Instead, like an idiot, he knocked again. "Everything okay with your daughter?"

A beat later, she opened the door. "Roni is fine. Thank you for asking."

He tried to pretend that he didn't see the dried tears on her cheeks. Besides being a fucking recovering pill popper, it turned out she was also a head case. *Why me?*

"I'm off to buy a barbecue, so you've got the place to yourself." He started to back away, then remembered he'd never given her a key to the house. "Hang on a sec."

He went out to his truck and returned with the spare. "Here you go. It works for both the front and back door locks."

"Thanks."

He was halfway out when he turned around. "You want to come?" He needed to get his goddamn head examined. *Say no. Please say no.*

"Uh...okay."

Great!

"Let's roll, then."

They were on their way to Farm Supply when she opened up. "My ex-husband wants me to come to his wedding."

"So? If you don't want to go, don't go."

"It's not that simple."

"Yeah, it is." He gave her a sideways glance, acutely conscious that the invite was the source of her crappy mood. "Why does he want you to come, anyway? Clearly, you're not over the dude. It seems kind of sadistic of him to ask that of you."

"I'm over him. This has nothing to do with it."

Bullshit, he thought to himself. "Then, what's the problem? Go to the damn wedding."

"It's so Roni will see us as one big happy family. Of course, I'm not really part of their family. So, where does that leave me with my daughter?"

"As her mother."

"You know where my daughter is right now?"

He didn't have the foggiest notion, but he was sure she was going to tell him. "Where?" he asked, resigned.

"With Brynn for her wedding dress fitting. Today is my day. My day." Her voice trembled. "I live for the weekends when I can see her. And yet, they…Brynn…had no hesitation taking her for the day."

"Did you tell your ex not to do it again? That you have rights."

She started to reply, then stopped herself. "I'm overreacting. It's just…"

"It's just what?" Jesus, why was he letting her suck him into her drama?

"I feel like I'm losing my daughter. That they have everything to offer her—a big house, a family, a damn trip to Hawaii—and I have nothing."

He pulled into the Farm Supply lot, cut his engine, and turned to her. "Nope. No one can ever take the place of a mother. Not a house and not a trip to Hawaii." He was living proof of that.

She reached into her purse, pulled out a mini pack of tissues, and blotted her eyes. Even an ugly smudge of black mascara couldn't mar her pretty face. Shit. First thing Monday, he had to tell Janine that he didn't care if she turned the state upside down. She had to find someone else.

"Ready to go inside?" he asked.

"Uh-huh. You must think I'm a total whack job."

"Yeah, a little bit." He grinned.

She laughed. But it came out like a snort, and she wiped her nose. "Whatever you think of me, I want you to know one thing. I'm really good at what I do. My patients always come first. I'm not just saying it to keep my job. It's the God's honest truth."

He didn't know why, but he believed her. Still, it didn't change the fact that she got under his skin. From the first day he'd seen her sitting alone in the Ponderosa, she'd captivated him. And that wasn't going to work. Not even a little bit.

"Let's go." He hopped out of the cab and didn't bother to wait for her to catch up.

The barbecues were outside, lining the exterior wall of the building. He inspected the different ones, looking specifically for a smoker. It had been a long time since he'd owned a barbecue. At the trailer park, he sometimes borrowed his neighbor's hibachi. Now he wanted to go full-hog, even if it meant shelling out some serious dough.

"What kind are you looking for?" Joey was back, and she'd cleaned her face.

"A smoker that has enough grill space to feed a crowd." Perhaps one of these days he'd invite Lucky and his family over for dinner.

Other than the Rodriguezes, he didn't know anyone well enough in Nugget to have over for a barbecue. For a long time, he'd avoided making friends or having any kind of close ties. He wasn't ready to change that, but it didn't hurt to occasionally feed his neighbors.

"My dad has this one. Swears by it."

It was a twelve-hundred-dollar smoker. He read the laminated card with the grill's features. The damn thing even had Wi-Fi, allowing you to control the heat from your phone. A little overkill, but hard to resist. He could start up the smoker before he even got home. Hot dog.

He examined a few of the cheaper models, but the pricier one kept calling his name. "What does your dad like about it?"

"The temperature's consistent, and the end result is delicious."

"Hmm, then I say we bring this bad boy home."

She smiled, her whole face lighting up. It stopped him in his tracks. A man could easily fall into a smile like that and drown.

"I'll go inside and pay," he said and rushed away.

Grace, the owner, was at the counter. Ryder had only met her a few times but she always remembered him.

"What kind of trouble are you up to today, Miss Grace?" He winked.

"Oh, just the usual trouble. How's the old Montgomery place treating you? I heard Colin Burke was by and refinished the floors. He said the house is shaping up nicely."

"So far, so good."

Out of the side of his eye, he saw Joey thumbing through the children's clothing.

"I'm glad to hear it," Grace said. "How can we help you today?"

He handed her the slip for the grill and slid his credit card across the counter. "You got one already built?"

"Because it's you, you can take that one."

"Why, Miss Grace, are you flirting with me?"

"Oh, honey, if I was only twenty years younger."

He told her to add a sack of pellets to his bill as she ran the card.

"I don't suppose you need help loading it up."

"Nah, I can handle it." He flexed his muscles.

Joey joined him at the counter, holding a frilly little denim skirt and a pink kid's top. He said good-bye to Grace and went outside to load up the grill while Joey paid for her items. Ryder had just finished strapping the barbecue down when she came out of the store.

"For your daughter?" He nudged his head at her package.

"It's not Hawaii, but Roni loves pink."

It was all he could do not to roll his eyes at her obvious attempts to buy her kid's love. But what the hell did he know? He'd never been a parent—never would be.

"You good to go?" He opened the passenger door for her.

"Ready when you are."

"I'm anxious to fire this baby up. You like steak? Or are you one of those anti–red meat people?"

"My ex-husband is a cattle rancher. What do you think?"

He got on the road and headed home. Home. The idea of putting down roots still unsettled him. It made him feel guilty, he supposed, like he was finally moving on instead of holding on to the past with both arms.

"Next, you need some patio furniture," Joey said. "It's a perfect day for eating outside."

He'd actually entertained the idea. "One thing at a time." He glanced over at her. "It must've been tough leaving the Circle D. It's a hell of a place."

The comment seemed to confuse her for a beat. "Oh, no, I never lived there. Ethan and I lived in Reno. The Circle D has been in his family forever. After the divorce, we sold our place in Reno, and he decided to relocate to California and build on his family's land."

"How come your daughter lives with him and not you?" He supposed it made sense given her work. An in-home caregiver couldn't be toting a kid around with her from job to job.

She sighed, and for a second Ryder thought she was going to tell him to mind his own business. It really wasn't like him to ask probing questions, but she'd started it by dumping her problems on him.

"I spent six months in a residential rehab facility," she said at last. "For consistency's sake, Veronica stayed with Ethan when I got out. Now, I'm here, too."

It certainly explained why she wanted this job so badly. He assumed with her credentials—she might not have a license, but she still had a nursing degree—she could probably name her job in Reno.

He swung into his driveway and made quick work of unloading the grill, which he set up in the backyard next to an electrical outlet near the kitchen door. Joey was right. The place could sure use some outdoor furniture. Even a picnic table.

Ryder read the instructions, and twenty minutes later he had the smoker preheating. Inside, Joey made a salad while he seasoned the meat.

"You like baked potatoes?" He'd grabbed a few while they were at the market, along with all the fixings.

"Love 'em. You want to throw them on the grill or bake them in the oven?"

"May as well use the grill."

It was strange having her in his kitchen. His kitchen. That in and of itself was weird. For the most part, he ate in truck stops and restaurants. Occasionally, he'd nuke a can of soup in his camper's microwave. This… well, it was making him feel claustrophobic.

He grabbed the potatoes out of the pantry and was just about to make a break for the yard when she took them from him.

"I'll get them ready."

He went out the back door and let himself breathe again, inhaling the fresh air. It was all he could do to stop the rush of memories. The sound of Leslie's voice. The smell of her cooking.

I miss you, baby.

He walked away from the house, out to a grove of pine trees and did his best to exorcise the melancholy that had overtaken him. It happened less often now. But sometimes all it took was a song or a picture for him to sink into a downward spiral.

In this case, it was Joey.

Getting a grip on himself, he walked back to the house to find her standing over the grill.

"It's too soon to put the steaks on," she said. "The potatoes will take a while." She'd wrapped them in foil and placed them on the upper rack of the barbecue.

He shut the lid. "I was thinking we could bring the table outside." There was a cracked concrete slab outside the back door that passed for a patio. It would be better than being alone with her inside the house.

"Good idea. I'll help you."

Together, they carried it out. He brought two chairs, and she gathered up napkins, plates, and silverware.

"This is great." She tipped her face up to the sun, and he had to look away.

"I'm gonna grab a beer. You want a soda or something?"

"A cola, please."

He found both in the fridge and got a glass out of the cupboard for her. They sat at the table, enjoying their cold drinks.

"How'd you find this place?" She stared past the yard to the broken-down fence that separated his land from the forest.

"Real estate agent. I wanted something where I could keep my tractor trucks and trailers." Renting space for them when they were out of service cost him an arm and a leg. Most of his drivers lived in apartments, where parking for an 18-wheeler wasn't easy to come by.

"It has potential. The land is gorgeous." She turned her head to the house.

"Yeah, the house not so much."

"I don't know about that. The outside definitely needs work. Some of the wood looks rotted, and it could use a paint job. Maybe something a little more cheerful than beige. But it could be cute. The wood floors inside are fantastic. And all the original trim gives the place character. It's just small."

He shrugged. "For you and my ma maybe. But it's all I need."

"Not if you start a family."

"That won't be a problem." He got up and pretended to check on the potatoes.

She must've sensed that the conversation of family was off-limits because she didn't press. "I suppose you could convert the two bedrooms into one large master."

"I hadn't thought of that. But yeah, it would be easy enough." He'd been splitting his time between his fifth wheel and the sleeper in his semitruck so long that small spaces weren't really an issue for him. But it wasn't a bad idea when his mom moved out.

"What about you? Any plans to get a place?" She must've had money from the divorce.

"I'd like to. We don't want to uproot Roni too much, so it would have to be here."

"You don't like it here?" Of every place he'd ever been, which was all over this great nation, Nugget appealed to him the most. The big trees, the rivers, the lakes, the mountains. It was the kind of place that lodged itself in a person's gut and just stayed there.

"I do, but work isn't exactly plentiful here. If I ever get..." she trailed off. But he suspected she was talking about her nursing career.

"Is there any chance of that...getting your license back?"

"I'm working on it," she said. "My situation isn't all that uncommon for people in my profession. But the board can be slow to respond."

"Situation?" He scratched his chin. "You mean drug addiction?"

She nodded.

He supposed it was a casualty of the job, having exposure to prescription drugs all day long. After Leslie, he'd taken to drinking a hell of a lot more than he should. But it had never gotten to the point where it interfered with his job or he couldn't just walk away from a bottle of booze.

"Can't your ex help you out on that end?" He would think that a doctor might have pull. But his sole experience with the medical profession were rodeo docs and physical therapists.

"Like, could he have influence with the board?" Joey pulled a face. "No, it doesn't work that way."

He hitched his shoulders as if to say, *What do I know?* "Say you get it back. What then? You return to working in a hospital?"

"Maybe. I was thinking Plumas General Hospital in Quincy. Something not too far away. But, of course, I'd stay with your mom until she moves to her senior community," she quickly amended.

She wouldn't have to wait that long because he still planned to find someone else. "I think we can put the meat on now."

"I'll get it." She started to get up, but he stopped her.

"I've got it."

He retrieved the steaks from the house and put them on the grill. Next time, he'd start them at a lower heat and leave them on the grill longer to maximize smokiness. But for now, he was too damn hungry to wait.

Joey got them more drinks and set out the salad. They couldn't have asked for better weather. And although he preferred his solitude, having a dinner guest was a nice way to christen the new place. More importantly, they seemed to have shed any residual embarrassment with each other over the kiss. But he'd be lying if he said he didn't still think about it.

"How do you like yours?" He flipped the meat over.

"Rare."

"Good girl."

She gave him a murderous glare, and he grinned, remembering one of the first times they'd crossed paths at the Ponderosa. He'd made the mistake of commenting about how good it was to see a woman unafraid to eat a big piece of pie. Her response was to rip him a new asshole. Basically, she'd called him a chauvinist.

He pressed the meat with his finger. "Two rare steaks coming right up."

It was a damn good meal, considering they'd whipped it up on the fly. "Not bad, huh?"

"Delicious." She filled her fork with baked potato.

"Too bad we don't have anything for dessert, like pie." He winked. "I know how you love your pie."

She gave him the finger and went back to her steak.

The sound of truck wheels on his gravel driveway got his attention. "You expecting anyone?" he asked Joey, who shook her head.

He walked around to the front of the house, where an old Ford pickup came up the hill. Ryder didn't recognize it, nor could he make out the driver. There was a dog in the bed of the truck, sticking its head out to catch the wind.

The Ford stopped short behind Ryder's Ram, and Ethan Daniels, holding a big bouquet of flowers, got out. He opened the back door of his pickup, and a little girl scrambled down the running board. She was a carbon copy of Joey.

The kid, blond hair flapping in the wind, ran across his front yard, her arms held wide. "Mommy, Mommy!"

"Roni." Joey, who had come up behind him, swept the girl up in her arms.

The dog started barking. Daniels yelled something at it, and the hound shut up.

He stuck his hand out to Ryder. "Ethan Daniels. We met last spring when you came to the Circle D to haul my cattle."

"Good to see you again."

"Great place you've got here. I hope we're not interrupting anything."

"Nope. We just finished dinner."

"Roni wanted to surprise Joey." He held up the flowers. "Congratulate her on her new gig. We won't be long."

"Take your time," Ryder said. "Beers and soft drinks are in the fridge."

As he headed to his camper to let them visit in private, he watched the trio huddle together. The kid had her arms flung around Joey's waist while Ethan gave his ex-wife a hug.

So, Ethan Daniels with his bundle of flowers the size of the rain forest was the ogre trying to steal Joey's daughter. He rolled his eyes and climbed into his fifth wheel.

Chapter 6

On Monday, Joey welcomed Siobhan Knight to her new home. She was a small woman who bore little similarity to her son in appearance, except for a matching pair of pale blue eyes.

Able to walk with the aid of a cane, she seemed surprisingly hale for a woman who had recently suffered a stroke. As far as Joey could tell, Siobhan, or Shiv, as she'd asked to be called, showed no signs of speech aphasia. And judging by the way she took in her new surroundings and complimented Ryder on the good investment he'd made, she was as sharp as a tack.

She was tuckered out from the nearly four-hour drive, though. Joey could tell that right away.

"Ma, would you like to relax a little while, before we sit down to dinner?" Ryder had said after they'd stopped for lunch.

"Just a short nap." Shiv looked relieved to be given a reprieve from all the newness of her situation and started for her bedroom.

"Let's see if the room is cool enough for you." Joey followed closely behind Shiv, trying not to hover. On Sunday, Ryder had installed screens on all the windows and had bought fans. It was getting warmer, and the house had no central air.

Ryder leaned against the hallway wall, watching Joey closely. She hadn't deluded herself into believing that Saturday's friendly barbecue solidified her job here. Her sense of Ryder was that he was a pragmatist, and if he didn't think Joey was right for the job, he'd sack her without a moment's hesitation.

That was fine. Because despite her ugly history, she was good at her job. So, let him watch and see for himself.

Shiv's room was in desperate need of window treatments. With the late afternoon sun streaming in, it would be difficult for her to sleep, never mind the privacy factor.

Joey turned to Ryder. "Do you have a dark sheet or a blanket we can use in here as a temporary curtain?"

He pushed off the wall, all six-foot-something of him, and went in search of a makeshift window covering they could use. At least there was a soft breeze.

Joey pulled down Shiv's covers. "Would you like me shut the window or leave it open?"

"Open is fine, dear."

Ryder returned with a hammer and nails, and a throw blanket with a picture of a man riding a bucking horse on it that looked a decade old. He reached up and tacked the blanket over the window, throwing the room into shade but not quite darkness. It would have to do for now.

"You two go on and let me get some rest." Shiv shooed them out of her room.

Ryder shut the door. "Sleep well, Ma."

He followed Joey into the kitchen, where she wanted to get a start on dinner. A healthy vegetable stir-fry with chicken.

"She looks good, right?"

"Uh-huh." Joey filled her arms with veggies from the refrigerator. "So far, from what I've seen, she's doing terrific."

He gave a crisp nod, seemingly reassured.

"But don't forget to get her that panic button we talked about. Did you look at the websites I sent you?"

"Yep, and I ordered it Friday. It should come in the mail sometime this week." He stood over her while she sliced bell peppers. She tried not to be affected, but his nearness made her jumpy. "You have a nice time with your kid yesterday?"

"I did." She and Roni had gone to Glory Junction, a cute ski resort town thirty minutes up the road. "What did you do?"

"Hung out. Took a crack at cleaning up the garage. Did some paperwork."

"For your trucking company?" She didn't know a lot about the business or what kind of records it entailed.

"Yeah. I've got a bookkeeper, but still...with fourteen drivers I have a lot of cargo to account for."

Her mouth fell open. "Fourteen drivers? They all work for you?"

"Yeah," was all he said, leaving her to believe that, unlike her brother, he wasn't one to brag or try to impress. "What're you making?" He motioned at her pile of cut veggies.

"A stir-fry. It'll be good for your mom."

"I'm gonna see if I can find blinds at the hardware store in Clio. It shouldn't take more than an hour." He shut the fridge for her as she carried more ingredients to the counter. "But I'd like to eat dinner with my ma."

"I'll wait." She found a big bowl to store the vegetables and began slicing the chicken breast.

"Do you mind if I measure your windows? They're the same size as the one in my mother's bedroom, and I don't want to disturb her."

"Go for it." She remembered too late that she'd hand washed two of her bras and hung them from her dresser to dry. Oh well. If the man got his jollies from wet lingerie, there was no helping him.

By the time she finished preparing the chicken, he was done measuring. She heard him drive away and went outside to call Roni.

Brynn answered. "Hi, Joey. How's your first day?"

"Good. Thanks for asking." Why did Brynn have to be so freaking nice? Joey would love to have hated her, but she made it impossible.

"I bet you're looking for Roni," Brynn said. "She and Henry just got home. Let me find her for you."

"Thanks." Joey leaned against the exterior wall of the house, enjoying the late afternoon sun.

"Hi, Mommy. Guess what?"

"What?" Joey smiled.

"I'm selling wrapping paper to raise money for school. Do you want to buy some?"

"Of course I do."

"Can you come buy it now?"

"Not tonight, sweet pea. I have to work. But soon. Save me a few rolls, okay?"

"It's not like that, Mommy. I have to order it, so don't worry, I won't run out. I have to go now to have a snack. Love you."

"Love you, too, baby girl. Talk to you soon." She clutched the phone to her heart, then went inside, afraid to be away from Shiv for too long.

She might seem strong, but Joey needed to watch for coordination and balance issues, common aftereffects of a stroke. Joey listened outside her door, and when she didn't hear any movement, quietly cracked the door open for a peek. Shiv was sound asleep.

Joey managed to occupy herself until Ryder got home. He came in, hugging three big bags from the hardware store, including blinds.

"My ma still in bed?"

"Yes, but I'm going to wake her soon. Otherwise, she'll have trouble sleeping tonight."

"I'll start on your room first," he said.

He spent the next thirty minutes making enough noise to wake the dead. Still, Shiv didn't rise. It concerned Joey, so she knocked on her door and went inside.

"Shiv," she whispered. When Ryder's mom didn't stir, Joey shook her. "It's dinnertime. Would you like to wash up first?"

"Oh, okay," she said in a groggy voice.

"Let me help you." Joey flicked on the light, then found Shiv's slippers in her suitcase and brought them over to the bed. "Come up slow." She didn't want her to get dizzy, another common aftereffect of a stroke.

She helped Shiv to the bathroom, where she could wash her hands and face and comb her hair.

"Come sit in the kitchen while I start the stir-fry. Ryder's going to install blinds on your window."

Shiv seemed less steady than before, but Joey attributed it to her still being half asleep. In the kitchen, she pulled out a chair from the table for her and fired up a fry pan she'd found in the cupboard.

In the background, she heard Ryder's drill and assumed he'd moved to Shiv's room. The man didn't let grass grow under his feet. She supposed he wanted to get everything done before he got on the road.

Joey tried to make conversation, but Shiv didn't seem interested in talking. Joey worried that Ryder's mother had taken an instant dislike to her, then told herself not to be ridiculous. It was more likely that Shiv took after her son, who answered most questions with monosyllabic answers.

Ryder came in and gave Shiv a peck on the cheek. "How you feeling?"

"Stop fussing. I'm fine."

Perhaps that was it. They were babying her too much.

"Dinner is almost done," Joey said. "I thought for Shiv's first night, we should eat in the dining room."

"Sounds good, right, Ma?"

She gave an imperceptible nod. Joey turned down the flame on the stir-fry and set the dining room table. Instead of using the plain white dishes they'd used for Saturday's barbeque, she chose the dainty blue and white china. They reminded Joey of her late grandmother's curio cabinet.

Everyone took their places at the table and Joey served the meal. Ryder didn't waste any time tucking into his food, stopping every once in a while to douse it with more salt. He cleaned his plate and served himself seconds.

Shiv leaned closer to Joey. "It's very good, dear."

But Joey noted that Shiv had barely touched her meal and had spent much of dinner pushing the food around on her plate. "Tomorrow, we'll go over the kind of things you like to eat."

"I'm not picky."

It was Shiv's first day out of rehab, Joey told herself. She just needed time to adjust. New house. New town. And a stranger invading her space. It was a lot of change for anyone to take in all at once.

"You're not hungry, Ma?"

So, Joey hadn't been the only one who'd noticed.

"We had such a big lunch," Shiv said.

Ryder appeared to accept that, putting Joey a little more at ease. Shiv was a tiny woman. She probably didn't eat much.

"If you two don't mind, I think I'll go rest now." Shiv started to get up, and Ryder quickly came to her side of the table to help her.

Joey followed them to Shiv's bedroom. "I'll take it from here," she told Ryder, and as soon as he left the room, she assisted Shiv with her nightgown.

"I can handle it, dear."

"Let me just help you to the bathroom."

Using her cane and Joey's arm, Shiv made it down the hallway. The day had clearly taken its toll on her. While she'd been stronger earlier, Joey could see she was flagging. Which was not unexpected.

Joey waited for Shiv to wash up and helped her back to her room.

"I'm just next door and a light sleeper," Joey told her. "If there is anything you need, just bang on the wall. Later this week, I'll hook you up with a button you can push."

"You're very sweet, Joey. Next time I'll help with the dishes."

"Don't you worry about that. That's my job." Joey darkened the new blinds Ryder had installed. "They look great, don't they?"

"My son's a good boy." For the first time that day, Shiv smiled. But it didn't quite reach her pretty blue eyes.

"He's a very good son," Joey agreed. But he was far from a boy.

She made sure Shiv was comfortably in bed before she left the room, then made her way to the kitchen to clean up. To her surprise, Ryder was at the sink, loading the dishwasher.

"I'll take it from here." She attempted to edge him away, but he wouldn't budge. It was futile trying to jostle a man who could sit on a 1,500-pound bucking horse for eight seconds, so she grabbed a dish towel. "Fine, I'll dry the pan." It was too large for the dishwasher.

"How do you think she's doing?" He bobbed his head toward his mother's bedroom.

"Honestly, Ryder, I don't know her well enough to say. I think today was a lot for her. The drive, the house, me. Was she pretty active before the stroke?"

"So much so that a lot of times I forgot she was sixty-six. She drove— God help us." He stared up at the ceiling for a beat. "She went out with her friends to restaurants, took exercise classes, was an avid gardener."

"How was she at lunch? Did she eat?"

"To tell you the truth, I didn't pay that much attention. I guess I should've."

"I'll track it. But my guess is that she's just a bit overwhelmed."

"Maybe that's it." He turned off the water and took the towel from her to dry his hands. "Thanks for dinner. I think I'll turn in for the night."

It was only seven. And despite herself, she'd looked forward to spending the evening with him. Why? She didn't know. The smart thing to do was put as much distance between Ryder Knight and herself as she could. But when had she ever been smart?

* * * *

Ryder crossed the yard to his camper and at the last second took a detour to his truck. It was too early to hibernate, and spending time with Joey was too much temptation. It had taken a fair amount of grit to watch her all afternoon in a pair of jeans without making a move. The woman didn't have to try to look hot, she freaking embodied it.

Too bad, because she was a hundred percent off-limits.

He got behind the wheel and dashed off a quick text before taking off. A short time later, he walked into the Ponderosa and pulled up a stool at the bar.

"That was fast," he said.

Lucky waved over the bartender and ordered them each a beer. "I was already here, having dinner, when you texted. Tawny and Katie went home, so you'll have to give me a lift."

"No problem." Ryder had nothing but time. "Good to see you."

"You, too. I keep meaning to get over to your new place, but there's always another fire to put out. How's your mother?"

"Getting by. What's going on with the dude ranch? I thought you guys were killing it."

"We are. But you wouldn't believe how high maintenance the hospitality industry is. We're coming up on our busiest season, and everybody's got something to bitch and moan about." The bartender brought their beers. Lucky took a swig and reflected. "It's mostly a great life, but there are times when I miss the simplicity of following the circuit."

Ryder laughed because there was nothing simple about it. Rodeo wasn't like other professional sports where you signed a contract and got paid whether you won or lost. In rodeo, if you didn't make it to the eight-second bell, there was no money. End of story. At least on his and Lucky's level, they'd had sponsors to get them through hard times. But the thing about sponsors was, they liked winners.

"How's the trucking business going?"

Ryder took a drink. "Can't complain. I've added hay to my cargo list. The money isn't as good as livestock, but it's steady. And it doesn't hurt to diversify."

Lucky nodded. "Smart." He swiveled to face Ryder and slapped him on the back. "I'm glad you're here. It's a good place…good people who look out for one another. Speaking of, I heard Ethan Daniels's ex-wife is taking care of your mom."

Nugget might be a good place, but word traveled fast around here. Too fast for a slow-paced town. Another reason not to play where he lived.

"Yep," was all he said.

"I heard she's good…knows her shit."

"So far, so good. What's the deal with Daniels?" Ryder found himself mildly curious.

"He's a top-dog pediatric orthopedic surgeon who's working on some kind of advanced stem cell study to fix severely broken bones and birth defects. Good guy. Totally down-to-earth. His family used to run their cattle here on the Circle D in the summertime. When his old man died a few years ago, he decided to relocate from Reno. Spent a fortune building the house and the barn."

"What happened with him and the first missus?"

"Ah, hell, I have no idea. They seem amicable, though. He's getting hitched to Brynn Barnes next month. She's a big-shot advertising executive. Does commercials for the Super Bowl."

"No shit." It was the first Ryder had heard of it.

"Yeah. She's done some work for Griffin Parks." When Ryder stared at him blankly, Lucky said, "The guy who owns Sierra Heights, that big planned community off the highway. You probably know him from the Gas and Go. He owns that too."

Ryder had been to the Gas and Go many times but wasn't sure if he'd ever rubbed elbows with the owner.

"We're thinking about hiring her to help us brand the Cowboy Camp."

Ryder's mouth hitched up in a mocking smile. Lucky insisted on calling his operation a "cowboy camp." Everyone knew it was a freaking dude ranch.

"What does something like that cost?" His trucking company had grown by word of mouth, but it wouldn't hurt to do some real advertising in ranching and ag magazines. Ryder had actually been thinking about it for some time.

Lucky made the *mucho dinero* sign with his fingers. "I had a pro do our website, but our message could use a little help."

Ryder didn't even have a website. Honestly, he'd been lax about that kind of stuff. Half the time he wrote his contact information on a scrap of paper because he'd run out of business cards and hadn't bothered to get new ones. Not real professional. It was something he planned to work on during his time off the road. That and getting an office built.

The goal was to eventually dedicate more of his time to dispatching instead of driving. Maybe get a few horses and breed bucking bronc stock while expanding the trucking business.

Paying Daniels's soon-to-be bride to do the marketing part of it would certainly lighten his load. But he felt an odd sense of loyalty to Joey. He didn't know whether there was a rivalry between the two women. If there was, for the sake of Joey, he didn't plan to get in the middle of it. He owed her that much for being willing to work for his mother on a trial basis.

And for the kiss.

The door swished open, and a group of women came in. From the looks of their getups—designer jeans, right-out-of-the-box boots, and straw cowboy hats with stampede strings—they were tourists up from the city.

Lucky waved to them and murmured, "Shit," under his breath.

"You know 'em?"

"'Girlfriends Getaway' at the Cowboy Camp. It's a cross-promotion with the Lumber Baron. Samantha Breyer's idea."

"Who's Samantha Breyer?"

"She's the wife of one of the owners of the Lumber Baron and an event planner. We do a lot of stuff together. And this week, we're doing a package for the ladies. Four nights at the Lumber Baron that includes horseback riding, a roping lesson, a barrel-racing exhibition, and an evening of line dancing at the Cowboy Camp," Lucky whispered. "Kill me now."

Ryder chuckled. In the backbar mirror, he watched the women, who'd been seated at a nearby table, throw appreciative glances their way. "Ah, come on, I remember a time when you used to love you some buckle bunnies."

"I'm married now." Lucky took a quick glance over his shoulder and cocked his brows. "But you're not. Bet they'd love to meet a two-time world-champion saddle bronc rider."

"Oh no, you don't." Ryder drained the rest of his beer and contemplated the wisdom of ordering a second. "You want another one?"

"You're driving, so why the hell not?"

Ryder signaled to the bartender for two more beers.

"Why don't you go over to their table and introduce yourself?" Lucky grinned in that goading way that made Ryder want to sock him.

"I'm good." He reached down the bar for a bowl of beer nuts and tossed a few in his mouth. "Didn't know you were dabbling in the matchmaking arts these days."

Lucky laughed, then turned sober. "Seriously, you seeing anyone?"

Ryder had never been good at heart-to-hearts. But he felt one coming on and wanted to cut it off at the pass. "I'm seeing lots of women, Rodriguez."

"You ever hear the saying, never bullshit a bullshitter?" He paused, letting the silence settle over them like a cold blanket. Then, in a low voice, he said, "It's been five years, Ryder."

Five of the longest years of Ryder's life. "You going to tell me it's time to move on?" He'd always thought that *"time to move on"* was one of the most callous sentences in the English language. Right next to *"get over it."*

"No, not move on," Lucky said. "But you've gotta live your life. Find happiness."

He was living his life the best he could. As for happiness? It was difficult to remember what that even felt like.

"We drinking, or are you preaching?" Ryder hadn't come to the Ponderosa to escape Joey only to have to think about Leslie. All he'd wanted was to spend time with an old friend, listen to country music on the jukebox, and drink in relative peace.

Lucky threw his hands up in the air. "Hey, you want to blow your shot at a night with a beautiful woman, that's up to you."

If Ryder was looking for a beautiful woman, he would've stayed home.

Chapter 7

Ryder woke the next morning to someone pounding on the door of his camper.

"Hang on a sec," he shouted, searching for his jeans. He'd tossed them somewhere when he'd stumbled in the night before.

Finding them in a heap on the floor, he managed to put on each pant leg as he hopped to the door. Joey stood outside, staring up at his bare chest. Her eyes moved over him and came to rest on the undone buttons on his Levi's.

His hand instantly moved to his fly. "What's up?"

"There are some weird people here who want to talk to you."

He stuck his head out and craned his neck. "Where?"

"At the front door of the house. I invited them in, but they said they'd rather wait for you outside."

"Did they say what they want?"

"Nope. But whatever it is, they aren't happy."

He scrubbed his hand through his matted hair. "Okay. I just need a sec to put on a shirt."

Ryder ducked back inside, found a clean Henley, and brushed his teeth. When he got to the house, there was a couple waiting for him dressed in identical khaki shirts embroidered with tiny bears and navy shorts with a sharp crease down the middle. Kind of a deranged park ranger vibe.

"Ryder Knight." He stuck out his hand, but neither the man nor the woman made a move to shake it. "How can I help you?"

"I'm Sandy Addison. This is my husband, Cal. We own the Beary Quaint up the road."

Ah, that explained the shirts. "Sure, I know the place. Nice to meet you."

They continued to stand there without responding.

"Uh, you want a cup of coffee?"

"It's after eight," Sandy said, as if that somehow answered the question.

Well, Ryder sure the hell wanted a cup and was tempted to say, *"You think we can wrap this up?"* But he was trying to be neighborly. And poor Cal already looked nervous. His eyes kept darting around, like he was expecting someone to unleash a pit bull on him at any moment.

Sandy rested her hands on her hips and pursed her lips. "This property isn't zoned for a campground."

Huh?

"Who said anything about a campground?"

Now Cal looked ready to piss his pants. Not Sandy, though. She stepped right into Ryder's personal space and pointed around the side of the house.

"You mean the fifth wheel?" he asked. "That's mine."

"Are you living in it?" Sandy jutted her chin at him in challenge. "Because this property isn't zoned for a mobile home park, either."

Ah, for Christ's sake. One trailer did not make a goddamn mobile home park, nor a campground. What the hell was wrong with these people? "I'm sleeping in it while my mother and her caregiver live in my house. What's the big deal?"

"You're breaking the law."

Ryder looked to Cal. *A little help here, dude.* But Cal's eyes fell to the ground. *Jeez, man up, you little worm.* What an odd couple. Whoever heard of complaining about a guy sleeping in his camper, for God's sake?

"Look, Sandy, there's nothing that says I can't spend the night in my fifth wheel if I want to." He wasn't hurting anyone. In fact, he'd probably increased their property value just by moving in.

The screen door squeaked, and Joey came onto the front porch. It hadn't escaped him that she'd been listening to the entire conversation through the window.

"Ryder, it's time for breakfast."

He gave her the one-minute sign, as he wanted to make sure the Addisons knew exactly where he stood. "The next time you want to come over here and—"

"We have the law on our side," Sandy interrupted him.

The hell they did. "Yeah, then call the police."

He swiveled on his heels, marched up the stairs, opened the door for Joey, and followed her inside. Together, they watched the Addisons get in their car and drive off.

"Shit. I'll be right back."

Joey trailed after him. "Do you think anything they said might be legit?"

"No. But I plan to make sure." He climbed into his camper and retrieved his phone, only to bump into Joey, who'd followed him inside.

"Wow." She turned in place, her mouth slack jaw. "This is nice. Like, really nice." She ran her hand over the sofa. "Is this real leather?" She strolled into the kitchen and did a double take at the granite countertops. "This is like a luxury condo on wheels."

"It's leftover from my rodeo days."

She continued to explore, poking her head in closets and opening doors. "It only has a half bath?"

He led her through the master bedroom. The bed was still unmade, and his crap was strewn across the floor. But she didn't seem to mind. Ryder gave her a tour of the full bath.

She took in the walk-in-shower and double vanity. "They sure didn't skimp on space."

"Check this out." Ryder took her outside, opened a panel on the exterior of the camper, and pulled down a set of metal stairs. "Access to the half bath."

She lit up, and he had to turn away to keep from staring at her. "Keeps you from tracking mud in after hiking."

Or, in his case, horseshit. "Look at this." He opened another side panel to reveal an outdoor kitchen.

"Holy Toledo. This is what you call glamping."

"This is what you call feeding a horde of hungry cowboys in a rodeo parking lot." He winked.

"That, too, I suppose." Her lips curved into a pretty smile, then she sighed. "I don't want to leave your mom for too long. She was still asleep when I came to get you. But by now she's probably awake and hungry for breakfast." She started to walk backward toward the house. "You coming?"

"Yep. Meet you inside." He closed everything up, and on his way to the house, dialed his real estate agent. She answered on the fifth ring, and he remembered that it was still early. "Hey, Dana, it's Ryder Knight. Hope I didn't wake you."

"I've been up for hours. Baby's been kicking. How's the new place?"

"That's why I'm calling." He went inside the house and followed the smell of coffee into the kitchen. His mother sat at the table in her bathrobe. Pre-stroke, she would've been dressed and ready to take on the world. He kissed her on the forehead and told Dana about his visit from the Addisons. "Is there any truth to what they're saying?"

"That you can't turn your property into a campground or a trailer park? Honestly, I'm not sure, because that wasn't an issue when you bought the place."

"And it still isn't. But is there anything that says I can't sleep in my camper?"

She sighed. "Technically, I suppose they could make a case that the camper isn't permitted for a full-time occupant. So if the county bugs you about it, which I highly doubt it will, just say you live in the house, but while your mother is staying with you, you've been sleeping in the camper."

"Okay. But what'll happen when I park my fleet of semis on the property? These folks seem like they're itching for a fight."

"We checked into the semi issue. You're zoned for agriculture, which includes commercial equipment. Good luck to them trying to argue otherwise."

He had a feeling that was exactly what they were going to do. Hadn't Donna Thurston warned him they were trouble? At the time, he'd figured it was idle small-town pettiness. Not so much anymore.

"What's these people's problem?" Everyone else in Nugget had been welcoming and warm.

She let out a small laugh. "They're a little different, for sure." It was an understatement, but Ryder could tell she was attempting to remain professional. "I've never had a problem with them," she continued. "But they've been territorial with others in the past. I think they feel like their position as Nugget's old guard is being usurped by newcomers. It was before my time, but Maddy Breyer-Shepard and her brother, Nate, went to war with them over the Lumber Baron. The Addisons didn't want the competition. It's a shame, because the Addisons could've benefited from joining forces with Maddy and Nate instead of alienating them. I would just try to avoid them."

It wasn't as if Ryder intended to invite them to happy hour. He finished his conversation with Dana and went straight for a mug of coffee, which he took to the table.

"You sleep okay, Ma?"

"Very well." She flashed a wan smile. She was still getting used to the move, he told himself.

"What was that about?" Joey leaned her rear end against the kitchen counter, holding a cup of coffee in her hand.

"My real estate agent. She says I have nothing to worry about."

"They were extremely unpleasant people." Joey turned to Ryder's mom. "Thank goodness you missed them, Shiv."

Siobhan stirred her coffee. "I heard a little of it from my bedroom. I hope they're not giving you trouble, Ryder."

"Nah, nothing I can't handle. What are your plans today, Ma?" He wanted to show her around the place more. Tell her his ideas for the future office.

"I thought I'd rest in my room for a while."

Ryder started to say that she'd just woken up, but Joey intervened. "Let's see how you feel after breakfast."

He liked how good she was with his mother. Not demanding, like some of the nurses were at the rehab home. Or patronizing. There was a physical therapist there who talked to her like she was a child with a mental deficiency. Joey was natural, more like a friend. But a friend who didn't take shit.

Joey grabbed a pan from the drawer. "How about eggs, toast, and fruit salad?"

"That sounds good, dear."

"Ryder?"

"Sure. You need some help?"

"I'm good." Joey got her ingredients from the fridge and began cracking eggs in a bowl. "How do you like them, Shiv?"

"Scrambled is fine."

"And you, Ryder?"

"I'm good with scrambled." He got up to set the table with napkins and plates.

After they ate, Joey helped Shiv shower and dress. He made sure his mother put on a pair of sturdy shoes and held her arm in his as they took a turn around the backyard. Joey used the time to tidy up Shiv's room and make her bed.

They got as far as the grove of pine trees when he released her arm. His mother was stronger than she looked. Then again, she'd always been a force of nature, weathering her husband's desertion and raising a small child on her own.

"What do you think?"

She lifted her hand and gently touched his face. "I'm so proud of you, Ryder." She gazed at the land, at the gently swelling hills. "Look at all you've accomplished. I wish Leslie was here to see it."

"Me too, Ma." He stared down at his own hands.

"This Joey, how'd you find her?"

"You don't like her?" His heart sank. "I can find someone else." He'd been planning to all along anyway.

She reached for him. "I think she's wonderful. And very pretty, too. I was only wondering how you found her. If maybe she was a friend of yours."

"I told you, Ma. The agency sent her." He assessed her to see if she was having trouble with her memory or if she'd seen through his smokescreen. He'd never been much good at keeping the truth from her. But what he did behind closed doors...well, she was better off not knowing.

She pinned him with a look but refrained from commenting. "Let's see your spot for the garage."

They were on the move again. This time she only used his arm to steady herself as she walked. He showed her what he had in mind for the garage and where he planned to put the office. It was a shady area, far enough from the house not to be an eyesore.

"It's a substantial piece of land." She scanned the distance from the end of the driveway to the opposite fence.

"Ten acres." Compared to Lucky's spread or Ethan Daniels's Circle D Ranch, it was a pittance. But he owned it free and clear. "The house isn't much, but it's enough."

"The house is lovely. It reminds me of the one I grew up in in Oklahoma. And that porch...it's a porch for rocking chairs, summer evenings, lemonade, and children."

The air suddenly got stagnant.

"Don't go there, Ma." He toed a dirt clod with the tip of his boot and watched it turn to dust.

"I just want you to be happy, Ryder. That's all I've ever wanted."

"I know. Should we return to the house?"

She took his arm, and they made their way back. Inside, Shiv retired to her room, making him feel like a first-class asshole. She'd loved Leslie as much as he had. But after all these years, he still couldn't talk about his late wife and all that he'd lost with her.

"You have a nice walk?" Joey came out of the kitchen, wearing rubber gloves.

"Don't let her fool you, she's tougher than she's leading on."

"I sort of came to that conclusion this morning when she got in and out of the shower on her own. There will still be some tough days ahead, but physically she's doing great. I'll let her nap for a few hours, then rouse her for lunch."

"I'm gonna go out for a while. I have to pick up a few things before I leave tomorrow. You need anything?"

"I'm good unless you don't want salmon for dinner. I was thinking of making it on your new smoker if that's okay.

"Knock yourself out." He grabbed his keys off his mother's old antique console and headed to his Ram.

His first stop was the Lumber Baron. The old Victorian inn took up an entire block on the square. An elderly couple sat on the front porch, watching the slow pace of the town go by. Ryder tipped his hat and went inside.

"Well, hello, stranger." Maddy gave him a big hug. "What brings you in?"

"Is there a private place we can talk?"

She raised her brows. "Sure, come into my office." Maddy led him to a small room off a narrow hallway that, in all the times Ryder had stayed at the inn, he had never noticed before. "This is where my brother, Nate, our corporate chef, Brady, and I have our offices."

Maddy's office wasn't as fancy as the rest of the hotel, but it was comfortable with a small sofa, big desk, potted ferns, and lots of kids' toys. Ryder remembered that she had a young daughter.

"What's up?" She motioned for him to take a seat on the couch while she sank into her office chair. "Is everything okay?"

"Yeah, yeah. It's all good. But I got a visit today from Sandy and Cal Addison. They're unhappy with my staying in my fifth wheel on the property. They actually accused me of using the land for a campground or a trailer park, which I'm not, and said it violated zoning ordinances. The big reason I bought the place was to park my tractor trucks and trailers. Dana says not to worry about them, that I'm within my rights to store commercial equipment. But I got the sense these people are hell-bent on making my life miserable. And I heard through the grapevine that you and your brother had your own dealings with them. So, I'm here to pick your brain."

Maddy tilted her chair back and let out a long sigh. "Oh, boy. They're at it again. I'd like to tell you that they'll go away, but they probably won't. They're the sourest people I've ever met and love to make trouble. My guess is, they liked it when the Montgomery place was vacant and are worried that you may threaten their precious motor lodge. Gag me. Have you seen that place?"

Ryder tried not to laugh, though nothing about this was funny. He'd just sunk his life's savings into the property, and if he couldn't house his trucks, the land was virtually useless. It had sat on the market for years before he'd purchased it, so it wasn't as if he could turn around and sell it tomorrow.

"I've seen it," he said and let out a breath.

"Unfortunately, they have pull with the city council and the county board of supervisors. They've lived here forever, and as cruddy as it is, the Beary Quaint is an institution in Plumas County. But if Dana thinks you're okay, I wouldn't worry too much about it. Would they be able to see your trucks from the road?"

Some of his trailers alone were fifty-three feet long. You try hiding that. "Probably. Eventually, I hope to build a garage for the trucks. But the trailers…it wouldn't make sense. Not cost-wise. And something that big would be more of an eyesore than the actual trailers."

"Because that's what they're going to complain about. The visual impact. Although their complaints aren't likely to get anywhere, I'm afraid they'll make your life miserable trying."

"You think I should try to talk to them? My trucks and trailers are out now. But maybe I should prepare the Addisons and try to smooth things over before the rigs get here."

Maddy shook her head. "From my experience, they're not the kind of people you can reason with. Believe you me, I tried when they attempted to force us to stop work on the Lumber Baron. They managed to mobilize much of the town against us. I don't expect them to do that to you. We were the competition, after all. You're not. I would just make sure of the zoning. Be completely prepared to shove it in their face when they come around again to complain. Do you know Flynn Barlow?"

"I hauled his cattle last spring but I doubt he'd even remember me. Why?"

"In addition to a cattleman, he's a lawyer. He might be someone good to talk to."

"Isn't his wife some kind of big deal, too?" Ryder remembered hearing something about her from Lucky but couldn't for the life of him recall what it was.

"Uh-huh. She's Gia Treadwell." When Ryder's face drew a blank at the name, Maddy said, "She used to have a show about financial planning on one of the big networks and now runs a foundation for disadvantaged women. Both of them are real savvy. I suggest you talk to them. I could introduce you."

"I'd appreciate that." Ryder didn't typically like to ask for help, but in a situation like this, it didn't hurt to rally the locals.

"Let me reach out to Flynn, and I'll give you a call."

"Thanks, Maddy." He got to his feet, hoping he hadn't taken up too much of her time.

"How are you liking the new place otherwise?"

"So far, so good. I've got my mother living there for now. Maybe one day I'll bring her by. She'd go nuts for this place."

"Please do. I'd love to meet her."

When he left, the same elderly couple he'd passed on the way in was still sitting in those rocking chairs. This time, they were holding hands. It made his throat grow thick.

He jumped in his truck and quickly checked his phone. There was a missed call from Comfort Keepers.

He immediately hit redial. "Hey, Janine, just saw you tried to reach me."

"I still haven't found anyone else yet. But I know you're anxious, so I was thinking of casting a wider net. Maybe someone in Sacramento or the Bay Area who's looking to relocate."

He fiddled with his rearview mirror and with some reluctance said, "Why don't we stick with how it is for right now?"

"But just yesterday, you—"

"I know, Janine." She'd sounded exasperated, and Ryder couldn't blame her. He was about as wishy-washy as a damn politician where Joey was concerned. "But my mom seems to like Joey, and I don't want to throw too much change at her at once."

"She's an excellent caregiver. Frankly, I didn't understand why you weren't thrilled…well, anyway. I'm glad your mother is happy. If you have any questions or concerns, don't hesitate to call me. Peter will be there later this week to relieve Joey."

"Thanks, Janine." He got off the phone and banged his head on the steering wheel. "Put a bullet in me now." What the hell had he gotten himself into?

He sat there for a beat, bewildered, then started his engine. His second stop was Colin Burke's workshop. He found the address at the top of Grizzly Peak easily enough. The house was impressive. A chalet with 180-degree views of the Sierra mountain range.

Ryder followed the brick walkway to the backyard and found a miniature version of the house. The sound of machinery assured him that he hadn't made the trip in vain. A dog came trotting down the path. Ryder held his hands out, and the dog sniffed them.

"How you doing, boy?" He scratched the dog's head, and the hound let out an appreciative whine.

The door was open to the workshop, and Ryder found Colin cutting wood at a large table saw. He stopped the machine as soon as he spied Ryder and shoved his goggles to the top of his head.

"Hey there. I didn't hear you come in."

"I hope it's okay that I just showed up like this. It crossed my mind the second I pulled up that maybe I should've called."

Colin flashed a big grin. "I'm always open for business. Everything good with your floors?"

"Yeah, they're great. I'm here about some rocking chairs."

"You came to the right place." Colin placed whatever he'd been working on next to the saw and led Colin into a back room filled with furniture.

Headboards, footboards, coffee tables, dining room tables, and on the far wall, rocking chairs.

"Looks like I hit the mother lode." Ryder ran his hand over the flat surface of a live-edge console table. "You do beautiful work, man."

"Feel free to browse. Everything except the crib is for sale."

Colin had mentioned to Ryder that his wife was pregnant. He assumed the crib was for their new baby and avoided it like he would a pandemic. Instead, he made a beeline for the rockers.

"What goes with a Craftsman? They're for my front porch."

Colin pulled several away from the wall. "Any of these would work on your porch."

Ryder sat in one with wide, flat arms and tested it. It was so comfortable he didn't want to get up. "You got two more like this one?"

Colin chuckled. "That didn't take long."

"Nope. I've never been much of a shopper, but I know what I like."

"My favorite kind of customer. Let me check the loft." Colin climbed up a ladder to a catwalk above. A short time later, he called down, "Can you grab these from me?"

He handed down two more chairs. "They're not exact replicas, but they're close."

Ryder actually liked that each one was a little different. It showed that they were handcrafted instead of factory-made. He lined them up next to each other and tried each one out.

Colin came down the ladder. "If that doesn't work, I can match the other one. But it'll take a few weeks."

"Nope. These three will do me." Ryder strolled through the shop, checking out some of the other pieces. The house was too small for anything else. But when his mother took her furniture to Cascade Village, he'd come back here to shop.

He reached in his pocket for his wallet and tossed Colin his credit card. "Plastic okay?"

"Plastic is my bread and butter."

"Great place you've got here," Ryder said while Colin ran his credit card. "You live here long?"

"About six years now. Harlee, my wife, has been coming up here since she was a kid. Her parents own a cabin down the road."

"Nice." Nugget was a long way from civilization, but somehow folks found it. "Did you build the house and shop yourself?"

"Yep. Originally, the house was one of those kit homes. But I modified it. Didn't want it to look too cookie-cutter, you know what I mean?"

Ryder nodded and gazed out over the white-tipped mountains. "You've got yourself one hell of a view up here."

"You should see it from the house." Colin handed Ryder back his credit card. "Come on, I'll show it to you."

Ryder followed Colin to the house. The inside was as impressive as the outside. Tons of windows with more sweeping views.

"You weren't kidding." He could see all the way to Nevada and the Feather River down below. It was almost dizzying.

The dog—Colin had called him Max—brushed up against his leg, begging for attention. Ryder gave him a good rub and proceeded to the great room, a huge open space with a big rock fireplace.

The kitchen was equally impressive. Lots of counter space and stainless-steel appliances.

"Did you make these cabinets?" he asked Colin.

"Yep. Most of the furniture, too."

"Pretty spectacular." If Ryder ever built a house, he was hiring Colin Burke.

"This is our latest project." Colin opened a door off the hallway into a room with drop cloths spread across the floor. It smelled like paint. "It's the nursery. I primed it last night."

Ryder backed out as fast as he could. "I'm sure it'll be great when it's done. Hey, thanks for showing me around. It's a fantastic place you've got here."

"Come by anytime. I'd like to introduce you to Harlee. She owns the *Nugget Tribune* and will probably want to interview you for her 'New Neighbor' column. Until you came along, Lucky Rodriguez was our only rodeo superstar."

Ryder stifled a laugh. Apparently it didn't take much to make the news in this town.

They went back to the shop, where Colin helped him load up the rocking chairs. On his drive home, his mother's words sifted through his head.

"*It's a porch for rocking chairs, summer evenings, lemonade, and children.*"

At least he could give her three of those things.

Chapter 8

Ryder left early Wednesday morning, and Joey was relieved to see him go. Having him so close was wreaking havoc on her senses. There had always been something about the man that made her want to break the rules.

But with him out of the way, she could focus all her attention on Shiv. Joey was worried about her. Since Monday, she'd barely eaten, slept too much, and appeared to have no interest in socializing. It wasn't unusual for someone who'd suffered a serious injury or illness to display signs of depression. Nor was it unusual for someone of Shiv's age to experience despair. But when they became hopeless, there needed to be medical intervention.

"Shiv?" Joey tapped on her bedroom door. "What do you say we sit on the porch for a while? It's a beautiful day." The temperature hovered around 75 degrees with a slight breeze. And the rocking chairs Ryder had brought home were heaven.

"All right, dear. Just give me a few minutes."

Joey had learned that minutes with Shiv was more like an hour because she didn't want to budge from her bed.

Not this time.

Joey let herself into Shiv's room with a basket of fresh laundry. "Here's a light sweater straight from the dryer. Let me help you get dressed."

"Oh, I'm fine to do it on my own."

"I'm sure you are. Then I'll just put these things away. I thought it would be nice for me to take a picture of you rocking away on one of those awesome chairs and send it to Ryder. What do you think?"

"Yes, that would be nice. I hope Ryder didn't spend too much on them. They look terribly expensive."

They did look expensive. Ethan had similar ones on his porch. Joey assumed they came from the same place. "We'll just have to show him how much use we're getting out of them."

She laid out the sweater for Shiv and dug through the pile of clean laundry for a pair of pants. As Joey began putting Shiv's things away, her phone rang. She dug into her pocket, secretly hoping it was Ryder. Not Ryder, Ethan, according to caller ID.

"Hey there. What's up?"

"Brynn missed her flight from New York yesterday and is catching the first one she can today. I'm stuck at work, Alma's in Reno, so there's no one to pick up Roni from school. Any chance you can do it? If not, I can try to foist her off on one of her friend's moms."

"No, I can do it." She'd just take Shiv with her. It would do her good to go for a drive, maybe do a few errands. "What about Henry?"

"He's got baseball practice after school. I'll be back in time to pick him up. Thanks, Joey. It's nice having you so close by."

A year ago, he wouldn't have said that. Deservedly, Ethan had been cautious about letting Joey back into their daughter's life after all the crap she'd pulled during the height of her addiction. But she'd worked hard to prove herself. And it looked as if it was paying off.

"That was my ex-husband," she told Shiv after the call. "He and his fiancée usually see to picking up my daughter after school. But today they're shorthanded. I hope it's okay with you that we go get her."

"Whatever you need to do, Joey. I'm fine with it. I could even stay here while you go."

Oh no, she didn't. "I think it'll be nice for us to go together. I can show you around Nugget." It was time for Shiv to venture away from the house. "And Roni's a good girl. She won't be any trouble."

It probably wasn't the best work practice to run personal errands on her first week of the job. But this was an emergency. Sort of.

Joey had a few hours until school let out. Still, it was a good excuse to go to town. Joey decided to take Shiv to lunch at the Ponderosa. Perhaps being out with people would cheer her up. They could always spend the evening on the porch.

Joey helped Shiv into her SUV and drove to the square. There was plenty of parking in front of the restaurant. Across the street, a few older men sat outside the barbershop at a folding table, playing cards. Ethan had once referred to the group as the Nugget Mafia. Later, Joey had learned that's what everyone called them.

"Ready?" Joey got Shiv's cane from the back seat and guided her onto the sidewalk. "They have an excellent Caesar salad."

Together, they went inside and were seated in the middle of the dining room. She recognized a few faces from previous visits. Shiv looked around, taking in the Western décor.

"Has Ryder been here?" she asked.

"Uh-huh." Ryder was a freaking regular.

Joey gazed over at the bar stool where he'd once propositioned her to join him in his room at the Lumber Baron. Despite trying to reconcile with her ex at the time, Joey had nearly taken Ryder up on the offer. To this day she wondered what would've happened if she had.

If his bedroom performance was anything like his kiss, she would've had quite a night. That much she knew. As for anything else...There was a reason why men like Ryder were still single. It was because they wanted to be. It wasn't as if she was looking for anything, either. After everything that had happened, including rehab, her divorce with Ethan, and losing her nursing license, she was trying to heal, not hook up with the first good-looking cowboy who came her way.

"It seems like the kind of place Ryder would like," Shiv said.

Joey nodded. "They play a lot of rodeo and PBR events here on the television." She pointed over to the bar, where there were three flat screens suspended from the ceiling. "He also likes their rhubarb pie."

Shiv quirked a brow. "How long have you known him, dear?"

"Not very long. We used to bump into each other here and there." *Bump.* That was a nice euphemism for it.

"Ah." Shiv quirked that brow again, gave Joey a long, knowing glance, and opened the menu. "So, you recommend the Caesar, huh?" A sly little smile played on her lips.

Joey was beginning to suspect that Shiv wasn't as out of it as she appeared. "Uh-huh, it's great with their grilled chicken. Not overly dressed, like some restaurants do."

"Then I'll have that, too."

A server came and took their order. Shiv continued to quietly take in the place.

"There's a bowling alley on the other side of that wall." Joey pointed. She'd taken Roni a couple of times.

"Really?"

Maybe Joey had just imagined it, but it seemed that Shiv had perked up. "Do you bowl, Shiv?"

"I was in a league ages ago."

"We should play one of these days."

Shiv waved her hand in the air. "It's been so long...I wouldn't be any good."

Joey started to say that she wouldn't know until she tried when a woman approached their table.

"Excuse me, I hate to interrupt, but are you Ryder's mom?"

Taken aback, Shiv said, "Why yes. How did you know?"

"I'm Maddy Breyer-Shepard. I own the Lumber Baron. Ryder came by the other day and said you were living with him, and I recognized...Roni's mom." Maddy turned to Joey. "Hi, we haven't formerly met."

"I'm Joey. Joey Nix."

"I'm crazy about your little girl. She and Henry play with my daughter, Emma."

That explained how Maddy knew Roni, which also meant she was friends with Brynn, who had probably mentioned that Joey was Shiv's caregiver. Oh, wouldn't Joey like to be a fly on their coffee klatch wall.

"Thank you." Joey scanned Maddy's finger and confirmed a wedding ring. Interesting that Ryder was friendly with all the pretty ladies in town. "It's nice to meet you."

"I just wanted to say hi and welcome Ms. Knight to Nugget."

Shiv reached across the table and took Maddy's hand. "That's very sweet of you."

"I know Ryder wants to show you the inn. So anytime you want to come over. Unfortunately, we just ended our Sunday high tea. It's become a local tradition. But we shut it down in spring and summer, which is the height of our tourist season. You would've loved it. Next year."

A server crossed the room with their salads.

"Let me get out of the way," Maddy said. "So nice meeting the both of you."

"Likewise," Joey said.

Joey watched Maddy cut a swath across the restaurant, stopping occasionally to chat with various diners. When she turned back to Shiv, Shiv was watching her.

"Nice lady," Shiv said.

"Uh-huh," Joey replied, suddenly feeling like an outsider, like the wicked pill-popping ex-wife. It was probably all in her head. But she couldn't help but compare herself to Brynn, who, for all her New York City sophistication, had seamlessly fit into this small town. To hear it from Ethan, Brynn was on every board, a member of every club, and sainted mother of the year.

The only members of Joey's social circle these days were her sponsor and twelve-step group.

They ate, or rather Joey ate. Shiv spent the meal pushing lettuce and chicken around the plate with her fork. Joey could tell by the way Shiv's clothes fit her that she'd lost weight. It was to be expected after a stroke. But now, they needed to work on her appetite.

After lunch, Joey persuaded Shiv to take a turn with her around the square. It was such a nice day that Joey hated to waste it inside. Besides, she wanted to ogle the Lumber Baron up close and personal. At least from the outside. And both of them could use the exercise.

It appeared that everyone else had the same idea, because the square was the most crowded Joey had ever seen it. The old guys were still outside, playing cards. There was a couple in the park, chasing a toddler around. A man walking a dog. And five teenagers on a blanket. It looked to Joey like they were studying.

As usual, there was a line of cars at the Bun Boy drive-through and every picnic table outside the hamburger joint was full. As they got closer to the Lumber Baron, she spotted three women on the porch rockers, sipping wine in the shade.

"It's a pretty little town," Shiv said. "And the inn is fabulous."

"You want to go inside?"

"Maybe another time, dear."

Joey was relieved. As nice as Maddy was, Joey couldn't help thinking she was Brynn's friend. It was incredibly petty of her, but that's where she was.

"We should probably get going anyway. School will be out soon, and parents start lining up at the curb early." Joey wanted to make sure Roni could find her.

On their way to Nugget Elementary, Joey pointed out the supermarket and the post office. Not that Shiv would go on her own, but Joey wanted her to soak in her son's new town.

As she'd predicted, cars were already snaked along the front of the school. Small groups of parents assembled on the sidewalk or in the grass, chatting as they waited for the afternoon bell to ring. She didn't know any of them. Though before Ethan had given her more visitation freedom, she used to lurk in the school parking lot just to catch a glimpse of Roni getting picked up in the afternoon. To this day, Ethan didn't know about her stalking.

The front doors of the school flung open, and groups of kids came jogging down the stairs. Joey peered out the window, waiting for Roni to appear.

"There she is." Joey hopped out of her SUV and waved her hands in the air. Even from a distance, she could see the excitement on Roni's face.

"Mommy!" She ran across the grass, her blond ponytail bouncing up and down, right into Joey's arms.

"How was school, baby?"

"Good. Can we get ice cream at the Bun Boy?"

Joey should've planned ahead for a snack. "Let's see how Ms. Knight's doing first. Come around here. I want you to meet her."

Roni followed Joey to the passenger side. Shiv had fallen asleep with her cheek pressed against the window.

Joey touched her lips with her finger. "Ms. Knight is tired, so we have to go home. But I'll make you a snack there. Just be real quiet, okay?"

"Okay, Mommy."

"Come here." Joey gave Roni a smooch on the top of her head. "I'm so happy we've got the afternoon together."

"Me too."

They made the ten-minute drive home, and Shiv stirred as they pulled into the driveway. "Are we home?"

"We are." Joey parked and helped Shiv out of the vehicle.

Roni trailed behind them as they went inside the house, being careful not to disturb Shiv. She was definitely the kid of a doctor and a nurse, sweet and nurturing.

"I think I'll take a nap," Shiv said.

Joey told Roni to wait for her in the living room while she helped Shiv get into bed. On her way out of the bedroom, she checked the time. Two hours. That's all she was giving Shiv, who was sleeping too much during the day. Joey could hear her stirring at night. Shiv needed a regular routine.

Joey called Roni into the kitchen. "Let's see what we've got." She searched the refrigerator. "How about carrot sticks and hummus?"

Roni pulled a face. "Grandma always has cookies."

Alma, Ethan's paragon of a stepmother, was a baker. Joey rummaged through Ryder's stash in the pantry. His diet was atrocious. For everything healthy Joey had gotten for Shiv, Ryder had matched it with junk. Oreos.

"Cookies it is. But first, eat a few carrots for me." Joey put a handful of veggies and a scoop of hummus in a bowl for Roni and poured her a glass of milk.

Roni sat at the small breakfast table, eating and describing in great detail lunch in the cafeteria. "The peas were disgusting. Jenny Fulton spit hers out right on her plate."

"You like Geema's peas."

"She makes them good." Roni finished her last carrot and reached for an Oreo.

Joey's mother cooked her peas in a pound of butter. So, yeah, they were delicious.

"Go easy on the cookies, baby girl. Leave room for dinner." She wasn't sure what time Ethan was coming to pick up Roni. But Joey planned to make turkey burgers on the smoker and hoped Roni stayed for supper. Every second she got with her daughter was precious.

"Can I play in the yard?"

"Sure." Joey had set Shiv up with the equipment Ryder had ordered. Now all she had to do was press a button to call Joey from anywhere inside or near the house. "I just have to keep an eye on Ms. Knight."

"How come she's so sleepy?"

"She's still recovering from being sick. It'll take a little while for her to get her energy back."

"Henry's legs were busted, and he never took naps."

"Henry's a lot younger than Ms. Knight. How's he doing nowadays?"

"Good. He rides Choo Choo almost every day. Daddy says horseback riding makes your legs stronger. Did you know that?"

"Uh-huh, I did. I'm glad he's doing better. How's Grandma Alma? Is she still planning to live with you after Daddy and Brynn get married?" Joey wasn't a fan of Alma. And Alma pretty much hated Joey's guts. But the woman had cared so tenderly for Roni while Joey had gone off the rails that she owed Alma a huge debt.

"She's going to live with us and in Reno. Daddy might build her a cottage on the ranch, like the one Henry and Brynn used to live in."

"That would be nice." Joey had a dozen more questions she wanted to ask but was afraid her nosiness would get back to Ethan or Brynn. For that reason, she was always careful about what she said around Roni.

"Can I go play now?"

"Yep. But stay near the house where I can see you from the windows."

Joey cleared the dishes and went to check on Shiv. Afterward, she planned to sit outside to watch Roni.

Her phone rang. She stepped away from Shiv's door. It was Ryder, FaceTiming her. Her pulse picked up. She fluffed her hair, wishing she'd worn makeup, and moved to the living room.

"Hey." She tried to sound casual. "How's the trip?" She couldn't tell for sure from the background, but it looked like he was in a parking lot somewhere.

"I'm making good time. How's everything going there? How's my mom?"

"She's napping right now. But I'll wake her up if you want to talk to her."

"Nah, let her sleep. I just wanted to make sure everything was under control."

"Everything is fine." She'd wait until he was home to discuss her suspicion that Shiv was clinically depressed. "We had lunch at the Ponderosa, took a walk around the square, and met your friend Maddy."

"Oh, yeah? Did you take my mom inside the Lumber Baron? She likes old stuff."

"Not today. Next time, for sure. Hey, I had a slight emergency and had to pick my kid up from school. Shiv was with me. Roni's here now until her dad picks her up." Joey glanced out the window. "I hope that's okay."

"Not a problem. My ma likes kids."

Right now, the only thing Shiv liked was sleep. But they were going to fix that.

"Thanks," she said. "We stole a few of your Oreos, but I'll replace them."

He laughed. "Just as long as she doesn't touch the good whiskey, I'm happy to share."

"When do you think you'll be home?" *Jeez, why did I just ask that?*

"I'm shooting for Sunday. But it'll depend on road conditions. Why, you miss me?" He grinned.

"Don't flatter yourself. I only asked for your mom's sake."

"Good to know." He bobbed his chin, reminding her of all the cocky doctors she'd worked for over the years. "Hey, I wanted to give you a heads-up that one of my drivers is scheduled to drop off a truck later this week. His wife is picking him up."

"Okay. Do I need to be here for that?" She had to take Shiv to a doctor's appointment on Friday, and there were bound to be a few grocery runs.

"Nope. He knows what to do. Just don't freak out when you see a new eighteen-wheeler in the driveway."

"I won't." She checked on Roni again. She was playing on one of the rocking chairs. "The rockers you bought are getting good use. I'll send a picture of your mother on one of them later."

"Of you, too," he said.

It was an unexpected thing for him to say. Except for his slightly flirtatious tone today, he'd been extremely professional since she'd started working for him. She tried not to read anything into it. He was simply being conversational.

Still, she would make sure to adjust the camera to get her good side. "I'd better check on your mom."

"Yeah, I need to get back on the road." Yet he seemed reluctant to hang up. "Hey...thank you for taking such good care of Siobhan."

"You're welcome." After she hung up, she held the words close. *Thank you.* It had been a long time since she'd felt worthy of them.

Chapter 9

Shiv felt a shadow hanging over her and wondered if it was death. If it had finally come to take her away.

She opened one eye slowly and squinted, trying to focus. Then just as slowly opened the other eye.

A little girl was standing next to the bed, staring at her. "Do you want to come outside and watch me play?"

At first, Shiv thought she was an angel. But it only took a few moments for her to clear the sleep from her head and remember Joey's daughter. Roni.

Shiv turned to the clock on her nightstand. Five o'clock. She couldn't recall what time she'd lain down, but it couldn't have been more than an hour ago. Though she was sleeping more and more now.

She moved to the edge of the bed and gingerly sat up. The little girl… Roni…offered Shiv her hand.

"I can help you."

"Where's your mother?"

"She's outside, starting the barbecue. I'm supposed be setting the table, but I wanted to check on you."

She was a beautiful child. Blond hair, like her mother's. The eyes were different, though. Hazel. Joey's were blue. Shiv often wondered if her grandson would've had blue eyes. Pale blue like hers and Ryder's.

"That's very nice of you to bother with an old lady like me, Roni."

"You're only a little old. You can still have fun."

Shiv laughed, and even to her own ears it sounded rusty. "Hand me those slippers, please."

Roni grabbed them from under the chair and brought them to the bed. "Do you want your cane?"

"Yes, please."

She scrambled to get it from the foot of Shiv's bed.

"What a lovely girl you are. Do you help your mother a lot?"

Roni nodded. "I might be a nurse when I grow up. Or a doctor, like my daddy."

"That's wonderful, Roni. When I was your age, I wanted to be a lawyer." But instead she'd fallen in love with Tanner Cole, then gotten pregnant, married, and divorced—all before her twenty-fifth birthday.

"Did you become one?"

"No, but I became a courtroom clerk, working for one of the smartest judges in California." And one of the best men she'd ever known. Just thinking about Morgan made her chest ache.

"Roni?"

"I'm in here, Mommy."

Joey came through the door. "Roni!" She put her hands on her hips and tossed her daughter a stony look. "Out, young lady. I'm so sorry, Shiv."

"For what? I was enjoying this darling girl." Shiv hoisted herself up, using her cane. "She said we're having turkey burgers for dinner." She hated turkey burgers. Why couldn't she just have a real hamburger?

"And a big, fresh green salad. Did you have a nice rest?" Joey glared at Roni.

"I did. I'll just wash up and meet you in the kitchen." As she headed down the hall to the bathroom, she heard Joey lecturing Roni.

The child's visit had been a bright spot in an otherwise dull world. But Joey was a good mother, teaching her daughter to be respectful and courteous. And that little girl was a sweetheart.

Shiv looked at herself in the mirror and saw an old, wrinkled woman looking back. She'd once been pretty. Not the kind of looker that Joey was, but attractive enough to turn heads. While petite, she'd had curves and breasts and even a nice behind. Now she was nothing but a bag of bones. Her clothes were dowdy, the kinds of things a hausfrau wore, and she spent more time in her slippers than in actual shoes. When she'd worked at the courthouse, she'd worn high heels and pantyhose. And smart suits.

She'd learned how to budget well and rewarded herself every month with a small extravagance. A nice blouse or a silk scarf, or a pretty pair of silver earrings. Now she had no one to dress for or anyone to impress. The fact was she had no purpose at all, except to be a burden on her son. Ryder was trying so hard to take care of her. But who was taking care of him? Leslie was gone, and with her went all of Ryder's light.

Though she'd seen rare sparks of…something…since Joey had come into their lives. Her son had been tight-lipped where the new caregiver was concerned, pretending there was no history between them. Bah. She might have had a stroke, but all her marbles were still very much intact. And her eyes worked just fine. No way was she imagining the chemistry between those two.

She finished washing up and joined Joey and Roni in the kitchen. Someone had picked wildflowers and arranged them in her cut-glass vase.

"Did you do that, Roni?" She nudged Roni and pointed to the bouquet.

"I picked them," Roni said proudly. "My mom made them pretty."

"Well, you both did an outstanding job."

"You have a lot of beautiful things." Joey repositioned the vase in the center of the table. "I mean, I'm assuming the dishes, the china, and the porcelain figurines are yours and not Ryder's."

"Thank you. I've collected a good many possessions over the years." The entire house had been furnished in the things Ryder had packed up from her town house. As far as she knew, her son ate off paper plates in that camper of his.

She'd never broached the topic of what Ryder had done with his and Leslie's lovely wedding gifts. The pain in her son's eyes whenever she attempted to discuss his late wife was palpable, so Shiv did her best to steer away from the subject. It probably wasn't healthy, but she didn't want to push.

"Speaking of Ryder, have you heard from him?"

"He FaceTimed earlier, but I didn't want to wake you," Joey said. "I told him we would send pictures of us on the rocking chairs later."

Shiv tacitly agreed but was so tired she didn't know if she could muster the strength to sit outside. Lately, all she wanted to do was pull the covers over her head and sleep. It wasn't as if she was useful for anything else. But for Ryder's sake, she tried to engage at least a little bit.

The sound of a car coming up the driveway startled the three of them.

"Were you expecting anyone?" Shiv asked Joey.

"It's probably Roni's dad." Joey got up from the table and went inside the living room. Roni scurried after her. A short time later, they returned. "It's him. Roni, finish your dinner."

Outside, a car door slammed.

"I'll get it." Roni started to dance to the door. But Joey told her to sit and eat her turkey burger while she let Roni's father in and brought him back to the kitchen.

He was a handsome man, tall with broad shoulders and dark hair. In his left hand he held a cowboy hat. Roni jumped out of her chair and ran to him, wrapping her arms around his legs.

"Hi, Daddy."

"Hey, Bonnie Roni." He leaned down and kissed the top of her head.

Joey introduced them, and Ethan tipped his head. "Nice to meet you, ma'am. You're in good hands."

He seemed genuine, and Shiv wondered about Joey and Ethan's relationship. After Tanner had left her, they'd had little contact. Shiv was lucky when she received a child support check from her ex, let alone a kind word. But things seemed amicable, even friendly, between Joey and her ex.

"Roni's finishing her dinner," Joey told Ethan. "Would you like something? I could throw a turkey burger on the grill for you."

"Nah, I'm good." He looked over at Shiv. "Sorry to have interrupted your supper."

Shiv waved him off. "It's not a problem. I've enjoyed your little girl's visit."

"I'm done!" Roni shoved the last of her burger in her mouth and threw her arms in the air.

"Please take your plate to the sink."

Roni listened to her mother and cleared her setting.

"You ready to giddy up?" Ethan lifted his daughter into his arms to fits of giggles.

"Can I go, Mommy?"

Joey kissed her daughter good-bye, leaving her alone in the kitchen with Shiv. Without Roni, a quiet sadness settled over the room like a dark cloud.

"You barely touched your dinner, Shiv. Don't you like turkey burgers?"

"I'm just not that hungry, dear."

"Okay," Joey said, sounding concerned. "Is there something else I can get you? It's important to keep your strength up while you're recovering. I'm trying to make things that are healthy, lots of greens and foods low in fat. But we can compromise. I'd like to see you eat a little more."

"A milkshake," she blurted, not entirely sure where the sudden yen had come from. Even before her stroke, Shiv hadn't had a milkshake in years. Not since Ryder was a boy and used to love going to the Dairy Queen.

"I can make that," Joey said with enthusiasm. "Let me see if I can find a blender. I think Ryder bought ice cream." She rifled through the freezer. Grinning, she held up a carton of vanilla. Chocolate was Shiv's favorite, but vanilla would do in a pinch.

Joey searched the cupboards for a blender and found Shiv's old Oster in the cabinet near the refrigerator. "Looks like we're in business." She cleared Shiv's plate away and got to work on the milkshake. "Roni doesn't know what she's missing out on."

Shiv couldn't imagine what it would've been like sharing custody of Ryder with Tanner. Her son had been her life.

Joey turned off the blender. "What do you say we drink them outside and enjoy what's left of the day?"

Shiv would've preferred to drink hers in bed, but she didn't want to be rude. She let Joey help her to the front porch, where she settled in to enjoy her shake.

"I'll be right back." Joey went inside the house and returned with two tall glasses. "Here you go." She handed Shiv her milkshake and tapped it with her own glass. "*Sláinte.*"

"This looks delicious." Shiv took a slow sip. It was thick and sweet and refreshingly cold. She'd forgotten just how good a milkshake was. In the hospital and rehab facility, she'd been served protein drinks that were as bland as the lime Jell-O they got with lunch.

Joey reached into her back pocket and handed Shiv a spoon, then took the rocker next to hers. "What a nice evening. It's so peaceful here."

Shiv couldn't argue with that. "It is. Where did you live before?"

"Reno. Ethan and I had a house there."

"He seems like a nice man."

"He is," Joey said.

To Shiv's disappointment, Joey didn't elaborate. She'd never been one of those women who stuck her nose in other people's business. But she confessed to being curious.

"What about you, Shiv? Have you ever been married?"

"To Ryder's father. But that was a long time ago. He lives in Colorado with his other family." That's how she'd always referred to Ryder's half-brothers. As the "other family." It had only been recently that she'd started to question whether Ryder would've been better off getting to know his father and his two half-brothers. After all, who would he have after she was gone?

"How long were you two married?"

"Only five years." He'd left to follow the rodeo circuit and had met someone else.

"Are he and Ryder close?"

"No. He fell in and out of Ryder's life so many times that I think Ryder wrote him off. He was never the most dependable person. How about you? Are you close with your family?"

"I am." Joey scooped out a spoonful of ice cream from the bottom of her glass.

For a long time they didn't say anything. The sun had started to set, and the sky was awash in oranges, purples, and blues. They'd had nice sunsets in Oakdale, but nothing like this. With the mountains in the foreground, it reminded Shiv of a Western painting. She stared out over the horizon, rocking on the new chair, enjoying the solitude.

"Oops, I almost forgot to take a picture to send to Ryder." Joey fished her phone from her pocket, pulled her chair closer to Shiv's, and took a selfie of the two of them sitting together. "What do you think?" She showed the picture to Shiv.

"My hair looks awful." She touched her gray locks self-consciously. Before the stroke and when she'd worked for Morgan, she'd colored her hair in the kitchen sink every five weeks. For more than twenty years, she'd had a standing appointment with L'Oréal's Age Perfect 8N.

Joey turned her attention from the picture and assessed Shiv's hair. "It could do with some TLC. I hear there's a woman in town who is a wizard. Should we make you an appointment?"

What was the point? It wasn't like Shiv had anywhere to go or anyone to see. "I'll think about it," she said just to be polite.

Joey sent the picture, and a short time later her phone beeped with an incoming message. "It's Ryder. He says to tell you he's glad we're getting use out of the rocking chairs and will call you tomorrow."

"Tell him I'm looking forward to it." The best thing she'd ever done in life was to have Ryder. He'd always been a stoic little boy with a heart as full as December. Tanner used to say that their boy took after her more than him. And in some ways Tanner had been right. She and Ryder had both been crushed by love.

Shiv managed to pick up her empty glass from the floor and hoist herself out of the chair. "The milkshake was wonderful, dear. It's been a full day, and I'm ready to turn in for the night."

Joey helped get her inside and into bed. It was there that she let herself dream that she was young again and could erase the mistakes that had left her alone and her heart broken.

* * * *

Ryder pulled in just past midnight Sunday. The house was dark, the front porch lit up only by the silvery moon. He parked his rig next to the Peterbilt parked in his driveway and jumped down from the cab. Tomorrow, he'd move both 18-wheelers to the other side of the property. But tonight, all he wanted was to crawl into bed.

He'd driven six hundred miles today, including the grapevine, a trucker's beast with its steep grade. Normally, he would've stopped and caught some sleep. But he'd been in a rush to get home. He couldn't remember the last time that had happened. It was because of his mother, he told himself, and pretended he wasn't lying.

His camper was hot and stuffy. That's what he got for keeping the windows closed for nearly five days. He popped a few open before getting in the shower and washing away the day's grime.

What he needed was a hot tub to ease his sore muscles from sitting in a truck all day. Who ever said bronc riding was bad for the body had never spent eight hours behind the wheel of a big rig. Eight seconds on the back of a bucking horse was nothing.

He turned off the water, toweled off, and climbed into bed. But as exhausted as he was, sleep evaded him. Ryder figured it was overtiredness. His body was simply too depleted to listen to reason and shut down for the night.

There was a Louis L'Amour book on his nightstand but his concentration was shot, so he just lay there thinking about things he ought not to. Like Joey.

The days he'd been away, she'd taken up healthy space in his head and didn't seem to want to leave. He found himself looking for excuses to call or FaceTime her. Or even text. It was bizarre because he enjoyed the solitude of being on the road. In the rare times he got lonely for female company, there were women. Women without strings attached.

He should've told Janine to keep looking for a new caregiver for his mother. But it was selfish. Joey was beyond competent, and his mom liked her. And Joey could be close to her kid. It was a win-win for everyone, except him.

By the time he nodded off, sunlight had begun to stream through the window blinds. He pulled a pillow over his head and caught a few more hours, then got up and greeted the day.

"Hey." Joey was on the living room sofa, folding laundry when he came into the house. She had on a dress that showed off a heart-stopping pair of legs. "What time did you get in?"

"Early." He valiantly tried not to stare. "Any coffee?"

"Let me make a new pot. Unfortunately, you missed breakfast. But I can make you some eggs."

"I can handle it." It wasn't her job to cook for him. "Where's my mom?"

"She's getting dressed. My relief is coming."

He hadn't remembered that it was her day off. Disappointment surged through him.

He nudged his head at her dress. "Where you going?" For all he knew, she had a date. He'd never stopped to consider whether she was seeing someone. Probably another doctor, since that seemed to be her jam.

"Roni and I are going to Reno for a day of beauty. Mani-pedis, facials, the works."

So, not a date. Despite himself, his insides did a little celebration. *Hey, stupid, it doesn't mean she's not with someone.* Ah, jeez, why the hell did he care?

She filled the coffeemaker with water and started a fresh pot. "I'd like to discuss your mom," she said in a soft voice and pointed to the wall that separated the kitchen from his mother's bedroom. Whatever she had to say, she didn't want Shiv to hear it.

Her secrecy had him anticipating the worst. He wrinkled his brow. "Is everything okay?"

"It's not an emergency," she assured him. "But I'd like to go over some things with you in private. Could we meet somewhere in Nugget around five? By then I will have dropped Roni off at her dad's."

"Yeah, sure. How 'bout the Ponderosa?" Under normal circumstances, he might've made an off-color joke about them meeting there. But she had him worried.

She reached out and touched his arm. "Don't stress about this. It's just some observations I've made and some things we can do to...well, I'll talk to you about it this evening. Let me go check on your mom." She got him down a mug and placed it by the coffeemaker before heading to Shiv's bedroom.

He watched her walk away, then poured himself a cup of coffee. Outside, he heard a car door slam, temporarily pulling him from thoughts about Shiv.

He wandered into the living room and found Joey greeting a big bald dude with a beard at the door. He announced he was Peter and came inside.

"I didn't know what the coffee situation was like out here, so I brought beans and a grinder. And Doughboys Donuts." He held up a bakery box.

"You didn't? I love Doughboys Donuts," Joey said.

He opened the box so she could pick one.

She sniffed and chose an apple fritter. "Keep the rest of them away from me."

"Janine told me you were a kick. Where's Miss Siobhan?" Peter searched the front room, his gaze resting on Ryder. "Well, hello there."

"I'm Ryder Knight, Shiv's son."

"A pleasure to meet you, Ryder. Here, have a donut." Peter pushed the box at him.

Ryder exchanged a glance with Joey, who hitched her shoulders and followed Peter to the kitchen. Trailing behind them, Ryder put the box on the kitchen table and snagged a jelly donut.

"Shiv will be right out," Joey said.

"You go have your day off, girl. I'll take it from here." Peter helped himself to a mug in the cupboard and poured himself a cup of coffee. One sip and he tossed it and the remainder of the pot down the drain. He came for Ryder's mug and dumped that as well. "Life's too short for bad coffee."

He plugged in his grinder and got to work making a new pot. Shiv wandered in, and Ryder kissed her hello.

"There she is," Peter said as if he'd known Shiv for years.

Joey made formal introductions, and Peter offered Shiv a donut.

Ryder thought Peter was a little kooky, but he'd brought donuts, so he'd give him the benefit of the doubt. If Shiv liked Peter, Ryder liked Peter. It was as simple as that. Now only time would tell.

"I'm taking off. If any of you need anything, I'm available on my cell." Joey held up her phone.

Peter gave her a peck on the cheek like they were best friends. "We'll be fine, doll."

"Have a nice day with your daughter," Shiv called and chose a cruller from the box.

Ryder walked outside with Joey. "Big guy, big personality, huh?"

"I'm already in love," she said, which made Ryder glower.

He scanned the front porch, then in a low voice asked, "Do you want to tell me about my mom?"

"She's depressed."

He'd also noticed she wasn't herself but figured it was par for the course after a major hospitalization. "I know. She'll bounce back, especially now that she's out of rehab." That place had been bad enough to put anyone in a foul mood, especially the food.

"That's the thing, Ryder. I don't think she will without help. This isn't just 'I've got the blues.' This is clinical depression."

"What's the difference?"

Joey glanced at the house. "I really don't want to talk about this here." She let out a breath and kept her voice only slightly above a whisper. "It's a severe form of depression, something that's beyond my skill set. I have some ideas, though. But let's talk about them later, when your mom's not within earshot. Okay?"

"Sure." He didn't know whether to be relieved or even more worried. But at least he knew what he was working with now, instead of flying blind.

He opened the door of her SUV. "Have a nice day with your daughter."

"You have a nice day, too. And, Ryder, don't worry. We'll work this out."

He watched her drive off, then climbed the porch stairs. By now, Peter's coffee was probably ready. Ryder needed a good strong cup.

Chapter 10

At four thirty Ryder drove into town, figuring he'd throw back a beer before Joey arrived. Peter had hustled Shiv into his Prius, insisting they get Mexican food at a taqueria in Clio. He said it had gotten excellent Yelp reviews.

The Ponderosa was even more crowded than usual for a Sunday night. Spring in the Sierra brought plenty of tourists out to see the wildflowers.

"Hey, Ryder." Sophie, one of the owners, was standing in as hostess.

"Hi, Soph. Any chance of getting a table tonight?" He usually settled for the bar, where he could watch pro rodeo on one of the flat screens.

"I think we can make that happen. For one?"

"Two, please."

"Give me a couple of minutes to get the booth in the corner cleared."

"Thanks." He gazed up at the TV and caught the tail end of a team roping event. A Dwight Yoakam song played on the jukebox.

There was a group of women at a table near the hostess station. One of them waved, and he turned around to see if she was greeting someone else. But there was no one behind him. When he looked back, the woman laughed and motioned for him to come over. Ryder didn't recognize her, nor any of her friends.

He stepped up to their table and tipped his hat, then remembered to take it off.

"You're Ryder Knight, aren't you?" asked the brunette who'd called him over.

"Yes, ma'am."

"Oh. My. God." She and her friends started shrieking while Ryder stood there, confused. "I saw you at the NFR six years ago when you won the world championship. You were amazing. Can I have your autograph?"

It had been years since anyone had recognized him, let alone asked for his autograph. Even back then, he'd never gotten the kind of attention someone like Steph Curry or Tom Brady got. For the most part, pro-rodeo guys weren't household names.

"Uh, yeah, sure." His hand automatically went to his shirt pocket, searching for a pen. "You have something I can write with?"

One of the women went through her purse and came up with a Sharpie.

"That'll work." He looked around for something to write on. "How 'bout a napkin?" He swiped one off the table.

"How about this?" The brunette pulled down her blouse, indicating that Ryder should sign his name on the top part of her breast.

He was too old to do the buckle bunny shit, but just wanted to get it over with. Ryder scrawled his name on her flesh, keeping his hand above her bra line.

Not to be outdone, the brunette's friend, a redhead who'd had too much to drink, squealed, "Sign both of mine." And proceeded to peel off her T-shirt.

"Whoa, whoa, this is a family restaurant." Already, folks from neighboring tables had begun to stare. "Let's stick with paper." He quickly signed the napkin, wanting to extricate himself from the situation as soon as possible. This was his hometown now. The last thing he needed was to make a scene. "You ladies driving?"

"We're staying at that hotel down the street," said a third member of their party, who seemed slightly embarrassed by her friends.

"How 'bout a round on me?"

The women cheered, and he motioned to a server to refill their glasses. Then he slunk away, backing right into Joey.

"Shit." He rubbed his jaw. "How much of that did you see?"

"Enough." She raised her brows. "But not as much as your new neighbors."

He scanned the dining room, and there were the Addisons, sitting adjacent to the women's table in matching bear shirts. This time, hoodies with paw prints up and down the sleeves.

"Ah, crap."

Joey laughed. "You should've seen their faces."

"I don't even want to know."

Sophie pulled out two menus and led them to a booth. Ryder waited for Joey to get in and took the bench seat across from her.

"A server will be right with you," Sophie said and rushed off to the next table.

"You get that often?" Joey asked him.

"What?" Ryder perused the meat entrées. He was considering a steak.

"Women wanting you to autograph their boobs."

"It's happened once or twice. Not any time recently, though. I was surprised to even be recognized, to tell you the truth." Usually it was only diehard rodeo fans, and not so much anymore. He motioned at the women's table. "I'm gonna wager a guess that they're bombed."

"Uh, that's not all they are." She smirked.

He lifted his gaze from the menu and locked eyes with her, staring into a sea of blue. The same color of the bluebells that grew wild in the field behind his childhood home. He knew she was thinking about the night he'd invited her to his hotel room, jumping to conclusions about the kind of man he was. She didn't know a damn thing about him.

"Maybe," he said. "But I'm not interested."

Her face flushed red, and she looked away.

"How was your day?" he asked to change the subject. He hadn't come here to argue with her.

"Good. How was Peter?"

"Ma seems to like him okay, and that's all that matters."

A server came to take their orders. He got the rib eye, and Joey got a salad.

"So, how bad is she?"

Joey took a sip of her water. "She's showing all the classic signs of clinical depression. Sleeping all the time, hardly eating, and she's lethargic. Obviously, you know her better than I do, but she seems sad. Does she seem sad to you?"

At first, he'd thought it was retirement. The months following her big send-off from the courthouse, she'd seemed out of sorts. Ryder had chalked it up to boredom and had told himself that all she needed was a new routine. And then she'd had the stroke, which would've depressed anyone. Hell, he'd been a bear to be around after breaking a few bones on the back of a bronc.

He'd told himself that her melancholy would pass, that it was all normal shit.

"Yeah," he said, guilt rushing through him. Why hadn't he been more proactive? Why had it taken a virtual stranger to see what was in plain sight? Ryder should've known right off. Not just because she was his mother, but because he'd been in a place so dark that it was a wonder that he'd ever emerged sane. If anyone should've recognized deep depression, it should've been him. "I guess I thought it would pass. I suck."

Joey reached across the table and took his hand. She was consoling him, nothing else. But he felt the zing of her touch ripple through him.

"No, you don't. The people who are the closest usually miss it, mostly because the person in trouble hides it from them. And I'm a trained professional, remember?" She gave him a weak smile. "But now that we know, we can do something about it."

"Like what? Antidepressants?" After Leslie died, everyone had wanted to push drugs on him. As if a pill could cure his pain. He'd turned to alcohol to dull it, but it never fully went away.

"Perhaps. Not my wheelhouse, though. We'll get her good professional help. Depression isn't uncommon after suffering a serious illness, Ryder. I want to find someone who specializes in it, which may mean Reno. I can take her."

He didn't know what to say. A year ago, Joey Nix had simply been a woman he'd desperately wanted to sleep with. Now she was his salvation.

"Thank you," he said. It was woefully inadequate, but all he had.

"It's my job."

He leaned in, never letting go of her hand. He didn't know what she was like before, when she had the drug problem. But he couldn't imagine taking on his mother's problems without her. Her assuring way put him at ease. "They should give you your nursing license back. The world needs you."

Her blue eyes pooled, and she looked away so he wouldn't see her crying.

"Shit, what did I say wrong?"

"You didn't say anything wrong." She blotted her eyes with her napkin. "It was actually the nicest thing I've heard in a long time."

Their food came, breaking the moment. They ate in companionable silence, both lost in their own thoughts. His never veered too far away from Joey.

"What are you looking at?" she asked.

"Nothing." His lips kicked up because he was lying. He'd been drinking her in like a man parched in the desert. "How was Reno?" He'd already asked her some version of that. But sitting so near her was destroying his conversational skills.

"We hit the salon, had lunch, did a little shopping, and I dropped her off at my folks for an hour so I could attend an AA meeting. Although it was too cool still for the pool, Roni got to dip her feet in. Then I dropped her home, so she could get an early evening in. Tomorrow's school."

"How was the good doc?"

"Fine, I guess. Busy planning his wedding."

"Why did you guys break up, anyway? If it wasn't the brunette, what was it?"

She stared down at her plate as if it held some secret significance. "It's not a pretty story."

"You cheat on him?" It was a really shitty thing to say. But the great Ethan sort of busted on Ryder's last nerve, even though he appeared to be a perfectly standup guy. Ryder suspected that was part of it.

"Worse," she said and turned her fork over in her hand. "I forged prescriptions in his name and nearly ruined his career. When I got caught, I got Roni up in the middle of the night, took her to a bad part of town to score oxy, and got carjacked at gunpoint. Ethan forgave me for the scripts. But having a nine-millimeter stuck in our baby's face was his breaking point."

"I could see that." It explained why the kid didn't live with her. "But it looks like he trusts you again."

She raised her face to him. "After that story, do you?"

He had no reason not to. So far, she'd been nothing but trustworthy. And his mother wasn't a seven-year-old. "People make mistakes. It's how they fix them that matters."

She gave an imperceptible nod but looked so sad he wanted to hold her.

"You went to a meeting, huh? You do that a lot?"

"Once or twice a week. I've been clean for nearly two years now. It's made me look at life differently. I'm much more grateful for what I have and don't want to risk ever losing it again."

He suspected she was talking about her daughter. "What about your ex? You ever wish you could get him back?" The question was overstepping for sure, but he couldn't seem to stop himself.

"There was a time I thought so. But our marriage was barely holding on before I became addicted to pills. Sometimes it's easier to fall out of love than it is to fall in it, you know what I mean?"

He didn't.

"How 'bout you and the brunette. You finding your way with her?"

"The brunette's name is Brynn. And she's actually a very sweet person. It's horrible of me, and I'll probably go to hell for it, but I just wish my daughter didn't love her so much."

His mouth quirked. "I'd say it's only human. But this I know for sure. No one can compete with a kid's mother."

"Not even a kid's father?" She pinned Ryder with a look. Clearly Shiv had been talking.

"Nope. Especially one who's a son of a bitch."

"How so?"

It wasn't something he talked about. But Joey had been generous with her secrets, he could at least tell her about Tanner Cole. "He left us when I was a kid. Took off for a rodeo in Abilene and never came back. A year later, he sent my mom divorce papers in the mail. As soon as the ink had dried, there was a new Mrs. Cole. The judge my ma worked for helped her change her name back to Knight. I took that name as well. Didn't want anybody knowing that man was my daddy."

"Did he at least pay child support or try to see you?"

"Sometimes he sent money. But mostly not. A few times he tried to see me. But it wasn't until I started making a name for myself in college rodeo that my long-lost daddy wanted back in my life. It turned out that besides his DNA, I'd inherited his skill at riding saddle broncs. He saw me as heir to his world championship throne. Too bad for him that by high school I didn't want any part of the man."

"Where is he now?"

Ryder hitched his shoulders. "Last I heard, living on his oldest son's ranch in Colorado."

"How many sons does he have?"

"Two. Both saddle bronc riders. How 'bout that?"

"Clearly it's in your family's blood."

"They're not my family," Ryder said and took a slug of his beer.

"Have you ever met them?"

"We've traveled in the same circles, bumped into each other a time or two. I wish them no ill will. But we ain't never going to sit around a campfire, singing 'Kumbaya'."

"It's kind of a shame. Whether you like your father or not, they're still your half-brothers. Is your dad still married to their mom?"

"He was until she died a few years ago. Cancer. Her death hit him hard, I guess. He came around, wanting to patch things up, try again."

"But you weren't interested?"

"Nope. I'm sorry for his loss. But I don't remember him being sorry for my mother's loss. And when Leslie di—"

"Who's Leslie?"

"My late wife."

She jerked back in surprise. "I'm so sorry, Ryder. When did she…What happened?"

"I don't talk about it if you don't mind."

"Okay. But I had no idea—"

He held up his hand. "We're done with that topic. Tell me about your brother. Is that the only sibling you have?"

"Jay." She stifled a laugh. "Yeah, it's just the two of us. He's not as bad as he seems. Sorry he tried to sell you a truck. He owns a dealership."

"I got that." Ryder cocked a brow. "He must do pretty well, then."

"To hear it from Jay, he does." She rolled her eyes.

"You don't believe him?"

"I do, but I think he spends more than he makes. The big house, the cars, the boat, the cabin in Tahoe. His monthly trips to Vegas. Who knows what the financial situation is there? We're not super close. But these last two years, he's been a good brother. Stood behind me during my darkest hours. I'll always love him for that."

Out of the side of his eye, Ryder saw the Addisons get up to leave. They were such a strange couple. The weird outfits were one thing. But they seemed like really miserable people. As far as he could tell, they'd eaten their entire meal in silence.

"I should get back to the house," Joey said. "Peter's off at six thirty."

Ryder called their server over to get the bill. When Joey tried to pay for her meal, he said, "Don't piss me off."

"Why? A woman can't pay her own way?"

"Seriously?" He shook his head. "This was about my mother. Consider it a business dinner." It wasn't a date, even though he'd liked the company. More than he probably should have.

They walked out together into a balmy evening. It was still light outside, and the scent of jasmine crept up on him.

"Where are you parked?"

She pointed to the barbershop. "I couldn't get anything close when I got here."

There were plenty of empty parking spaces in front of the restaurant now. In a couple of hours, all of Nugget would go dark. That's how it was in ranching towns. Early to bed and early to rise.

"I'll walk you," he said.

She looked at him like he was crazy. It was Nugget, after all. But he told himself he needed the exercise. They slowly strolled down the street. His hand accidentally brushed against hers, and he quickly shoved it in his pocket.

He could smell her perfume, something soft that mingled sweetly with the jasmine. Ryder remembered it from the first time they'd met. And later, when they'd clung to each other outside the Ponderosa.

"I'm right here." She pressed her fob, and the red SUV beeped.

He opened the driver's-side door for her. But instead of moving away, he boxed her in. He knew even before he caught her mouth with his that he'd regret this moment. That it would upend any professional boundaries he'd tried to set. Yet he was powerless to stop himself.

He pulled her against him and kissed her. She moaned against his lips and laced her hands behind his neck. Ryder rocked into her as he took the kiss deeper, letting his hands caress her sides and resting them in the dip at her waist.

She was soft and curvy, and he itched to touch her skin instead of the fabric of her dress. He cupped the back of her head while he explored her mouth with his tongue. She pressed against his groin, silently pleading for more. He wanted to lift her onto the hood of her car, but they were in a public place. So, he settled for the taste of her kiss. It reminded him of springtime. Warm, like a May morning with all the comfort of coming home.

Yeah, she felt like home.

He shut that thought down as soon as it entered his head. There was no room in his home for anyone other than him. This was sexual attraction and nothing more.

Her hands slid down to his ass and into his back pockets, and he felt himself grow harder. She whimpered, and he nearly lost his mind. He maneuvered her away from the open driver's-side door and pinned her against the side of the SUV. His hands were everywhere, touching her arms, her breasts, her bare legs. The kiss grew rougher with a need he didn't know he possessed.

She groaned again and went for his fly. In two seconds, they'd be naked, and he'd have her on her back.

"Shit." He hadn't realized he'd said it aloud until she stopped mid-kiss, her blue eyes dazed and heavy with desire. "We've got to shut this down."

Jesus, what had he started? He pulled away and tried to collect himself. Tried to tell himself that it was nothing. Just a kiss. Tomorrow, they could go back to normal.

But the whole way back to his truck, he knew he'd screwed this up for good.

Chapter 11

Joey didn't know whether to be angry or relieved that Ryder had stopped before they'd taken their kiss further. The last time they'd kissed like that, it had taken months to erase it from her mind. This time, there was no telling how long it would take.

Ryder Knight could kiss, that was for sure. There was more to him, though, than a pair of lips. Tonight, she'd shared her worst shame with him. It was something she didn't tell anyone, let alone an employer. He'd listened intently without showing a scintilla of judgment. Then he'd blown her away with his own story. Well, partial story.

A wife.

And perhaps a tragedy. At least that's what it sounded like to Joey, though he'd made it abundantly clear he didn't want to talk about it.

No, there was more to Ryder than a ruggedly handsome face and a hard, chiseled body. A puzzling man with a complex story. But if she was smart, she'd let the mystery about him be.

She beat him home and dashed inside before he drove up. Peter was alone in the living room, watching a rerun of *Say Yes to the Dress*.

"Hey there. You have a nice day off?"

"I did." She hoped she didn't seem flustered, or worse, disheveled. In her rush to beat Ryder home, she hadn't thought to check herself in the mirror. "How did it go with Shiv? Is she in bed?"

"I wore her out." Peter's mouth slid up. "Have you been to Roberto's? It's fabulous."

She'd heard of the taco stand, knew Ethan liked to go there, but had never tried it herself. "Did Shiv eat?"

"Not much."

She sat next to Peter on the couch and huffed out a breath. "Does she seem depressed to you?" Joey wanted a second opinion. Even though Peter had only just met Shiv, as a caregiver he'd been trained about the warning signs.

"Yes," he said. "Physically, she's a rock star. But she sleeps too much, hardly ate today, and has the demeanor of a clinically depressed person. Do you plan to talk to Hunkomatic about it?"

Joey laughed because it didn't take an advanced degree to know who he was talking about. "Yep. We met for dinner to discuss possible solutions." *And then we made out on the sidewalk like two high school kids.*

"Dinner?" Peter waggled his brows. "With the cowboy? How do I get one of those? What did he say?"

"That he's okay with me booking her an appointment with a good therapist. I'm going to ask my ex-husband to talk to his colleagues about a recommendation. Do you have one?"

Peter shook his head. "My last client had lots of medical issues, fortunately depression wasn't one of them. But Janine can probably give you a referral."

Joey lightly rested her hand on Peter's leg. "Janine told me about Fred. I'm sorry for your loss, Peter."

Peter's brown eyes watered. "The old man was a hoot, reminded me of the father I never had. Loved me like a son. He was eighty-six and lived a hell of a good life. The angels have him now." He pulled a handkerchief from his pocket and wiped his nose. "Miss Shiv is still a baby. We've gotta bring her back to the land of the living."

"Hear, hear!"

Peter got to his feet. "I'll be back on Saturday. What do you know about that inn downtown? I was thinking of treating myself next weekend and booking Saturday night. It'll save me a drive to and from Reno and looks positively divine."

"I've never been inside, but I hear it's gorgeous. Judging from Shiv's taste"—Joey waved at the antiques around the room—"she'd love the place. The owner invited us to take a tour. So, if you get a room, we'll drop by for a few minutes."

"Fun! Let me know if you need anything from the big city. I'll bring something delicious on Saturday."

"Drive carefully, Peter." They'd only known each other for fifteen minutes, but she was already in love with him.

After Peter left, she checked on Shiv, who was sound asleep, and weighed whether to hide in her bedroom on the chance that when Ryder got home, he'd come inside. It was just too darn early. Without a TV in her room or even a book—she reminded herself to buy a few or find the e-reader she'd left at her parents' house—she'd go stir-crazy in the small room.

So, she parked herself on the sofa and continued to watch *Say Yes to the Dress*. It was a marathon. She kept one ear open for Ryder's truck to come up the driveway. *Coward.*

An hour went by, and she started to get concerned. It wasn't as if Nugget had a bar row. By now, the Ponderosa had rolled up for the night. She supposed Ryder could've gone to Reno or headed to a honky-tonk or biker bar along the highway.

God only knew what he was doing right now. Walking away from that kiss had nearly killed her.

She told herself she didn't care and changed into her pajamas. A few minutes later, she was back on the sofa, channel surfing. A person could only take so many wedding gowns. Halfway through a *Friends* episode, she heard the familiar sound of Ryder's Ram engine.

She'd convinced herself that he'd head for the comfort of his fifth wheel when those broad shoulders of his passed through the front door. He did the dude head bob when he found her on the couch.

"I wanted to say good night to my mother."

"She's asleep." It took all her willpower not to ask where he'd been.

He rubbed his hand down his face, sat in the wing chair, and plopped his boots on top of the coffee table. "I guess we should talk about what just happened."

"I'm good," she said, but she really wasn't. Besides the fact that he'd left her frustrated in a cold shower kind of way, she was worried about getting fired.

"We can't do that again."

"You started it, not me."

"Are you taking lessons from your seven-year-old now?"

Yeah, she'd sounded kind of childish.

"There's something about us…some kind of chemistry. But I don't want there to be. Not just because you work for my mother, which in and of itself makes this impossible. But because I don't want a woman in my life."

"If you want a man, Peter might be interested."

For a long time, he didn't say anything, just hung his head back against the chair and stretched his long, denim-encased legs across more of the coffee table. "Do you understand what I'm saying?"

"I don't think you could've made it any clearer. And for your information, I'm looking to put my life back together, not to find a man. So, I think we're both on the same page. It was just a kiss, Ryder. We'd confessed hard truths about ourselves to each other, and at the end of the day we just wanted someone to hold on to. That's all."

"Is that what it was?" He stood up. "Good to know."

* * * *

Joey spent most of Monday trying to avoid Ryder. She wasn't sure when he was leaving again, but the sooner the better. He'd spent much of the morning re-parking and washing the two giant trucks that had been taking up space in the driveway.

During Shiv's nap, she called Ethan, who actually had time in his day to talk.

"Sorry to bother you, but I was hoping you could make a referral or at least know someone who can."

"Okay. Hit me."

"I need a psychiatrist or psychologist who specializes in depression for a mature adult."

"A little out of my wheelhouse. Is this for your patient?"

It was nice of him to use the word "patient," knowing Joey was no longer a nurse. "I'm not at liberty to say." They were both well versed in HIPAA privacy rules.

"I'll have to ask around. You want someone in Reno?"

"Preferably Quincy." That's where Shiv's new primary care physician was. "But Reno would work."

"Let me see what I can do. How's the job going?"

"Good." In the old days, they used to discuss their patients without identifying anyone's name. She didn't miss being married to Ethan, but she did miss talking shop with him. "It's challenging in its own way." Especially living only a few feet away from a man who confounded her beyond reason. "How 'bout you? Anything new?"

"Just wedding twenty-four-seven. Did you get our invitation?"

Oh, goody.

"Not yet. I haven't had my mail forwarded. Next time I visit my folks, I'll get it." It wasn't surprising that her mother hadn't passed the envelope along to her on Sunday. She'd desperately wanted Joey and Ethan to reconcile. Lou Ellen had said it was for the sake of Roni, but sometimes Joey wondered if her mother liked the cachet of her daughter being married to a world-renowned surgeon.

"I hope you'll consider what we talked about and will attend. If nothing else, the food will be good."

Her lips tipped up at his sense of humor, then she sighed. "I'm not going to lie to you, Ethan, it's awkward. But for the sake of Roni, I'll think about it."

"I appreciate it, Joe. Veronica said she had a good time yesterday. But Joey, you don't have to buy her something every time the two of you are together."

She bristled at his lecture. She was Roni's mother, and if she wanted to buy her daughter things that was her business.

"Don't forget to get me a referral. I have to go now." She hung up, trying not to be angry. They'd come so far. And after all she'd put Ethan through, his generosity still floored her.

She peeked in on Shiv, debating whether to let her continue sleeping when the screen door slammed. Joey girded herself.

"My ma still asleep?" Ryder came up behind her.

"Uh-huh." She quietly shut the bedroom door. "I'll give her thirty more minutes, then I'm taking her downtown to get her hair done." Initially, the stylist had been booked but had called an hour ago with a cancelation. "I'm hoping it'll perk her up a bit."

"Did you find someone for her to talk to? Maybe I should start looking around."

She motioned for Ryder to move away from the door and out of the hallway. "I just got off the phone with Ethan. He's going to make some inquiries. He'll find someone good."

The weight of the world was etched on Ryder's face.

She couldn't help herself and reached out to take his hand. "We'll work this out, I promise. We've just got to get your mom back into the sunlight. It'll happen."

"I've gotta haul a load on Wednesday to the Central Valley, pick up a new load, and truck it to Sacramento. It's a two-day trip, max. One, if I make good time and drive through the night. If you can get an appointment on Friday, I can go with her."

"Ryder, I don't think we'll get in to see anyone that soon. A good therapist is usually booked out for weeks. But let me see what I can do."

"Yeah, all right. But I'd like to get her an appointment as soon as possible."

"Message received. I'll do the best I can." She started to walk away.

He gently grasped her shoulders. "I wasn't complaining. My mom lucked out with you."

"Thank you," she whispered. It was the second time in twenty-four hours he'd complimented her job performance. He had no idea how much she needed the reinforcement.

"I'm going out for a few hours. Anything you want me to pick up?"

"We're good. After I take your mom to her hair appointment, I'll hit the grocery store."

"See you around, then." He started to go when Joey stopped him.

"How do you feel about me removing the wallpaper in my room?"

His mouth curved up. "That bad, huh?"

She waggled her hand from side to side. "I thought it might be a good project for your mom and me. If it works out well in my room, we can start on your mom's. Maybe paint both rooms a cheerful color."

"Knock yourself out. If you need any help or supplies, let me know."

After he left, she marveled at how normal their exchange had been. Professional and friendly without any residual weirdness over what had happened the night before. She was a good actor because his nearness—the feel of his hands—had sent tingles up her spine.

"Joey."

She rushed to Shiv's room. "I'm here. Everything okay?"

"Yes, dear. I got a little dizzy trying to get up is all."

"Here, let me help you." Joey hoisted Shiv to her feet. "Just stand there for a couple of minutes and see if you feel better."

Shiv's balance appeared fine. She was able to stand on her own without her cane. The dizziness could've easily been caused by dehydration.

"I think it's gone."

"Why don't we walk around a little bit. See how you feel?"

They took a turn around the house, and Shiv was able to walk on her own.

"I'd like you to drink a tall glass of water," Joey said. "Then we've got to head out to make your appointment."

"I'm not really feeling up to it." Shiv's gaze fell to the floor.

"I think once we get out, it'll change your perspective. Plus, if we cancel now, Ryder will get stuck with the bill," Joey lied. Unlike the high-end salons in Reno, the Nugget barbershop hadn't asked to put a credit card on file. She could probably cancel, but it wouldn't be nice after the stylist went to such trouble to fit them in. Besides, Joey suspected that some pampering might be just what the doctor ordered.

It hadn't gone beyond Joey's notice that at one time Shiv had cared about her appearance. She had a closet full of nice things. Pretty silk scarves, quality blouses, high-heeled shoes, and a toiletry bag full of department-store-brand makeup. Pictures scattered around the house portrayed a put-together, fashion-conscious career woman.

Joey found a pale blue wrap dress hanging in Shiv's antique armoire. "This is lovely. It matches your eyes." She handed it to Shiv to put on.

"Oh, I'll look silly."

"Why would you think that?" Granted, jeans, Western shirts, and cowboy boots seemed to be the uniform in Nugget. But the dress was simple enough to be perfectly appropriate for a country town.

"It's a work dress," Shiv said. "And I'm sure it no longer fits me."

"There's only one way to find out."

Shiv reluctantly put the dress on. The fitted style came alive on her small frame but even Joey had to concede that it was too large. A good seamstress could probably take it in. For now, a few strategically placed safety pins would have to do the trick.

"Hang on a sec." Joey went to her room and returned with her sewing kit. "A tuck here and there and it'll fit beautifully." She found a few discreet spots to pin. It wasn't perfect, but the dress was better than it was before. "What do you think?" She moved Shiv to the mirror behind her door.

Shiv stood there, staring at her reflection. "It used to be one of my favorite dresses." She lifted her hand to her hair and muttered, "I look like death."

"You don't look like death. And after we get your hair cut and colored, you're going to feel so much better." Joey returned to Shiv's closet. "Now let's find you some shoes." She chose a pair of silver ballet flats. Heels probably would've accomplished more of the effect Joey was going for. But in case Shiv got dizzy again, the flats were a more cautious choice.

"These are adorable. Where did you get them?"

Shiv looked down at the shoes Joey had placed at her feet. "A boutique in Modesto, I believe. I haven't worn them in years."

"How do you feel about pantyhose?" Joey never bothered with stockings, but her mother would never wear a dress without them.

"Have you seen my legs?" Shiv ran her finger over a series of blue veins that crisscrossed the back of her calves. "This is what happens when you get old."

"I have them, too, and I'm hardly old." Joey was thirty-six. And along with her varicose veins, she'd never been able to get rid of her pregnancy stretch marks. "I consider them a badge of my accomplishments."

Shiv put on the pantyhose. The final product was a sharp-looking middle-aged woman. Yet Shiv seemed unimpressed with what she saw in the mirror. Joey only wished Shiv could see what she did. Maybe a fresh hairdo would turn things around.

"You ready to go?" Joey didn't wait for an answer, just grabbed a couple of protein bars and hustled Shiv out of the house before she changed her mind.

They got to the square five minutes before Shiv's appointment. Joey didn't know what she'd expected, but the barbershop did not fill her with confidence. It was clean with the usual accoutrements you'd find in a men's barbershop. What it was missing was the feminine trappings of a hair salon. Except for a chair with a hair dryer and shelves filled with expensive styling products, there were no pictures of hair models, no pretty mirrors, no tea and coffee station (Joey's Reno salon served sparkling wine). Even the choice of reading material consisted mostly of outdated hunting and outdoor magazines with a couple of *Cosmo*s and *People*s thrown into the mix.

The stylist, a woman named Darla, was also of grave concern. She had a pink hairpiece clipped to the top of her head, with matching plastic hoop earrings the size of bagels, and she had penciled a Marilyn Monroesque beauty mark near her upper lip.

Darla cut Brynn's hair, which was always flawless. But Darla's getup wasn't instilling a whole lot of confidence in Joey. Shiv looked too tuned out to care. But Joey did. She wanted Shiv to leave the salon, or rather the barbershop, with a fresh outlook.

"That blue is so good on you, right?" Darla picked a piece of lint off Shiv's dress, then started fluffing her hair.

Joey was just about to make up a fake emergency to get them out of there when another client came in.

The client gave one of the drinks she was carrying to Darla. "Do you have time to give me a blowout?" She rested her hands on her stomach. Other than being hugely pregnant, she looked normal. That is to say, no weird hairpieces or fake moles.

"As soon as I'm done with Ms. Knight," Darla said and gave her a pointed look as if to say, *Do you not see that I have clients?*

The woman turned to them and smiled. "Sorry, I didn't notice you guys when I came in. Half the time, I walk around in a haze."

Joey still remembered her pregnancy fog. Walking into the kitchen and forgetting why she'd come. Looking for her cell phone when it was right in her hand. "When are you due?"

"A couple of weeks. But if I could get this baby out of me right now, I would."

Joey chuckled. "It'll be over before you know it. Congratulations, by the way."

"Thank you. I complain a lot, but we're really excited."

"You ready, Ms. Knight?" Darla led Shiv to a chair. "I'm going to double-smock you because I don't want to get any color on your pretty dress. What are we thinking? Light blond?"

"I usually go a darker blond."

"Really?" Darla took a strand of Shiv's hair and examined it, then appraised her face. "I think we should lighten you up and add a few lowlights. It'll keep your hair from looking brassy. It'll be pretty, trust me."

Joey wanted to scream, *"We don't,"* but it looked like the ship had already sailed. Darla went to the back to mix the color.

As if the pregnant woman had read Joey's mind, she said, "Don't worry, Darla is like John Frieda good."

Joey had no idea who John Frieda was, but she assumed he was a big name in the hair industry.

"Is that your mom?"

"No, I'm Shiv's caregiver." Joey stuck out her hand. "Joey Nix."

"I'm Harlee Roberts. Darla's my best friend. Do you two live around here?"

"Shiv is Ryder Knight's son. He moved here not too long ago. We live with him."

"Oh, on the old Montgomery place. My husband redid the floors and built the porch ramp there. Ryder's the rodeo star, right?"

"Yes, he was. Now he owns a trucking company."

"That's what Colin said. Colin's my husband. I should get Ryder's phone number from you. I've been meaning to do an interview with him."

"Interview?"

"Uh-huh." Harlee took a big gulp of her drink. "I own the *Nugget Tribune*."

"Wow. I'll let Ryder know." Joey suspected Ryder would love a story about himself. The notoriety would mean more women's breasts to sign.

Darla returned with a bowl of color and foil for the lowlights. At least she appeared to know what she was doing, and Joey took some solace in the fact that Harlee had a great layered cut. Joey assumed Darla had given it to her.

"I'll get your color on, and then we can talk about what kind of style you want." Darla told Shiv, who gave a small nod.

Their so-called day of beauty wasn't having the effect on Shiv Joey had hoped for. She wasn't joining in the conversation and didn't seem to care what Darla did to her hair.

Harlee managed to heave herself out of her chair and waddled over to Darla, where she assessed Shiv's hair from all sides. "A layered bob."

"That would look so good, right?" Darla brushed color onto a few strands of Shiv's hair and wrapped it in foil. "Lots of texture and body. Super youthful."

"What do you think, Shiv?" Joey asked.

"Whatever you girls decide."

Joey nodded to Darla that she should go ahead with a bob and prayed that Shiv would like it. Though, at this point, it didn't seem like Shiv would care if Darla gave her a Mohawk. What they needed was a good referral for a shrink.

Harlee returned to the waiting area and sat next to Joey. "Are you from around here?" she asked Joey.

"Reno. But my ex-husband owns the Circle D Ranch. We have a daughter together."

"Ethan Daniels is your ex?"

Small towns. "Uh-huh."

"So, Roni must be your daughter. I love that kid."

A smile stretched across Joey's face. "Me, too. Who knows, in the not-so-distant future she may be babysitting yours."

"I would love that." Harlee stretched her back as her hand rested on her stomach. "You and Ethan must be on good terms."

Harlee had stated it as fact, but Joey knew it was a question. A personal one. Then again, the woman owned an online newspaper.

"We are," Joey said because they were.

The bells on the barbershop door jingled, and that awful Addison woman came in. Today, she had on a T-shirt with a bear applique. It looked like something a four-year-old would wear.

"Where's Owen?" she asked without greeting Darla, and the sour expression she'd had at the Ponderosa the other evening was still on her face.

"Day off," Darla responded in the same terse way in which the Addison woman had asked.

She stomped off without saying good-bye, letting the door clang closed behind her. Darla and Harlee burst out laughing, then, remembering they had clients, stopped.

"What's her deal?" Joey asked. "She seems perpetually unhappy."

"Sandy Addison?" Darla glanced at Harlee.

"She's a giant pain in the butt," Harlee finished. "Up in everyone's face. When Maddy and her brother began rehabbing the Lumber Baron, Sandy tried to turn the whole town against them. Did the same to me when I first took over the *Nugget Tribune*. Can you believe she threatened to sue me over a story I did about how forecasters were predicting another El Niño year, claiming that I was intentionally trying to keep tourists away from her precious Beary Quaint? As if anyone brave enough to stay at that dump would be afraid of a winter storm."

"Do people just ignore them?"

"For the most part. But because they've been here so long and for a while owned the only lodging in town, they've got their fair share of backers. It's best to steer clear of them." Harlee scrutinized Joey as if she'd suddenly sniffed out a potential story. "Sandy hasn't hassled you guys, has she?"

Joey didn't feel it was her place to discuss the Addisons' confrontation with Ryder. That was his story to tell. But Harlee had confirmed what Joey had already figured out. The Addisons were big fat troublemakers.

"I'd forgotten that the Beary Quaint is next door to the old Montgomery place," Harlee continued.

"I'm closer," Darla said. "Just over the hill. But on the other side."

Joey hadn't known that Darla was a neighbor. From Ryder's, you couldn't see another house, only fields and forest.

"No, nothing like that," she fibbed, earning a skeptical glance from Harlee. "They came over the other day to talk to Ryder. I'm sure it was just to introduce themselves."

Darla put her empty color bowls on a cart. "Oh my gosh, we are so rude for not coming over. It's just that Wyatt's been filling in for Jake while he and Cecilia are on vacation, and I've taken on more hours here. Don't hate us, Shiv."

Shiv patted Darla's hand. "You're fine, dear. And you're always welcome."

Darla led Shiv to another chair to let the color set while she washed Harlee's hair at the sink bowl. Joey got a call from Ethan and took it outside.

"Did you find someone?" she asked by way of a greeting.

"I got three referrals. But, Joey, have you discussed this with Ms. Knight's primary physician?"

It was a good point. One Joey hadn't thought of, reminding her how out of practice she was. "I'll do that. But give me the names." She rummaged through her purse to find a pen and something to write on.

Ethan rattled off the numbers. One of them was in Quincy, and hopefully Shiv's doctor knew him and could get them in as soon as possible. It would give Ryder a sense of relief to know this was handled before he took off for work.

"I can't believe how quickly you got these. You are a good man, Ethan Daniels."

"Yeah, I'm not that bad. I've got a favor to ask, though? Brynn and I would like to get away for a weekend in San Francisco. Alma has plans Saturday. Any chance you could take both kids until Alma gets home in the late afternoon? I know it's a big ask, and if you can't, we'll make other arrangements."

Joey couldn't decide whether she was thrilled that she'd won Ethan's trust or skeeved out that her ex had basically set the picture for a romantic weekend with his fiancée. "Henry is always welcome. You know that. I'll plan something fun."

"You're a champ, Joey. I can't tell you how badly Brynn and I need this weekend."

Why? Trouble in paradise? Not that Joey wished them any ill will. She only wished her life was going as well as theirs, not that she was complaining. Compared to a year ago, she was in a good space.

"Sure. No worries. But I better go. Again, hats off to you for those referrals."

When she got inside, Darla was blowing out Harlee's hair with a big, round brush. The result was gorgeous. Large, bouncy curls that framed Harlee's pretty face. Joey's initial doubt about Darla began to evaporate. She definitely appeared to know what she was doing.

Darla spun Harlee around in the chair, giving her a 360-degree view. "You look adorbs. Feel better?"

"Yeeees." Harlee folded her hands over her heart. "I wish you did pedicures, too. I don't know the last time I could actually see my feet, let alone paint my toenails."

"Soon, girlfriend."

"Love ya." Harlee got out of Darla's chair and gave her a peck on the cheek. On her way out, she threw kisses to Joey and Shiv. "Nice meeting you both. I've got to get back to work."

They waved good-bye. Darla washed Shiv's hair out, and Joey amused herself with one of the year-old *People* magazines lying around. She could hear Darla trying to engage Shiv in conversation. At least Shiv was responding. But Joey got the impression it was more out of politeness than anything else.

Joey helped Shiv back into the barber chair, and Darla went to work. Even wet, Shiv's new color lit up her face. And as Darla began to snip away at Shiv's hair with a pair of scissors, Joey could see a shape taking place. But the real transformation came when Darla got out the blow-dryer and the same round brush she'd used on Harlee to style Shiv's layers into one of the most flattering haircuts Joey had ever seen. Darla was a magician because Shiv took one look at herself in the mirror and did a double take. A literal double take.

"It looks so good, right?" Darla rubbed styling product through Shiv's hair and fussed with the ends until each lock was perfect. She turned the chair, so Shiv could see her profile. "What do you think?"

"I love it," Shiv said with an enthusiasm Joey hadn't heard before.

Darla demonstrated the technique she'd used so Shiv could style the new cut on her own. "If you have any trouble, come back and I'll show you what you're doing wrong. But you have good hair. It'll probably look like this even if you let it dry naturally."

Shiv leaned closer to the mirror and ran her fingers through her hair. "I never would've thought of going this light. The color changes everything."

"Told you." Darla took Shiv's cape off and brushed the back of her neck. "You look beautiful."

When they got to Joey's car, loaded down with styling products, Shiv flipped down the visor mirror and took another look at herself. "I hope I can do this myself."

"You can," Joey assured her. "And if we have to come back for another lesson, we will." Joey checked out herself in her own mirror. "I'm thinking I should let Darla do my hair, too."

Shiv waved her hand in the air. "You couldn't be any prettier than you already are. But that Darla knows what she's doing."

By the time Joey pulled into the driveway, she was feeling more optimistic about Shiv's state of mind than when they had left that afternoon. Shiv had been upbeat the entire drive home, which Joey considered a major victory.

All in all, a good day. The sun was shining. Joey had made two new friends in a town where she knew no one. Ethan trusted her to care for Brynn's son despite their history. And she and Ryder appeared to have weathered their mutual attraction like responsible adults.

Silently, she celebrated. But her zen moment came crashing down the minute her cell phone beeped with a text from her mother.

"A letter from the California Board of Registered Nursing came in the mail today. Do you want me to open it?"

The letter held the key to her future. So, if anyone was opening that envelope, it would be Joey herself.

Chapter 12

Ryder stayed away from the house for as long as he could. It was ridiculous. He'd spent his life's savings on a place where he could hang his hat, put his feet up, and chill when he wasn't on the road. But because of one curvy caregiver, he'd banished himself from the goddamn property.

Last night, after they'd tangled tongues, he'd sat in his truck for hours up on a fire trail in the middle of nowhere, trying to get his head on straight. Of all the boneheaded moves. Even after their little talk about how it couldn't happen again, Ryder wanted an encore performance.

But he couldn't stay away forever. He had paperwork he needed to do, and he wanted to check in on his mother.

Maybe he could duck in the house for a few minutes, careful to avoid Joey, then hole up in his fifth wheel for the rest of the evening.

But that plan was laid to rest when he pulled up the driveway. Joey was sitting on the front porch. He bobbed his head at her and got out of his truck.

"How'd it go?"

"Good. Your mom's taking a nap before dinner."

"Another nap, huh?" He raised his brows.

She patted the rocker next to hers. "I got some names of therapists from Ethan. He suggested we talk to her primary physician first. I can do that, but it might be better if we did it together. Today was good for her, though. Getting out, being fussed over, a new hairstyle—which, by the way, she loves—perked her up. I'll try to plan some more excursions similar to today. Perhaps a mall in Reno. She could use a few things that fit her. She's lost weight."

"I noticed." He sat. "I should probably take her, maybe show her around Cascade Village. What do you think?"

"She'd definitely enjoy spending time with you. Maybe wait on Cascade Village, though. Let's see what her doctor and therapist think."

He glanced over at her. She was wearing the same jeans and shirt she'd worn this morning. In the afternoon light, the blouse was kind of see-through, and Ryder had to avert his eyes not to stare. Last night, she'd felt so good pressed against him. But there weren't going to be any instant replays.

"You have a productive day?" she asked to break the silence.

"It was okay." If he considered finding errands to keep him busy okay. He'd bought a ratchet set he didn't need at the hardware store, a pair of boots from Lucky's wife that were finer than anything he'd ever have need for, and a goddamn birdhouse from Farm Supply. A birdhouse. So far, Joey was costing him a fortune.

"I ordered a table, chairs, and an umbrella for the backyard," he said. "Delivery is in a few days."

Joey eyed the birdhouse he'd rested on the porch railing, and her mouth slid up. "Aren't you the homemaker?"

He wanted to tell her it was her fault he'd gone on a shopping spree. He'd bought more crap today than he had in the last two years. "I like birds."

She eyed him skeptically. "Where's the birdseed? I'll hang it for you."

Shit. Grace hadn't said anything about birdseed.

She laughed, reading his mind. "Tell you what, I'll get birdseed if you'll sit with your mom for a couple of hours this evening."

"You got a thing with your daughter?" he guessed.

"No, but I need to run to Reno."

"Everything okay with your folks...your brother?" Or maybe she needed to hit a meeting. It wasn't his business, but then again, it sort of was. He was entrusting her with the well-being of his mother.

"I have to pick up my mail." She paused and let out a breath. "A letter came from the state nursing board."

He leaned back in the rocker and propped his boots up on the railing. "Good news?"

"I don't know yet. I wouldn't let my mother open it."

He could feel her tension radiating across the porch. A career and everything she'd worked toward hung in the balance. He couldn't blame her for wanting to go tonight.

"I'll take you."

She jerked in surprise. "I can drive myself. Someone has to stay with Shiv."

"I could probably find someone to hang out for a few hours." Though he didn't know who. Lucky or Tawny maybe, but it was a big ask. "We could always bring her along. But you shouldn't do this alone."

"You think it's bad news?" She squeezed her eyes shut.

"You'd know better than me. But you deserve your license, Joey." He scrubbed his hand over his face. "Hell, you've been nothing short of great for my mom. No matter what the letter says, you should be with someone when you open it."

She pinned him with a look. "Why? You think if it's a hard no, I'll fall off the wagon?"

To be frank, it had crossed his mind, though he wouldn't confess to it. "I didn't say that. But is moral support such a bad idea?"

"No." She let out a sigh. "I could use it. I've waited for this for over a year. I would've had my mother read it to me over the phone, but...I couldn't. Too humiliating if the answer is no. They've already seen me at my lowest point. I don't want to go there again."

"You don't have to worry about me," he said. Lord knew, his lowest point hadn't been pretty. "No judgment here."

She got to her feet. "Let me make a call. I may have a solution so your mom can stay home." She disappeared inside the house.

Good going, Ryder. He'd spent the entire day hiding from her, only to offer to be alone in a car with her for two hours. Hey, everyone needed a friend every now and again. Even an asshole like him recognized that.

He'd go with her to Reno, read the letter, and come home. No kissing. No nothing. End of story.

She returned a short time later to the porch, a sweater draped over her arm. "Ethan said he'd do it."

At first, he thought she meant that her ex was going with her to Reno, which would've pissed him off if he hadn't quickly realized she was leaving the surgeon with Shiv. "You're kidding me, right?"

"What? You don't trust a doctor? Brynn's coming with him." She rolled her eyes. "The kids are with Ethan's stepmother. I didn't tell him about the letter, just said a last-minute meeting came up with the Cascade Village folks about a vacancy for your mom. So, don't spill the beans."

"You and your ex have a strange relationship," he said, shaking his head.

Thirty minutes later, he and Joey were on the road. "Why didn't you tell your ex?" He slid her a sideways glance as he merged onto the interstate.

"I guess for the same reason I didn't want my mother to know. I'm tired of letting everyone down."

"Letting everyone down? It's out of your control and in the hands of the licensing board, right?"

"Yeah, but their decision is based on my screwups."

There wasn't a whole lot he could say to counter that. At least she was accountable. There was a lot to say for that. After Leslie died, he'd done a lot of crazy shit. It had taken him a long time to man up to his mistakes. Even longer to accept that if he didn't change his lifestyle, he was going to wind up dead, too.

"Should we make a plan?"

"A plan? For what?"

"Bad news. How to handle that."

She pressed her forehead against the passenger window. "After a year of not hearing from them, I pretty much accepted that I wasn't getting reinstated. I'm prepared for the worst."

He hesitated to ask, but he knew she had to be thinking it. "What if the answer is yes?"

"I'll start looking for a job at a hospital." She twisted around to face him. "But I won't leave you in the lurch. I would never do that."

He believed her.

"But, Ryder, it's a safe bet that it isn't going to happen. I'll be sad, but in my heart I've accepted it."

The fact that she was rushing to get the letter was proof to the contrary, he thought. But he didn't argue the point.

As they got closer to Reno, Joey's anxiety became palpable. Ryder could feel it emanating across the cab of his pickup. Despite his self-imposed no-touching policy, he reached for her hand and held it.

"Whatever the letter says, you'll be fine, Joey Nix. You'll be just fine."

"I know, yet my stomach is turning inside out. It's just that all I ever wanted to be was a nurse. Science was my thing, you know? I couldn't write my way out of a paper bag, and classic literature put me to sleep. But I aced biology, chemistry, anatomy and physiology. And most of all, I love helping people. Even when I was a kid, I volunteered at Renown two days a week, working as a Candy Striper. And every holiday season I read to the seniors at the retirement home near our house. At the risk of sounding corny, nursing was my life's calling. And while I've accepted that there are other ways to use my skills, losing my vocation is like losing myself."

"I get it," he said, switching lanes to get out from behind a slow-poke late-model Chrysler. "It was a lot like that for me when I left saddle bronc riding."

"Why did you leave?"

He usually told people that he'd gotten too old for the sport, but that was a straight-up lie. He'd still be doing it today if things were different. "I was taking too many crazy chances. Riding when I was either too drunk or too injured to walk."

"Why?" She turned in her seat. "Did you need to win that badly?"

He'd always wanted to win. But never to the point of stupid.

"Nope, death wish." Ryder had never told anyone that. Some people went in their garages, shut the windows and doors, and turned their car engines on. Instead, he'd climbed up on raging horses and ignored the rules. "After my wife died, I didn't want to live anymore."

He couldn't believe he was talking about it. But she had opened the floodgate.

"I'm so sorry, Ryder. What about...Are you doing better now?"

What was better? Sadness eating away at him until he was nothing but a shell of a man who could barely drag himself out of bed in the morning? Or a numbness that had him going through the motions without actually having a life? Joey had been the first woman since Leslie who had made him feel things again. Things he didn't want to feel.

"Do I still want to kill myself?" He let out a mirthless laugh. "I've got too many people relying on me."

"But that's why you don't compete anymore?"

"That's why I stopped. Then I found that owning a trucking company was more profitable." Not as exciting as bronc busting, but it paid the bills. Rodeoing was a rush, and when he won, the money was good. But it had always been a gamble.

"Tell me how she died?"

"I will." He swallowed hard. "But not today." Today was about Joey. "Let me know which exit to take."

Joey gave him directions, and they rode the rest of the way in silence. He wondered if he'd told her too much. If the wound he'd opened had repelled her. Ah, what did he care?

They pulled up to a sprawling ranch house. It looked like most of the homes in the San Joaquin Valley, where he'd grown up. American cheese sandwiched between two slices of white bread. Comforting, but nothing fancy.

An overweight dog, a cross between a rottweiler and a retriever if Ryder had to guess, howled at them. Within a few seconds, the mutt lost interest and stretched out in a sunny spot in the front yard.

An older version of Joey with poufy red hair came out the front door. In her younger days, she'd probably been a bombshell. She gave him a once-over, and a big smile lit her face.

"That was quick. Come inside and say hi to your daddy."

Joey gave Ryder an apologetic glance and introduced him to her mother. He noted that she'd made sure to emphasize that he was her employer. The house held the faint scent of cigarette smoke. They passed through the front room, which, despite the slider that opened to a nice-sized built-in pool, was dark. A big-ass flatscreen hung on the wall, and the bookcases were cluttered with knickknacks and pictures. Lots of Joey during various stages of her life. Horse shows, prom, cheerleader, graduation, wedding. He was surprised that last one was still up.

Ryder would've liked to have taken a closer look, but they were moving at a fast clip to the kitchen, where the table had been set for dinner.

"Hi, Daddy." Joey hugged her old man, a big guy with jowls and an older version of Joey's brother.

He got up and wrapped his daughter in a bear hug. "You staying for supper?"

"No, we've gotta get back."

Joey's dad darted a glance at Ryder, and she made the introductions like she had with her mother.

Lou Ellen and Ace.

He gave Ace a firm handshake, wondering how it stacked up against Ethan's. The meet-the-family thing was kind of surreal.

They stood around in the kitchen for a while, making small talk while Lou Ellen put the finishing touches on a casserole.

"Where's my granddaughter?" Ace asked.

"She's home, Daddy. We have a meeting with the senior coordinator of the planned community where Ryder's mom is going to live. I just wanted to drop by and say hi."

Ryder watched as Joey and Lou Ellen exchanged glances. They disappeared for a few minutes, leaving him alone with Ace.

"So, you own a trucking company, huh?"

"Yes, sir."

"You should talk to my son, Jay. He owns a Ford dealership."

Ryder didn't really know what a trucking company had to do with Jay's Ford dealership, but he nodded anyway.

Joey returned with her mother and nudged Ryder. "We've got to get going if we want to make our meeting on time."

It was all Ryder could do not to roll his eyes. Lou Ellen walked them out and whispered to Joey, "Call me as soon as you open it," loud enough for him to hear. Clearly, she was in on the subterfuge and not Ace.

When they got in his truck, he asked, "Why all the rigamarole with the bullshit meeting?"

"My dad doesn't know about the letter, and I don't want him to until I have had time to absorb whatever it says."

"But your mom knows."

"She's the one who collects the mail. Not much I can do about that."

"Where do you want to open it?" He turned on the ignition, assuming she didn't want to read the letter in her parents' driveway.

"I don't know yet. Just drive."

He did what he was told, heading in the direction of the interstate. They could either go back to California or drive deeper into Nevada. "Nugget or Winnemucca?"

She chewed on her bottom lip. "Nugget."

He swung onto the 395. She took the letter out of her pocket and studied the return address, then flipped it over.

"I can pull over when we get to the California side."

"Or maybe I'll just wait until tomorrow."

"Why? You won't get any sleep tonight. Just get it done with." It was easy for him to say. His career wasn't hanging in the balance.

Ryder exited on CA-70 and pulled over at the first safe turnout.

"I'm not ready yet." She shoved the envelope in her purse as if she was afraid that he'd take it from her and rip it open himself.

He got out of the truck, went to the passenger side, and pulled her out of the cab. The sun had started to set, and the desert sky, streaked in orange and violet, seemed to go on forever. The temperature was cool with a soft breeze, and the smell of creosote filled the air. Miles of scrub brush stretched out before them. It was haunting and lonely and so beautiful it made Ryder's chest ache.

He gathered Joey up in his arms and kissed her. Slow at first, then with an intensity that made him lose himself. She returned the kiss with the same fervor. Breathless and desperate. Clinging to him, she hummed into his mouth a low, needy moan, urging him on. He cupped the back of her head and tilted her face so he could go deeper, bruising her lips with his.

His fingers combed through her silky hair, which smelled like sunshine. Her hands moved under his shirt, brushing against his abs, making him suck in his breath. He wanted to touch her, too. Her skin, her breasts.

A series of cars whooshed by, breaking the mood, and they both backed away.

Joey touched her lips. "What was that for?"

He'd gone and broken his own goddamn rules. He scrubbed his hand through his hair. "Hell if I know."

She leaned against his truck, trying to catch her breath. He flipped the tailgate down and motioned for her to sit next to him. A few more cars passed, but for the most part, this stretch of highway was quiet. There was only the occasional cry of a red-tailed hawk in flight.

"I guess I thought it would distract you from the letter. Maybe give you the courage you needed to open it." It was as good a reason as any for the kiss.

She closed her eyes and tilted her head back, letting the last rays of sunlight beat down on her face. "Should I just do it?"

"It's up to you. But yeah, I think you should."

"Okay." But she didn't make a move to retrieve her purse.

He took her hand, lacing his fingers with hers. Together, they leaned back on their elbows, staring up at the sky. The moment felt more intimate than the kiss. Ryder's first instinct was to pull away. But he couldn't. It was as if something vital in him would wither if he broke contact.

"I guess I need to do this. I told Ethan we'd only be a few hours." She scooted off the tailgate, opened the passenger door, and returned with the envelope. "Ready?"

"The question is, are you ready?"

"Not really, but I don't think I'll ever be." She tore open the seal and pulled out what looked like a form letter. "Here goes."

With shaking hands, she read it to herself, then folded it up and stuck it back in the envelope.

"What does it say?"

Her shoulders shuddered, and she wiped at her eyes. "I can't freaking believe it."

"You gonna hold me in suspense, or are you going to tell me?"

"They're considering my appeal and the process could take up to six months. That's it." She waved the envelope in the air. "All that buildup for a whole lot of nothing. I've already waited a goddamn year, and this is the best they can do." She crumpled the envelope in her hand.

"I don't understand," he said, sitting upright. "Hadn't they already told you they were taking up your appeal?"

"No, but I assumed it was automatic. A union rep said they'd either reinstate or deny me. I didn't realize they could refuse to consider the appeal altogether."

"Then this is good news, right? It means they're at least willing to hear you out, which, in my mind, takes you that much closer to getting your license back."

"I guess." She huffed out a breath. "It's just that I thought it was finally over and that I'd know one way or another and could move on with my life."

"In my experience, bureaucracies don't work that way. They like to drag things out and keep you hanging on by a thread. But all in all, I'd say this is very hopeful."

"You think?" She swiped at her eyes again.

"Yeah. Clearly they haven't written you off."

"Not yet anyway."

She hopped off the tailgate and offered him a hand. "We should get going."

He got in the driver's seat, waited for her to buckle in, and nosed out onto the road.

"Sorry," she said. "Had I known all the letter said was that the board was taking up my appeal, I wouldn't have been so dramatic about it."

"No worries. It was a nice drive."

She poked him in the arm. "Driving is work for you, not something you want to do on your day off."

Not usually. But she was going above and beyond for his mom, so it was the least he could do. *Yeah, right, keep telling yourself that.*

"Ryder?"

"Hmm?"

"What's going on with us?"

He thought about blowing off the question, turning it into an off-color joke. But Joey was too smart for that, she'd see right through him. Furthermore, he had too much respect for her to throw out some cheesy line.

"I think it's pretty clear we're attracted to each other. I was from that first day you walked into the Ponderosa. Maybe not you. Not that first day. But evidently I grew on you." He glanced over at her and grinned. "I'm trying to stop, but apparently I'm doing a piss-poor job of it."

"How do you stop being attracted to someone?" She twisted to the side to face him. "I'm not being flip. In all honesty, I want to know."

"Beats the hell out of me. If you figure it out, let me know. But, Joey, I meant it when I said I don't want a woman in my life. Even beyond complicating our work situation, I...can't be with someone."

"You don't date? Not at all?"

He let out a sober laugh. "Dating is not what I would call it."

"What does that mean?"

"It means exactly what you think it means." He gave her a pointed look, and the truck cab filled with silence.

They were ten minutes away from Nugget when she said, "Is it because of your wife? Like, anything more meaningful than a random hookup would be disloyal?"

Not disloyal. Leslie would want him to move on, he knew that. He simply couldn't. Not after everything he'd lost.

He cleared his throat. "No. I just can't."

"That's sad because you're a good man, Ryder. You deserve happiness and someone to love. Someone who loves you."

That was the thing. He didn't.

Chapter 13

The week sped by, and before Joey knew it, Ryder was gone. It was a short trip this time. But she found herself spending much of Friday watching the driveway for his semitruck. He'd gotten waylaid on his way back and hadn't been able to turn his deliveries around in one day. He was due in sometime this afternoon.

Why she was pining for him was beyond ridiculous. He'd been crystal clear that they were a nonstarter. The idea that she was even interested told her that she needed way more than a twelve-step program. Her baggage was heavy enough. She didn't need his, too. But he had been a good friend at a time when she had none.

She wandered into the front room, where Shiv was working with her physical therapist on her balance. Patrice, the PT, had Shiv on a wobble board and was barking orders like a military sergeant. Trying to be encouraging, Joey gave her a big thumbs-up. Shiv in return stared daggers at her.

"I'm running into town for a few groceries. Is there anything special you want?"

From the look on Shiv's face, a bayonet. "Surprise me."

Joey was heartened to hear a little spunk in Shiv's voice. Her doctor had signed off on any of the three therapists Ethan had recommended. The one in Quincy was only part-time and had a full roster of patients. So Joey had gone with a Reno psychologist who specialized in "midlife" patients. Her office wasn't far from Cascade Village. Joey thought they could drop in after one of Shiv's sessions and tour the gated senior community.

There was hardly anyone in the Nugget Market parking lot when she got there. She took it as a good sign that she could get in and out. Her good fortune ended at the produce aisle, where she nearly collided with Brynn.

"Oh, hey there." Brynn flashed her perfect toothpaste-ad smile. "I'm just stocking up for Alma and the kids."

Right, she and Ethan were going to San Francisco this weekend. When Joey had been married to her ex, he hadn't had time to take her to a Motel 6 in Carson City.

"Thanks for taking Henry Saturday."

"It's my pleasure," Joey said. She really did adore the boy.

Brynn moved her shopping cart closer. "Um, I hate to ask this, I really do."

Joey's hackles immediately went up. She was half-expecting Brynn to ask for a drug test. "What's that?" she asked in her most saccharine voice, which Brynn either chose to ignore or had missed altogether.

"Ever since the accident, I've become neurotic about Henry doing anything remotely adventurous. Every time he climbs onto Choo Choo's back, my heart is in my mouth. Ethan said something about you taking the kids on a fun activity, and I would appreciate it if it was—"

"Say no more." Joey held up her hands, feeling like a bitch. Nearly two years ago, an all-terrain vehicle accident had killed Brynn's husband and had left Henry severely injured. The boy was lucky to be alive. How could anyone blame Brynn for being paranoid? If it had been Roni, Joey would've reacted the same way. "I heard The Farm had cherry picking. I was thinking of taking the kids there."

Brynn's expression turned to relief. "That's perfect. And again, thank you. Knowing that you're a nurse…well, it's another layer of reassurance that Henry is in good hands."

Brynn was making it difficult to dislike her. In all honesty, Joey had never disliked her. But it was easy to be jealous of all that Brynn had.

"Henry will be fine. We're going to have a good time." She glanced at her watch. "I left Shiv with the physical therapist and have to run. I'll see you Saturday morning."

She grabbed her groceries and got back to the house to find that Ryder had beaten her there. His semi was parked in the driveway. She managed to squeeze her Ford around his big rig and park close to the kitchen door.

Before going in, she flipped her visor mirror down and checked her face and hair. She'd taken a little more care than usual with her blow-out and makeup. Liking what she saw, she grabbed a sack of groceries from the trunk and went inside.

Ryder was leaning against the counter, eating a sandwich with some of the leftover chicken she'd made the night before. "You need some help?"

"I've got two more bags in the back of the car."

"I'll get 'em." He put his sandwich down, went outside, and returned hugging both packages. "Where do you want 'em?"

"Over there." She pointed to the counter next to the fridge. "How was your trip?"

He hitched his shoulders. "Noneventful, just the way I like it. How'd it go here?"

"I made an appointment for your mom with a therapist in Reno." Joey started putting the perishables away in the refrigerator. "She wasn't too thrilled about it. So maybe the two of you could have a conversation…You could tell her how important it is to you. That will probably have more sway than me telling her there's no stigma about suffering depression after a major health crisis and discussing it with a professional."

"I'll talk to her." He grabbed a bottle of beer from the fridge door and stood there drinking it while she continued to unpack the groceries.

She wondered if he had looked forward to his return as much as she had, then inwardly chastised herself for being an idiot. She really needed to get herself a hobby. Or an online boyfriend.

There was a knock at the front door. Joey hadn't heard anyone drive up. Then again, between Ryder's 18-wheeler, the physical therapist's car, and her Ford, there wasn't room for another car in the driveway.

"You expecting anyone?"

"No." She closed the fridge and followed him to the front room, where Shiv was wrapping things up with Patrice.

Ryder opened the door, and there were the Addisons. As usual, they wore their bizarre matching camp counselor clothes—shorts embroidered with tiny bears and white polo shirts with the Beary Quaint logo stitched across the pocket—and their sour dispositions.

"Afternoon." Ryder tried for a pleasant smile, but Joey could tell it was forced.

He stepped onto the porch, and Joey joined him. "My mom's with her PT. Otherwise, I'd invite you in."

Joey doubted it. Ryder wasn't particularly good at hiding his displeasure. And right now, he looked as if he'd been bucked off one of his rodeo broncs. Her gut told her the Addisons weren't here on a social call. She was guessing Ryder had come to the same conclusion.

"What can I do for you?" he asked.

Sandy Addison turned and pointed to his semitrailer. "You can't park those here."

Ryder leaned against the porch rail in that loose-limbed, lazy way that said he was all cowboy. Not a care in the world. But underneath his calm exterior, he was fuming, Joey was sure of it.

"Why's that?" he asked.

"It's against code. This is zoned residential."

"Is that so? How is it then that you're able to run a motor lodge less than a mile away?"

"It's all there in the planning department," said snippy Sandy. "Where Bear Creek Road meets the highway is the cutoff point. Everything east of that is zoned commercial."

"The planning department, huh?" Ryder pushed off the railing and stepped closer to the Addisons, whom he towered over. "I suggest you do your research. This is zoned agricultural and all that entails, including my trucks. Look, I don't come over to your place of business and give you a rash of trouble. Why are you making problems? We're neighbors, let's try to get along."

Sandy harrumphed. "We've given you fair warning. Don't blame us when you find a notice from the county taped to your door and are forced to pay a fine."

"Do what you've got to do. But be prepared for a fight." Ryder put his hand at the small of Joey's back, guided her inside, and slammed the screen door.

"What's those people's problem?" She'd never met anyone ruder, and she'd worked in a hospital full of officious doctors with God complexes.

Ryder let out a frustrated breath, started to say something, then noticed that Shiv and Patrice were both staring.

"What happened?" Shiv asked.

"It's nothing, Ma. Don't worry about it." He went back to the kitchen.

Patrice took off, and Joey helped Shiv into the shower. Peter had gotten a three-night deal at the Lumber Baron and had offered to take Shiv this afternoon on a tour of the inn to give Joey a few hours. It was so kind of him. She planned to pick Roni up from school for a little mother-daughter time, maybe drive through the Bun Boy and grab burgers and ice cream.

While Shiv was in the bathroom, Joey returned to the kitchen to finish putting away the dry goods. Ryder was halfway through his beer and working on a second sandwich.

"Are you worried about what they said?"

He went to the pantry and brought the chips back to the table. "Not worried. Just irritated. I don't have time to deal with their bullshit."

"Is this really zoned agricultural?" She nudged her head at the window. Joey hadn't seen any ranches or farms on Ryder's road, not like the Circle D, which was surrounded by ranchland.

"Yep. And my business is hauling livestock. Can't get any more agricultural than that."

"You think you should talk to someone? Like maybe a lawyer, just in case."

"On it." He held up his phone. "A friend of mine knows a local attorney, who also happens to be a cattle rancher. From people I've talked with, the Addisons are famous for pulling this kind of crap. It's how they get their jollies. I've sunk too much money into this place to put up with it."

"We should all go on Yelp and give their creepy motel bad reviews."

Ryder chuckled. "Nah. I'll take care of it." His eyes roved over her red shift dress. "How come you're all duded up?"

She ran her hands down the skirt, suddenly feeling self-conscious. "While Peter takes your mom on a tour of the Lumber Baron, I'm going to get an hour in with my daughter. Pick her up from school and take her to that drive-through for ice cream."

"That's nice." His eyes met hers, but she had the feeling he was still fixated on her dress. "I thought Peter doesn't come until tomorrow."

"He got some kind of package deal at the Lumber Baron, so he came a day early. I think he and your mom are going to tag along tomorrow when I take Roni and Brynn's son to The Farm to pick cherries."

"Doesn't sound like much of a day off." He hitched his brows.

"It'll be fun. You should come, too." She threw out the invitation, knowing full well he would find an excuse not to accept it. Still, a part of her hoped he'd join them.

He brought his plate to the sink and put away the chips. "Have fun with your little girl. That lawyer said he's got time to talk. I'm meeting him at the Ponderosa. You want me to get take-out for dinner?"

"Uh, sure. It'll be a nice treat for your mom. I'll take a salad."

"Yeah, I know. Cesar with chicken."

Either she was incredibly predictable, or Ryder had been paying attention.

* * * *

Flynn Barlow didn't look anything like a lawyer as far as Ryder was concerned. According to Lucky, Flynn had been an FBI agent, a federal prosecutor, and was currently a corporate lawyer, who dabbled in a little of everything. In a Stetson, jeans, and boots, he looked like a typical rancher to Ryder.

But Lucky had assured him that Flynn knew his stuff. Flynn waved to Ryder from across the bar.

"Recognized you from the PRCA," he said and motioned for Ryder to take the bar stool next to his. "Saw you win the world championship in 2014 in Vegas. That was a hell of a ride."

Flynn flagged the bartender over. "Sierra Nevada and whatever my friend here wants."

Ryder got the same. "Thanks for taking the time. I don't know how much Lucky told you." Hell, for all he knew, Flynn was friends with the Addisons.

"Enough to get the general gist. Can't say I'm surprised. You're fresh meat for Sandy and Cal, who never met a newcomer they didn't harass."

"Yeah, man, what's their problem?"

Flynn hitched his shoulders. "Who knows? Too much lead in the paint in that motel of theirs? Everyone here gets along. We may fight over politics, gossip about each other, envy our neighbor's farm equipment. But at the end of the day, we've got each other's back. Except the Addisons. Those two are all about themselves."

It was true about the town and how everyone here came together to help one another. A perfect example was the other day when Ethan Daniels and his new woman rushed over to sit with Siobhan for a few hours just because Joey had asked. Or Lucky and Maddy, who'd hooked Ryder up with the town lawyer. Or the town lawyer, who was sitting here right now, having a beer with a total stranger, doling out free legal advice.

Ryder liked that about his new home. He'd never been one to lean, but it was good to know that if he ever needed to, this town could shoulder the weight.

"First, they came to hassle me about sleeping in my fifth wheel, accusing me of turning the property into a mobile home park. Then, today, they complained about me parking my semitrucks and trailers on my land. Dana assured me when I bought the place that it was zoned agricultural and I could park my rigs here. Otherwise, I wouldn't have purchased the place."

"There's no question it's zoned agricultural," Flynn said. "I researched it when my wife and I were looking to buy it a year ago. My wife, Gia, runs a nonprofit and was considering expanding it into the old Montgomery place. It didn't pan out. But the point is, Dana's right. She's as honest as they come and wouldn't have steered you wrong on this. However, I'm not entirely sure the Addisons don't have a case about the trucks and trailers."

That wasn't what Ryder wanted to hear. "Why's that?"

"Just to play devil's advocate here, an argument could be made that long-haul trucking isn't ag."

"But I haul livestock."

Flynn nodded. "Yup, and you could certainly make that argument. That's the funny thing about the law. It's not cut-and-dried. It's up to interpretation."

"Well, hell." Ryder dragged his hand down his face. "What do I do if they take this to the county? I've got a lot invested in the place, and it's worthless if I can't park my rigs there."

Flynn took a drag of his beer. "I'd say try to reason with them, but they're not reasonable people. So maybe a preemptive strike."

"Like what?" Ryder wasn't following.

"I suspect there's plenty that isn't up to code at their motor lodge. I'd be willing to bet the motel isn't earthquake retrofitted." Flynn's mouth quirked. "To get it up to code could cost in the hundreds of thousands."

"How could I find that out?"

"Colin Burke might know. He's done work for them in the past. But we bluff. We send them a letter that says it's come to our attention that their entire lodge is out of code. We don't have to specify. It's basically a veiled threat. You screw with us, we screw with you."

It seemed kind of iffy to Ryder. "What if they know everything is up to code?" The Addisons came off as the kind of people who were sticklers for those things.

"In my experience, nothing is ever entirely up to code, especially not a commercial business. But we throw it out there and hope it sticks. See if we can scare them. It certainly doesn't lose us anything."

Sure. Why not? "Can I hire you to write the letter?"

"I'm happy to write the letter pro bono. These people have been a thorn in the sides of my friends for too many years. It's time someone shows them what it feels like to be on the other side."

"Sounds good to me." Ryder tipped back his beer and ordered another round. "The next time you need your calves hauled, you call me."

Clay McCreedy, another cattleman, joined them while his wife got her hair done over at the barbershop. Flynn filled him in on the Addisons' bullshit.

"They never quit," Clay said. "Everyone else here tries to get along, except them. My old man, who never had a mean word to say about anyone, couldn't stand 'em. They tried to oust Rhys as police chief when he first got here. Messed with Maddy and Nate over the Lumber Baron, which is

Nugget's shining attraction. I wish someone would buy their motor lodge and they'd move away."

"Yeah, not happening," Flynn said.

They sat at the bar for a while, talking about rodeo, ranching, and life in Nugget. Flynn and Clay were good guys. And as it turned out, they and Ryder knew a lot of the same people. Big state, small world.

On his way out, he bumped into Rhys. "You and your mom getting settled in?"

"Yep. And thanks for the drive-bys." The patrol car that cruised up Bear Creek Road late at night hadn't gone beyond Ryder's notice.

"We aim to please. See you around."

The sun was shining, and the square was full of teenagers stretched out on the grass, eating take-out from the Bun Boy. Ryder shielded his eyes with his hand and stared across the square at the burger joint's parking lot, then wandered in that direction. He found Joey and her kid, sitting at one of the picnic tables on the lawn underneath a shady tree.

Ryder told himself that he'd say a quick hello and go, leaving Joey to spend what he knew was coveted time with her daughter.

"Hey." She waved to him, and the little girl turned around on her bench to stare.

"You guys eat?"

"We're waiting for our names to be called. I didn't think about the after-school crowd." They both gazed at the long line at the window.

"You remember Mr. Knight?" Joey asked Roni.

"I remember you." The kid stood on the bench so she was eye level with Ryder.

"Sit on your bottom, Roni."

Ryder surprised himself by squeezing in next to Joey's mini me. "Whaddya get?"

"A burger, the fries that go like this"—Roni made a swirling motion with her finger—"and a chocolate shake. How 'bout you?"

"I thought I'd just steal from your plate." He winked.

"I'll share with you, Mr. Knight."

"You can just call me Ryder. 'Mr. Knight' makes me feel old."

"Is your mom coming?"

Ryder looked to Joey, who said, "Not today, baby. Ms. Knight is with Peter."

Joey's name was called, and Ryder told her to stay put. Roni followed him to the window. "Here you go, kiddo." He handed her the shake.

"I can take more."

"I've got it." He gave her ponytail a playful tug.

This time, he took Joey's side of the table and snagged one of her fries. "How'd your meeting go?"

"Good. I'll tell you about it later." He'd lived here long enough to know there were big ears everywhere.

He snuck another fry. "I'd better help you with this so you'll still have room for dinner."

"You can have some of mine." Roni pushed her carton of curly fries to the middle of the table. Damn, she was a cute kid.

He snatched one.

"You want a bite?" She offered him her burger.

"I'm good with just fries. But thanks."

Joey cut her burger in half. "Have this. I only got it so Roni wouldn't eat alone."

"Looking forward to that Caesar salad, huh?" He took a bite and shoved a couple more fries in his mouth.

He'd only planned to stay a few minutes. But it would be rude to eat and run, he told himself.

"Ryder, how come you don't have a dog?" Roni's question was sort of out of the blue.

"I travel a lot for work, so there would be no one to keep him company."

"I could or my mom could. You should get one," she said around a bite.

"Roni, sweetheart, don't talk with your mouth full."

"Maybe I will." He took another bite of his half burger. "Someday I'm planning to get a few horses. You like horses?"

"I love horses," Roni said. "Henry and I share Choo Choo, but my dad said we might get a new horse just for me. A bay. Do you know what that is?"

"Yep. Brown with a black tail and mane. Real pretty."

"You should get a bay, too."

"Definitely something to consider," he said. He liked a kid who knew her horseflesh. "You gonna eat those?"

"You can have them." She gave him the rest of her fries and sucked on her shake straw. "I'm full."

Joey finished her half burger and put all their wrappers on a tray. Ryder carried it to the garbage.

"I'll see you back at the house," she said. "I've got to get Roni home."

"Thanks for letting me crash your party," he told Roni.

She looked somewhat confused at first, then hopped up on the bench again, latched on to him for a great big hug. Stunned, he didn't know what to do. Joey laughed at his befuddlement.

"Okay, Bonnie Roni, let's bust a move."

She jumped down, reached for her mother's hand, and they took off across the greenbelt.

Ryder watched them disappear inside Joey's SUV, feeling a little off-kilter. What had just happened?

Chapter 14

Shiv took the letter to her room. It had been sitting in the mailbox when Peter had dropped her home. He was such a lovely young man. So kind and considerate. And despite herself, she'd enjoyed her tour of the Lumber Baron and its friendly innkeeper.

They'd been served wine and cheese in the dining room and given special attention. It was because of Ryder. The innkeeper was quite fond of him. Apparently, he'd been a regular at the inn before getting a place of his own. She was glad her son had availed himself of the small extravagance. Since Leslie died, Ryder had withdrawn so much that sometimes Shiv didn't recognize the once outgoing man whose quick charm had earned him legions of fans on the rodeo circuit.

She'd never been crazy about him riding broncs. But it ran in his blood. Tanner himself had been a world champion, and despite their estrangement, Ryder had followed in his father's footsteps. But he'd left all that when he'd lost his wife. Secretly, Shiv had given thanks that his rodeo days were behind him. Ryder had become reckless in that last year, and Shiv had feared for his safety.

The trucking company had seemed like a stable job with good financial possibilities. But Ryder became a workaholic, burying himself in building a new business to hide from the world. As far as Shiv knew, he didn't date, he rarely saw any of his old friends, and he denied himself any of the fruits of his labor, spending most of his time behind the wheel. It was no way for a young man to live.

So, she'd been heartened to hear that he had at least allowed himself a little bit of luxury on his long treks across the state. And there was this home. The first real reward he'd given himself for all his hard work.

And now, she lived in it, not him. With all of Shiv's medical needs, her son didn't even have privacy in his own home. For all intents and purposes, he'd been relegated to his camper. She was filled with guilt over how she'd become a millstone. How could Ryder ever move on with her living underfoot?

At least he and Joey appeared to be friends—and maybe more. Shiv wasn't so old that she couldn't see the way Ryder looked at Joey and Joey at Ryder. It dawned on her that she needed to do more to push them together.

But first, the letter. Before she could tear it open, Joey tapped on the door.

"Everything okay, Shiv? Ryder just called. He's on his way home with dinner."

"I'm changing. Be there in a few minutes."

As soon as she heard Joey's footsteps retreat down the hall, she slipped the letter under her pillow. She wanted time to read it at her leisure, to savor it. Perhaps even pen something back.

While she'd been in the hospital, Morgan had sent flowers and get-well cards. Once, shortly after her retirement, he'd emailed her. But there had never been a letter. Not once. There was something intimate about it, something old-fashioned and romantic.

You're being ridiculous, she told herself. He was probably just checking in to see how she was adjusting to her new town. A simple gesture of concern for an old friend and employee.

She pushed the thought out of her head, changed into one of her exercise outfits, and joined Joey in the kitchen. The table had been set, and Joey was on her phone, texting.

"Peter said you guys had a good time today." Joey put her phone down on the counter.

"It's a gorgeous inn with so much history. It was nice of Peter to spend time with me on his day off. I feel like I've become such a responsibility to everyone."

"Why do you say that?" Joey took her usual seat at the table.

"I just feel like an old woman who is in constant need of babysitting."

Joey put her hand on top of Shiv's. "You're not old. But you are recovering from a major health scare. A stroke is no joke, Shiv. It can happen to anyone at any age. We're taking precautions until you're a hundred percent again. That's all."

When Shiv didn't respond, Joey said, "If you could have your life any way you wanted, what would it look like?"

The question caught Shiv off guard. Not because she hadn't thought about life after retirement or what would make her happy. But because what she wanted was impossible.

"Come on," Joey insisted. "At least name one thing."

"For Ryder to be happy," she blurted. "For him to have a family and to give me a grandchild."

There was a long stretch of silence. Shiv wondered if Joey even knew about Ryder, Leslie, and the baby. It wasn't something her son talked about, but perhaps he had with Joey.

"Unfortunately, that's out of your control, Shiv. You only have control over yourself. What could you do to make yourself happy?"

Shiv thought about it for a while. "To be young again." To be in love with a man who would give her adventure and something to hold on to in her darkest hours.

"Why?" Joey looked her straight in the eye. "You really want to trade the experience of a life well lived for..."

Shiv let out a bark of laughter. "Boobs that don't sag, hair that doesn't gray, a body that doesn't give out on me? Hell, yeah." But that wasn't really it. She just didn't want to feel so damned alone, so useless, so...over.

"It happens to all of us." Joey looked down at her perfectly firm breasts. "That's what good bras, good stylists, and good physical therapists are for."

Despite herself, Shiv smiled.

"Chow's here," Ryder shouted from the front room and came into the kitchen a short time later with a big to-go bag from the Ponderosa, which he unpacked. "Let's eat."

Shiv wished she could take her dinner to her room and leave the two young people alone together. She was nothing but a dark cloud hovering over the kitchen anyway.

But Ryder had gone to the trouble of bringing in her favorite dishes, and everyone was so worried about her that it would only cause a fuss. For that reason, she sucked it up and went through the motions of enjoying a group dinner.

All the while, the letter sat, waiting to be opened.

* * * *

Joey helped Shiv to bed. It was only eight. But Shiv swore she had a good book she was dying to read. Joey didn't believe her, but what could she do?

As soon as Joey returned to the front room, Ryder made an excuse to disappear inside his camper. Without company, there wasn't a whole lot to keep her occupied. She considered peeling the wallpaper in her bedroom, but at the last minute decided it was too late to start on such a messy project. There wasn't much on television. In the old days, she would've poured herself a glass of wine. And while alcohol had never been her problem, it wasn't a good idea.

Nothing addictive was. Something she should remind herself whenever she was around Ryder. He'd been so cute with Roni at the Bun Boy. It made her wonder if he and his late wife had ever considered having kids.

She went in the kitchen and popped her head in the pantry, looking for a snack, even though she wasn't hungry. Finally, she settled for a banana and ate it, sitting on the counter. She threw away the peel and stepped outside for some fresh air. The moon lit the sky, casting shadows in the trees. It should've been eerie. Instead, Joey found it peaceful.

She walked around the house, telling herself she needed the exercise. In truth, she wanted to peek at Ryder's fifth wheel. See if the lights were still on. *And if they are, so what?*

The camper was lit up like Macy's at Christmastime. Lord knew what he was doing in there. Probably watching rodeo or some other sporting event. She sat on one of the rockers and watched the bugs buzz around the porch light.

It was a beautiful night. Still, with the perfume of jasmine in the air. As quiet as it was, she could hear the highway a few miles away. Somewhere in the distance, a train whistle blew, reminding her that Nugget was a railroad town. There was even the faint rush of the Feather River. Funny, she had never heard any of those sounds during the day, or maybe she hadn't taken the time to listen.

There was a rustling near the camper that put her on alert.

"You spying?"

She stood up and walked closer to the railing. "No. Are you?"

Ryder came closer. His shirt was open, leaving his chest bare. And the top button on his jeans was undone. "What are you doing?"

"Nothing. Just taking in the night air."

"Bored, huh?" He quirked a brow as if "bored" was a euphemism for something else. She didn't like the inference.

"It's stuffy in there." She started to go inside, but he came up behind her, clasped her around the waist, and guided her into one of the chairs.

"Don't leave on my account." He took the rocker next to hers and stared up at the sky. "Nice night. Bright moon."

"It is. What were you doing?"

He hitched his shoulders. "Not much of anything really. I had high hopes of getting some paperwork done but was too distracted."

"By what?"

He didn't respond, letting his silence speak for itself. It was her cue to flee. Go inside, where she intuitively knew he wouldn't follow. But she resisted, even though she sensed it was the right thing to do. The sane thing. But from that very first day in the Ponderosa, she'd been drawn to him like the fireflies to the porch light.

Joey didn't fully understand that kind of attraction. It was fodder for movies and novels but never real life. Though, here she was. And nothing good could come of it. Ryder wasn't in the market for a romance, nor was she. Which only left one thing.

Sex was a slippery slope. Inevitably, someone always got hurt. And she didn't have the wherewithal for it to be her.

"What are you thinking?" she dared to ask.

He let out a rusty laugh. "You don't want to know."

They let silence stretch between them, each aware of what wasn't being said.

"I should go inside." Ryder leaned back and tilted his head up to the sky. "Alone."

"You should," she whispered and held her breath, hoping that he wouldn't.

"Or you could come inside with me, and we could finish what we started a year ago."

She stood, powerless to stop herself, and walked to the camper without glancing back to see if he was following.

Inside, the TV played with the sound turned off. Ryder came up from behind her and flicked it off. He pushed her against the wall, boxed her in with his hands, and kissed her. The hot pull of his mouth felt and tasted so good that heat spread through her like a flame. She twined her arms around his neck and went up on tiptoes to take more of his kiss. To take more of his tongue, which delved deeper.

She moved her hands to his fly, running them up and down his button placket. He sucked in a breath and wrestled her hands away, putting them once again around his neck. Then he lowered his lips to her throat, where her heart stopped. There was something so sensual about the way he moved over her that she nearly forgot to breathe.

The tension curled in the pit of her stomach and spread lower until she was panting. Though she tried to push him toward the bedroom, he wasn't finished kissing her yet.

His lips circled around the whorl of her ear, whispering words of encouragement. "I want you so bad." He pressed into her groin, proving his desire. "God, you're beautiful."

She caressed his chest, feeling his muscles bunch. His skin was hot to the touch. She kissed his pecs, tasting the saltiness of his flesh, and skimmed his stomach with her hands. For sitting in a truck all day, the man kept in shape. His abs were taut and sinewy. Hard as a rock.

She hooked her fingers in the waist of his jeans and pulled him closer, trying to fill the need pulsating between her legs. He ground into her, and she about lost her mind.

"Ryder?" She fell to her knees, tore open his pants, and freed him from his shorts. He was thick and hard. She covered him, taking him into her mouth.

He let out a moan, then quickly lifted her head away, tugging her to her feet. "You want to end this before we've even started?"

Ryder swooped her up in his arms and carried her to his room, kicking the door closed behind them. He laid her in his bed and fell down on top of her, coming up on his elbows to cushion her from his weight.

"Get this off." He rucked up her red dress and tried to drag it over her head.

When the dress got tangled around her shoulder, she held up her arms to help him with the rest. He tossed the dress on the floor, leaving her in nothing but a red lace bra and matching panties. Ryder pulled away to look at her, his eyes heavy-lidded and heated.

A pool of warmth swamped her insides at the look of arousal on his face.

He touched her breasts, molding each one in his hands. "Damn," he mumbled, then suckled her through the lace. Tired of the fabric barrier, he unclasped her bra and dropped it somewhere near her dress. He went back to fondling and kissing her until she couldn't take any more.

"Ryder, please." She pushed off his shirt and went for his pants, trying to slide them over his hips.

Impatient, he shucked off his jeans and briefs in one fluid motion. He moved one leg of her underwear to the side and tested her with his finger. "You're so ready for me."

She bowed up and wiggled out of her panties, leaving herself completely exposed. "Do you have...anything?"

He reached into his nightstand and plucked out a handful of foil-wrapped condoms. For a second, she let herself wonder how many women had come before her. And how many would come after?

But he washed away the thought as he covered her mouth with his, kissing her like she was the only one.

She straddled him, but he rolled her onto her back. "There's time for that later," he said in a husky voice that sounded strained.

He opened one of the condom wrappers with his teeth and rolled it on. Then he spread her legs and entered her in one forceful thrust.

She called out, and he instantly stopped moving. "You okay? This okay?"

"Yes." She adjusted beneath him, trying to accustom herself to his size. "Don't stop. Just go slow at first."

"We can just hang out like this for a while." He went up on his elbows again and gazed down on her, his pale blue eyes filled with desire.

She wrapped her arms around his neck. He felt so good she couldn't help rocking into him.

"Or not," he said and slowly started to thrust in and out of her. "Man, you feel so good."

She whimpered, moving her hips up and down to meet his strokes. Each one feeling better than the last.

"This good?"

"So good. Don't stop."

He nuzzled her neck. "No chance of that, I promise."

She moved her hands to his butt, which was as firm and muscular as his stomach, and urged him to go deeper.

He hiked her legs up so that they were bent at the knees and her feet flat on the bed and reentered her. This time, deeper, filling her until she nearly came undone. It was so good that she cried out.

"More," she begged.

He obliged by picking up the pace, pumping harder and faster. She wrapped her legs around his hips to keep up. It took a few minutes until they found their rhythm. And then it was like a primal dance. They felt so attuned to each other, each knowing exactly where to touch for maximum pleasure that it was mesmerizing.

He continued to kiss and caress her, exploring her body with his hands… his mouth.

"Oh, Ryder." She tipped her head back on the pillow, sensation filling her every molecule.

He brushed a strand of hair off her face, the gesture so tender it ripped her apart.

She arched up and kissed him, then rolled him underneath her, so she could be on top. He held her hips as she rode him and watched her body sway in the moonlight that filtered through the blinds.

His hand moved between her legs, and he worked her with his finger. She leaned back, holding on to his shoulders for leverage, and pumped faster. Heat coalesced in her stomach, and her body began to shake as she reached her climax.

Joey called out Ryder's name, then fell forward, her hair cascading over his chest. He reversed their positions and plunged into her again, working his hips like a piston back and forth, going faster and harder.

She felt that moment when his breathing changed, and his body began to spasm. His grunts became guttural, half-calling her name, half-muttering something nonsensical. Afterward, he collapsed on top of her.

"Am I crushing you?" he asked after a few minutes.

"No." His warm body felt good, like one of those weighted blankets that people used to help them sleep. She held him so close she could feel his heartbeat.

They just laid like that until suddenly he swung his legs over the bed and without a word grabbed his clothes off the floor and headed to the bathroom. He couldn't have made the message any clearer. She found her underwear and dress and quickly slipped them on, not knowing whether to leave or wait for him to return.

She heard the shower come on. Trying not to feel humiliated, she made her exit and rushed inside the house. There was no light coming from underneath Shiv's door. Joey cracked it open just enough to make sure Shiv was sleeping comfortably.

Then she headed to the bathroom for a long, hard cry and a shower.

Chapter 15

The next morning, as Joey and Shiv were eating breakfast, there was a knock at the front door. Assuming it was Peter, Joey called for him to let himself in. It was perfect timing. She needed to pick up Roni and Henry so Ethan and Brynn could get on the road.

But it wasn't Peter who came into the kitchen. It was a tall, handsome cowboy, whom Joey had never seen before.

He took off his hat. "Hey there. I'm Flynn Barlow, a friend of Ryder's. He around?"

"He's in the camper outside." She held her breath, hoping the cowboy didn't expect her to get Ryder for him. Joey intended to stay out of sight today.

"You must be Ms. Knight." He shook Shiv's hand and then waited for Joey to introduce herself, which she supposed she should've done in the first place. She was too busy planning her getaway before Ryder could make his morning coffee appearance.

"I'm Joey. Pleased to meet you."

"Roni's mom," he said.

Her lips curved up. "That would be me."

He continued to stand there, so she offered him coffee or juice.

"Sure, I'll take a cup of coffee." He grabbed a seat at the table and gazed around the kitchen. "Cute place. It didn't look this good the last time I saw it."

"My son has done a lot of work," Shiv said. "And Joey keeps it spotless."

It was nice praise. She supposed the nurse in her brought out the clean freak.

"Good morning." Peter bustled into the kitchen, carrying a pastry box. "I hope you don't mind that I let myself in. I found this fabulous farm stand with the most incredible desserts." He searched through the cupboards until he came up with a platter and started spreading out an assortment of muffins and little cakes.

He put the plate on the table and pecked Joey on the cheek. "How are you, doll?"

"I'm good, but I've got to run." She noted the logo on the pastry box. "This is the farm stand I told you about, where we're going berry picking. Do you and Shiv want to meet me there in a couple of hours? I'm going to take the kids to breakfast first."

"We'll be there." Peter worked his way around the table and just like he had with Joey, gave Shiv a peck on the cheek. "And who is this?"

Flynn introduced himself while Joey gathered up her purse and a light sweater in case it got chilly.

"I'll see you in a little while," she called over her shoulder.

She was almost out the door when she smacked into something hard. Ryder's hands came out to right her.

"Sorry, I should've watched where I was going." She tried to get around him, but he blocked her way.

"You never said good-bye last night."

"Shush." She put her finger to her lips and in a whisper said, "It didn't seem necessary after you ran off to hide in the shower."

"Is that what I was doing?"

She shrugged. "I don't know, was it? I'm going to be late, Ryder."

He moved out of her way. "Say hi to Roni for me."

She got in her SUV, took a deep breath, and hightailed it down the driveway. Just what she'd been hoping to avoid. And to make matters worse, she'd sounded bitter. *I did sound bitter, didn't I?* Why couldn't she have treated Ryder with the same air of indifference as he'd treated her after they'd slept together?

She took the curve at the end of Bear Creek Road too fast and nearly hit a mailbox. By the time she got to the Circle D, she'd calmed down. Ethan was loading the minivan with luggage. Joey didn't miss that Brynn's were designer and monogrammed. Ethan's was still the same battered leather duffel that he'd always used when he and Joey were married. At least some things didn't change.

Roni came out onto the porch in her pajamas. "Hi, Mommy."

Ethan shook his head. "Hey, Roni, I thought I told you to get dressed."

"I can't decide what to wear."

Ethan gave Joey a look and she smothered a laugh.

"We're going berry picking, baby. Wear something comfortable. Jeans and a T-shirt."

Roni skipped away.

Joey leaned against her SUV. "So, San Francisco, huh? That sounds nice."

"Yeah, we're looking forward to it. A weekend without wedding stress. Maddy Shepard over at the Lumber Baron got us a deal at the Theodore. Her brother owns it."

"Nice." Joey didn't know the Theodore but figured it was probably pretty hoity-toity because…Brynn. Ethan had never been much for fancy accommodations, but Brynn was from money, so everything was first class. At least she wasn't snobby. It was one of the things Joey admired about her.

"How's Ms. Knight holding up?"

"Okay. I took her to get her hair done, and that seemed to pick her up a little bit. We'll see how it goes." She really couldn't say too much about Shiv. She'd only said what she had because Ethan was a doctor and had given her the referrals.

"The Knights are lucky to have you," Ethan said. "Still nothing from the board, huh?"

She deliberated on whether to tell him about the letter, ultimately deciding to wait until she had actual news. "Nope. I'm sure they'll get around to it eventually."

"Can the caregiving gig sustain you?"

"When it covers my room and board, yeah. But at some point, I'd rather not do twenty-four-hour care." Then she would need her own place. And while rent was probably cheaper in Nugget than it was in Reno, it would be tight. "I should be flush in a couple of months and won't need the alimony checks anymore."

"That's not why I asked, Joey." He slid the van door closed and joined her.

"I know. But it's time. You're starting a new life, and…I'll be fine."

"I know you'll be fine. That's not the point. I want good things for you."

The words left a lump in her throat. For the first time in two years, she was ready to shed the history that had flogged her and move on. From her addiction, from Ethan, from depending on her parents. She was striving for a new life in which her daughter was front and center. To make that happen, she needed to be here in Nugget, near Roni's school and friends. She needed to have a place with a second bedroom and an environment that felt like their home, not someone else's.

All that was dependent on her getting her nursing license back.

Brynn came out of the house and waved. "Henry is so excited. Thanks again for taking him for the day."

It was the second or third time Brynn had gushed gratitude. It made Joey realize that navigating the blended family thing was as awkward for Brynn as it was for her. They at least all had each other. It was Joey who was the odd person out.

"It'll be fun," Joey said.

Brynn came down the porch stairs carrying a toiletry bag. As if the luggage Ethan had already loaded wasn't enough for a weekend getaway. Ethan must really be in love, Joey thought. Though he was a distinguished surgeon, he'd always been a cowboy at heart, traveling light.

"There's coffee in the house," Brynn said. "Can I fix you a cup before we take off?"

"Nah, I'm good. Feel free to hit the road. I'll round up the kids. I was planning to take them to breakfast before we head to The Farm."

"Let me give you some cash for that." Ethan reached into his pocket.

Joey glared at him and under her breath said, "Don't you dare."

He must've realized that he'd embarassed her in front of Brynn because he put his wallet away.

Joey started up the stairs. "Have a great trip. I'll drop Roni and Henry home around five. We'll send you pictures from the orchard."

She rushed inside the house and called for the kids. Roni had changed into jeans and the pink tee Joey had gotten her at Farm Supply. Henry looked like a mini replica of Ethan in a pair of Levi's, a pearl-snap Western shirt, boots, and a Stetson.

"You guys hungry?"

"Yes!" Roni jumped around in circles.

"Then let's get. We'll grab breakfast at the Ponderosa and head to The Farm." She loaded them into her Ford Edge and made sure they were buckled in.

By the time they got to The Farm, the kids were sticky with pancake syrup and hopped up on hot cocoa. But their giggles were so sweet. Henry, who'd given Joey a complete summary of the book he was currently reading, had really come out of his shell from a year ago. Back then he'd been a shy little boy who'd been grappling with the accident and his injuries.

There was a tractor hitched to a straw-filled trailer parked in front of the store. Annie, the owner, and a nice-looking man who was holding Annie's baby—Joey assumed he was Annie's husband—were helping folks onto the trailer. As soon as Annie spotted them, she came over to give Roni and Henry hugs.

"Hey, kiddos. Are you here to pick cherries?"

"Yes," they chorused, and Annie beamed.

"We're just waiting for two more." Joey searched the parking lot for Peter's Prius.

She thought she recognized Ryder's Ram but told herself it couldn't be him. Then, much to her surprise, he came walking toward them across the parking lot with Peter and Shiv in tow. Peter waved.

"There they are," Joey told Annie. "I guess we're six."

Annie gave Ryder a big hug, which also surprised Joey. Ryder hadn't struck her as a hugger. Annie, on the other hand, had that earth mother vibe that brought out the hugger in everyone, Joey supposed. Still, a wave of jealousy hit her so hard that it shamed her. Joey had never been the jealous type. Not even with Ethan, who was Renown Children's Hospital's pinup doctor and every single person within a five-mile radius' wet dream.

Roni ran up to Shiv and took her hand. "You want to sit by me in the hay wagon?"

"I most certainly do." Shiv had fixed her hair the way Darla had done it, and it made her look younger than her sixty-six years.

Peter winked at Joey as if he'd noted the hairstyle, too. It was a positive first step.

"This is Henry, everyone." Joey made the introductions.

"Nice hat, Henry." Ryder shook Henry's hand.

"Is it true that you're a world champion bronc rider?" Henry gazed up at Ryder with pure adoration.

"Two-time champ. Yes, sir."

It was the first time Joey had ever heard Ryder boast about his rodeo days. She suspected he didn't do it with adults, just excited little boys. Ethan must've told Henry about Ryder, and it had obviously made an impression.

"I'm a roper myself," Henry said and puffed out his chest.

"Oh, yeah? Tie down or team?"

"Team with Ethan. My mom won't let me do tie down."

Thank God. Joey could only imagine all the ways a kid could hurt himself jumping off a horse, throwing a calf to the ground, and tying its three legs together with a rope. Brynn would have a heart attack.

"You the header or the heeler?" Ryder asked.

"Header."

Annie called for the small crowd to start boarding the hay wagon. The man next to her handed Annie the baby and helped people up. Ryder wrapped his arm around Roni's waist and swung her up into the trailer to fits of giggles.

She went to the wagon railing and put her hands on Ryder's shoulders. "Again!"

Ryder grinned and lifted her into the air, then slowly let her down. Joey caught the expression on Shiv's face. The only way to describe it was astonished. Before Joey could remark that Ryder was Roni's new best friend, he swung his mother up onto the wagon. Henry was next. Peter got himself up and wedged in next to Roni, who was practically in Shiv's lap.

Ryder offered Joey a hand. She could get herself up without help but didn't want to appear petty. He held on as she climbed up and his warm, calloused hand sent a shiver through her. Joey found a spot next to Henry. Ryder was the last to get on, then he grabbed the wheel well on Joey's other side.

She was still processing why in heaven's name he'd come. A hay wagon filled with children and happy couples wasn't at all his thing. Perhaps Shiv had pleaded with him to join in. There wasn't anything Ryder wouldn't do for his mother.

Joey tried not to be self-conscious with him tagging along, turning her focus on what had turned out to be a beautiful day. The sun was shining, and the day was so clear you could see all the way to Nevada. The Sierra mountain range was still capped in white. Yet it was warm enough to go without a sweater.

Roni was keeping up a steady stream of conversation with Shiv. Joey couldn't hear what her daughter was saying, but occasionally Shiv would break into a big smile. She caught Ryder watching with interest. Easygoing Peter leaned back, letting the sun kiss his face. And Henry focused all his attention on Ryder.

The wagon hit a series of ruts as the tractor towed it along a dirt road to the cherry orchard. Jostled, the kids laughed, grabbing on to the railings. Ryder reached his arm out to hold Joey and Henry in place. A family of tourists, ultimately on their way to Yosemite, couldn't get over the countryside, oohing and aahing over how green everything was.

They crested a hill and parked near a row of cherry trees. A table had been set up with white paper bags, buckets, and a few fruit scales. Annie and her family had followed in a pickup. Her husband stationed himself at the back of the wagon and helped the passengers safely get out.

Ryder hopped over the side, reached up, and lifted Roni and Henry out. When the wagon was cleared, they all gathered around the table, where Annie gave picking instructions. Then everyone scattered across the orchard. Joey corralled her crew and found a shady row of trees where they could get started. Ryder hung back to talk to Annie and her husband, not that Joey was paying attention. Peter and Shiv took one tree and the kids found another where there was lots of low-hanging fruit.

Joey went back to the table to fetch another bucket so she wouldn't have to share with Roni and Henry.

"Hey." Ryder wandered over, his thumbs hitched in his pockets.

"I wasn't expecting you to join us."

"No? Why? You invited me."

She hitched her shoulders. "It doesn't seem like your kind of thing."

"A warm day in the country, how could that not be anybody's thing?"

He had a point. "I assumed you were avoiding me."

"Not avoiding, Joey. That would be kind of impossible since you live under my roof. I'm just not looking for anything beyond what we had last night, which I was up front about from the beginning. Same with you, I thought. Or at least that's what you told me. Did I somehow misread that? Because if I did, I'm sorry. But it doesn't change anything."

She glanced over at the tree where the kids were happily picking away. "I'm not looking for anything, Ryder. What happened last night was a one-off." She started to leave, but he gently took her arm.

"It's not you, Joey. I like you. I like your kid. I'm just not built for anything more."

She held his gaze, staring into his eyes for what seemed like an eternity. "Got it."

He took the bucket from her and followed her back to the corner of the orchard she'd claimed.

"Ryder, can I get on your shoulders?" Roni grabbed a fistful of his T-shirt and jumped up and down. "I want to get those cherries, but they're too tall for me."

"Yup, let's do it." He crouched down so Roni could climb up, then rose to his full height.

Henry watched enviously.

"You're next, buddy." Ryder mussed his hair.

Joey shielded her eyes with her hand and searched the orchard for Peter and Shiv, who were a few rows down. Peter was carrying on a lively conversation with her, but she was distracted, watching Ryder with the kids. She wanted grandchildren, Joey remembered Shiv saying. Poor lady. Ryder couldn't commit to a postcoital cuddle, let alone a child.

By the time the kids had filled their bucket with cherries, they'd run out of steam. Joey had packed a picnic basket with refreshments. She spread a blanket on the ground and set Roni and Henry up with PB&J sandwiches and juice boxes.

Great minds thought alike, because Peter had brought along a similar setup for him and Shiv, including a bottle of hand sanitizer and a bottle of sparkling cider. They came over to join the kids while Joey went in search of a restroom or Porta Potty.

"It's over there."

She turned to find Ryder behind her. "How is it that you're so familiar with the place?"

"I'm not. But truckers have pretty good mental GPS for bathrooms. You having fun?"

"I am. It's a gorgeous day, and I get to spend it with my daughter. Nothing could be better." She saw a flash of something in his eyes. Sadness, maybe. But it was gone so quickly she thought she might have imagined it. "How 'bout you?"

"Sure. My mom seems to be having a good time, and that's what's important. She seems pretty taken with your daughter."

Joey let out a chuckle. "The whole town of Nugget is. I swear, Roni's going to be president one day."

"What's the deal with the boy...Henry?"

"He's Brynn's son. A real sweetheart. A while back, he was in a horrible accident. His father was killed, and they didn't know if Henry would ever walk again. Ethan got him into his medical trial, and...well, look at him."

"What kind of accident?"

"An all-terrain vehicle. Apparently, the father was a real daredevil. But who the hell does that with a little kid?"

Ryder blanched and quickly walked away.

Joey caught up to him and grabbed his arm, which he abruptly pulled away. "Ryder, what did I say wrong?"

"Nothing." He stopped walking and leaned against a tree. "I overreacted. Don't worry about it."

"Please, just tell me."

He pushed himself off the oak and continued to the row of blue outhouses on the other side of the dirt road with her trailing him. "Do me a favor and change the subject."

She couldn't force him to discuss something he didn't want to talk about. But she'd clearly touched a nerve. The obvious conclusion was that his late wife had died in an accident.

"Who was the man that came to see you this morning?" She hoped the question was neutral enough. She didn't want to ruin the day, especially given the weirdness over them sleeping together.

"Flynn Barlow? He's that local lawyer I met with the other day. He wrote a letter to the Addisons that he wanted to show me."

"What kind of letter?"

Ryder glanced around to make sure they were alone. "A cease-and-desist with an added incentive to make them go away."

Her eyes grew round. "You're not paying them off, are you?"

He laughed. "Not even close."

Ryder lengthened his strides, and Joey had to practically jog to keep up.

"Wait up," she called. "What do you mean by 'incentive,' then?"

"Their own code and zoning violations. They report me, I'll report them."

"Do they have any?" What was that saying about people in glass houses not throwing stones?

"We don't know for sure, but Flynn seems to think it's likely and the kind of thing to get them off my back."

It seemed like a long shot to Joey. But an attorney would know better than her. "I hope it works."

"Yeah, me too," he said but sounded worried.

Chapter 16

Shiv read the letter again that evening. She'd thought about it all day in the cherry orchard. She could hear the deep cadence of Morgan's voice with every word she read. Sometimes, when he'd spoken from the bench, she'd gotten lost in the melodic quality of it. His family had come to California during the Dust Bowl, and his speech still held a touch of Oklahoma. The accent was rich and reminded her of storytellers.

He wrote, asking how she was, how she liked her new home, and whether she was feeling better. All the things she'd known would be included in the note, written in his efficient handwriting on the letterhead he reserved for his personal correspondence.

There was nothing hinting of romance in the letter—and she knew there wouldn't be—although his tone suggested he missed her. Or maybe she was delusional, misconstruing things that weren't there.

Hadn't that always been her problem? Believing that they were someday fated to be together. And here she was. Alone.

How had she not learned from Tanner? Those first few years, she'd left the porch light on for him, believing that one day he'd wake up and come home to her and their little boy. That other woman forgotten. But Shiv and Ryder had been the ones to be forgotten.

By the time Ryder went to middle school, she'd stopped waiting by the window for her cowboy. Any feelings she had left for him disappeared the day she walked into Morgan Lester's courtroom. Unlike Tanner's muscular build, Morgan was tall and rangy. An elegant man, who reminded her of Gregory Peck. He had a wall of diplomas that rivaled Tanner's silver buckles.

The other way Morgan was vastly different from Tanner was that he stayed true to his vows.

She neatly folded up the letter and placed it on top of her dresser. At some point, she would write Morgan back. But not now, when she was feeling sorry for herself and frankly a little exhausted after the day's outing.

It had been wonderful to be outside with the children. That Roni was a little charmer and Henry so polite. His mother had raised him right. She still couldn't get over the fact that Ryder had joined them. When he'd offered to drive them to the orchard, she'd assumed he would drop them off and leave. She hadn't bothered to invite him to participate, knowing that family-type activities were difficult for him.

And then, wow. Watching him with the children had filled her with a combination of wonder and a deep, abiding sadness. It wasn't fair that he wasn't a father. It wasn't fair that his unborn child had been snatched away from him in the blink of an eye. Then again, when had life ever been fair?

She rolled over on her side and closed her eyes, but for the first time in months, sleep, her solace, evaded her. As the clock ticked by, she tossed and turned until finally giving up. Slipping into a robe, she padded to the front porch. The wooden boards felt cool and worn under her bare feet.

It wasn't so late. Just a little past ten. Peter had long gone back to his hotel, and Joey was probably in her room, reading. The light was still on in Ryder's camper. She held the railing tight, and instead of using the ramp, took one stair at a time, then crossed the yard to his door with the moon to guide her.

She gently tapped, deciding that if he didn't answer, she'd turn around and go back to bed. But he swung the door open and seemed surprised to see her standing there.

"Who were you expecting?"

"Ma, what are you doing up?" His eyes took in her robe and stopped at her bare feet. "Are you okay?"

"I'm fine, just couldn't sleep."

"Where are your slippers?" He reached down and offered her an arm to come inside.

"I think I'm about ready to burn them."

"Yeah?" He scratched his chin, then led her to the sofa. "Let me get you a glass of water."

She wasn't thirsty but took the drink anyway, and a quick glance around.

"Nice place" for a trailer. He should be living in the house he bought, sleeping in the room he'd given to her.

Ryder's eyes quickly darted across the room, presumably checking to see if the camper was tidy. "I guess you've never been inside before."

She shook her head. "You never invited me."

His mouth ticked up. "Nope. Didn't think you'd approve."

She didn't. He worked hard and should have a real home, not one on wheels. But she supposed wheels were good for running. "It was fine for when you were rodeoing but now…What do you hear from that retirement community you put me on the list for?" Retirement community, ha. It was an old-age home.

"Why are you asking me that, Ma? You want to run off on me?"

She reached over and held his chin like she used to do when he was a little boy. "I want you to stop running from life. I want you to be that man in the cherry orchard today."

Ryder huffed and got to his feet. "I want you to be the happy woman you were before the stroke."

She hadn't been happy long before the stroke. It had started with retirement, when the days seemed to stretch on forever and she'd wandered around without any purpose. "What would go a long way to making me happy is seeing you happy."

"Where did you get the impression that I wasn't happy?" He sat in the recliner and kicked the chair back.

"Ryder? I'm your mother." She scowled at him. "Roni and Henry adore you. And judging by the way Joey looks at you and you look at her…It's time for you to move on. You've grieved Leslie and the baby long enough. You've punished yourself long enough. Grab some happiness while you still have time because one day you'll wake up old and lonely and it'll be too late."

"Is that what happened to you?"

Her eyes filled, and she turned away to wipe them. "Yes, and I don't want it to happen to you. You, my greatest joy, deserve better."

He got up and sat next to her on the couch. "So do you. Why didn't you find someone else after Tanner?" Ryder had stopped calling him "Dad" in high school. She used to think it was poetic justice. Now it filled her with guilt. She should've pushed harder for them to have a relationship, instead of taking secret pleasure that Ryder had rejected his father in solidarity with her. "I know there were men who were interested. You think it was for the love of planting that Mr. Brigham joined your garden club? The man didn't know a damn annual from a perennial, and his backyard looked like shit."

"Language, Ryder."

"Sorry. My point is, there were men. Jonsie Christian's dad spent two years trying to get you to go on a date with him. There were all those lawyers in the courthouse. Don't tell me there wasn't a single one in the lot you weren't interested in."

The one she was interested in she couldn't have. "I didn't want to bring someone into our lives who would disappoint you."

"Ah, that's the biggest bullshit excuse I've ever heard. You just couldn't get over Tanner."

She did a double take. "Is that what you think? Because it couldn't be further from the truth."

"Then you tell me what the problem was. Because it doesn't make sense. Why the hell did you give up on love, Ma, if it wasn't for Tanner?"

"I was putting my energies into other things…career, improving myself. Anyway, this is about you, not me. Why can't you open yourself up again, Ryder? Why do you want to live all alone in this sardine can?"

"I thought you said you liked it." His mouth quirked.

"For camping, not for hiding away."

"I'm not hiding away. If you haven't noticed, I'm running a good-sized company, I bought a house and moved to a nice, small town, and I went cherry picking today. I don't know what you want from me."

She turned sideways and took his large hands in hers. "I want you to stop pretending to go through the motions and really live. As difficult as I know it is, I want you to let Leslie go."

He turned away and stared out the window into darkness. "I've let her go, Ma. I did that a long time ago. But nothing has ever hurt so bad. Not Tanner leaving, not losing the career of my dreams, not anything. I can never…I just can't."

"Ah, honey, you can't let what happened crush your spirit. Love is taking risks. Would you have traded away your life with Leslie if you'd known that it was going to be cut short?"

He tilted his head back and stared up at the ceiling. "No. But that's different. We were so young, our lives so intertwined. I'd loved her since the ninth grade. She was my best friend."

"Nothing can replicate what you had with Leslie. That doesn't mean you can't have something equally special with someone else. A family, Ryder. Something to hold on to."

Someone knocked. The sound reverberated through the trailer with a tinny sound. Ryder got up and opened the door.

"Your mom wouldn't happen to be in there with you?"

"She is."

"Thank God."

Shiv peeked around the corner to find Joey flushed with relief. Did the poor girl think Shiv had run away?

"Sorry, dear. I couldn't sleep, and Ryder's light was on. Come in." Shiv got to her feet. "I'm going back to bed. Joey, do me a favor and keep Ryder company." She started for the door.

"Let me help get you situated." Joey tried to follow.

"I'm perfectly capable of getting myself situated. I've got the button if I need anything." Shiv held up the ridiculous alarm apparatus she'd sworn to wear around her neck. She patted Ryder's cheeks. "Think about what I said. And you, Joey, need to let me do more for myself. I'm not an invalid."

She got down the steps herself, then turned around to face her son and caregiver, who'd been stunned silent. "Tomorrow, I want to see this Cascade Village. Make sure it's up to snuff."

* * * *

Ryder watched his mother's back retreat behind the front door.

"Should I go help her? Or is that going to provoke her?"

"Provoke her." He stepped into the kitchen, stuck his head in the fridge, and tossed Joey a soda. "Were you sleeping?" She had on pajama shorts and a tank top. No bra and a pair of tennis shoes that weren't laced up.

"I woke up, checked on your mom, and nearly had a heart attack when I couldn't find her."

Ryder grabbed himself a beer and gestured with the neck of the bottle for her to take a seat. Her hair was poufy and kind of wild around her face, the same way it had looked after they'd had sex the other night. The memory made his groin tighten.

"What's going on with her? Am I coddling her too much? Is she annoyed? Because she sounded annoyed."

"With me," Ryder said. "Not with you."

"Why is she annoyed with you? She seemed tickled pink today when you joined our field trip to The Farm."

"It's a long story, Joey."

She kicked off her tennis shoes and curled her legs under her butt. "I've got time."

"I don't even know where to start." He rested his head on the back of the couch. "Long story short, she wants me to live a different life than I've chosen."

"And what life does she want you to have?"

He let out a long breath. "The house, the wife, the kids, the dog, a four-door sedan."

"My brother could probably hook you up on that last one."

He sat up and took a swig of his beer. She was funny. He'd always liked that about her. "I reckon he could."

"But you don't want any of those things because of your late wife."

The woman didn't mince words. "Something like that."

"How'd she die, Ryder?"

He dropped his head between his knees, then came up slowly. "Car accident. A fucking seventeen-year-old swerved into the oncoming lane while texting her boyfriend and hit Leslie head-on. She died in the ER."

"I'm so sorry, Ryder."

"She was seven months' pregnant with our little boy. They couldn't save him, either."

"Oh, Ryder. I...I didn't know."

"Well, now you do. Leslie was my high school sweetheart. My everything. We were planning to buy a ranch outside of Modesto, breed horses, plant a garden, raise our kid in the country. And just like that, it was all taken away. Two lives and a dream killed before I could even say good-bye."

"I don't know what to say, Ryder. It's that awful."

It was better to say nothing than spew bullshit platitudes. *It was God's will. She and your son are in a better place now. The Lord never gives us more than we can handle*—that one was his personal favorite. How the fuck would they know?

"There's nothing to say." He tilted the rest of his beer back and killed the bottle with one swallow.

"You're living the best you can. You built a business, bought this place, you're taking care of your mother." She pulled him in for an embrace.

His initial instinct was to pull away. But she felt good, like a harbor of hope. He wrapped his arms around her and tucked her head under his chin, letting himself revel in the sweet scent of her hair. She nestled against him, and he held on. Whatever she was willing to give, he'd take because he was sick and tired of feeling alone and wounded.

And she fit. Later, it would scare the hell out of him how well she fit. But now he needed her like he'd never needed anyone before.

She pressed her mouth against his heart, and that simple gesture broke him. He lifted her face and with bruising force took her mouth with his, kissing her deeply. She returned the kiss with the same ferocity.

They fell back on the couch, and he crawled over her. His hands were everywhere. Her legs, her hips, her sides, her breasts. She dragged his T-shirt over his head and dropped kisses across his chest. Her lips were warm and soft, the closest he'd ever come to heaven.

He stripped off her tank and kissed her beautiful breasts, molding each one in his hands. She arched up, giving him better access. He dragged his mouth down her chest to her belly, tasting her skin. Her desperate murmurs fired him up.

He slid her sleep shorts down and spread her legs, dipping his fingers in to see if she was ready for him. She was so wet his chest expanded with the knowledge that he could do this to her. That he could arouse this beautiful woman to such a frenzied height.

She rocked into his fingers, silently pleading for him to fill her. He strained against the fly on his jeans, growing harder.

"Please," she begged. "I want…I need…more." She tore at the buttons on his jeans.

He lifted up, pulled down his pants just enough to free himself, and entered her with one powerful thrust. She moaned with pleasure, wrapping her legs around his waist so he could go deeper.

She was so tight and hot that he nearly climaxed. Then he realized he'd forgotten protection and slowly pulled out, holding his breath.

"Shit."

"No, no, no. What are you doing? Why are you stopping?"

"Condom." He rolled off the sofa and ran to the bedroom, trying not to trip over his pants. "Don't move."

He found her in the same position he'd left her. Spread out on the couch, her blond hair fanned out behind her, her plump pink lips formed in the shape of an *O* with her eyes closed. She was so damn sexy his heart stopped.

He ripped open the foil wrapper, suited up, and mounted her. Not a second later, he was moving inside her.

"Oh," she cried out. "Oh, Ryder."

He kissed her neck, loving the taste and smell of her, a combination of salt, perfume, and woman.

"This is good," he whispered, his strokes slow, drawing out every inch of pleasure. "So damn good."

Her hands were in his hair, on his scalp, and she was kissing him. Her body bowed up, giving him as much as he wanted. A veritable feast. And he took and took and took, careful to give as much back as he could.

He sucked her breasts, laving them with attention. He touched her between her legs, finding what she liked the best. Changing the tempo from slow to fast, he pumped harder. Deeper.

Ryder took her to the brink three or four times, making it last until she thrashed her head from side to side, begging for sweet release. He didn't know how he was able to hold on so long. It was either force of will or the knowledge that once he let go, he'd be right back where he started. Alone. And for right now, he needed to lose himself in her and forget about the past.

"Please," she murmured.

He kissed her long and hard. The hot pull of her mouth set him on fire. Reaching under her, he lifted her ass so he could go even deeper. His thrusts became more powerful, more desperate. The couch wasn't big enough for them, but by sheer will he kept them from falling.

"Ryder." Joey arched her back as she met him stroke for stroke. Her body began to tremble as she reached her peak.

He could feel her clench and then she let out a long "Ohhh" as she came apart under him.

"Joey," he called and threw his head back, seeing only stars.

They moved together for a little while, milking their climaxes to the very end. Then, he rolled off her. But there was nowhere to go but the floor. He lifted her in his arms and carried her to his bed.

"Sleep," he said and wrapped himself around her.

Chapter 17

Joey snuck away the next morning, careful not to wake Ryder, who was sleeping soundlessly. She needed to check on Shiv before Peter arrived. But mostly she needed time and space. She was getting in too deep with Ryder. Her world couldn't take any more disappointment, and he was disappointment with a capital *D*.

It was only a matter of time before this job would be over. Shiv was already making noise about leaving to live at Cascade Village. As soon as the retirement community had an opening, she would go, Joey was sure of that. And then there was Joey's nursing license. If the gods were smiling, maybe she'd be reinstated and could start looking for a nursing job.

Her life was completely up in the air, and here she was, falling for a man who was completely unavailable.

She tiptoed into the house, praying that Shiv was still asleep. It was only seven, plenty of time for her to shower and dress before putting on a pot of coffee. She cracked open Shiv's door to find her still in bed, then rushed to the bathroom.

After bathing, throwing on a pair of jeans, and applying a little makeup, she strolled into the kitchen to find Peter at the table.

"You're early."

"I wanted to take advantage of that fabulous breakfast at the inn before the rest of the guests woke up. I stuffed my face and found myself with nothing left to do. What's on tap today for you and your daughter?"

"I was thinking of going riding. My ex has horses, and he's gone for the weekend. It's only his wicked stepmother. She probably wouldn't mind if Roni and I availed ourselves of a couple of horses. The ranch is five hundred acres, so she won't even have to see me."

"That bad, huh?"

Joey wagged her hand from side to side. "A lot better since Ethan got engaged to someone more suitable." She made finger quote marks in the air around "suitable."

"Oh, honey, she's crazy if she doesn't think you're suitable. I'm in awe. The way you're able to juggle being a mom and an amazing caregiver. Color me speechless."

"Peter, where have you been my whole life?"

He chuckled. "Miss Shiv had a good time yesterday. She's smitten with Roni, you know? Thanks for letting us tag along."

"It was my pleasure."

"I was a little surprised about Cowboy Beef Cake."

Joey nearly dropped the coffeepot, she laughed so hard. "Cowboy Beef Cake? Yeah, me, too. It was good for Shiv."

"Honey, it was good for all of us. You do know the man has the hots for you?"

He had something for her, something physical. "Nah, he's worried about his mother and just needs a friend."

"I could be there for him."

"Be there for who?" Ryder came into the kitchen, sporting a good case of bedhead.

Both Joey and Peter exchanged glances, fearing they'd been overheard. If they had, Ryder didn't let on.

"Coffee will be ready in few." Joey turned on the machine.

"What did you bring us, Peter?" Ryder searched the kitchen counter. "No donuts?"

"Nothing this morning, I'm afraid. The Lumber Baron ought to do take-out. They'd make a fortune."

Ryder stuck his head in the fridge and pulled out a carton of eggs. "Anyone want an omelet?"

"I couldn't eat another bite," Peter said and rested his hand on his stomach. "I'll wait to have breakfast with Roni. But thanks."

He glanced over at her and nodded. No one observing would ever guess that they'd spent the night having some of the best sex of her life. That was sort of Ryder's MO. Hot and cold.

He got down a mixing bowl and found a pan in the cupboard. "My mom's not up yet?"

"I'll give her until eight, then rouse her. I know she wanted to see Cascade Village today, but I'm doubtful they're open for tours on Sundays."

Peter perked up. "Really? I'd gotten the impression she wasn't too excited about Cascade Village. Though Cascade Village is like no senior community I've ever seen."

"You know it?" Ryder asked.

"I worked there as a caregiver for two years. It's gorgeous. The apartments and homes are spacious, and there's three restaurants, an enormous pool, tennis courts, a fabulous gym, twenty-four-hour concierge, on-site health care. I'd move there if they'd take me."

Ryder hunted through the fridge for cheese. "Will they let her tour the place today?"

"That I don't know. Call the concierge. They used to have models of the homes, but they may have sold those by now. From what I hear, it's hard to get in."

"We're on a waiting list," Ryder said. "Yesterday was the first time my mother ever showed interest in the place. I'm hoping she likes it and that it will give her something to look forward to. Get her out of her funk."

"She definitely won't be bored. There's tons of social activities." Peter got up, gathered a few mugs from the cupboard, and set them on the table with a container of milk.

Joey checked the clock. "How early do you think he can call?" she asked Peter.

"Any time. They're there twenty-four hours."

Joey went to wake Shiv and found her sitting at the edge of her bed.

"Morning. You want coffee and breakfast first? Or a shower?"

"A shower." Shiv got to her feet. "I'll meet you in the kitchen."

Joey couldn't gauge Shiv's mood, but she'd made it clear that she wanted to get ready on her own. Fair enough. There was no reason Siobhan couldn't be more independent. Her balance was getting better, and the dizzy spells were infrequent.

While Shiv was in the bathroom, Joey used the opportunity to strip her bed and gather up a load of laundry. She'd start the wash before she headed off to the Circle D. On her way out, she spotted a towel on top of the dresser and added it to her pile. A piece of stationery fluttered to the ground, and Joey dropped her load to pick it up.

She didn't mean to pry but couldn't help but notice the letterhead. It belonged to the judge Shiv used to work for. On occasion, she'd mentioned him, always with a degree of reverence that had made Joey wonder about their relationship. Shiv had never indicated that it was anything other than professional. Still, Joey had detected something there. A kind of longing that she'd initially attributed to Shiv missing her job and the prestige of serving an important judge.

Joey peeked at the first paragraph, and before she knew it, she had read the whole letter. It was fairly generic, the kind of note an employer who over the years had become a friend would send, asking after Shiv's health. Yet, there was something about it that made Joey think there was more. The sentence: "I miss you," which was quickly followed up with "We all miss you." It was as if the judge realized the original sentiment was too revealing and tried to correct himself. There were other things, too, like "My dearest Siobhan." It seemed like rather antiquated language for a friendly missive. To Joey, it was the way you would start a love letter. But older, proper people (maybe he was from England) spoke like that.

Besides, it was none of her business. She folded the note and returned it to the dresser.

Peter and Ryder were chatting when Joey got back to the kitchen. She poured herself a cup of coffee and sipped it, leaning against the counter. It was still too early to show up at the Circle D. If Ethan was there, she wouldn't have cared. But Alma would act put out.

"If I can't get in today, you want to come with me tomorrow?" Ryder asked and she assumed they were still talking about Cascade Village.

"Sure, I'd love to see it."

"What about you, Peter?" She didn't want him to feel left out. He was also Shiv's caregiver, and since he'd worked at Cascade Village, who better than him to come along?

"I have a client on Monday. But I'm free Thursday and Friday. Besides, I'm hoping they let us in today."

Ryder locked eyes with her. She knew he wanted her to go with them but didn't want to come right out and say it. It was her day with her daughter, after all. And the fact that they'd slept together—not once, but twice—made navigating the work thing a ticking time bomb. Another reason why she needed distance.

But Sundays were also her days to hit meetings in Reno after her visit with Roni, so she'd be there anyway. And, of course, she wanted to make sure Shiv would be happy in the retirement community.

"Try to get an appointment for the afternoon, so I can spend a few hours with Roni." She washed her cup and grabbed her bag. "Call me."

She made it to the Circle D in less than ten minutes and sat in the driveway, deliberating on whether it was still too early to go in. But Alma saved her from having to decide by coming out onto the porch.

Joey prepared herself for Alma's usual condescension and got out of the car. "I hope it's not too early." She shaded her eyes with her hand to block out the morning sun.

"Roni just woke up. She's getting dressed," Alma said in that superior, you're-a-bad-mother tone that always left Joey feeling guilt ridden. Her sponsor had told her to ignore it. Easier said than done.

The only woman more perfect than Brynn was Alma—okay, it was a toss-up. Alma was a retired news anchor, the toast of Reno, looked ten years younger than her age, and had helped raise Roni while Joey had been too stoned to do it herself. She'd taught Roni how to bake cookies, to always say please and thank you, and that red and purple clashed. Currently, she was teaching her Spanish.

From day one, Alma had made it crystal clear that she thought her stepson was too good for Joey. The sad realization was that she'd been right. Joey had been a terrible wife, a party girl who wanted to play more than she'd wanted a committed relationship. She'd never cheated on Ethan, but she'd gone out of her way to attract male attention.

Resentful of Ethan's long hours, she'd spent more time in bars with her girlfriends than making their house a home. When Roni was born, she'd told herself it was time to settle down and be a mom. In those first years, she'd doted on her family. Then, she found opioid analgesics, and that became her life.

"Are you coming in?" Alma stared down her nose at Joey.

She climbed the stairs. "I thought I'd take Roni to breakfast." It would be better than sitting around in the kitchen while Alma insisted on making something. "Henry, too."

"Henry's got a playdate."

Joey followed Alma inside, stood at the staircase, and called up to Roni, "I'm here, baby. Hurry up so we can go to breakfast."

Roni came out of her bedroom, still in her PJ's. "Okay, Mommy. Should I wear a dress?"

"If you want to. But I thought we could go riding after we eat. So maybe jeans and boots."

"I get to ride Choo Choo." She danced back into her room.

Joey found Alma in the kitchen, making coffee from the fancy built-in machine.

"Would you care for a cup?"

"No, thanks. I had some before I came."

Joey sank into a stool at the enormous marble island, noting a stack of wedding materials in the corner. It was next Saturday. She'd received her engraved printed invite, hand-addressed in calligraphy. She still hadn't sent back the elegant RSVP card, which was beyond rude, but she hadn't decided whether to attend.

The idea of going was right up there with having a colonoscopy. But if it would smooth the transition for Roni, she didn't see how she could avoid it. *One big, happy family.*

Who knew? Maybe she'd meet the man of her dreams at the reception, not that she was looking. The thought conjured an immediate image of Ryder, naked, on top of her. She tried to shut it down, but it didn't seem to want to go away.

"How's the job going?" Alma asked, trying to be pleasant.

"Good. Ms. Knight is a lovely woman." *Unlike you.*

"Nothing on your nursing license, huh?" Of course, Alma knew. Joey wondered if she asked just to be mean.

"Not yet."

"How are your folks?" Alma hated Joey's parents but was trying to make small talk to make up for how uncomfortable this was. Ordinarily, Ethan was here to be a buffer.

"They're fine and send their regards." What the hell was taking Roni so long?

She didn't know why she said it, but it just fell from her mouth. "You must be really excited about the wedding. I hear you're all going to Hawaii."

"Yes, the wedding should be lovely. And the kids are thrilled about Hawaii. It was very sweet of them to invite me along," she said, but without the victorious tone Joey had expected. She almost sounded like she wanted to downplay it for Joey's sake.

"Of course, they would invite you. Ethan and Roni love you, and I'm sure Brynn and Henry do, too."

A soft smile lit Alma's face, and she reached out and ever so slightly touched Joey's hand. That's when Roni came running into the room.

"I'm ready!" She held up her foot so Joey could admire her pink cowboy boots.

"Ooh, where did you get those?" It was the first Joey had seen of them.

"Brynn got them for me from Katie's mom."

"Who's Katie's mom?"

"Tawny Rodriguez," Alma said. "She's a well-known boot designer, who happens to live in Nugget."

Joey had a sudden memory of Annie telling her about the custom boot maker when they'd run into each other at Farm Supply. As Joey recalled, Annie had also said her cowboy boots were prohibitively expensive. A wave of agitation hit her so hard it nearly knocked her over. She did her best to hide her ire, afraid Roni, or even Alma, would pick up on it.

"Daylight's burning." It was something Ethan always said when he wanted to get everyone out of the house.

"Let's go," Roni shouted.

"You sure Henry won't feel left out?" she asked Alma.

"No." Alma waved her off. "He's still asleep and will be excited about meeting up with his friend."

Roni chatted endlessly on their trip to the Ponderosa. Even though Joey wished there were more sit-down restaurants in Nugget, you couldn't beat the Ponderosa for breakfast. Really for anything. For such a tiny town, the restaurant was good.

"What're you going to get?" she asked Roni as they went inside.

"Waffles."

The waiting area was packed with people who spilled out onto the sidewalk. The owner, Mariah, spotted them and bobbed her head in greeting.

"Looks like we'll have to warm one of these benches for a little while." Joey grabbed a seat at the entrance and pulled Roni onto her lap to give an elderly man room to sit.

Two women across the restaurant waved, and she had to look closely to see who they were. Darla and her friend, Harlee. She waved back.

Roni jumped off her lap to run over to their table to say hello and returned a few seconds later. "They said to come sit with them."

"Really?" That was awfully nice.

Roni took her hand and dragged her to their table.

"You sure?" she asked the two women.

"Uh, yeah." Darla flipped her hair. Today it was platinum blond and Joey was pretty sure a wig. "Eat with us. We haven't even ordered yet, and we have this whole table to ourselves."

"Thank you." Joey pulled out a chair for Roni and joined them. One look at Harlee and she tried not to laugh at how far she had to sit from the table. "Any day, right?"

"Ugh." Harlee threw her head back. "Why can't this baby be born already?"

"Can I hold it when it's born?" Roni got up and touched Harlee's belly.

"Yep. You can even babysit when you get older."

Roni's eyes grew round, and Joey laughed.

A server came and took their orders. Both women got virgin Bloody Marys, and Joey decided to get one, too. She ordered Roni a waffle and a side of scrambled eggs. She'd never eat it all, but at least there'd be some protein on her plate.

Roni saw a friend from school, and she sprinted across the dining room to greet her.

"Is this a regular thing for you two?" Joey asked Harlee and Darla, liking the idea of a ladies' brunch.

"Not really," Harlee said. "My husband is doing some work on the Barlow place, trying to get caught up before the baby comes. And Wyatt had to work today."

"He's a cop," Darla reminded Joey. "The department is so small that everyone has to pull a weekend shift every month. At least he'll be off for Brynn and Ethan's…" she trailed off, remembering that Joey was the ex-wife.

"It's okay. Even I got an invitation."

The two of them looked at her, surprised. Good, at least it wasn't just her who found the whole being invited to her ex's wedding bizarre.

"Ethan thought it would be good for Roni if I was there. A way to show that I was giving my blessing."

"Are you?" Harlee asked. "Giving your blessing?"

Joey had opened the door. Still, the question startled her. She thought about it. When he'd first met Brynn, Joey had been insanely jealous and had done whatever she could to win him back. Somewhere along the line, though, she discovered that it was the idea of him that she loved more than it was Ethan himself. The truth was, the marriage had been in peril long before she'd become a substance abuser. And despite everything they'd been through, Ethan continued to be her stalwart supporter and friend. He was a good man, possibly the best man she'd ever known.

"Ethan deserves to be happy, and Brynn does that for him," Joey said at last. "So, yes, he has my blessing."

"Wow, that's, like, so refreshing." Darla turned to Harlee. "Right?"

"If Colin and I ever got divorced and he married someone else, I'd slip laxatives into his breakfast cereal and post his fiancée's profile on Tinder. And that's before I truly got creative."

"You would not. That's just the hormones talking," Darla said.

"Talk to me in a few months when you look like me." As soon as the words left Harlee's mouth, she covered it with her hand. "Oops, sorry."

Joey stifled a laugh. "I guess congratulations are in order."

"We're not telling anyone yet." Darla smacked Harlee's arm. "I've got another week until we're out of the woods."

"I won't tell a soul." Joey pretended to zip her lips shut. "Promise. We won't even discuss it." She understood wholeheartedly.

"Thank you."

Harlee gave Darla a hug and let out a little squeal. It was so sweet that Joey reminded herself to get a best friend.

"Let's circle back to the wedding," Darla said and turned to Joey. "Does that mean you're going?"

Joey let out a puff of air. "I haven't decided yet. Although he has my blessing, I'm not sure I can withstand the awkwardness of it."

"You should take a date," Harlee said.

"A super-hot guy," Darla added.

Ryder came to mind. As if. A man who didn't do relationships wasn't likely to do weddings either. Even as a guest. "Yeah, maybe. We'll see."

"If nothing else, you should go to witness the spectacle," Harlee said. "I hear it's going to be glitzy, like a wedding on steroids. Brynn hired a caterer from Manhattan, who's coming all the way here."

"Brady must be pissed." Darla filled her glass with ice water from the pitcher on the table.

"Who's Brady?"

"He's a local chef who works for Nate Breyer's hotel chain. He always caters the weddings around here." Harlee did a quick look around to make sure no one could hear them. "Brynn said she wanted him to be a guest, not a worker."

"I can see that." One of Joey's college roommates was a photographer. She had once confided in Joey that she hated shooting their sorority sisters' weddings. Not only had she felt left out, but the pressure was worse when it was a friend.

"I heard she's also having some of the members of the New York Philharmonic do the music," Harlee said.

Joey wasn't surprised. "Her father is the conductor."

Harlee nodded. "Weddings around here are big to-dos if they're held in Lucky's barn. You can only imagine how everyone is talking about this one."

Joey could relate. She and Ethan had gotten married at his family's ranch outside of Reno. The wedding cake had come from Costco. Ethan's dad had donated a half side of beef. Alma had worked a week straight, making her famous tamales. The music had been provided by a country-and-western band that played at a bar not far from the hospital. And Joey had worn an off-the-rack wedding dress.

She was stunned that Ethan was going along with a big, showy shindig. It wasn't at all his style. But that's how crazy he was about Brynn.

Roni skipped back to their table, and the conversation turned to other residents of Nugget, including the Addisons.

"I heard a rumor that they may be interested in selling the Beary Quaint," Harlee said and stopped talking when the server brought their food.

"Where'd you hear that?" Darla asked as soon the waitress left. She sounded skeptical.

"Sources. But yeah, I have my doubts about the credibility of the information."

"If I were you, I wouldn't go to press with it just yet." Darla drowned her eggs in hot sauce. When she realized Harlee and Joey were watching her, she said, "I'm craving spicy like you wouldn't believe. So good, right? Anyway, I find it highly unlikely that the Addisons are selling. They've owned that relic of a lodge since the beginning of time."

Harlee shrugged. "Keep your ears open. You never know, and it would make a hell of a story."

Joey wondered why, if the Addisons were trying to sell, they would be hassling Ryder. Then again, perhaps they thought Ryder's trucks would scare away potential buyers. She stored the information so she could tell Ryder about it later.

In between bites of her waffle, Roni entertained everyone with a story about her new best friend. It was a thoroughly delightful morning. Yet Joey couldn't shake their discussion about Ethan's upcoming wedding. In just a few short years, everything had changed. Yet it still felt as though she was the one standing still.

Chapter 18

Cascade Village had been beautiful. Different from what Shiv had expected. She'd pictured something akin to a convalescent home, not a sprawling community of single-family houses, condos, and apartments. There was a big lodge with an indoor and an outdoor swimming pool, a clubhouse, a gym, a library, and a couple of restaurants.

The residents ranged in age from sixty to much older. There were clubs and activities and even a bus that shuttled residents to shopping and shows at the area casinos. The grounds were immaculate, with views of the surrounding desert. It looked like any other high-end planned community. The only difference was that medical assistance was included in the price of living there.

She was interested in buying a small condo. Because there weren't any available, she'd been shown brochure pictures and a video tour of what had previously been the models. Everything was gorgeous. One level, spacious rooms, top-of-the-line appliances, and big picture windows that let the light in.

Of course, the promotional material would only show the best. But Shiv was confident it wasn't a bait and switch. The place wouldn't be full if it were.

What had been missing were her friends. Most of her former colleagues had lived near her Modesto neighborhood. They'd frequently met for coffee, or she and a few of the other court clerks and bailiffs had gathered for happy hour at one of the bars near the courthouse. Morgan never joined them, but she'd always felt connected to him through the others.

Cascade Village would be good, she told herself. A new start.

"So, what did you think?" Joey asked that evening. She'd met them there and had parted ways after the tour to run errands.

"Very impressive."

"It was. But is it somewhere you can picture yourself living?"

Ryder was in the other room, pretending to watch a sporting event. Shiv knew he was eavesdropping.

"Absolutely," she lied.

Joey flashed a wry smile. There was no fooling her. It was one of the reasons Shiv liked Joey so much.

"It's been a long day. I think I'll turn in, maybe watch a little TV in bed."

"I changed the sheets. Would you like me to draw you a bath?"

"Dear, I'm perfectly capable of drawing my own bath. But thank you. And thank you for meeting us in Reno. It's your day off…your day with Veronica. And you gave it up for me."

"I didn't give it up. I had the whole morning and most of the afternoon with Roni. I wanted to see the place." She walked Shiv to the bedroom, and when they were out of earshot of Ryder, she said, "Your son wants you to be happy more than anything in the world, Shiv. You don't have to pretend. If Cascade Village isn't for you, we'll come up with a better solution. There is no rush to make a decision. Rest well."

Shiv waited until the sound of Joey's footsteps faded down the hallway. Then she reread Morgan's letter before rummaging through her top drawer for her stationery. She sat at the tiny desk in the corner of her room and began to write.

Dear Morgan,

It was lovely to hear from you. I hope all is well and that things have settled down at home. My thoughts and prayers go out to Dolores. Hang in there. I know how difficult it is.

I'm feeling much better these days, and my physical therapist thinks that in a few weeks I'll be back to a hundred percent.

Ryder has been wonderful, and his new home is so peaceful and serene. His new lady friend, Joey, and I sit out on the porch every evening, enjoying the beautiful countryside. On weekends, our friend Peter drops by. He's always up for a good time. Yesterday we went berry picking at a lovely cherry orchard near Ryder's place.

Today we took a trip to Reno to visit a retirement community where I'm thinking of buying a condo. It was very fancy but shockingly affordable. No wonder Californians are flocking to Nevada.

I appreciate hearing from you and look forward to your letters. Please send my regards to Gary and Erin, who I hope are doing a good job for you. I miss you all and think about you often.

Sincerely,

Siobhan

She read the letter several times, then folded it neatly into thirds. Before sliding the note into an envelope, she gave it a faint spritz of Chanel No5, reconsidered the part about looking forward to his letters, then quickly sealed it up before she could change her mind.

* * * *

"Hey, are you really watching this, or do you have a few minutes to talk?"

Ryder flicked off the TV. "What's on your mind?"

Joey sat in the chair opposite him. "I need a favor."

"What's that?" He kicked his feet up onto the coffee table and waited for her to continue.

She squeezed the bridge of her nose. "I need a date next Saturday to my ex-husband's wedding."

"I thought you'd decided not to go."

"No. I was contemplating it and have decided it's the right thing to do. But it would be easier if I didn't have to do it alone. Will you go with me?"

He leaned his head back and scrubbed his hand down his face. "Come on, Joey. You know me better than that."

"For goodness' sake, it's just a party, Ryder. We don't even have to dance. I just need Roni to know I'm there, wish the bride and groom well, and we can leave. Don't make me do this by myself. Please."

He got up and paced the room. "You've gotta know someone else who can do this with you. What about Peter? I bet he'd love to go. I can stay with my mom."

"Forget I even asked," she said and snuck off to her bedroom, mortified that she'd resorted to begging.

She kicked off her boots and sat on the edge of the bed. It was too early to go to sleep. *Note to self: Get my own TV.*

She stared up at the fading wallpaper. It was beyond time to get rid of it. She found a seam in the center of the wall where a corner of the paper had curled up. Tearing at it, she peeled back a large swath. For the next twenty minutes, she became immersed in ripping the paper off piece by piece. She stood back to appraise her handiwork. It was like a patchwork quilt with strips of stubborn paper still clinging to parts of the wall. The blank spaces were covered in glue that had yellowed over time. She'd need a scraper and soapy water for the rest. Even steam. Then she had three more walls to go.

But the peeling and stripping was cathartic. She supposed part of the pleasure was seeing instant results. Life rarely gave you that kind of immediate reward. In rehab it had taken weeks, even months, before she could go a few hours without thinking about getting high. It had taken her two years to see that she could have her life back, even if it was a different life than the one she'd had with Ethan.

She was about to start on the next wall when there was a tap on the door.

"Come in." She quickly glanced at her medical alert pager to make sure she hadn't missed a call for help from Shiv.

Ryder stood in the doorway, one shoulder propped against the jamb. His pale blue eyes looked sadder than she'd ever seen them. "I would if I could, but I can't. I just can't."

"I understand." And she did. Before, she had reacted to his rejection. Now she could see that it wasn't so much rejection as it was the fact that the wedding would be a trigger for him.

He came into the room and assessed the wall. "You've been busy."

"I was bored."

He hitched his brows as if to say, *I know how to fix that.*

No more.

Their sex rendezvous had to stop for more reasons than Joey could count, starting with the fact that it wasn't healthy for either of them. They both had lives to fix, and while recreational sex was a nice distraction, it wasn't getting the job done. Never mind the fact that it was completely unprofessional.

"Hang on a sec." He disappeared down the hallway, only to return a short time later with two spackling knives. "This might work."

He began scraping the rest of the wallpaper.

"I'll get something hot to loosen the glue." She went to the kitchen and filled a pot with sudsy water, adding a spot of laundry softener.

For a while they worked in companionable silence, pushing her bed to the other side of the room so they could begin scraping and peeling a second wall.

"It's making a mess of the new wooden floors." She stared down at the heaps of paper that had fallen to the ground.

"I've got a couple of old moving blankets in the shed we can use for a dropcloth." Ryder went outside to get them while Joey got a trash bag to throw away the scraps.

They were making good headway with the second wall when Joey remembered what she had learned in town that morning. "I heard a rumor that the Addisons may be selling their motel."

He jerked his head up. "Really? How reliable is the rumor?"

"I heard it from the woman who owns the *Nugget Tribune*. She hasn't been able to confirm it yet. I don't know who her source is, but I thought it was worth passing on. I did promise not to tell anyone, so please keep the information to yourself. I just hoped it would come in handy in case it turns out to be true, especially given your hassles with them."

"I wonder if that's why they've been messing with me. They don't want my trucks to screw up a potential deal."

"That was my initial thought. But the rap on them is that they enjoy getting into tussles with the townsfolk. So, who knows?"

"Dana, my real estate agent, might know if they've listed it. Would you mind if I asked her? I don't have to say where I got the information from."

Joey chewed on her bottom lip. "I promised Harlee I wouldn't say anything. Is there a way you can ask Dana without alluding to the rumor? You know, like just say you have a friend who's interested in buying a hotel in Nugget if she knows of any for sale."

He snorted. "Yeah, that sounds plausible. I just happen to have a friend who's clamoring to get himself a hotel in a town so off the grid you can't even find it on a map. I'll just ask her why she thinks the Addisons are giving me such a hard time. If she knows something, she'll tell me."

"That works." Joey tore a long piece of wallpaper off the wall.

"Thanks for the tip. I think your friend might be on to something."

"If she is, hopefully the new owners won't be such turds."

Ryder laughed. "No one is going to buy that dump. Unfortunately, I'll be stuck with the Addisons till the cows come home."

Joey thought he was probably right. She'd driven by the motor lodge many times, and while she wouldn't call it a dump, it didn't have the greatest curb appeal. Chainsaw bears of every size and color had taken over the front yard. And the exterior of the little cabin-style rooms could use a face-lift. Besides the chipping paint, they looked ratty and tired. She could only imagine what was going on in the inside.

The place had potential, though, and could be quite cute with some TLC. And its only competition was the Lumber Baron, which Joey assumed was much pricier than a motel.

"You missed a spot." Ryder used his knife to peel away a big piece of paper. It had sort of become a contest. Who could get the largest strip with one pull?

"What do you think your mom thought of Cascade Village?" Joey had her own thoughts on the matter but was curious what Ryder's take had been of the visit. He knew Shiv best, after all.

"Yeah, she liked it. There really wasn't a whole lot not to like. Whether she wants to live there is the real question. I don't think so. But she sure put on a good act."

"For you, right? She thinks she's a burden, doesn't she?"

"I don't know why. She can live here the rest of her life as far as I'm concerned."

Joey's heart melted. For all his baggage, he was a good man.

"I just thought she'd want a community, a group of women she could hang out with, go to the movies, shopping. She can't really have that here. And half the time I'm traveling."

"No, she needs her own place. What was wrong with where she was living before?"

"For one thing, it's four hours away. I don't want her that far. For another, her health. After what she went through, I want to know she's got assistance. Twenty-four-hour care, if need be. Cascade Village was the closest setup like that and by far the nicest. What I liked about it was she could live independently but still have a professional healthcare staff looking after her."

"It is pretty perfect except for the not-so-small matter that I don't think she's too thrilled about it, even if she says she is. Let me ask you something. What was her deal with the judge she worked with?"

"Judge Lester? What do you mean?"

"I happened to see a letter he sent her. It was out in clear view, so I wasn't snooping. I don't know, I sort of got the impression there might be something there."

"Something there? Like romantic?" Ryder glowered.

"What?"

"He was her boss. Good guy. Treated her great. Threw her a big party at his fancy country club when she retired. But definitely not her boyfriend. The truth is, I don't think she ever got over Tanner."

"Your father?"

"More like my sperm donor. But yeah." He sponged the wall with water that had long ago turned cold. "What did you think you saw?"

"It wasn't anything concrete. Just a tone."

"A tone? What the hell does that mean?"

"We need more hot water." She nudged her head at the wall where he was chipping away at the paper one tiny piece at a time.

"I'll get it. First explain."

"It's nothing I can really put my finger on, just a woman's intuition."

He put down his scraper and folded his arms over his chest. "Basically, you let your imagination run away with you."

"No." She huffed. "I picked up a vibe."

He shook his head, grabbed the kettle, and headed to the kitchen.

"Maybe boil some water," she called to him. "Steam may work better."

The second wall was turning out to be harder than the first. The plaster was in pretty bad condition, and the room was a mess. Attempting to rid the bedroom of the hideous wallpaper might've been a mistake, Joey thought as she waited for Ryder to return with hot water.

"What about the steamer from an iron?" Ryder placed the pot of hot water in the center of the room.

"That could work. Let's see how this goes first. So, maybe I was wrong about the letter. But until proven otherwise, I'm sticking with my gut."

"Why don't you just ask her?"

"Why don't you? You're her son, after all."

Ryder held his hands up in the air. "I'm not getting involved in my mother's lov— Personal business."

Joey let out a laugh. "You can't even say it, can you?"

He pretended to shudder. "Nope. And stop reading other people's mail."

They went back to scraping, letting wet pieces of wallpaper fall on the old blankets Ryder had spread on the floor. Every so often, Joey scooped up the remnants and threw them in a big plastic trash bag.

"Somehow I don't think this is how you planned to spend your evening," Joey said.

"Not even a little." Yet he seemed as determined as she was to finish the job. "What are you thinking for the walls?"

"I don't know, maybe a soft gray. Something neutral." For whoever got the room next.

"You don't strike me as a neutral type."

"What's that supposed to mean?"

He stopped and held her gaze. "It means I equate neutral with plain Jane. And you're no plain Jane."

"Is that a compliment?" She thought it was, but with Ryder you could never tell.

He moved closer and lifted her chin with his finger. "Not a compliment, just a fact. You've got to know how beautiful you are. How sexy."

Her throat clogged. It had been a long time since anyone had said those things to her. Worse, it had been a long time since she'd felt worthy of the words. She backed away, afraid that he'd see her vulnerability. See the desire shining in her eyes.

"Yet you won't be seen with me at a wedding," she joked.

"What made you decide to go, anyway?"

It was a good question, one she hadn't altogether thought through, but she knew it was the right thing to do. "A lot of stuff happened between Ethan and me, most of it my fault. I kind of count it as a miracle that he's still my friend. The wedding is a big day for him. The start of a new life with the woman he loves. He asked me to be part of it, and it seems to me that I would be doing him a great dishonor if I turned my back on something so generous."

Ryder cocked a hip against the dresser and gave her a long, appraising look. "I was going to call bullshit, but I think you're actually telling the truth. Good for you. Damn evolved if you ask me. I'd say the good doc is a lucky man to have a friend like you."

The words touched her more than he could know. The trick was getting through the wedding without breaking down. Although everything she'd told Ryder was genuine, seeing Ethan move on while she continued to stagnate…well, she'd be lying if she said it wasn't going to hurt. The worst part was Roni. Ethan was giving their daughter a new brother and stepmother under one very luxurious roof. Joey couldn't even provide her daughter with a bedroom.

Ryder scanned the room, checking out their progress. Two walls down, two to go. "What do you say we call it a night and start fresh in the morning?"

"Good idea." Peeling half-century-old wallpaper was hard work. Her hands hurt.

She started to push the bed to its old spot. Currently, they had to climb over it to get out of the room.

"Leave it," Ryder said, taking a slow visual stroll down Joey's body. "Come back to the camper with me." His meaning was clear.

The temptation to spend the night in his arms—in his bed—overwhelmed her. But as tempted as she was, she shook her head no.

Ryder blinked, like he couldn't believe someone was actually turning him down. "Why not?"

She looked at him. Really looked, seeing the man he was, the man he could be, knowing that another night with him wouldn't change a goddamn thing. She summoned all her strength and, with as much conviction as she could muster, said, "I'm through with broken."

Chapter 19

The week passed quickly. On Monday, Joey finished removing the rest of the wallpaper herself and had the entire room painted by Wednesday. She'd gone with a pretty pale periwinkle that picked up the color of her eyes. An article she'd once read said you should paint your walls in a color that would cast a flattering glow on your skin tone. Ryder hadn't said no, so why the heck not.

Shiv loved it. They were tackling her room as soon as Shiv got home with Ryder from her therapy session. He'd volunteered to take her to give Joey a few hours with Roni on her last day of school and a pre-birthday celebration. Roni would be in Hawaii on her actual birthday.

June had snuck up on her. But Joey aimed to make up for the milestones in her daughter's life that she had missed. She'd brought homemade cupcakes to share with Roni's class and sat with the other mothers and fathers as the teacher called out each student, handing them a brightly colored diploma someone had made on a computer. It was so cute that Joey had taken a dozen pictures.

Afterward, they'd gone to Farm Supply to get a few things for Roni's Hawaii trip and an early birthday gift. Brynn might have gotten Roni the expensive pink cowboy boots, but Joey planned to make sure it was she who dressed her daughter for summer. Call it a point of pride.

By the time she'd dropped Roni off, the Circle D Ranch was buzzing with workers. Big white tents, outdoor heaters, round tables, and wooden folding chairs were scattered across the lawn. Two-bathroom trailers— one for men, the other for women—had been set up and were the fanciest Porta Potties Joey had ever seen. Real toilets, pedestal sinks, and finger towels embroidered with the bride and groom's monograms. Not Ethan's idea, that was for sure.

Unable to help herself, she snooped a little. Okay, a lot. Both Ethan and Brynn were too tied up with caterers and wedding planners to notice. Roni had wanted her to see her junior bridesmaid's dress—it was lovely how Brynn had included her—but the last thing Ethan needed was another person traipsing through the house.

"It'll be a great big surprise tomorrow," she'd told Roni. "I can't wait."

She'd left, dreading the day, only to drag herself back the following afternoon. If the weather was a predictor of Ethan and Brynn's marriage, it would be sunny, warm, and perfect.

Joey had come by herself, wearing a simple blue sheath dress, wedge heels, and a lightweight sweater. But the second she was escorted to her chair, she regretted her decision. Not the dress, which rode the line between not quite dressy enough and completely appropriate for a first wife, hoping to not call attention to herself during her ex-husband's second wedding.

No, the mistake was in not inviting Peter to be her plus-one. Despite her understated attire, she felt as if she stuck out like a two-headed baby. Having Peter by her side...well, safety in numbers. Plus, he was so gregarious and likeable that it would've taken the onus off her. As it was, people probably thought she was a barracuda, here to stick her sharp teeth into Ethan and ruin the party.

She scanned the crowd—there were at least two hundred people spread across Ethan's backyard—and landed on Harlee and Darla, who were sitting with what she assumed were their husbands a good ten rows down on the bride's side. *Can't go there.*

She focused instead on the white wooden arbor, adorned with enough roses to open a nursery, where Ethan and Brynn would say their vows. A tall, slender woman in a dress too elegant for a working cattle ranch stood to the side, having a conversation with someone in a black suit and headset, probably the wedding planner. Based on the slender woman's age and the family resemblance, she had to be Brynn's mother.

Joey thought of her own mother and the scratchy peach lace dress she'd gotten at Kohl's and had worn to both Jay and Joey's weddings. Joey was suddenly glad that her parents hadn't been invited.

Alma and Ethan's siblings, along with their families, were ushered to the front row. Thank goodness they hadn't spotted Joey. Ethan's sister, Mary, had never been Joey's fan. Even when things had been good between her and Ethan, Mary had been distant. It was as if Mary didn't view Joey as good enough for her brother. Looking back on it, Joey had always walked on eggshells around the entire family.

Well, she didn't have to anymore. It was both liberating and sad. There was a part of her that felt as if she had something to prove to them, especially after they'd pushed for Ethan to get full custody of Roni during the divorce. In the short term, it had been the right decision. The best thing for Roni. But it still hurt that they had openly encouraged Ethan to take her daughter away from her.

Again, Peter came to mind. This all would've been easier with a partner. She checked her watch. Five minutes to showtime if the ceremony started on time. The orchestra had begun to play. Joey didn't know anything about classical music. She listened to country. But the piece they were playing reminded her of spring. For some reason, it conjured flowers blooming while the earth woke up from a long winter's nap. It was nice. And classy.

A few doctor colleagues of Ethan's squeezed into her row. She kept her head bowed, hoping they didn't recognize her. Though her transgressions had been a private personnel matter, hospital workers were notorious for gossiping. Everyone from the cleaning crew to the chief resident knew what she had done, she was sure of it.

She busied herself by setting up her phone camera to take pictures when Roni walked down the aisle. Someone from the orchestra announced that everyone should take their seats, then the music shifted into a rousing piece that suggested things were about to start up. That's when Joey noticed that Ethan was now standing underneath the arbor, looking dashing in a dark suit.

There were murmurs from the back seats. Joey turned around to see her daughter, dressed in a pale-pink chiffon dress with a crown of baby's breath in her hair, coming down the aisle with Henry. A sob caught in Joey's throat, and her heart came out of her chest. Roni looked so grown-up. So beautiful.

She wished she'd chosen a seat at the end of the row, so she could get close-ups of Roni. As her daughter made her way toward the arbor, Joey leaned over the person sitting two chairs over to capture a photo. The guest, whose big hat hid her face, shot Joey a dirty look and an admonishment that Ethan and Brynn had hired a professional wedding photographer.

Since when was it a crime to take pictures at a wedding?

Joey took a closer look and instantly recognized Ethan's former partner's wife. Renee knew exactly who Joey was. She and her husband had attended numerous dinners and parties with Joey and Ethan. Renee also knew about the stolen scripts. When Ethan had faced the disciplinary board over what

Joey had done, it had been his partner who'd gone to bat for him. Renee was being intentionally nasty.

Instead of making a scene, Joey put her phone away. When Roni got closer, Joey waved. But Roni was staring adoringly at her father and didn't see Joey. Renee looked positively victorious. Joey wouldn't let Renee rile her. She was here because Ethan had asked her to come for the sake of their daughter. When it was over, she could check the box and move on, knowing she'd done the right thing for Ethan, Brynn, and especially Roni.

The music changed to something Joey recognized. It wasn't the "Wedding March," but a piece she'd heard played at other weddings. More hushed voices came from the rows behind Joey, and soon everyone was standing. Brynn came down the aisle on the arm of her father in the most beautiful gown Joey had ever seen. Like Roni's, it was a pale pink. It clung to Brynn like a second skin and had a low-cut cowl neck that reminded Joey of the maid-of-honor dress Kate Middleton's sister wore to the royal wedding.

It was so breathtaking that some of the guests audibly gasped as Brynn made her way toward Ethan. Joey had never seen her ex-husband look at her the way he was looking at Brynn. His face glowed with pure adoration.

"God, she's beautiful," Renee murmured under her breath just loud enough for Joey to hear.

"Finally, the right woman for Ethan. Someone who can raise that sweet little girl."

The words hit Joey like a sucker punch. Her face burned like it was on fire. Never had she wanted more to run away, to be anywhere, even the depths of hell, than to be here.

An arm caught her around the waist, and she jumped.

"It's just me."

She turned away from the bride to find Ryder standing next to her. "When...where?"

"Just got here." He pointed his Stetson, which he held in his hand, at the outside aisle. "And not a minute too soon." He glowered at Renee.

He'd heard, which should've mortified her. Instead, she'd never been happier to see him. "You said you couldn't—"

"Shush." He put his finger to his lips and nudged his head at the altar, where the officiant had started speaking. His arm never left her waist.

She leaned into him, pretending to listen to Ethan and Brynn's marriage vows while she inhaled his scent. She swatted at her eyes, which had begun to leak.

When he held her gaze, she whispered, "Thank you. I know how hard this is for you."

He shrugged and wiped away one of her stray tears with his thumb. Using his strength to hold her up, the ceremony went by in a blur. The orchestra started up, and the recessional began. Ethan and Brynn led, beaming and holding hands. Brynn's best friend and Ethan's brother came up the aisle next. And then there was Roni and Henry.

Just the sight of her little girl spread warmth through Joey's chest.

Ryder squeezed past her, reached across Renee into the aisle, and gave Roni, who lit up at the sight of him, a high five. "Your mama wants a picture." He nudged his head at Joey.

"Mommy!" Roni rushed down their row of seats into Joey's arms. Henry followed Roni and gave Joey a big hug.

Renee stared daggers at them. Ryder stared right back. Of the two, he was more intimidating, and Renee kept her mouth shut.

"You guys look amazing." Joey crouched down so she was eye level with Veronica. "Look at your beautiful dress. Let me get a picture of the two of you."

Ryder maneuvered the four of them out of the way so Joey could shoot a few photos with her phone. She got a couple of Roni and Henry together. Then snapped some of Roni, standing by a big blue oak tree a few yards away from the arbor. Little by little, folks were migrating to the white tents for cocktails before the reception started.

Midway through Joey's impromptu photo session, Ethan came looking for the kids. "Hey, guys, we've got pictures. The photographer is waiting."

"Sorry." Joey hoped Ethan wasn't angry.

He bobbed his head in acknowledgment, rounded up the kids, and herded them up the hill.

"Was that rude?" she asked Ryder.

"Him or you?" He stared after Ethan's back.

"Me. Maybe I should've waited to get pictures."

"It took all of five minutes, Joey. Hardly a capital offense. What was rude was him insisting you come to his goddamn wedding, and then when you do, he gives you the cold shoulder."

"He's just harried. This"—Joey waved her hand at the opulent setup— "isn't his thing. There must be more than two hundred people here, not counting the staff."

"I don't care what his thing is. That right there was bullshit." Ryder put his hand at the small of her back. "Let's get a drink."

"I don't drink, remember?"

"Yeah, but I do."

He guided her to the bar, his gait stiff. She felt annoyance coming off him in waves.

"We don't have to stay." She took his hand and tugged on it. "Roni knows I was here, and Ethan saw me. I honored my commitment."

"No, we're staying."

She didn't get why he was being so insistent, but they were too close to other guests for her to argue. He got a Jack and Coke and her a cola. They wandered over to a table to retrieve their seating assignment, which seemed too formal for a country wedding. But what did Joey know? The guests at her wedding had been seated on bales of straw at a row of folding banquet tables that had been pushed together. Jay's wedding had been more upscale, held at his wife's family's country club. Still, the guests had sat wherever they'd wanted.

If any of Ethan's colleagues from the hospital were seated at their table, she didn't care what Ryder said. They were leaving. Their table was in a far corner, far away from the dance floor. She discreetly scanned the name tags the other guests had left next to their wineglasses before going off to mingle. There wasn't one name she recognized.

Why should she be surprised? Brynn was too sophisticated to commit the social faux pas of sticking Joey next to anyone who'd been part of her and Ethan's past. While relieved, she wished they'd been seated at the same table as Harlee, Darla, and Annie.

"You want to sit or circulate?" Ryder glanced around the tent where pockets of people stood in groups, gabbing and munching on passed hors d'oeuvres.

"I don't know a lot of people." The truth was, she wanted to get through this as quickly as possible.

"Come on, I'll introduce you around." He took her hand and slipped through the crowd toward a circle of men in cowboy hats.

"Ryder." One of the guys waved them over.

"That's my friend, Lucky, and his wife, Tawny," He spoke into her ear, so she could hear him over the din of the gathering. "You'll like them."

He made the introductions. She recognized Flynn from the time he came to the house, and she met his wife, Gia. A third couple, Clay and Emily McCreedy, joined them a few minutes later.

"How do you know Ethan and Brynn?" Emily asked.

"Uh, I'm Ethan's ex-wife." Emily didn't seem remotely phased by the acknowledgment. Still, Joey quickly added, "We thought it would be good for our daughter if I attended."

"She looked so beautiful in her little dress."

"Thank you," Joey said, even though she'd had nothing to do with Roni's dress. Brynn had chosen it.

"Well, look who the cat dragged in." Donna Thurston, the owner of the Bun Boy, did a hip bump with Emily. "I don't think we've had a wedding like this since yours."

"Mine wasn't nearly this lavish," Emily said.

"I bet your food was better."

Donna, whom Joey only knew from seeing her behind the counter of the Bun Boy, turned to her. "You're the first wife, aren't you?"

"Guilty as charged." Joey started to give the same spiel she'd given Emily but stopped herself. She didn't owe anyone an explanation.

"I guess that's the way folks do it now. One big, happy family. It's crazy if you ask me, but you didn't." She laughed. Joey wasn't sure what to make of the woman. "I'm Donna. I've seen you at the Bun Boy with Roni and hear you're taking care of Ryder's mom."

"I'm just helping out," Joey said, wanting to protect Shiv's privacy.

"It's got to be tough having that guy underfoot." Donna looked over at Ryder, who was deep in conversation with Flynn, and fanned herself.

Donna didn't know the half of it. "We manage to not trip over each other."

"It's got to be nice for Roni to have her mom so close. What is it, four miles from the old Montgomery place to the Circle D?"

"Three and half," Joey said and felt herself flooded with gratitude for no other reason than someone besides herself recognized the importance she played in Roni's life.

Soon their group grew to include Maddy from the Lumber Baron and her husband, Rhys, Nugget's police chief. For the first time since she'd arrived, Joey didn't feel like a wedding crasher. Everyone was so kind and respectful.

The band leader announced that dinner would soon be served, their cue to be seated. As they made their way to their table, the bride and groom entered the party to thunderous applause. Joey stopped and watched as well-wishers exchanged hugs and handshakes with the couple. Ethan wore an ear-to-ear smile. The only time Joey could remember seeing him that happy was when Veronica was born.

Ryder saw her watching, and something moved across his face. Anger maybe. Before she could ask him about it, they'd arrived at their table, where eight other couples were being served their salads.

"Just in the nick of time," Ryder said as he slid into his chair.

Everyone went around the table introducing themselves and sharing how they knew the bride or groom. It quickly became clear to Joey that these were the "Z" list guests. That Joey had been seated at the "Z" list table. She told herself to stop being petty. This wasn't a social event. This was an obligation that, by the grace of God, would be over soon.

"You know a lot of people in Nugget," she told Ryder between bites of the freshest salad she'd ever eaten.

"Not really. Lucky and I used to follow the circuit together. He hooked me up with Barlow. I know Rhys through Maddy from my days staying at the Lumber Baron. Today was only the second time I'd met McCreedy, which could turn out to be good for business. He runs one of the largest herds in Northern California."

"I hope for your sake it does. I can't begin to tell you how much you showing up when you did meant…means…to me."

"Who was the woman in the hat?"

"The wife of Ethan's former partner. Believe it or not, she used to claim me as a friend. That was before I caused Ethan to nearly lose his license… before I went running around in the middle of the night with my small child, getting us carjacked at gunpoint."

"She still shouldn't have spoken to you like that."

Joey stared down at her sensible wedge heels.

"Hey." He gently clasped her chin and turned her face up until they were staring into each other's eyes. "Don't do that. You're not that woman anymore. You're a great mother, a great caregiver, and a good person."

Her eyes watered. "So are you, Ryder."

It was at that moment that Ethan approached their table. He greeted the other guests, whom Joey was pretty sure he'd never seen before this day, then pulled an empty chair up to hers. "Sorry about earlier. I meant to say hi, but things were more chaotic than the OR, if you can believe that."

She smiled. "No worries. I probably should've waited on the photos."

"Nah, it was fine. I know Roni loved seeing you here."

"It's a beautiful wedding."

"It's all Brynn." He let out a sigh. "You know me, not really my scene. But if it makes her happy…" His gooey smile made Joey throw up a little in her mouth. She stole a sideways glance at Ryder, whose fists were clenched at his side.

"You remember Ryder Knight?" Joey said.

"Of course. Good to see you again. Glad you could come."

Ryder returned a curt nod.

Roni came bounding toward them, shouting, "Mommy," and then climbed into Ryder's lap.

Joey didn't know who was more surprised, Ryder or Ethan.

Roni clasped both of Ryder's cheeks between her hands. "Where's Mrs. Knight and Peter?"

"At home, kiddo. You were the best flower girl I've ever seen."

"I'm too old to be a flower girl. I was a junior bridesmaid."

Ryder tossed his hands in the air. "Forgive a cowboy for not knowing that kind of stuff."

"You're forgiven." She scooted off his lap. "Fix my flowers, Mommy." Her crown was askew. Joey readjusted the bobby pins to right it. "I'll be back later." Roni ran off to talk to Cody, the nice boy Ethan had hired to muck stalls.

She and Ethan exchanged smiles.

"She's something else," he said.

"She is that."

For a second, it was like the old days, when she and Ethan had been a family, besotted with the little creature they had made.

"Well, I'd better make the rounds." Ethan got to his feet. "I've been ordered to mingle. Nice seeing you again, Ryder. And, Joey, thanks for coming. It really means a lot to Brynn and me."

As he walked away, Joey heard Ryder exhale and mutter something unflattering under his breath.

"What?" she asked him.

"He's an asshole, and you're still in love with him, aren't you?"

She quickly glanced around the table to find that everyone was too caught up in their own conversations to hear theirs. "You're wrong. I love him like I love a member of my family, but I'm not in love with him. And why are you calling him an asshole?"

"Because you don't do that to a person. You don't guilt your ex, someone who was…is recovering…into coming to your goddamn wedding and force them to watch your new happy life unfold. It's fucked up, not to mention cruel."

She reached up and stroked his face. "Do you see my life as so unhappy?"

"I see you as still in love with the guy."

"You're wrong, Ryder. But it would probably be better than being in love with a man who is so stuck in the past that he can't look toward the future." Her eyes clouded, and she got to her feet. "Excuse me, I have to use the restroom."

She made her way to the fancy bathroom trailer, wondering what had come over her to say such a thing. Was she in love with Ryder Knight? If she was, she needed to get her head examined. Her mind wandered to that very first kiss in front of the Ponderosa more than a year ago. She'd been drawn to Ryder even then. She let out a mirthless laugh. Clearly, the universe wasn't done testing her.

When she came out of the bathroom, he was waiting for her. "Did you think I was really headed to the bar?"

"I don't know, were you?"

She rolled her eyes.

"You made your appearance, we ate that salad with the shit they call lettuce, we can go now."

That's what she got for dropping her bomb. "I want to say good-bye to Roni first. I'll meet you at home."

He tipped his hat, and she watched him cross the lawn to his truck in the makeshift parking lot.

Cut and run. It was Ryder's MO.

Chapter 20

On Monday, Ryder went to Dana's real estate office, figuring it was easier to fish for information in person than it was over the phone. He'd managed to lie low for most of the weekend.

Joey's comment about being in love with a man who was stuck in the past had thrown him. Ryder didn't care to delve too deeply, so he'd dodged the whole conversation completely by hiding out in his camper. Luckily, he had a short-distance haul set up for Wednesday and wouldn't return until late Thursday. By then, he hoped things between them could return to normal. Whatever normal was.

Dana was at her desk when he walked in, but she stood and gave him a big hug. He noticed that folks in Nugget were huggers. She had the air-conditioner going, and the cool blast was a nice respite from the June heat. The office was small, just two desks, a conference room, and a reception area. But everything was new. He'd heard somewhere that the agency had burned down in a fire and Dana and her partner had had to rebuild.

"To what do I owe the pleasure? Interested in more real estate?" Dana looked hopeful.

"Nah, I came to pick your brain over this whole Addison deal."

Her face fell. "Oh gosh, are they still bothering you?"

He took the chair in front of her desk. "As predicted, they've threatened to turn me in to the county over my tractor trucks and trailers."

"I'm sorry, Ryder. This is the last thing you need after buying a new place and having your mom to think about. But they don't have a leg to stand on."

That wasn't exactly what Flynn had said. But he was a lawyer and in Ryder's limited experience, attorneys tended to air on the side of ultimate caution. "What do you think their motivation is?"

"Besides being jerks? I don't know. I would guess that the vast majority of their guests come off the highway, not Bear Creek Road. So, they can't argue that your trucks are creating an eyesore that's hurting their business. But they're just that prickly."

"Is there a chance they're looking to expand, maybe have an entrance on Bear Creek Road that would require some of their customers to drive by my place?"

"I don't know. You could check the county for permits. They'd have to get one if they planned to build anything."

Ryder put his hat on the top of Dana's desk and scratched his head. "Any chance they're getting ready to sell and want to mitigate anything that might lower their property value?"

"If they do, they sure haven't approached me. I would've told you, Ryder."

"You think that's even plausible, given that you're the only game in town?"

"It could be. Unless it's a working farm or ranch, I don't typically handle commercial real estate. Once or twice, I've been the listing agent for small, family-owned B and Bs, but never a hotel or motel. If the Addisons were selling, they'd list with someone who specializes in that kind of property. Honestly, I wouldn't even know where to begin. Still, I think it's a long shot. The Addisons have been here forever, and the Beary Quaint is their pride and joy, such as it is." She scrunched up her nose. "But you know who would know? Nate Breyer, Maddy's brother. He's a hotelier, and my guess is, if he doesn't study what's out there, he'd know where to find it in less than a second. You want me to call him?"

He'd promised Joey not to blow her source. At the same time, it sure would be great to put the rumor to rest once and for all. "I don't know. Folks around here sure love to gossip, and I wouldn't want to start a rumor."

"I could just tell him I have an old client who's looking to buy an operating B and B or motel in the area, not even mention the Beary Quaint, and ask him where to look."

"If you wouldn't mind, that would work."

"I'll do it right now." She went over to a mini fridge in the corner. "Would you like something to drink?"

"I'm good," he said, anxious to get this over with. Ryder wasn't sure what would be more beneficial to him. A sale, which would get the Addisons out of his hair? He suspected that if they stayed, they'd be a perpetual problem. Or new owners, who might be up his ass even more.

She brought a bottle of water back to the desk and popped the cap. To Ryder, she looked even rounder than she had before. He gauged that her due date was right around the corner.

"Let me just find his number." She scrolled through a list of contacts on her computer. "Have you met Nate yet?" When he shook his head, she said, "He and his wife, Sam, are two of the nicest people. They commute back and forth from here to San Francisco, where their hotel offices are. Here he is."

Ryder waited while she dialed the phone, worried that Dana would somehow slip up and give away his suspicion about the Beary Quaint going on the market. Then he'd be guilty of breaking his promise to Joey.

"Hey, Nate." Dana nodded her head at Ryder. "This is Dana. I was hoping you could help me out. I have a client who is interested in buying and operating a lodge in the Sierra, preferably around here." She paused, then laughed at something Nate said. "Nothing could ever compete with the Lumber Baron, Nate. I think they're looking for something much more modest. Do you have any idea where I could find motel or B and B listings?"

She put her finger to her lips and turned the phone on speaker.

"With Airbnb and VRBO, bed-and-breakfasts are a hard sell these days. But far be it from me to advise your clients otherwise." Nate chuckled. "I don't know of anything off the top of my head, but you can check a few websites." He rattled off several names, which Dana wrote down. "Is this anyone I know?"

"No, I don't think so." Dana looked at Ryder and worried her bottom lip. He felt like a jerk asking her to lie. "Honestly, I don't know how serious they are. I think right now it's more of a little retirement fantasy. But I wanted to at least sound somewhat knowledgeable."

"Sure. Let me know what you find out. If there's anything good out there, I might be interested."

"I'll give you first dibs, Nate. That was some wedding on Saturday. Samantha did a great job."

"She always does. It was great seeing you and Aidan."

"You, too. Take care, Nate. And thanks for the info." She hung up and turned the notepad toward Ryder. "Should we take a look?"

"Sure." He moved his chair around to her side of the desk where he had a better view of the monitor.

She went to the first site on her list, and together they scanned the listings. There was a B and B in Glory Junction and a motor lodge off Highway 80 on the way to Tahoe, but nothing in Nugget.

They moved along to the next site, which had more listings than the first and appeared to specialize in country lodges for sale.

"This looks promising," Ryder said.

Wow, from the looks of things, Nate was right. People must really want out of the bed-and-breakfast business. There were at least a dozen Victorian inns on the market, another dozen roadside motels, and even one historical hotel in downtown Napa. But not one in Nugget.

Dana plugged in the third site, which showcased a smattering of coastal properties with names like the Crusty Crab, the Beach Bum, and the Riptide. They looked more like crack houses than any place he'd want to stay. And he'd stayed in some shitholes over the years.

"Nope." She closed out of that one and went to the fourth site.

He recognized a motel he frequently stayed at on his route to Wyoming, called the Wagon Wheel. It was off the 80, outside of Elko, Nevada. It was clean, and the service was friendly. Who knew it was for sale?

He skimmed down the listings, checking out the pictures for anything that resembled the Beary Quaint. Nothing.

"Take a look at this." Dana highlighted a pictureless ad for a "Unique opportunity to live at and own one of the most beautiful places on earth."

Well, that couldn't be it.

"Check out the location." Dana hovered her cursor over the bottom of the ad, where instead of listing an address, it simply said, "Located in a small railroad town in California's Sierra Nevada mountains. Call for more information."

"What do you think?" A lot of places fit that bill in Northern California.

"One way to find out." Dana picked up the phone and dialed the number on the listing. "Hi, I'm Dana McBride, a real estate agent representing a couple who are interested in buying an operating motel in the Sierra. I saw your listing and was wondering if you could tell me more." She put the phone on speaker again.

"It's a darling twenty-room motor lodge," said the other agent. "The owners are willing to share their financial records from the last three years with serious buyers and might be convinced to carry. Are your clients preapproved?"

"Uh, yes, they are. Where exactly is it, and are there pictures?"

The agent cleared her throat. "Absolutely. I can email them to you. It's off Highway 70 in a little town about an hour away from Tahoe." Dana's mouth fell open.

Ryder wrote, "Which town?" on the scratch pad Dana had used to write down the websites and pushed it under her nose.

"What's the town's name? My clients were hoping for something near Glory Junction."

"You're in luck because it's less than thirty minutes away. Are you familiar with the town of Nugget?"

"I am," Dana said and mouthed to Ryder, *"Oh my God."* "I'd love to see those photos. Could you also send the price? I'd like to send as much information to my clients as soon as possible."

"Would you like to set up a showing? I'm based out of San Francisco but would like to be there," the agent said.

Kind of pushy, Ryder thought.

"They're out of state," Dana replied. "But for the right place, they'll fly out. Let me get that price and photos to them first."

"On it."

Dana signed off. "I'm stunned. It has to be the Beary Quaint, don't you think?"

"Check to see if she sent the pictures." He had no idea how this was going to affect him, but if it was the Beary Quaint, it solved the mystery of why the Addisons were so intent on harassing him.

"Not yet," Dana said. "Let's give it a few minutes."

Ryder checked the time. He had a phone conference with three of his drivers in forty minutes. But damn, he wanted confirmation.

"The Addisons sure went to a lot of trouble to keep their sale secret." Dana took another sip from her water bottle. "Seems sort of counterintuitive. With real estate, especially something as unique as a motor lodge, you usually want to spread the word. But they've always been kind of sneaky."

"Maybe they're worried people will be reluctant to book for the summer if they know the place is on the market. If I was the new owner, I'd take a little time to fix the place up." And fumigate.

Dana was on the same page because she laughed. "Nate is going to die when he hears the news. He and the Addisons hate each other."

"Who do you think would buy a place like that?" The new owners might not be any better than the Addisons. *What was that saying about the devil you knew?*

"I'm hoping Nate. And I'm hoping he uses me as his agent."

Ryder suspected that kind of sale would bring in a tidy commission. Even a dump like the Beary Quaint cost coin. What did they say in real estate? Location, location, location. Commercial property off a state highway on the way to ski resorts was nothing to sneeze at.

"It's in," Dana squealed and clicked on an email from the Maven Group. "Take a look."

Ryder scooted his chair closer as Dana opened the first photo, which showed the Beary Quaint's neon sign of a bear sleeping in a sleigh bed. "Holy sh—"

"That's it." Dana enlarged the picture. "It's the Beary Quaint. I can't believe it." She continued to scroll through the pictures, which looked professional and a far cry from what the place actually looked like. "Someone did some staging and some fancy camerawork."

"Yup. What's the price?" he asked out of curiosity.

Dana scrolled down to the bottom of the email. "One point five, which seems outrageous to me."

"Really? I was thinking at least three mil. Shows what I know."

"Honestly, I have no idea what a motel goes for. But Nate would know. Do you mind if I call him?"

After all Dana had done for him, he wanted her to make the sale. And if Nate was anything like his sister, Ryder was certainly down with having him as a neighbor. At the same time, he didn't want to mess up Joey's friendship with Harlee. "Can I make a call first?"

"Sure," Dana said but looked puzzled.

He stepped outside and direct-dialed Joey. "Hey."

"What's up?" she asked, her voice tinged with irritation. Either he'd caught her at a bad time, or she was mad at him for intentionally staying away.

Well, it wasn't as if she'd made an attempt to seek him out. He'd bet she'd been dodging him as much as he had been her.

"You can tell your reporter friend to run with the story," he said. "The Beary Quaint is on the market."

"What? Are you kidding me? Even Harlee thought it was a bad tip. How'd you find out?"

"I talked to Dana. But I promise I didn't give anything away."

"Are you sure? I don't want Harlee to think I'm a loudmouth."

"You're good. Besides, you're about to make her day, so she's got nothing to be mad about."

"Who else knows?" Joey asked.

"For right now, just me and Dana. But Dana wants to tell Maddy's brother. He's partners with her in the Lumber Baron and owns other hotels. She thinks he might be interested."

"Wow. Kind of crazy, huh? I guess this tells us why they were so awful to you."

"I don't know. From what I hear, they're assholes to everyone. But this certainly gives them more motive. Anyway, I wanted to give you a heads-up before Dana calls Maddy's brother. Everything okay over there?"

"Everything's fine. Your mom's doing her exercises with her PT."

"Does she seem...better? Less depressed?"

There was a long pause. "It's not something that just goes away, Ryder. But I think her session with the psychologist was helpful. We can talk about it later." Which was Joey's hint that his mother was close by and could hear every word.

"Hurry up and make your call to Harlee before this thing blows up. Nothing stays secret long around here."

"I'm going to call her right now. And, Ryder, thanks."

"You're welcome." He hung up and stayed outside, trying to gather his thoughts. Not about the Addisons, but about Joey.

"It would probably be better than being in love with a man who is so stuck in the past that he can't look toward the future."

The words kept looping through his head, making him angry. She didn't know what it was like to lose her whole world in one fell swoop. She didn't know the guilt he lived with.

The sun beat down on his head, and he realized that he'd left his hat inside. Besides, Dana was waiting for him to give her the go-ahead with Nate. And he was anxious to see how this deal with the Addisons was going to play out. Getting rid of them would be one less headache if the right buyer took over.

He went inside. "Go ahead and call him. You mind if I sit in?"

"Nope. If it wasn't for you, I never would have thought of looking. Plus, if Nate buys it, you won't have to deal with the Addisons' shenanigans anymore."

While he waited for Dana to get Nate on the phone, he texted Flynn about meeting later. It wouldn't hurt to get him up to speed.

He was cutting it close for his phone conference, but he supposed he could do it from his truck in Dana's parking lot. The crap with the Addisons took precedence. If they continued to try to run his business off his property, he'd be in a world of shit.

"Nate"—Dana motioned to Ryder that she had him on the phone—"I'm putting you on speaker. I've got news."

"You find a motel for your clients?"

"I think I found a motel for you. You're not going to believe this, but the Beary Quaint is on the market."

"No way." There was a pause, and then Nate yelled, "Maddy, come in here. I'm about to blow your mind." Nate had switched his phone to speaker because Ryder could hear Maddy in the background asking Nate what he wanted. "The Beary Quaint is for sale," he told her.

"Oh. My. God."

Dana looked at Ryder, and they both grinned. "Are you guys interested?"

"No. Yes," they both said at the same time.

"What do you mean no?" Maddy was talking to Nate now.

"What would I want with the Bates Motel? The place gives me the creeps. All those freaking bears."

"How much are they asking?" Maddy said.

"One-point-five million."

Nate started laughing. "You've got to be kidding me. What's the cap rate?"

Dana went back to the email from the Maven Group. "Uh, it doesn't say. But I could find out."

"Whatever it is, I can tell you that one-point-five is too much. It'll take that much just to renovate the place. What is it, twenty rooms?"

"Yep," Dana said.

"I can't see them getting more than seventy-five bucks a night."

"Eighty," Maddy chimed in. "But if you added kitchenettes to the rooms, a pool, maybe a game room, you could attract guests who wanted to stay a week or two at a time, and we could get more. It would be like a mini version of Gold Mountain."

"When I bought Gold Mountain, I knew the ski resorts in Glory Junction would carry it," Nate said.

"The Beary Quaint is right next to the Feather River. We could offer whitewater river rafting, inner tubing, kayaking, and fishing expeditions," Maddy argued. "The place does well in the summer, Nate. And that's without the Addisons realizing the motel's full potential."

"'Full potential'?" Nate let out a bark of laughter. "The one and only time I was in that place, they had fuzzy covers on the toilet seats."

It was like a Ping-Pong match between them.

"Just because they're asking one-point-five doesn't mean we can't get the price down," Dana added.

Go, Dana.

"I don't know. Let me think about it," Nate said. "In the meantime, can you find out the cap rate, Dana? If I can't talk any sense into my sister, we'll also want to see the financials."

"Absolutely."

"Let's do this on the QT," Nate said. "There's no love lost between us and the Addisons. I'd almost like to buy the place in absentia just to see the look on their faces when the deal closes and they figure out who bought it. They put us through hell when we bought the Lumber Baron. I'd like to return the favor."

Remind Ryder never to go up against Nate Breyer.

"My lips are sealed." Dana motioned to Ryder that his better be, too.

He nodded, knowing how to keep a secret.

He made it to his truck just in time for his meeting and to home in time for lunch. Joey was on the front porch when he got there.

"Ma resting?" He came up the stairs.

"Yeah, the PT work really knocks her out."

"Anything to eat?"

"There's leftover chicken in the fridge." Ordinarily, she would've fixed it for him. But today she didn't budge from her rocking chair.

"Still pissed at me, huh?" He took the seat next to her.

"Nope." She shook her head. "Just avoiding things that are bad for me."

He couldn't help himself from flashing a wry smile. It was true. He wasn't good for anyone.

"I told Leslie to meet me that night." He paused, letting the words sink in before saying, "Did you know that?" Of course, how could she? But he wanted Joey to understand, he needed her to see why he was incapable of being the man she wanted him to be. "I was at a rodeo in Santa Maria, heading to another one in Texas the next day. I'd been away from home for three weeks, traveling the circuit. I missed her so much that sometimes I'd call twenty times a day just to hear her voice. But the baby was on the way, and we needed the money.

"She wasn't feeling well, a combination of her pregnancy and something she'd eaten. Still, I asked her to get in her car and drive two hours so we could spend the night together after my event and before I had to leave in the morning. I had the best ride of my life that evening, knowing that I'd be seeing her that night. The whole day had been like a high. I'd planned to make her dinner in the fifth wheel, just the two of us. But she never made it."

He stopped, unable to go on. Even after all these years, it was still raw. Still like a knife in his heart. How many times had he asked himself what if he hadn't told her to come? What if she'd just stayed home that night?

He closed his eyes. "She'd still be alive if it wasn't for me."

Joey shifted in her seat and in a tearful voice said, "What happened was beyond tragic, Ryder. Losing someone you love…well, if anything ever happened to Roni, it would destroy me. But blaming yourself? Blame the kid who was texting and driving. All you did was love your wife. All you wanted was to hold her, to be with her. And she died knowing that. It was your love that brought her peace in her final moments. Think about that."

She reached over and took his hand, and they sat like that until the afternoon sun faded.

Chapter 21

Shiv awoke to voices in the kitchen. She got out of bed and peered out the window. It was dusk, which meant she'd been sleeping for hours. Ordinarily, Joey would've stirred her, afraid she'd been sleeping too long.

It had gotten to be a problem, even Shiv recognized that. The psychologist Joey had made Shiv see believed she suffered from clinical depression, likely triggered by her stroke. Shiv wouldn't have put such a fancy title to it. Back in her day, they just called it the blues. Even so, she didn't seem able to shake it. Frankly, it took too much energy to be happy.

The voices grew louder. Shiv got curious, so she put on a decent pair of jeans and a blouse and shuffled off to the kitchen. There, she found Ryder and the lawyer who'd been at the house before.

"Hey, Ma, you remember Flynn?"

The young man stood to greet her. "Nice to see you again, Ms. Knight."

"Has there been a development?"

"Turns out the Addisons have put the Beary Quaint on the market," Ryder said. "We suspect they want to clean up the neighborhood to impress potential buyers. And that's why they've been harassing me about the fifth wheel and my semis."

"Oh my." Shiv reached into the fridge for the pitcher of Joey's sun tea. "Is this good news or bad?"

Flynn chuckled. "Hard to say at this point. The good news is, if the Addisons sell, we'll be rid of them."

She poured herself a glass of tea. "Can I offer anyone else a glass?"

"No thanks," Flynn said.

"Where's Joey?" she asked.

"She ran to the market."

Shiv had suspected as much when she didn't see her. The sweet girl was always running here and there to make sure Shiv had everything she needed.

"So, what do you do now?" she asked Ryder and Flynn. "Do you still send the letter?"

"That's what we were discussing," Flynn said. "On the one hand, it's a nice little threat to hold over their heads. And if we actually find a code violation, they'd have to disclose it to any potential buyers. On the other hand, it might behoove us just to lie low and hope the Addisons sell the Beary Quaint fast and get the hell out of Dodge."

"I could certainly see the dilemma."

"What would you do, Ma?" Ryder turned to Flynn. "My mom used to work for a big-time Superior Court judge in Stanislaus County." His expression was filled with pride, which both delighted Shiv and broke her heart. Now she was just an old, irrelevant woman.

"No kidding. Which judge?"

"Judge Morgan Lester," Shiv said, her voice a little too reverent because Ryder looked at her funny. "Have you gone before him?"

"No, ma'am. My practice is farther north, primarily serving Sacramento and Plumas counties. And back when I was a federal prosecutor, I didn't see the insides of too many county courthouses. What did you do for Judge Lester, if you don't mind me asking?"

"Not at all. I was his courtroom clerk."

"You don't say. How long?"

"Thirty years."

"She read the verdicts in the highway murder case," Ryder said.

It had been one of the highest profile cases in California, right up there with O.J. Simpson and the Scott Peterson trial. Every day, Morgan's courtroom had been packed with reporters from all over the country. The *New York Times*, the *Sacramento Bee*, the *San Francisco Chronicle*, and the *Los Angeles Times*, to name a few.

It had been a capital case, and Shiv had read verdicts during both the guilt and penalty phases, which had been aired on all the network and cable news channels. For a while, it had sort of been like being a celebrity. People at the market, at restaurants, and even at gas stations had recognized her from the trial.

"That must've been something else," Flynn said.

Despite being an established lawyer himself, Flynn seemed legitimately impressed.

"It was," she said, a sadness sweeping over her. "But I'm retired now."

"Well, if you ever decide to come out of retirement, let me know."

She sipped her sun tea. "Why's that?"

"I could use someone like you on my staff. Doris, my right-hand woman, left me high and dry." His lips tipped up. "Nah, she's semiretired. Only works for me a couple of days a week in Sacramento and spends the rest of the time with her grandkids. I could use someone to fill in the rest of the week in my office here. Someone who knows their way around legal jargon and can sweet-talk court clerks." He winked.

"You have an office here?" Ryder asked, surprised.

"Yeah, it's called my ranch." He turned back to Shiv. "I commandeered one of the outbuildings and had Colin work his magic. You'd have your own office, your own coffee mug, even your own parking spot. No pressure, though."

"My ma's recuperating from a stroke."

"I'm fine," she said, excitement coursing through her. "Ryder and Joey like to fuss over me. But my physical therapist and doctor have given me a clean bill of health." Her doctor hadn't given her any such thing. But if she asked her, she probably would. Shiv hadn't had any of the debilitating headaches she'd gotten in the weeks following the stroke, nor had she experienced dizziness like she had before. And her balance was nearly back to normal. She wasn't sure she was ready to drive again, though.

Oh, for the love of God, why was she even considering a job? She was retired, for goodness' sake.

Because I miss getting up every morning with purpose. Stop it, she told herself. She was moving to a retirement community in Reno.

"There's no rush," Flynn said. "Take some time to think it over. We could always try it, and if you find it's too much, no hard feelings. In the meantime, why don't you, Ryder, and Joey come over for dinner one of these nights and meet my wife, Gia? You'll love her."

"That sounds lovely," Shiv said, and they went back to debating the pros and cons of whether to send the Addisons the letter Flynn had composed.

* * * *

Joey lay in bed, listening to the breeze rustle through the trees in the night. Ryder was back to hiding in his camper. When she'd gotten home from shopping—and taking a detour to drop off some freshly baked cookies from The Farm at the Circle D for the kids—he'd declined dinner and had taken off for a few hours.

She had no idea where he'd gone and tried not to think about it. Around eight, she'd heard him pull up, then the sound of his creaky camper door open and close. He'd exposed too much of himself earlier and was salving his pain by holing up with his two best friends, Pity and Sorrow.

She got it. Hers used to be Oxycodone and Fentanyl.

She rolled over and closed her eyes, but sleep eluded her. She kept thinking about what Ryder had told her. How he'd blamed himself for the death of his wife and child. How he'd lived with the guilt all these years and let it fester like a malignant cancer. It broke her heart.

It also should've reinforced that he was broken and that trying to fix him would only bring disappointment. But she was a nurse, for God's sake.

She got up, threw on a pair of shorts and a T-shirt, and followed the now well-beaten path to his front door. He opened it before she could even knock as if he'd been waiting for her or at least anticipating her visit.

He didn't speak, just pulled her into his arms and kissed her until he made her forget what she'd come for. Or maybe she'd come for this. It had always been this way between them. Sex-driven and hot. But there was more. In the short time she'd come here, they'd become friends. Champions for each other. Confidantes. Companions.

And somewhere along the line, she'd fallen in love.

His hands moved over her in a frenzy. Unlike the other times, when he'd taken the time to seduce, he rushed to get her clothes off, clumsily wrestling with her buttons and clasps.

She was too turned on to care, though she should've. But if he needed her body to escape his pain, she'd give it to him willingly at the risk of her heart.

"Here or in bed?" he asked breathless, dragging his shirt over his head.

She wanted the bed but had a feeling they wouldn't make it. He pressed her against the wall, rocking into her so that she felt his thickness through his jeans. She clawed at his fly, trying to undo his buttons, feeling as frenzied for him as he was for her.

He pushed her hand away, got his pants open just enough to free himself, seemed to pull a condom out of thin air, and thrust inside her. Their height disparity made it difficult, so he lifted her up. She wrapped her legs around his hips and let him take her against the wall.

He was ruthless, pounding into her again and again. The friction and the desperation in each one of his powerful thrusts brought her to orgasm almost instantly. She clenched around him, calling out his name, overcome by the intensity of the moment.

Ryder climaxed at almost the same time, his body shuddering as he took his release, his arms straining to hold on to her. When it was over, she slid down the wall onto the floor.

The sex had only lasted a matter of minutes, yet she'd never experienced anything as passionate or as powerful in her life.

She sat there naked and flushed, covered in a sheen of sweat. Ryder stood over her, panting for breath. At some point, he removed the condom and threw it away.

She thought this was it. Now he would turn his back on her. But he surprised her by lifting her off the floor and carrying her to his bed. He stripped off his clothes, and she felt the mattress dip with his weight. Soon, his hands were on her, fondling her breasts while his lips strung kisses across her neck.

He murmured something inaudible, and she whispered back, "I love you."

His hand moved between her legs, and he stroked her until she was writhing and rocking against him for more. His mouth slid down her chest, over her belly, and dipped lower until he was there, tasting her. She took fistfuls of the sheets in both hands and cried out with the sheer pleasure of his tongue lapping against her.

He brought her to the brink, then kissed his way up her thigh until he was at her breasts. She felt him grow hard again and expected their foreplay to turn frantic as it had before. But he took his time, touching and laving every inch of her body with his mouth. He moved over her and kissed her deeply. Reverently.

She closed her eyes, her heart coming out of her chest as he whispered in her ear, "You're so beautiful." But he never once uttered the words she wanted to hear.

The nightstand scraped open, and he rolled on another condom. This time when he entered her, he went slow, only moving a fraction inside her. Still, she felt every inch of him, every pulse, every twitch. Every word that went unsaid.

Warm moonlight seeped through the window blinds and washed over them, casting a glow over Ryder's broad back. She loved the way his muscles bunched, the way his strong arms felt around her, and the way his pale blue eyes seemed to see inside her soul.

He brushed her hair away from her face and kissed her lips, soft as a whisper. She could feel his heart beating with every stroke. He reached under her, holding her up, so he could go deeper and increase his pace.

She met him thrust for thrust, falling into a perfect rhythm. A dance as old as time. They climaxed like that, almost exactly at the same time. When he tried to roll off her, she held him tight, afraid to let go.

"Love me," she whispered.

He turned his face away, and in a cracked voice that sounded a million miles away, said, "I can't."

Chapter 22

On Wednesday, Joey watched Ryder leave at the break of dawn towing his mile-long semitrailer behind him.

She drew the shades and considered going back to bed, but she wasn't tired. So, she went into the kitchen and made a pot of coffee.

Shiv joined her. "You're up early."

"You, too." It was a rare day when Joey didn't have to wake her.

"I didn't tell you, but that nice young man, Flynn Barlow, offered me a job."

"He did?" Joey's eyes widened. "What kind of job?"

"Secretarial work. He has an office on his ranch and is apparently shorthanded. And of course, I have legal experience from all my years working as a court clerk."

"Are you considering it?" It wasn't as if Shiv needed the money. According to Ryder, she had a nice pension and the proceeds from the sale of her town house. And Joey suspected that Ryder would always contribute financially to anything Shiv needed, including partly paying for Cascade Village, which didn't come cheap. And then there was her health, though Joey didn't think an office job would be too terribly taxing.

"I don't know," she said. "I think I might miss working. And this would only be part-time."

Joey poured them each a cup of coffee and took them to the table. "How does Ryder feel about it?"

"He's worried that I'm not up to it. What do you think?"

Joey didn't like being thrust in the middle. But she saw how animated Shiv was about the prospect of working again and thought a part-time job might go a long way toward helping with her depression. "Well, it would depend on how physical the job is, how many hours you worked a day, and the conditions. For now, I'd be worried about you driving. But this is really something for you to discuss with your doctor. She would know best."

"Shiv, can we have a real conversation about Cascade Village?" This time Joey wasn't going to let Shiv blow smoke up her behind.

"Of course, dear."

"You don't really want to live there, do you?"

There was a long pause. Joey could tell that Shiv was deliberating on how much to say, which told her everything she needed to know.

"It's a beautiful community," Shiv finally said. "More amenities than my condo had. And I suppose it makes sense to be in a place where I would be able to eventually transition to an assisted-living situation."

"But?" Whether Shiv said it or not, Joey suspected there was more.

"I don't know anyone there." Shiv stirred her coffee, unable to meet Joey's eyes.

"And?"

"It made me feel old, like the best part of my life was over and I was going there to die."

The words made Joey want to cry. No one should ever feel that way about the place where they lived, even though the planned community hadn't given Joey that vibe at all. To her, it was a posh and activity-filled way to spend your retirement years. But clearly Shiv wasn't enjoying retirement.

"You have to tell Ryder," Joey said. "You can't let him believe that you like the place simply because you think that's what he wants for you. I know for a fact that all he wants is for you to be happy."

Shiv let out a long breath. "I suppose I'm confused about what happiness for me looks like. I thought it would be retirement."

"But it's not. Did you talk about this with your therapist?"

"A little bit. But I'm able to better articulate it with you." Shiv reached across the table and patted Joey's hand.

Oh, how Joey adored this woman. "You've only had one session with Debra Miller. You'll open up more with time."

Joey paused, then plowed forward. "Can I ask you another personal question, Shiv?"

"Anything you'd like."

"Were you and the judge you worked for romantically involved? Does that have something to do with why you're so sad?"

Shiv jerked in surprise. "What makes you think that?" The defensive way she asked it let Joey know she was on to something.

"You left a letter from him open on your dresser. And although it was wrong of me, I confess to having glanced at it." It was such a violation of

Shiv's privacy that Joey couldn't bring herself to tell her that she'd read the entire note. *Coward.* "And while there was nothing explicit, I just got a weird feeling that there was something between you two more than a work situation."

"Honey, when you work with someone for thirty years, there's a certain familiarity that passes, I suppose. We're friends, that's all."

Perhaps Joey had been wrong. But she didn't think so. There was more to this story than Shiv was saying, Joey was willing to bet on it. She shouldn't have pressed, but she couldn't help herself. "Maybe he had feelings for you and you didn't reciprocate them?"

"Morgan is married."

If Joey had a dollar for every married doctor who'd put a move on her, she'd have a tidy savings by now. She pinned Shiv with a look.

"His wife has ALS, Lou Gehrig's disease. She's suffered for a long time, and he's been with her every step of the way."

"That's very sad," Joey said. Either she was letting her imagination run away with her, or she was seeing things very clearly now. "And you were in love with him."

Shiv went back to stirring her coffee, apparently finding something inordinately interesting in the way the liquid swirled around the cup.

"Shiv, you can tell me to mind my own business if you want. But I think we're on to something here. And I'm a lot cheaper than Debra Miller."

Shiv chuckled. "My insurance covers Miller." She was silent for so long that Joey had just about given up on taking the conversation any further when Shiv closed her eyes and said, "Deeply. I love him deeply."

"And does he return those feelings?"

"I don't know. But he loves his wife. I'm sure of that."

Joey swallowed hard, feeling Shiv's pain as if it were her own. "Did things ever get…did the two of you have an affair?"

"Never." Shiv said it so emphatically that Joey believed her. "He would never be unfaithful to his wife, and I would never want him to be. When Tanner left Ryder and me for someone else, the pain was excruciating. I would never wish that on another woman. One of the reasons I love Morgan is for his unwavering loyalty to Dolores. He's the most honorable man I've ever known. Kind, gentle, and dependable."

It seemed ironic to Joey that the thing Shiv loved most about Morgan was the thing that kept them apart. Yet, she understood. Joey herself had released Ethan of any noble ideas of reconciliation so he could be with the woman he truly loved.

"But there was still something special between you two, right?"

"We were friends," Shiv said. "Wonderful, lasting friends."

"I can only imagine how difficult that must've been. Working side by side with a man you loved but couldn't have. I'm so sorry, Shiv."

Shiv's eyes filled. "I think it must've been why I retired. It had gotten harder and harder to see him struggle with his wife's illness while I tried not to imagine what my life could be with him."

They sat in quiet for a long time, both lost in their own thoughts while their coffee went cold. Joey knew the judge felt the same way about Shiv as Shiv felt about him. She'd felt it in his letter but knew it was hopeless.

"Is there a chance you could fall in love with someone else?" Joey asked after a while.

"I'm sixty-six years old, dear. My dating days are behind me."

"That's ridiculous," Joey said. "There's no age limit on love."

Shiv patted Joey's hand again. "You are a wonderful girl. Be patient with my son. Life has thrown him so much tragedy that he hasn't stopped reeling from it. But someone like you would be so…just try to be patient, Joey."

No, patience wouldn't win Ryder. Couldn't Shiv see that Ryder was a lot like her judge? Completely unattainable. He would never let go of the ghost of his wife and son. And Joey wouldn't let herself wind up like Shiv, working for a man whom she constantly yearned for but who couldn't return her love.

Joey's phone rang, shattering the sudden stillness and saving her from having to respond. According to caller ID, it was her mother.

"Is everything okay?" she asked in lieu of a greeting.

"Can't I call my daughter without an emergency?"

Joey's parents weren't much younger than Shiv. She couldn't help but worry. "Of course you can."

"A little birdie told me that you went to Ethan's wedding over the weekend."

That little birdie must've been Jay. She knew it had been a mistake to tell him. First, because he had this weird rivalry with Ethan. And second, because he couldn't keep his big, fat mouth shut to save his life.

"Ethan and I decided it would be good for Roni if I attended."

"What about for you?" Lou Ellen's disapproving voice came through the phone loud and clear. "Was it good for you to watch your ex-husband marry another woman?"

Joey opened the back door and took her conversation outside. "Mom, he was going to marry her whether I attended or not. He and I are over. And I'm good with that. You're the only one who seems to be having a problem with it."

"I don't believe in breaking up families."

"Our family isn't broken." It was just different now. The idea of that struck her in a way it never had before. Family could just as easily include the people you loved as much as the people you were related to by blood or marriage. Ethan would always be part of her family, even though they were divorced, just as Shiv had become a new member. Joey even considered Brynn part of her familial circle.

"I worry about you, Joey. I worry that you're more fragile than you think." The underlying context there was that Lou Ellen feared that Joey would start popping pills again.

"There's nothing to worry about, Mom. I'm in a good place." It was the truth. For the first time in years, she felt strong. That's why as much as it would break her heart, she knew her time here was up. She had to move on. Shiv would be fine without her.

Lou Ellen let out a long-suffering sigh. "The real reason I called is because there's mail here for you, an envelope from the nursing board. You want me to come over, and we can open it together?"

Joey felt her lungs squeeze tight and forced herself to slowly exhale. "I'll come there as soon as I can break away." Maybe Peter was available to sit with Shiv for a few hours.

"You sure? I can read it to you over the phone."

Joey was conflicted. She desperately wanted to know, but at the same time she was scared to death. Her inner strength told her to rip off the Band-Aid and find out her fate once and for all. The coward in her wanted to put off the board's answer for as long as possible.

Last time, it had been Ryder who'd given her that extra ounce of courage to open the envelope. He'd made her bold.

The knowledge that he couldn't do the same thing for himself hurt. Not just because she wanted him to love her, but because she wanted him to be happy.

"Joey? What do you want me to do?"

"Open it." She braced for the worst, telling herself that no matter what, she'd be okay.

* * * *

Ryder got home early Friday morning. The trip to Idaho, carrying twenty-four tons of hay, had taken longer than he'd expected. Forty-eight hours was a lot of time to be alone with your thoughts. Ordinarily, Ryder used those hours to plan the future of his business. But lately, the only thing that filled his head was Joey, who wanted more from him than he could give.

He considered catching a few hours' sleep in his camper but wasn't particularly tired. Cowboy up, he told himself and headed to the house.

He hadn't seen Joey since their night together and knew he'd have to face her sooner or later. Better to get it done and make his position clear, even if it meant shutting down the physical aspects of their friendship. That wasn't going to be easy. She'd made him feel alive again. She'd reminded him what it was like to be a man.

The smell of freshly brewed coffee hit him as soon as he walked in, and he followed the scent to the kitchen. There, he found Joey hunkered over a cup at the breakfast table. She greeted him with a slight bob of her head. Her blond hair was loose and still wet from her shower, and she smelled faintly of perfume.

His body instantly reacted. He busied himself at the coffeemaker until he got himself under control.

"How was your trip?" she asked.

"Noneventful. How 'bout here?" He assumed if there had been anything important to report, she would've called him. But the only calls he got were from a Colorado area code, which he chose to ignore, as he always did.

"A little bit of news."

He jerked his head in surprise. "Like what? Someone buy the Beary Quaint?"

"Not that I'm aware of." She got up, brushed by him, and poured herself a second cup.

His first inclination was to catch her around the waist and give her a proper greeting, the kind a man gives his woman when he's returned home from a long trip. But she wasn't his woman.

"I was hoping we could talk before Shiv gets up," she said.

He stiffened. *Hoping we could talk.* They were the most dreaded words in the English language.

"What's up?" He sank into a chair at the table.

"Your mom wants to try working for that lawyer friend of yours, and I think she should."

He rubbed the back of his neck. "Seems like a lot of stress for a woman who just got over having a stroke. And if she wanted to work, then why the hell did she retire in the first place?"

"She had her reasons." Joey gave him a pointed look.

"Ah, jeez." He pinched the bridge of his nose. "Judge Lester?"

"It's her story to tell, not mine."

"Not if he did something to her. Then you damn well better tell me."

Joey took her cup to the table. "It's not like that, Ryder. I don't think there are two people in this world who have more respect for each other, who care about each other, more than they do. But all they can ever be is friends. And that's terribly difficult when you love someone. When you yearn for them."

He had to look away. Joey might have been talking about his mother, but the pain he saw in her eyes was like a dagger through his chest.

"In any event, she misses working," Joey said. "She misses feeling useful. I'm not a doctor, but I think she's up to the challenge. Maybe not driving at first, but arrangements could be made. Of course, this should all be discussed with her physician, who should confer with her physical therapist. But I don't think a few hours a day to start would hurt her."

"What about Cascade Village?"

"That's the second thing I wanted to talk to you about. It's not for her, Ryder. It's beautiful and luxurious but…it makes her feel old."

"She told you that?"

"Not in so many words. She doesn't want to disappoint you. She doesn't want to feel like a burden. But she's said enough that I can read between the lines."

"Does she want to live here?" He glanced around the tiny kitchen and looked outside the window, where there was nothing but trees.

"That's something you'll have to discuss with her. My suspicion is that she wants some independence."

Ryder blew out a breath. "I thought she'd be happy there. That she would have a social life and still be close enough to me that we could spend time together. You think she wants to move back to Modesto?" He scratched his chin. "I guess I jumped the gun by selling her town house so fast."

"Those are all things you two will need to talk about. But I suspect she doesn't want to go backward, Ryder. Only forward."

He nodded.

"That brings me to the next thing I wanted to talk about," she said.

"What's that?"

"I'm giving my notice. I'll stay until you find someone else, but I don't think she needs twenty-four-hour care any longer. Again, this is something you and Shiv should discuss with her doctor. But let's face it, Ryder, I've been a glorified companion. Your mom's recovery has gone so well she doesn't need me anymore."

He looked at her. Really looked.

Her voice dropped. "I can't stay, Ryder."

That was the real reason. Them, not the fact that Shiv had improved. He wanted to protest, to say he needed her, Shiv needed her, but that would be unfair. Selfish. In the long run, it would be easier for them to part ways. Yet, the idea of her leaving made him feel so damn empty inside that it was painful.

"Where will you go?" he said at last.

She fidgeted with the handle on her cup. "I heard back from the nursing board." There was a catch in her voice. "They've decided to reinstate my license."

He blinked. "When did that happen?"

"The letter came to my parents while you were gone."

"Wow." It felt wrong that he hadn't been there to share the news with her. He went in for a congratulatory embrace but stopped himself. Cold turkey. Otherwise, he wouldn't be able to let her go. "Congratulations, Joey. I'm so freaking proud of you." Seriously, his chest swelled. "I guess that means you can work at a hospital again. Get a place of your own, with a room for Roni."

"Yes," she said. "But, Ryder, that's not why I'm leaving."

"I know." He held her gaze, trying to sort it out in his head. She was going, walking out of his life. Forever. She hadn't said as much, but as long as he couldn't return her feelings, that's what this came down to.

That's when the walls started closing in on him. He needed air. "Excuse me for a sec. I forgot I've got to make a call."

He made a break for the back door, circled around to his fifth wheel, and pressed his forehead against the siding, letting the cool aluminum soothe his throbbing head. What the hell was his problem? He'd find somebody else for Shiv and get on with his life. Then why did he feel like someone was scaling the insides of his gut with a fishing knife?

Just fucking breathe, he told himself, coming up with a hundred and one reasons to insist she stay. None of them included the one she wanted. But he couldn't. He just couldn't. Losing Leslie and his son had destroyed him and sucked him so dry he had nothing left to give. Not to Joey. Not to her little girl.

His phone vibrated in his back pocket, and he took a moment to collect himself before staring at the screen. It was the same Colorado area code but a different number. *Nice trick, old man.* But Ryder wouldn't let himself be fooled into answering his father's call, and he let it go to voice mail. Lord knew, he had enough weighing him down. The last thing he had time for was dealing with Tanner's repeated requests for reconciliation.

Why the hell couldn't everybody just leave him alone?

Chapter 23

Joey went as far as the departure gate and waved as Roni boarded the plane. Her first flight, and Joey wouldn't even be with her. At least Roni would have Alma and Henry. Still, Joey yearned to see the wonder on Roni's face as the plane took off into the sky and pushed through the clouds as Reno grew smaller and smaller.

At least when they landed in Hawaii, Alma had promised to call. And Joey was sure that Ethan would take lots of pictures of their baby playing in the surf and sand. Still, she had the jitters. It was Roni's first big trip, and Joey wouldn't be there.

It will be fine, she told herself. Roni had three adults who would watch her like a hawk.

She left the airport, zigzagging through the crowds, feeling lonely in a sea of people. A whole weekend stretched before her with nothing to do. Peter was with Shiv. And Ryder was soon going out on the road. Not that it would've mattered. She was doing her best to cut all ties with him. As much as she would've liked to have stayed friends, it hurt too much. He was everything she wanted and couldn't have.

She found her SUV in the parking lot and drove aimlessly around Reno. The pool was open at her parents' house. She could always go over there and jump in the water. It was hot as hell. But it would take her mother all of fifteen seconds to surmise Joey's mood and then try to pin her down on the reason for it. If Joey refused to tell, her mother would simply assume it was Ethan's honeymoon. That his newfound happiness had brought Joey pain.

She hated to admit it, but once upon a time, it would've been true. And she would've wallowed in self-pity. But now, she fervently hoped that Ethan had truly found his soul mate and that they lived together forever in wedded bliss. Most of all, she wanted her daughter to see what a good marriage looked like. Because at this rate, Joey wasn't much of a model.

She'd let herself fall for the unattainable. And instead of celebrating that she'd won her nursing license back, she was suffering over a man who was too damaged to let himself reach for happiness with both hands.

Quickly nixing the idea of going to her parents', Joey took the road back to Nugget. She could spend the rest of the day charting out hospitals where she could send her résumé. She'd already dropped off one at Plumas General, and she was scheduled to have a telephone interview with a person from HR next week. Because of its proximity to Nugget, it was her first choice. But even if she had to commute to Reno or Glory Junction, she would because the salary would allow her to rent a place large enough for her and Roni.

She swung into the Bun Boy on her way home. There was a long line of cars at the drive-through, and she considered giving up. But she hadn't been eating too well these past few days, and she craved something salty, like French fries. She parked and walked to the window. But the line was equally as long there. The tourists were out in droves. Summer in the Sierra.

"Hey, Joey," someone called.

She turned to find Darla, sitting at one of the picnic tables in the shade, and waved.

"I'll save you a spot," Darla said.

The line moved quickly. Joey put in her order and wandered over to Darla, who'd commandeered extra bench space.

"Sit here," she said.

"Where's Harlee?" Joey had never seen Darla without her sidekick.

"She had her baby! A boy. Eight pounds, six ounces. His name is Charlie." Darla beamed.

"That's fantastic. Are they home?" At some point, Joey wanted to swing by their house and drop off a gift for the baby. Joey didn't know Harlee well, but both she and Darla had made her feel welcome here.

"They just got home from the hospital a few hours ago. Connie and I went over and decorated the house with a big 'Welcome Home, Charlie' sign. Connie had to put in a few hours at work. She's the nine-one-one dispatcher at the police department. And I didn't want to crowd Harlee and Colin on their first day with the baby, so we both left about twenty minutes ago. He is so cute."

"How are you?" Joey asked, covertly sliding a glance at Darla's belly.

"So far, so good," Darla whispered. "We're still keeping it on the down-low, though."

"Gotcha." Joey could keep a secret. Well, at least sometimes. "Did Harlee get her scoop before she had Charlie?" Joey hadn't had a chance to check the *Nugget Tribune.*

"About the Addisons selling the Beary Quaint? Yep. Can you believe it? I mean, I thought they'd die in that place, wearing their little bear suits."

Joey had to stifle a laugh. Darla certainly had her own weird style, but unlike the Addisons' creepy bear infatuation, her penchant for loud colors and big, plastic earrings had flair.

"Boy, did they bite Harlee's head off for printing the story. You'd think they'd want the publicity, right? The story was like a freaking free real estate ad. But noooo. First thing they did was threaten to sue."

"Oh no. She's not worried, is she?" Joey had seen how strong the couple had come on with Ryder, who wasn't easy to intimidate. Yet, the Addisons, not exactly what you would call imposing figures, had gone toe-to-toe with him. "It's true. They are selling. So, what could they possibly have to sue her over?"

"Nothing. Absolutely nothing." Darla waved her hand in the air. "They're submental. Anyway, did you hear the news that there may be a buyer? Word is that someone's made an offer. Without Harlee, we'll have to wait until escrow closes to know who the new owners are. So frustrating, right?"

Joey hoped for Ryder's sake that whoever it was left him alone. Her name was called over the loudspeaker, and she dashed over to the counter to retrieve her fries and shake. Not the most nutritious meal, but today, Joey was allowing herself to eat her feelings.

"I got to get going," Darla said and gathered up her wrappers. "Date night with Wyatt."

"Have a good time, and if you see Harlee, tell her I'll be dropping something by for the baby next week."

"Will do."

Joey watched Darla disappear inside the barbershop and went back to her fries.

When she was finished, she started for home. *Home.* She supposed in the last two months that's what the little 1920s Craftsman had come to mean to her. Each lovingly stripped wall, each paint choice.

After she and Siobhan had peeled off the wallpaper in the master bedroom and painted the walls in Palladian Blue—Shiv liked the way the color matched her eyes—they'd made big plans to start on the kitchen. Perhaps Shiv could now do it with Peter.

Joey had already begun searching for a place in the area. The houses for rent tended to be on the dumpy side, with some that didn't even have central heat. Just a wood-burning fireplace. Roughing it wasn't exactly her style. She'd considered calling Ryder's real estate agent, but she wanted to wait until she got a job first.

They were waiting to talk to Janine about finding Joey's replacement until Ryder and his mom met with Shiv's physician to see if a twenty-four-hour caregiver was even necessary any longer. Whatever they decided, Joey had offered to train the new person.

The always-intuitive Shiv had taken Joey's resignation with somber understanding. No words had passed between the two women about Joey's real reasons for leaving. But if anyone understood the pain of that decision, it was Shiv.

"I will be right here in town, and we will remain friends," Joey had promised her.

Shiv had replied, "I will hold you to it." She had taken Joey's hand and with tears in her eyes had said, "I'm sorry."

And that's where they'd left it.

Peter was in the living room working on a scrapbook he'd been putting together for weeks. "Hello, sunshine. Did little Roni make it off okay?"

"I've never seen her more excited."

"Then what's with the resting bitch face?"

Joey laughed and sprawled out on the sofa next to Peter. "I guess I've got a lot on my mind. Shiv napping?"

"No," Peter said brightly. "She and Ryder went over to that lawyer guy's place to check out his digs. I was dying to see it myself."

"And?"

"I thought mom and son could use a little alone time."

"Then why don't you take off for the rest of the day? I'm here, and I suspect Shiv will be over there for a while. I hear the guy's married to some famous self-help guru and his home is on steroids. The whole place. I'm sure you could salvage the rest of the day."

"That's the thing. I don't really have anything else to do." Peter's voice cracked. "Fred, my last client, had sort of become my whole world."

"Ah, Peter. I'm so sorry." She'd always avoided any conversation about Fred's passing as she knew Peter was still grieving.

He swiped at his eyes. "Occupational hazard. Don't ever become too attached."

"I know what you mean. I'm going to miss Shiv like crazy."

He shot her a look. "And the son? Will you miss him like crazy, too?"

Joey closed her eyes and nodded. No sense in playing coy. Peter was a smart man with eyes. He knew what was going on.

"Shiv still thinks he'll come around," Peter said.

"You two have talked about it?" Joey was surprised.

"A little. Nothing that amounted to us gossiping behind your back. Okay, we gossiped. Shiv thinks he's in love with you."

"He's not." He was in love with a ghost, a ghost Joey could never compete with. Nor did she want to. "Take my word for it."

Peter let out a heavy sigh. "I'm sorry, Joey. You probably don't want to hear this right now, but there will be someone else. You're a catch, sunshine."

She kissed him on the cheek. "Thank you." It took all her willpower not to cry. "What is this scrapbook you've been working on?"

"It's for Fred's daughters. Pictures of his last years. Holidays, family gatherings, that sort of thing."

"That's really sweet of you, Peter. Have you given much thought to doing another live-in situation? It might be time." She shrugged her shoulders.

"Actually, I was thinking that I might apply for your job."

Joey looked at him to see if he was kidding. It would be the perfect solution. Shiv adored him, and Ryder seemed to mesh with Peter fine. The question was whether she needed someone anymore.

"I love it," Joey said. "I'd feel so good knowing she was in your hands. But, Peter, what if her doctor says she's past the need for full-time care?"

"Your words to God's ears. If that's the case, I could go part-time. Maybe have Janine hook me up with a few clients in the area. There's got to be a need around here. If there is, I'd find a place in Nugget. You need a roommate?" His lips slid up to show he was joking. "But seriously, I'm thinking of relocating, finding a slower pace. A place that's cheaper."

"I know that Shiv, Roni, and I would be thrilled to have you here. But I'd worry you would get lonely. I don't think there's much of a dating scene in Nugget."

"Well, honey, you and I will have to go to Reno for that. The good news is, it's only fifty minutes away."

She reached over and hugged him. "I'm so glad I have you in my life, Peter."

"Right back at you, sunshine."

* * * *

Across town, on a ranch that reminded Shiv of a TV set, she sipped iced tea poolside while Flynn, Ryder, and a few other ranchers talked cattle. She hadn't been aware that her son knew so much about the beef industry. Then again, he hauled livestock for a living.

It was a lovely party. When Ryder said they'd been invited over to Flynn's home, she'd assumed it would be just them. But they arrived to find a gathering of more than a dozen people, including Ryder's friend, Lucky, and his lovely wife.

Owen, the barber from town, had planted himself next to Shiv. He was a nice-looking man, but he talked too much. She could barely get a word in edgewise.

Flynn's wife, Gia, wasn't anything like Shiv expected. Years ago, Shiv had caught Gia's financial advice show a few times and had found it helpful. In fact, one of the programs had spurred Shiv to begin socking away a small fraction of her weekly paycheck for Ryder's college fund. It turned out he got a scholarship to Cal Poly, but the money Shiv had saved helped him kick off his rodeo career.

On screen, Gia had seemed so glamorous and intellectual. But here, she was as down-to-earth as a ranch hand, serving drinks to her guests in a simple sundress and a straw cowboy hat that had seen better days.

The conversation turned to the Beary Quaint. There'd been an article on the local news site about it being up for sale, and there was a lot of speculation on potential buyers.

"I wouldn't be surprised if Tom Bodett took it over," Owen said. "He'll leave the light on for ya."

Flynn chuckled and shook his head. "My money is on Nate and Maddy."

"They wouldn't want that ridiculous place," Gia said, dismissing him with a wave of her hand. "I'd say that place needs a cool million just to give it a face-lift and clear away all those freaky chainsaw bears. Otherwise, I would've considered buying it for my program." She explained to Shiv that she had founded a residential job-training program for women down on their luck. "It would've been a great opportunity to teach my students the ups and downs of the hospitality industry."

"Just as long as it ain't none of those Hiltons," Owen said. "They're trouble. Them and those Kardashians."

Clay McCreedy, Flynn's neighbor, choked on his beer. "I don't think the Kardashians are in the hotel business, Owen."

"They've got their hands in everything, those women do, including the NBA."

"I hope whoever buys it is willing to do some cross-promotion with my cowboy camp," Lucky added. "When I approached the Addisons about the idea of creating some package deals together, they practically spat in my face. *Adios*, mofos, don't let the door hit ya on the way out."

"Don't dismiss Griffin," said Annie, the lovely girl who owned the farm stand with the cherry orchard. "He can afford to buy it and do all the renovations without making a dent in his bank account."

"Who's Griffin?" Shiv asked.

"He owns the Gas and Go and Sierra Heights, that white elephant planned community off the side of the road," Owen said. "It used to be a hotbed for meth cookers."

Clay rolled his eyes.

"It's not a white elephant anymore." Gia refilled Shiv's glass. "Ever since Brynn took over the advertising, Griff has been selling homes left and right. The place is gorgeous."

Shiv noted that Dana, Ryder's real estate agent, sat off in the corner, saying nothing. Shiv would bet money she knew exactly who the buyer was.

Flynn got to his feet. "You ready to check out my office?" He offered Shiv a hand. "Ms. Knight and I have business to discuss while the rest of you continue to get drunk on my booze."

He led her down an impressive flagstone path, past the outdoor kitchen and gazebo, around Flynn and Gia's huge log home, which took Shiv's breath away, to a matching side building that was larger than Ryder's Craftsman. They stepped into the front room, which was decorated in leather sofas, kilim rugs, and bookcases sagging with law books. Off the parlor was a small kitchen and two offices. The first one was Flynn's, judging by the pictures of him and Gia scattered across the desk and the photographs of cattle on the wall. The second was bare except for a desk and loveseat.

"This would be yours. Sometimes my investigator, whom we call Toad, comes in and uses the computer." He jutted his chin at a Mac on the desk. "But for the most part, he works out of my Sacramento office."

The room was large with picture windows that looked out over a pond and the Sierra Mountains in the foreground. It was a far cry fancier than the corner of the courtroom where she'd worked before.

"You can do anything you like with it," Flynn said.

He took her to the back of the building, where there was a small conference room. "I use it for depositions and meetings with clients."

"It's beautiful." The room was painted in a soft taupe, and there were portraits of Western landscapes with picture lights hung on the wall. The conference table was a gorgeous slab of wood with a live edge. The chairs were done in soft brown leather. The whole suite of rooms, even the empty office, was elegant. They made Shiv think Flynn was very successful.

"Just say the word and I'll give you the code to the gate and a key to the door. You can pick your days and hours."

A smile blossomed in her chest. She hadn't realized just how much she missed working until she'd smelled the leather bindings of the law books. It reminded her of Morgan's chamber. Only this time, the memory of him didn't make her sad.

"I still have to check with my doctor," she said. "There are times when my balance isn't good, and I'm going to guess that driving won't be an option for a while, so I'll have to figure out the transportation situation. But if I can start with only two short days a week, I think I could build up."

"That works for me. When do you want your start date to be?"

She and Flynn worked out a tentative schedule, and Shiv couldn't wait to get home to tell Joey and Peter that she was taking the plunge.

She thought about Morgan, about all the years she'd worked in his courtroom and all the years she'd loved him.

He'd been a driving force in her life and had taught her that good men still existed. He'd given her an important job when all she'd had was a high school diploma. It was a job where she could grow, and more importantly, support herself and her son. He'd believed in her.

There were husbands who weren't as supportive of their wives as Morgan Lester had been of her. Lord knew, Tanner had never been, leaving her to fend for herself with a young child, while he cheated and lied.

Though Morgan couldn't make a life with her, he'd been her guardian angel. The best friend she'd ever had. And for that, she considered herself lucky to have known him. But it was time to let go. Time to forge ahead without him.

Maybe if Shiv had been more like Joey, able to move on after unrequited love, she would've met someone else. Would've had someone with whom to spend her twilight years. Now she was just old and alone.

But the job Flynn offered, this town with its quirky characters, and living so close to her son, who in his own way needed her as much as she needed him, could be a new beginning for both of them.

The possibilities made her feel lighter and free of the melancholy that had wrapped around her like a boa constrictor.

She walked with Flynn back to the party, planning to sit next to the barber again. And perhaps this time she'd make a real effort to talk to him.

Chapter 24

The rest of June passed in a whirlwind. Roni came home from Hawaii tanned and brimming with stories. She'd brought Joey a shell necklace as a souvenir, which Joey had worn to the Fourth of July barbecue Annie and some of her neighbors had thrown at The Farm.

For once, Joey hadn't felt like an outsider. Harlee, Colin, and baby Charlie were at the party. Darla came with her husband, Wyatt, and an evident baby bump. And of course, Shiv and Peter had joined Joey. The three of them had become a tight little clique.

The only one absent from the gathering had been Ryder, who'd been out on the road most of the latter part of June. The distance between them had come with a combination of welcomed relief and a soul-searing sadness.

"Stay occupied" had been her mantra.

And she had.

She'd interviewed twice more with the chief nurse and the head doctor on the orthopedics ward at Plumas General and had been offered a job. Nurses were in short supply in California's rural counties, and they'd jumped at a chance to get someone with Joey's credentials and experience, despite her past issues. Unfortunately, drug abuse in her field was all too common. Fortunately for her, Plumas General was willing to take a chance. She'd accepted the job and started in two weeks.

Shiv had been given a clean bill of health, though her doctor didn't want her to drive or operate heavy equipment. The latter wouldn't be a problem. The former had been solved by Peter, who'd volunteered to be her chauffeur until she got the go-ahead to drive again. The two of them had cooked up all kinds of plans, including renting a place in Nugget together. Ryder hadn't taken the news well. He wanted Shiv to continue living with him.

"A grown man shouldn't live with his mother," Shiv had argued. "It's time for you to start a life in this house."

He'd walked away in a huff.

Undeterred, Shiv and Peter began their house hunt in earnest. It had only taken them a week to sign the lease on a lovely three-bedroom in Sierra Heights, the only planned community in Nugget. The house was owned by a San Francisco Bay Area couple who planned to retire in Nugget. But that was ten years off, and in the meantime, they wanted it to generate an income. It was only a few miles from Flynn Barlow's law office and had as many amenities as Cascade Village, though it wasn't a senior community with an assisted living component. But rooming with Peter, a trained caregiver, gave Joey confidence that Shiv would be well taken care of.

Janine had found Peter a couple of clients in the region who needed part-time help. Peter thought it would be enough to sustain him financially. And even if it didn't, his late client had left him enough money to live on as long as he was frugal. What he said he needed more than a good-paying job was change. New scenery. Joey worried that he would get lonely in Nugget, but he'd assured her that he was looking forward to the slow pace here. He'd already begun making friends, including Annie, who'd offered him hours at The Farm if he didn't find enough work as a caregiver.

The best part was that he'd be close. In the short time Joey had gotten to know him, they'd clicked. She predicted they'd wind up being friends forever. As would Shiv, though it would be tricky keeping her separate from Ryder, whom she desperately needed to get over. She loved him so much that it physically hurt to get up in the morning, knowing he would never be in her life.

At least she was moving out. She'd found a place in town, which coincidentally belonged to Ryder's rodeo buddy's wife, the bootmaker. Ryder's real estate agent, who apparently had some history with the house, had helped Joey find it.

The home wasn't anything fancy, just a two-bedroom, one-bath. But it was plenty spacious enough for Joey and Roni, who could have her own room on the days she stayed over. There was a cute yard, where Joey could put in a swing and maybe a tetherball pole. It wasn't the Circle D by any stretch, but Joey could make it feel like a home.

In fact, she was on her way to the house so Dana could give her the keys. Shiv and Peter were over at their new place, taking measurements. Everything was moving so quickly that Joey barely had time to catch her breath.

Dana was sitting on the front porch step when Joey got there. "Congratulations, it's officially yours." She tossed Joey the keys and managed to get to her feet without toppling over. It seemed to Joey that half the town was pregnant. "Ready to do the walk-through."

"Absolutely."

They went in through the front door. Last time Joey had been in the house, it had been filled with furniture and moving boxes. A railroad worker had been renting it and got transferred to another crew-change site. It looked bigger empty and frankly a little shabbier than she remembered. Furniture would change everything, she told herself. She'd buy a cute sectional, maybe a big ottoman that could be used as a coffee table, and hang lots of pictures on the wall. She and Roni would also need bedroom sets, a dining table and chairs.

Suddenly, she was having second thoughts about the whole thing. *Stop it.* This was everything she'd worked toward. A house where Roni could feel at home. Yet, something about it left her cold. She kept returning to Ryder's little Craftsman. Although it wasn't much as far as creature comforts, it felt right. Warm and safe. Like there had been love in that house. A hundred years of love.

Ironic that Ryder, a man who'd closed himself off from love, now owned it.

"It's month to month, right?"

Dana looked at her. "Yes. What's wrong? You don't like it anymore?"

"I do. I'm just…you know, new job, new place. I want to make sure it's right."

"No worries," Dana said. "It's only month to month, and there is no shortage of people who would be happy to take it over from you. As you may have noticed, rentals in Nugget are scarce. There's a lot of cabins around here, but few are winterized. And there's Sierra Heights. The few unoccupied homes there are for sale—not for lease. Shiv and Peter lucked out with their deal. The police chief owns a duplex and rents out both apartments. But I can't remember the last time either place was vacant. Now, if you want to buy, that's a different story. But currently the inventory is thin. A couple of large ranches and farms and a few fixer-uppers close to town."

"No, I don't want to buy." Joey wanted to get past her three-month probationary period at the hospital before she committed to a mortgage. And she wasn't in the market for a fixer-upper. "This will be fine." She gazed around the front room. "I think I'm just experiencing a little buyer's remorse is all. Once I get some paint on the walls, some rugs on the floor, and make it my own, it'll feel better."

"It's a good place, Joey. I fell in love with my husband here." Dana smiled at the memory. "We were roomies after my house burned down. The arson investigator and the anal-retentive real estate agent who left a candle burning too close to a pile of rags covered in turpentine. I swear, someone could write a romance novel about us."

"Really?" Joey squinted at Dana to see if she was telling the truth. She'd never heard the story before, and in a town like Nugget, everyone knew everything about their neighbors, even a newcomer like Joey.

"Just ask anyone. Aidan thinks it's hilarious. Tells everyone he meets that I burned down my own house. He does not, however, find the story of the arsonist who burned down my real estate office so funny. But that's a story for another time. Let's continue the walk-through in the kitchen."

The appliances were all new, which should've made Joey inordinately happy. But a wave of homesickness for Ryder's bungalow hit her so hard she rushed the inspection. If it wasn't for Dana taking time away from her busy day to do the walk-through, Joey would've fled. Instead, she went through the motions, nodding her head at everything Dana said.

By the time Joey left with the keys, she had a throbbing headache. It was from the heat, she told herself. The temperature had reached triple digits. But deep down inside, she knew it wasn't the heat. It was the finality of moving away from Ryder. It was writing the end on a love story that had never gotten off the ground.

Things went from bad to worse when she got home to find that Ryder had returned from his latest haul and was washing his semitruck shirtless in the driveway. It was time to tell him she was moving out.

* * * *

The sun pounded on Ryder's back as he hosed down his tractor unit. He had another run to make on Friday, and his windshield and tires were caked with dirt from his last haul. The semitrailer was ready to go, though. He'd scrubbed it clean and sanitized it for the load of lambs he was transporting to a feedlot in the Central Valley from the Sacramento Valley.

It was a day's worth of work, and he hoped to find a load for his return trip. Nothing worse than a deadhead, otherwise known as an empty trailer.

Joey pulled up behind Peter's Prius in her red SUV. He knew she'd been house hunting and suspected it was just a matter of time before she packed up and left. It was for the best, under the circumstances.

And though it was a small town, Ryder was gone so much of the time that the chances of them running into each other were low. It had been wrong for him to have gotten involved with her in the first place. But there'd always been that pull between them, an attraction that transcended reason.

He tried to tell himself that he'd gotten her out of his system. And when that didn't work, he fell back on the fact that she'd be better off without him.

He gave her a quick nod as she went inside the house, then dragged the shop vac from storage and vacuumed the cab of the tractor. Afterward, he polished the dashboard and seats. The heat was relentless, and his torso was slick with sweat. He hopped out of the cab, turned on the hose, and showered himself with tepid water. Perhaps, later, he'd walk down to the river and take a cool swim.

An army-green pickup he didn't recognize nosed up his driveway. He wondered if the Addisons had sent reinforcements to harangue him. Ever since news broke that the Beary Quaint was on the market, they'd given him a rash of shit. Everything from threatening to sue him for slander— they'd gotten it in their heads that he'd started a campaign against them—to accusing him of trying to sabotage their chances of selling the motel by continuing to park his big rigs on his property.

"If you consider me having to hire a lawyer because of your constant harassment a 'campaign against you,' then I'm guilty as charged," he'd told them. "As far as my trucks, keep it up, and I'll make this place look like a used car lot." And he would.

According to the rumor mill, a sale was pending. He thought that would finally shut them up. But he suspected the pickup meant otherwise. He lowered his sunglasses to get a better look, only to be blinded by the sun.

The truck came to a stop, and the driver jumped out. As Ryder stared at the man, it was like looking in a mirror. Last time he'd seen Kale, he was a skinny eighteen-year-old with a bad case of acne.

Joey, Peter, and Shiv came out of the house and stood at the porch rail, interested to find out who had come to visit. Ryder glanced over at Shiv, who was openly staring at Kale. She'd never seen him before, but there was no mistaking that he was Ryder's half-brother. Tanner's son.

"You ever answer your phone?" Kale approached him with the legendary Cole swagger. "I've been trying to reach you for a week."

"Well, here I am."

Joey and Shiv came down the stairs to join Ryder. Kale acknowledged them with a tip of his cowboy hat and had the audacity to give Joey a once-over.

Then he focused his attention on Ryder. "Our father's dying. He's asked to see you. If you'd answered your goddamn phone, I wouldn't have had to drive here all the way from Colorado."

It was like someone had knocked the air out of Ryder. Tanner. Dying. In the background, he heard Shiv gasp. Or maybe it was Joey.

Ryder looked at Kale, a million thoughts swirling in his head, and all he could manage was, "How'd you find me?"

"Tanner knew where you lived. Said you bought a place in the Sierra Nevada."

Ryder turned to his mother, who shook her head. The old son of a gun must've been keeping close tabs on Ryder to know about the move.

"I hadn't heard he was sick," Ryder finally said.

"Lung cancer. He was diagnosed a year ago but didn't tell anyone until two weeks ago, when his breathing got so bad that we had to take him to the emergency room."

Yeah, that sounded like Tanner. Ryder remembered seeing his old man being nearly stomped to death under the hooves of an angry bronc. Tanner had managed to hoist himself up and walk out of the arena on a broken leg with a concussion. The crowd had cheered like he was a returning war hero.

Lung cancer, huh? That, too, made sense. Every time Ryder had ever seen him, he'd either had a damn cigarette or a wad of chew in his mouth. The son of a bitch.

Ryder put the hose down and hitched up his wet jeans. "I'm sorry, Kale. For you and your brother. Tanner, too."

Kale squinted at Ryder, confused. "Does that mean you ain't coming?"

"I've got to haul a load of sheep."

Joey's hand slipped into Ryder's, and she squeezed it. It was a small thing. But until she'd done it, he hadn't realized how much he'd needed the physical contact. The support.

"Would you like to come inside the house for a cool drink, Kale? Maybe we could give Ryder a little time alone...What do you say?"

Kale looked from Joey to Ryder and then back to Joey. "Yeah, okay. Thank you, ma'am."

He followed Joey inside the house. Ryder watched Peter trail behind them while Shiv stayed behind.

"You should go, Ryder." Shiv put her hand on Ryder's shoulder. "Make your peace with him before it's too late. Otherwise, you'll regret it."

"No, I won't. The man's nothing to me but a sperm donor."

Shiv flinched, and Ryder wished he hadn't been so coarse. This had to be affecting her, too. Tanner had been her husband, after all, and until recently, Ryder had been under the impression that she'd never fully gotten over him.

"Sorry, Ma." Ryder toed the dirt with his boot. "But he did us wrong. And I won't absolve him of that just because he's dying."

"I don't think he would want you to. What I do know is this is your only chance to say good-bye. You didn't get that with Leslie, and you've carried it around with you for more than five years. Don't do it with your father."

Ryder jerked his head up. "Don't compare Leslie to that sumbitch. I loved Leslie. All I have for Tanner is contempt."

"That may be so, but he's your father, Ryder. He's the man who brought you into this world. If you don't take this opportunity to say good-bye I know you'll wind up being sorry. Don't do it for him, do it for you. Now, I'm going inside to get better acquainted with your half-brother."

He waited until Shiv was gone, took a deep breath, and banged his head against the newly cleaned hood of his tractor unit. He wished he could get in it and drive away. Instead, he went inside. Kale was in Ryder's kitchen while Joey served him that sun tea she was always making.

"How long did it take you to get here?" he asked Kale, though he'd already calculated the mileage in his head.

"I left at three this morning, about fifteen hours give or take a few minutes."

Ryder let out a puff of air. "You got a place to stay tonight?"

"Nah, there's no time. After this"—he held up the glass of tea—"I'm driving back."

A straight thirty hours on the road…Ryder was a professional trucker, and even he wouldn't attempt it. He couldn't believe what he was about to do. What had the old man ever done for him? "I'll drive your truck and take a flight back."

"That'll work," Kale said.

The kid had grown up. Ryder figured he must be in his mid-twenties by now. Kale's older brother, Lawson, had to be about thirty. Last Ryder heard, Lawson's saddle bronc ranking would get him to the National Finals Rodeo in December. Another Cole carrying on the legacy, such as it was.

"You got a minute?" he asked Joey.

She nodded and reading his cue, opened the back door and stepped outside. He joined her and motioned for them to walk away from the house.

"You find a place?"

"Uh-huh," she said, staring off into the distance. "Your agent friend has been very helpful. Thanks for the referral. I wanted to talk about timing… but you've got your hands full right now. I'm sorry about your father, Ryder. I know to say that the two of you weren't close is an understatement. But losing him…well, it's still gotta hurt."

Ryder was too numb to think about anything other than logistics. "When are you leaving, Joey?"

She let her gaze drop to her sandals. "I got the keys to my new place. Tomorrow the beds come. This is my last day."

Tomorrow...He'd known it would be soon, just not this soon. But it was good. Perfect, actually. She'd be gone when he got home from Colorado. A clean slate.

"I'll look after Shiv until you get back. She still has her alert button, and I can drop by in the evenings to check on her. Between her new job and packing for her move, she'll have plenty to keep her occupied." She headed to the kitchen door, turned around, and said with tears in her eyes, "Drive safely, Ryder. And thanks for entrusting your mother's care to me. I appreciate all you've done to help me get back on my feet."

Just before she went inside, she whispered, "Stay well."

Chapter 25

Ryder drove all night, watching Idaho disappear in his rearview mirror and miles of Utah desert stretch before him. Kale slept most of the way. And when he was awake, he worked the phones.

Tanner was back at the ranch. According to Lawson, he'd convinced the hospital staff to let him die at home. Someone from hospice was there. Tanner was holding on until Ryder and Kale got there, Lawson said.

"Was that your wife?" Kale asked in the darkness of his pickup cab.

"Huh? Who?"

"The pretty blonde. Joey."

"No. Where'd you get that?"

The moon peeked out of the sky, and Kale gave a half shrug. "I don't know. You seemed like you were married, that's all. She your girlfriend?"

"She's my mother's caregiver. Was my mother's caregiver. She's a nurse and is starting work at a local hospital soon."

Kale shuffled in his seat and cleared his throat. "I was sorry about Leslie. Dad told me."

It had been more than five years ago. Kind of late for condolences. But whatever. It wasn't as if Ryder and his half-brother knew each other. This was the most time they'd ever spent together and the most words—such as they were—they'd ever exchanged.

"Thanks," he said and turned on the radio.

"I'm thinking of moving to California."

"Yeah. Why's that?"

"Sick of the cold. And figure I'm on the road most of the time, so why not?"

To Ryder that seemed like a better reason to stay in Colorado. "California's expensive." He'd seen Kale's bronc riding standing this year. Beverly Hills wasn't an option. Then again, next year could be better. The Coles tended to dominate the sport.

"You ain't kidding. I've been checking out the real estate."

"Where you looking?" Frankly, Ryder didn't care, but the conversation was keeping him awake.

"I don't know. San Diego looks nice. Maybe I'll learn to surf." Kale chuckled.

"San Diego's a big city." Most of the guys who followed the circuit lived in rural parts of the country. "Wouldn't it make more sense to live on Lawson's ranch when you're not out on the road?" The kid didn't strike Ryder as the sharpest tool in the shed.

"Yeah, maybe. But I've lived in Colorado my whole life. Might be nice to experience something new. See the ocean."

Okay, Ryder got that. One of the things that appealed to him about being a trucker was getting to see so much of the country. Back in his rodeo days, all the towns had looked the same. And the only place he'd wanted to be was back home with Leslie.

"I was even thinking I could do some stunt work in Hollywood."

The kid was delusional. But let him find that out for himself. Who was Ryder to tell him? He just wanted to get this over with. Say his final good-bye to Tanner and get the hell out of Dodge. If he timed it right, he could still make his run on Friday, then move his stuff into what would soon be an empty house. Empty. Just him and the walls, the way he liked it.

"Dad talks about you all the time, you know?"

Ryder slid Kale a sideways glance. "Nope." He was tempted to tell Kale exactly what he thought of Tanner Cole, but what would that accomplish? His half-brother had obviously had a different experience with the old man. Why taint it?

"He says you'll get inducted into the ProRodeo Hall of Fame."

Ryder hated to disappoint the kid, but he didn't give a shit. And the fact that Tanner went around bragging about a son he hardly knew pissed Ryder off. He might have gotten his father's rodeo genes, but Ryder had worked damn hard at the sport all on his own. If there was anyone to thank for Ryder's success, it was his high school and college coaches. Tanner didn't get to take credit for any of it.

By the time they got to Lawson's ranch, daylight had broken. The sky was streaked in bronzes and oranges as the sun rose over the horizon. From what Ryder could see, it looked like a nice spread. Flat land fenced for cattle.

Kale told him how to get to the house, which sat on top of a hill. It was a one-story wood-sided home with solar panels on the roof and an untended flower garden in the front yard. Ryder didn't know whether Lawson was married or if he had kids. Hell, he wasn't even sure he'd recognize him outside of a rodeo arena.

Ryder parked Kale's truck behind two pickups. "This okay?"

"Yeah," Kale said and was halfway out the door.

Ryder followed, feeling a little awkward about just going in. The house was quiet, like everyone was still asleep. It was barely six. Ryder looked for a place to rest his hat.

"You can hang it from one of the hooks."

Ryder spun around to find an older version of Kale in the foyer. Lawson. His hair was darker than Ryder's and his eyes were brown, but no one would miss that they were related.

"I'm glad you came." Lawson scratched a night's worth of stubble on his chin. "He's been in and out of it. But when he's lucid, he asks about you."

Ryder gave a curt nod. "He asleep?" He wanted Tanner to say his piece so Ryder could hitch a ride to the Denver airport as quickly as possible.

"Yeah. The hospice worker is in the room with him. You want a cup of coffee?"

"Sure." Ryder looked around for Kale.

"He hit the head," Lawson said.

Ryder could use one himself. "You got another?"

"You can use mine." Lawson directed Ryder to the master bedroom. "I'll be in the kitchen."

Ryder did his thing and splashed some water on his face. Later, he'd grab a shower. The house showed no signs of feminine influence. It was tidy enough but lacked the same kind of touches Joey had left on his. She'd painted, hung pictures and shelves, and put up a frilly shower curtain. There was always fresh flowers. And his house smelled nice, too. Like lemon furniture polish. This house had a musty odor.

He found his way to the kitchen, where Lawson was making a fresh pot of coffee and Kale was frying eggs.

"You hungry? I'll make you some breakfast."

If nothing else, his half-brothers were hospitable.

"I could eat," he said.

Kale threw a couple more eggs in the pan and a few slices of bread in the toaster oven. Lawson poured them all steaming mugs of coffee. They drank in silence, none of them knowing quite what to say.

"How much time does he have?" Ryder finally asked.

"Not much." Lawson topped off his cup. "He's been hanging on for you. I guess he's got things he wants to say before he goes." He looked down at his scarred boots as a pall fell over the room.

Ryder knew this was as emotional as it would get. Cowboys tended to keep their feelings to themselves. He didn't know why, but he thought about Joey. She would've known what to say at a time like this. She would've made everyone feel better.

Ryder glanced around the kitchen to keep from having to look at Lawson or Kale. It was a pleasant enough room. Bigger than his kitchen, with oak cabinetry and granite countertops. Other than that, it was run-of-the-mill.

His had been downright shabby until Joey had come along. In the last week or two, she'd peeled off the fifties wallpaper and had painted the room a "buttery"—her words, not his—yellow. It had gone a long way to cheering up the place.

Kale plated Ryder's eggs and put them on the table. Kale ate his standing up.

"Nice place you've got here." Ryder wanted to ask how many acres Lawson had but held off. For ranchers, it was like asking how much money they had in the bank.

"Thanks. Half the cattle are Dad's. That's probably part of what he wants to talk to you about."

Ryder didn't want Tanner's damn cattle. He didn't want anything from the old man. He was here for himself, not for Tanner Cole to buy him off.

"Hear you're going to Vegas," Ryder said to Lawson for the sake of changing the subject.

"Yeah. Made the finals. Doubt I'll beat your record, though."

According to his standing, Ryder thought there was a good chance of his half-brother breaking his record. Lawson was good, one of the best saddle bronc riders Ryder had ever seen. "I don't know about that."

"How's the trucking business?" Lawson asked. Mostly everyone on the circuit knew that Ryder hauled livestock now.

"No complaints. I'm looking to diversify, maybe invest in a few more trailers to haul farm equipment, produce, that sort of thing." Ryder cleaned his plate with the rest of his toast.

Lawson refilled Ryder's coffee mug and joined him at the table. "Dad says you bought a place in Northern California."

Ryder still didn't know how Tanner had found out about that unless Shiv had told him. He hadn't been aware that his mother kept in touch with the old man. "Just ten acres and a small house, nothing like this."

"You run your business from there?"

"Yeah." At least until the Addisons or the new owners tried to stop him. "Nice."

A woman came into the kitchen. She looked to be about Shiv's age. Lawson stood and got down another mug. Kale offered to make her eggs.

"Thank you," she said and looked at Ryder. "You must be the oldest son." Ryder nodded and introduced himself.

"I'm Fran from hospice care. He's awake and would like to see you now."

Ryder scrubbed his hand through his hair and followed Fran to Tanner's room. The old man was on a hospital bed and hooked up to tubes. Joey probably would've known what everything was. To Ryder, it just looked like a bunch of clear plastic spaghetti.

Tanner lifted his head and then dropped back onto the pillow. "You came," he said in a scratchy voice that was barely above a whisper.

"I'm here." Ryder took the chair next to the bed and heard Fran slip out the door. "I'm sorry you're sick."

"I'm not sick." Tanner pulled himself up into a half-sitting position, which proved too much, and he let himself flop back down. "I'm dying."

Ryder didn't know how to respond to that, so he remained silent.

"I've got a few things to say to you," Tanner continued. "I'm going to say it fast because I want to get it all in."

Ryder nodded.

"I was a lousy father to you." He let out a rusty laugh that turned into a cough. "I guess 'lousy' is an understatement. I was lousy to your two brothers, too. I pushed them, rode 'em hard. But I raised 'em. I had no hand in raising you. Maybe that's why you turned out so good." Tanner's lips curved into a pained smile. "I couldn't be any prouder of the man you've become. Of the man your ma helped mold. I have too many regrets and too short of time to name them all. The biggest, though, is the distance between us."

Ryder started to say it was Tanner's fault but stopped himself. It wasn't altogether true. Every time Tanner had reached out, Ryder had rejected him. He'd learned that it was safer to be an island than to build bridges. First, when Tanner had left. And later, when Leslie and the baby had been killed.

He reached over and touched Tanner's gnarled hand. "I'm here now."

Tanner's skin was so pale it was nearly translucent. And his lips held a blue tint. Ryder hardly recognized the once robust cowboy he'd idolized and then hated.

"I'm leaving a third of my cattle and a third of my money to you. It ain't much, and I know it can't make up for all those years I never…" Tanner trailed off. Ryder couldn't tell if it was too physically challenging for him to complete the sentence or he was simply having trouble saying good-bye.

Good-bye. It was so permanent.

Suddenly Ryder wished they had a little more time together. Perhaps just so Ryder could tell Tanner what a shit father he was. Or maybe just to get to know the man who'd given him life. The last thing he expected was to feel regret. But here, in this dimly lit room that smelled of death and disappointment, he wondered what would've happened if he'd at least met Tanner halfway. If he'd just once returned his father's calls. Or hadn't walked away from Tanner as his father tried to shake his hand in a crowded rodeo arena.

Now he'd never have the chance to find out.

"Get to know your brothers," Tanner said. "Whether you like it or not, they're your family. Blood's thicker than water, boy. And now they've got no one but you. Open your heart a little. It's good to have people, Ryder. It's good to be loved."

Ryder's chest tightened as he squeezed his father's hand.

"I love you, son."

Ryder tried to say it back, but the words wouldn't come. They were stuck in his throat like a wishbone while he struggled for air. It was now or never. From the looks of things, Tanner wouldn't make it to the end of the day.

He thought about lost chances. He thought about his mother and what she'd said about regret. He thought about Leslie and how she had more love in her than anyone he'd ever known. He thought about what she would've wanted him to do and how she would've wanted him to carry on without her.

Ryder squeezed his eyes shut and felt warm tears sliding down his cheeks. "Dad"—his voice cracked—"I love you, too."

* * * *

Tanner passed away that evening. Ryder stayed the week at Lawson's to help with the funeral arrangements. It was a well-attended service. Neighbors, ranchers, and a number of Tanner's rodeo buddies came to send him off in style.

Ryder left, feeling an unexpected camaraderie with his half-brothers, with whom he now owned a herd of cattle. Nothing had been decided on that front. Ryder, Lawson, and Kale had chosen to put off talking business until his half-brothers had had time to grieve.

In his own way, Ryder grieved, too. For the father he never really knew, and for the missed opportunity of getting better acquainted.

He returned to Nugget to an empty house. Joey's room had been cleaned out and left bare. And the only hint that Shiv still lived here was the bed in her room. Little by little, his mother had begun transferring her belongings, including much of her furniture, to her new house. She and Peter planned to be fully moved in by the end of the week.

He walked the wooden floors, hearing his bootsteps echo through the sad little house.

"You should start fresh," his mother had told him before she'd gone to work at Flynn's. "Furnish the place with things you like. Things befitting a young man, not an old lady." She'd pulled his head down for a kiss.

Yeah, as if furniture shopping was top on his to-do list, he thought to himself as he stood in Joey's empty bedroom. The faint scent of her perfume still clung to the air. He continued to stand there, inhaling her smell and holding on to her memory. Everything felt different without her. Lonely and dull.

She's just down the road apiece, you jackass.

He could visit her if he wanted to, but that would be sending mixed signals. *I want you, I don't want you.* Better to go cold turkey, he told himself.

He wandered outside, sat on one of the rocking chairs on the porch, and tried to convince himself that he was looking forward to the solitude. Finally, he could move out of the fifth wheel and have a little breathing room. Maybe he'd get one of those couches with the reclining seats and a larger flatscreen. Watch TV in his BVDs if he wanted to.

He sat there, staring out over the Sierra Nevada Mountain Range, watching the clouds float in the sky like big, fluffy pillows. Instead of enjoying the peacefulness of being alone, the desolation depressed him. It gave him too much time to think, too much time to wallow in his own sorrow.

"It's good to have people." His father's words came back to him. *"It's good to be loved."*

He grabbed his keys from his camper, and before he could change his mind, got in his truck. As he passed the Beary Quaint, he noticed the chainsaw bears that had once cluttered the grounds were nowhere to be found. It made the place look a little less "mountain hillbilly." The "no-vacancy" sign was on, even though there were no cars parked in front of the cabin rooms. Ryder suspected the new owners would be taking over in the next few weeks. He'd find out who they were soon enough.

There was a line of cars at the Bun Boy, and families jostled for space at the picnic tables. He checked the clock on his dashboard, surprised to see that it was suppertime. The days were longer, and he'd lost track of time.

He crossed through town, turned on a residential street into a neighborhood he wasn't all that familiar with, and parked in front of a blue house with a white picket fence.

He sat there, trying to gather his thoughts and put them into words that made sense. Words that would convey what a fool he'd been. And that's when he saw her through the big picture window that looked out onto the front yard. His pulse picked up, and he crossed the driveway to her door and rang the bell.

Joey appeared in the doorway, as beautiful as ever. It had only been a week since he'd seen her last, yet it felt like an eternity had passed. He couldn't help himself, and he pulled her into his arms.

"What's this?" she said, surprised. "Hey, you okay?"

"I am now."

She backed away a few steps to look at him. Their eyes met, and then she quickly looked away. "I heard you stayed for the funeral. That bad, huh?"

"No…I mean, it was sad. But I'm glad I was with him in his final hours. Glad I spent time with my half-brothers."

"That's good, Ryder."

They both stood awkwardly at the threshold.

"Come in," she finally said and led him into an empty living room. "Furniture is coming in a few days. There are chairs in here."

He followed her into a sunny kitchen. Under different circumstances, he might've looked around, checked out the place. But he only had eyes for her. God, how he'd missed her.

"Shiv at work?" she asked, clearly curious why he was there.

"Yeah. She seems to like it." He rolled his eyes. "I don't know why she bothered to leave her first job."

"Because she was in love with her boss and couldn't have him. I suppose that takes a toll on a person." She held his gaze, her message clear.

He took off his hat, rested it on the countertop, and rubbed his hand down his face. "Come back, Joey."

"What?"

"The house is empty without you."

She just stood there, looking at him like she was trying to understand. He wanted to say how he'd fallen hard for her, but the words got stuck in his throat.

"I think it happened that first time you kissed me," he said.

"You kissed me."

He hitched his shoulders. "Okay. But that's not how I remember it."

"You think what happened?" Joey put her hands on her hips and stared at him, leery.

"I learned how to love again. I didn't want to, so I stopped going to the Ponderosa when I thought you'd be there. But I never stopped thinking about you. Sometimes I'd lie awake at night reliving that kiss, reliving that first day I saw you sitting by yourself in the restaurant. I played you a song on the jukebox. George Jones." His mouth curved up at the memory. "And that day you showed up to interview for Shiv's caregiver…damn, I was gone. You don't know how hard I tried to find someone else for the job, someone who wasn't you."

Her eyes filled. But instead of going to her, he stayed planted by the counter. He had stuff to say, things he should've told her the night she'd asked him to love her.

"I couldn't tell you then, but I can tell you now. I love you, Joey. I didn't think I could ever be happy again. But you make me so damn happy. I don't know what I'd do without you in my life. So, come home."

Standing stock-still, she didn't reply.

"Joey, do you not love me anymore?" The prospect of losing her made his chest constrict so tight he found it hard to breathe.

She started to cry. "I still love you." She choked on a sob. "But I thought…Oh, Ryder."

He swept her up into his arms. "So, you'll come home?"

"What if you change your mind?" She rested her head on his shoulder. "What if you discover that I can't match up to Leslie? I can't do this again, Ryder. I've finally started getting my life back. A nursing job, this place, a bedroom for Roni. I don't want to compete with a ghost."

"It was never about that, Joey. Leslie will always have a place in my heart. But I'm in love with you. You." He placed his hand above her breastbone. "As much as I tried to fight it, you're everything to me. I can't lose you. And as for Roni, I'll add on an entire wing for her if it'll make you happy. Let's be a family, Joey. You, Roni, and me."

She swiped at a stray tear and wiggled out of his arms. "Are you sure you're ready for that?"

"Never been more sure of anything in my life. Let's do this, Joey. I don't want another day to go by without you in it."

"Be careful what you wish for, cowboy." Joey pulled his face down and clasped her hands on both sides of his cheeks. "Because I plan on holding on to you forever. Can you do forever?"

His lips slid up into a lopsided grin. "I'll raise your 'forever' to an eternity. And no one knows how to hold on better than me. I'm a two-time world champion, baby."

Joey locked eyes with him. "I love you, Ryder." She glanced around the kitchen and let out a long sigh. "I guess we'd better call Dana."

"Yep. Tell her to put the place back up for rent because you're coming home. But"—he pulled her back into his arms—"do it later. We've got lost time to make up for."

Epilogue

Roni ran through the yard, their new puppy, Ringo, chasing at her heels. Joey sat on the front porch, laughing.

"You ready to fire up the grill?" she asked Ryder.

"Huh?" For the last hour, he'd been staring at the architectural plans Colin had delivered that morning. "I'm sorry, what did you say?"

"That it's time for dinner." She pointed at the blueprints. "Those must be pretty darn interesting."

He rolled up the plans, a wide grin covering his face. "When the project's done, we'll have one hell of a house. Colin managed to get in everything we put on our wish list."

"That's great. But you know I'm happy with the house just the way it is, as long as I have you."

He leaned over and kissed her. "I want Roni to have a place she can bring her friends home to. And when we decide to grow our family, there'll be plenty of space. In the meantime, I've got a surprise for you."

Ryder had done nothing but shower her with surprises since they'd gotten engaged two weeks ago. "What is it?" She looked down at her ring and watched the sunlight glint off the diamond.

"I reserved the Lumber Baron for our reception."

"I thought we decided it cost too much. That we should save our money for the house."

"That was before I sold the fifth wheel, which I did today. And for a nice chunk of change."

"Why?" She reeled back. "You love that camper."

"Nah, it's outlasted its use." He winked. "Besides, it's parked where my new office is going." They'd already carved out a neat section of the property for Ryder to keep his semitractors and trailers, providing them plenty of space for the house add-on. "But if you don't still want the Lumber Baron for our party, we can choose somewhere else."

"Are you kidding? It's a dream come true, Ryder. You know I love the hotel. It's so elegant. And Brady's food...well, it's off the hook." Her mouth watered just thinking about his cinnamon roll French toast. She'd only had it once when Maddy had invited her and a few other women for brunch at the inn, but it had been to die for. "Wow. I can't believe you did this for me." She got up, sat in his lap, and threw her arms around his neck. "I love you."

He kissed the bridge of her nose. "Maddy said the whole month of February is open. Unless you're worried about snow."

"Jay will get my folks here, even if it's a blizzard. Maybe Valentine's Day? Or is that too cliché?"

He shrugged. "You're asking me? I just want to make it official. Whatever day works for you works for me."

"I can't believe we're going to rebuild this house." Her eyes swept over the front porch. "And plan a wedding at the same time. Are you sure we can afford all of it?" She was making good money at the hospital, but not enough for a full-scale remodel and a fancy wedding. It was mostly Ryder picking up the tab.

"Business is good, and Lawson says beef prices are up."

Ryder and his half-brothers had become closer since Tanner died. Kale had shown interest in becoming one of Ryder's drivers when he wasn't following the circuit. And they'd gone to San Francisco to watch Lawson ride in the Grand National Rodeo at the Cow Palace and had had dinner together afterward at a fancy restaurant in the city.

"Plus, I'd like to give Maddy and Nate the business, after all they've done for us."

To no one's surprise, except of course the Addisons', Nate and Maddy had purchased the Beary Quaint. After Dana had negotiated the price down, it was a deal Nate couldn't resist. Maddy and Nate had hired Peter to run the motor lodge. Given the lack of qualified innkeepers in Nugget, they hoped Peter's big personality would make up for his lack of experience.

"They've been great neighbors," Ryder continued. "Despite all they're doing to spruce up the place, they don't care about my trucks or my trailers. Good riddance to the Addisons."

The couple had left Nugget with little fanfare. Joey had heard through Harlee that some of the old-timers had thrown the Addisons a small party. But most people were happy to see them go.

"Yesterday I drove by the motel to pick Roni up from school," Joey said. "I can't believe how much they've gotten done. The pool is amazing. I never thought I'd say this, but the place is adorable. I predict they're going to kill it, especially with Peter. He's so good with people. I just know the guests are going to love him, and I think the change will do him good."

"My ma says he's excited about running the place. I've gotta give Maddy and Nate credit for taking a chance on a novice. They're either on to something, or they're crazy."

"Maddy is putting him through an intensive training course. He'll be great. Besides, she's just down the road if he needs help with anything." Joey pulled down the brim of Ryder's trucker cap. "You better fire up that grill. We've got company coming."

"I'd rather sit here with you." Ryder's hand wandered down Joey's back until he landed on her butt.

She swatted his hand away, laughing. "We're not alone."

He stood up, lifting Joey with him. "Hey, Roni," he called across the front yard, where Roni was trying to teach Ringo how to fetch, "want to help me with the barbecue?"

She and the pup bounded over. Ryder put Joey down and swept Roni up under one arm, carrying her sideways as she squealed with delight.

Joey followed them to the backyard, where she'd set up a couple of picnic tables for their guests. Shiv and Peter were due to arrive any minute to help with the preparations. The rest of the gang was supposedly coming at six. But you never knew. This wasn't the kind of town where people followed protocol.

Joey was still surprised at all the new friends she'd made. Even Brynn had become part of her clique. As long as it didn't interfere with her nursing shift, Joey regularly met up with Harlee, Darla, and the police dispatcher, Connie, for nachos and virgin margaritas at the Ponderosa. Sometimes Connie's best friend, Sloane, a detective with Nugget PD, joined them. Other times, Lucky's wife, Tawny, met them at the bar.

Harlee and Darla, who was getting closer to her due date, occasionally organized a bowling party that was a blast. It was a good little town, where everyone watched out for one another.

Roni was thriving here, especially now that Ethan had relented and let Joey have their daughter fifty percent of the time. But living so close, they remained flexible. Alma and Shiv were always available to pitch in with child care when Joey, Ryder, Ethan, and Brynn's work schedules interfered. Roni—and Henry, for that matter—loved having a third grandmother in their lives. Shiv spoiled both kids rotten and hadn't been subtle about her wish for more grandchildren.

Her job with Flynn Barlow's law firm had given her a new lease on life. And Peter had been an excellent influence, pushing Shiv into social situations where she could make new friends. It was paying off. She now had a network of women she palled around with, including Ethel from the Nugget Market, Grace of Farm Supply, and Lucky's mother, Cecilia. The four ladies met weekly for pastries, coffee, and a good gossip session at The Farm.

Ethel, Grace, and Cecilia had also invited Shiv to join the Baker's Dozen, a local cooking club. Joey and Ryder had been the happy recipients of all the new dishes Shiv made.

Though Shiv loved living at Sierra Heights, Ryder and Joey had incorporated a mother-in-law unit into their building plans if she ever wanted to move back. Until that day came, they were all taking advantage of the amenities at the gated community as Shiv and Peter's guests. Roni and Henry adored the pool.

Ryder sent Roni into the house for a bag of ice to fill the drink cooler.

"We're ready for company." He pulled Joey into his arms. "And I'm ready to tell them to go home early so you and I can spend some quality time together." He nudged his head at the bedroom, making her laugh.

"You and your one-track mind."

The guests began arriving after five. Word had gotten around, and even people who hadn't been invited showed up. Ryder just threw more burgers and dogs on the grill. The more the merrier. The Baker's Dozen had brought enough dessert and Annie enough corn on the cob from her farm stand to feed the entire town, anyway.

The Nugget Mafia set up a folding table on the patio and kept themselves busy by playing a rousing game of Texas Hold'em, while the kids ran around the yard, chasing the new pup. Darla and Dana sat in the shade, fanning themselves, looking ready to pop. Good thing there was a nurse and doctor in the house.

Ethan came up beside Joey. "You done good, Joe."

She gazed over at Ryder, who was still manning the grill, her heart full to bursting. "I sure did."

Later that evening, they built a bonfire, and everyone toasted marshmallows. Shiv, Peter, and Donna passed around graham crackers and chocolate so the kids could make s'mores.

Ryder pulled Joey into his lap. "You happy?"

She snuggled closer. "The happiest I've ever been. How 'bout you?"

"You, Roni"—he glanced around the circle at the people who'd become their friends, and his voice hitched—"this town. Best thing that ever happened to me."

"Me, too," she said. "We're going to raise our children and grow old together here. And all these people…" Joey also choked up a little. "Family. They're our family."

He wrapped his arms around her. "Yep. But you and Roni…you're my heart."

CPSIA information can be obtained
at www.ICGtesting.com
Printed in the USA
LVHW021511150621
690286LV00002B/332